Caroline Beecham grew up at the English seaside and relocated to Australia to continue her career as a writer and producer in film and television. She has worked on a documentary about Princess Diana lookalikes, a series about journeys to the ends of the earth, as well as a feature film about finding the end of the rainbow.

Caroline decided on a new way of storytelling and studied the craft of novel writing at the Faber Academy in 2012. She has an MA in Film & Television and a MA in Creative Writing and lives with her husband and two sons by Sydney Harbour.

Eleanor's Secret is her second novel.

Also by Caroline Beecham:

Maggie's Kitchen

CAROLINE BEECHAM

Eleanor's Secret

EBURY
PRESS

1 3 5 7 9 10 8 6 4 2

Ebury Press, an imprint of Ebury Publishing
20 Vauxhall Bridge Road,
London SW1V 2SA

Penguin
Random House
UK

Ebury Press is part of the Penguin Random House group of companies whose
addresses can be found at global.penguinrandomhouse.com

Copyright © Caroline Beecham, 2018

Caroline Beecham has asserted her right to be identified as the author of this work
in accordance with the Copyright, Designs and Patents Act 1988

First published in Australia in 2018 by Allen & Unwin Book Publishers
First published in the UK in 2018 by Ebury Press

www.penguin.co.uk

Typeset in 10.2/15.5 pt Minion Pro
by Integra Software Services Pvt. Ltd, Pondicherry

A CIP catalogue record for this book is available from the British Library

ISBN 9781785035364

Printed and bound in Great Britain by Clays Ltd, St Ives PLC

Penguin Random House is committed to a sustainable future for our business,
our readers and our planet. This book is made from Forest
Stewardship Council® certified paper.

For my grandmother,
Ellen Mary Taylor,
for sharing all your stories

And for my parents, especially my mother

PART I

The Children in the Attic

'What did it look like? They will ask in 1981, and no amount of description or documentation will answer them. Nor will big, formal compositions like the battle pictures which hang in palaces; and even photographs, which tell us so much, will leave out the colour and the peculiar feeling of events in these extraordinary years.'

War Pictures by British Artists,
OXFORD UNIVERSITY PRESS, 1942

One

LONDON, MARCH 1942

This was Eleanor's last chance: she hadn't been able to find the last four artists she had been sent to sign, and Mr Steadman was losing patience. *One for the forces, one for us,* he had told her, huge eyes magnified through his glasses, expression grave. But it seemed as if she was always a fraction too late; each artist she tracked down had already signed up or recently packed out. It was looking more like 'four for the forces, one for us'.

Eleanor felt even more irritated now because she and her driver, Clive, were lost—either that or all the roads looked the same. Just as she felt like giving up, their Austin Eighteen fought another pothole, rattling towards the junction, and she spotted the unmistakable yellow of Yorkstone through the trees.

'That's it!' she said.

'Very good, miss,' Clive replied from the driver's seat, glancing at her in the rear-view mirror.

'It's much bigger than I expected,' she said, as she wondered if the rumours about the place were true.

The three-storey Victorian building was shrouded by thick canopies of oaks and pencil-thin trunks of silver birch. It was also half-hidden from street view by large detached Wandsworth houses, home to the city's up-and-comers until war had wrenched them away. Eleanor had plenty of time to peer through their elegant windows as the large saloon crawled past, and she imagined the works of art that might be languishing inside.

Her journey from Portman Square had taken twice as long as it should have because of diversions through the bomb-damaged streets—and thanks to Clive's overly cautious nature. The first reason was unavoidable but as for the second . . . She had to bite her tongue as Clive drew the car to an excruciatingly slow stop on the gravel driveway.

She had grown used to working out the routes with fewer street signs than before the war, but she would never get comfortable with being chauffeured when cars were being requisitioned and the manpower was needed just as badly. She was quite sure she could do a better job of driving than Clive too. If only Mr Steadman would agree to let her take her driving test, but there was little chance of that—only last week, the divisional officer had commented that she wasn't ready yet: *It is highly irregular for a woman to take her test after only two months of lessons, Miss Roy.*

Well, they were living in highly irregular times.

Eleanor double-checked inside her leather satchel, making sure that the papers and contract were all there, and then stepped from the Austin and into the shadow cast by one of the Gothic towers.

The Royal Victoria Patriotic Building really was much bigger than she had expected, altogether more imposing, and it made her think of the stories she had heard about the place. It had been built as an asylum for the orphaned girls of the Crimea, and some said they haunted it still, while others said that it was inhabited by the ghosts of Great War soldiers who had died within its walls.

That morning, before Eleanor's workmate Maura had left the office, she'd leaned over the desk and clutched Eleanor's hand. Her soft Irish brogue had been hushed and full of exaggerated kindness. 'Good luck, my dear. You *do* know they torture spies and traitors there, don't you?'

Eleanor had laughed, assuming her friend was joking. But as she looked up at the building's French-style turrets, and at the roofs that were a sinister grey, like an ominous sky before a thunderstorm, she thought that perhaps it might be true.

She straightened her wool skirt and told herself to stop being ridiculous. She was there for a purpose that was unlikely to take very long, anyway. In just an hour she would be back at the Ministry of Food, spinning Maura an outlandish tale about the ghosts she had seen—or maybe she should feign injury and make up a story of how she had been tortured but released when her captors realised she didn't have any intelligence to share.

While the building was foreboding, its vast gardens were inviting. To the east, manicured lawns led down to a lake surrounded by a cathedral of trees; a refreshing wind barely moved the branches, whistling through the long, fragile grasses. They were only six miles from the Ministry's office at Portman Square, but it was strangely peaceful. Quiet, except for the chatter of finches. The noisy, battle-scarred streets could have been a hundred miles away as the afternoon slowed to its natural rhythm. For just a moment, Eleanor felt as if she and Clive were the only people there—until a door banged inside the building.

She lowered her head to her driver's window. 'I shan't be too long, Clive,' she said, her hazel eyes holding his gaze. 'You will wait here, won't you?'

It was more of a request than a question, and he winked up at her, tapping his grey cap with crooked fingers. 'Certainly will, miss.'

She hoped that he meant it this time, that he wouldn't park the car and stroll around as he had done before—especially when she might be eager to get away. The woodland and birdlife might prove too much of a temptation for him, and she really didn't want to be stuck here any longer than necessary.

'You don't need to stretch your legs then?' she asked.

'Oh no, miss,' he said, extending them out under the steering wheel. 'I reckon they're just about as long as they're going to get!'

'Jolly good,' she said, smiling.

Inside, the building was not nearly as impressive—the painted walls were flaking badly and the plaster had come away in places, leaving large areas of exposed brickwork. The air was so thick with dust that Eleanor wanted to throw open the windows to let the building breathe but they were bolted shut with grimy locks. Maybe she wasn't in the right place after all; it didn't look like somewhere to bring grieving children for comfort and support.

A large entrance hall extended into a reception area with three doors and a wide staircase, but the only noise came from the floors above. She followed the echo upwards, slowly trailing behind dust motes that chased the sun before they disappeared into the roof-light.

Voices drifted from somewhere higher up, and so she carried on: past the first floor, where rooms stretched along unlit corridors that disappeared into shadows at either end, and up the second set of stairs. The voices were becoming clearer, and she could make out words—the closer she drew, the stronger they became, tiny voices, some barely more than whispers, singing 'Ring-a-Ring O'Roses'.

Up here the walls were in an even poorer condition. Splintered planks of bare wooden studwork gave glimpses into the room behind, where a small group of children sat cross-legged on the floor at the feet of a woman seated on a stool. The woman, in her mid-twenties like Eleanor, flipped through a book as they started on a new nursery rhyme.

> *Sing a song of sixpence, a pocket full of rye,*
> *Four and twenty blackbirds baked in a pie,*
> *When the pie was opened, the birds began to sing . . .*

When the woman glanced up, Eleanor raised her hand in greeting. The woman waved back as she continued to sing.

Eleanor drew closer, so she was level with the door, and was so absorbed by the children's singing that it was a moment until she noticed the outline of a man. His tall frame would have looked awkward, arched forward as it was over the easel, had he not moved so gracefully, white shirtsleeves rolled up to reveal unusually sun-tanned skin.

On the walls around him was a scattering of black-and-white sketches: some depicting the children grouped together, others of them individually. These pictures weren't as beautiful as Murillo's seventeenth-century street children, but they were mesmerising in their detail, a fretwork of greys and blacks. Eleanor moved forward, drawn to the startlingly intricate lines that built the shading, with smaller lines indicating where an eyebrow might be or the edge of a smile.

The artist was sketching a girl of about six, and every time he looked up his dark hair fell across his face, hiding it from view.

The room was an old dormitory—skeletons of bedframes were spaced along its length, and windows with rails but no curtains were higher up on the walls. Across the narrowest part of the room, a simple line was strung, now home to delicately coloured paintings from the same hand as the sketches. The artist must have been here for some time, Eleanor realised, since there were several of these watercolour pictures, raw in form but each capturing the expression and characteristics of the child.

Eleanor glanced across the frayed and dirty creatures with their slumped backs and earnest faces. They presented a strange contradiction, not because such sweet song arose from them, but because of the enthusiasm with which the tribe did their best to sing and the woman her best to lead them. Perhaps they were bewildered by their recent fate and exhausted, allowing themselves to be easily shepherded and cajoled. The last thing Eleanor wanted was to disturb them, so she stood quietly as they sang and the artist sketched; she imagined it to be minutes of welcome abandon for them all.

Then the artist twisted round, exchanging his pencil for a brush, and she noticed how quick and fluid his movements were. She supposed he would have to be nimble to go where he went, to do what he did. And as she watched him drawing, she wondered what other qualities a man like this would need. People were used to seeing beauty in nature, to seeing its magnificence reflected back and preserved in great works of art: there had been centuries of it, from Constable to Monet, from landscapes to monuments. But now British artists were engaged to record the atrocities of war—all that was base and deplorable in humankind. And yet here were watercolours so beautiful, the children so vulnerable, that they were some of the most haunting images she had ever seen. She knew the artist's work, had seen his book illustrations and some of his portraits, but these were something different. He had captured the souls of these children, brought the angels out of them, preserved their innocence before the war had the chance to pluck it away.

Eleanor was so engrossed in watching him work that as she took another step, her foot hit a loose plank. The wood squeaked, and the artist turned around.

He glanced up, dark eyebrows knitting in a momentary frown, then he smiled. As his green eyes bore into her, her cheeks burned. It was clear now that, as his name suggested, he was of Mediterranean descent. He was also much taller than she had expected, and altogether stronger and more poised, with the physique of an athlete rather than an artist.

It was dark here in the attic, with less air circulating, fewer windows to open; perhaps that was why she felt overwhelmed. Then she remembered why she had come. She stepped towards him, offering her hand. 'Hello, Mr Valante. I'm Eleanor Roy, from the Ministry of Food. I'm here with the contract for you to sign.' She had been ready to be efficient and businesslike, get the contract signed then return to the office as soon as possible, but all she could think about was how this unexpected man could create such extraordinary work. He looked vague, though, his expression so remote that she continued: 'We wrote to you about having some of your pictures decorate our British Restaurants.'

Her purpose must have finally registered because he came towards her, rubbing his hands on a rag, until he was as close as the narrow ceilings would allow. He carried the scents of turpentine and tobacco.

'Pleasure to meet you, Miss Roy,' he said, extending his hand. 'Call me Jack.'

His skin felt warm and smooth, not the dry and callused palms she experienced from days spent painting and long nights cleaning equipment and brushes.

'You too, Jack,' she said brightly, 'and I must just say, I am a huge admirer of your work.'

She was so relieved to finally be speaking with an artist, she had got carried away. As soon as she'd spoken the words she regretted them; self-conscious, she looked about to see what the children were doing. The infants were lying on their bellies, while the older ones sat cross-legged, their singing now muted as they drew or painted.

'Oh, really,' Jack said, sounding surprised. 'Where have you seen it, Miss Roy?'

'At the Slade School of Art—they had two of your pictures on loan last year.'

'Yes, *The Warrior* . . .'

'And *Excavate*. Stunning pieces.'

'Thank you. Do you go to many exhibitions?' he asked, his arm resting on the beam overhead, his body filling up the space.

'I try, but I was a student there . . . until last year.'

'Really? You must have worked with Aubrey Powell?'

'Yes, I did,' she said. 'He is a tireless advocate for his students . . . in fact, he put me forward for our decoration scheme.'

'Oh.' Jack looked at her more intensely. It was an artist's gaze: one that she recognised, one that assessed the subject. 'And what do you like to paint, Miss Roy?'

He'd caught her off guard and she hesitated. 'Well, I don't get to paint much anymore . . . but I really am much more useful at the Ministry,' Eleanor said, hoping she sounded convincing. 'Anyway, unless I was as talented as Anna Airy, then I doubt very much that anyone should miss me,' she added with a forced laugh. Anna Airy was her hero. Also a former Slade student, Anna had painted during the Great War, often in very difficult circumstances, and had shown Eleanor how female artists could share the stage with men.

Jack smiled warmly. 'So tell me again, what brings you here, Miss Roy?' he asked.

'I have the contract for you to sign,' she said. She raised the document towards him.

He took the paper and glanced over it, then handed it back. 'I am sorry, Miss Roy. I'm afraid there's been a misunderstanding.' His smile turned apologetic, and he moved away from her, going back to his painting. He picked up a brush and traced the outline of a child's silhouette. Then he glanced round and smiled again. 'Please thank the Ministry for its interest, but—'

'What sort of misunderstanding?' she asked.

'I cannot sign any contract. I'm truly sorry you came all the way here.'

The wind was picking up outside, reminding her of Clive waiting in the drafty car to drive her back into town—and of the irritation she would be greeted with from Mr Steadman at her failure.

The children also carried on with their artworks, so she watched them as she decided what to do; an artist had never just flatly refused to sign a contract before—at least as far as she knew. Surely there must be some protocol or procedure to follow, but she couldn't think what it was.

'You do know that it really is quite an honour,' she said, her heart beating faster, her breathing constricted beneath her navy woollen suit.

'How so?' Jack asked.

'A great many artists would be flattered to have their work as part of this scheme. Dozens, in fact, would jump at the chance.'

'Well, perhaps you should ask one of them, Miss Roy.'

Eleanor was about to tell him that she had clear instructions to get the contract signed, and that she needed a date for the completed lithographs, when there was a heavy tramping on the stairs.

Two men appeared in the doorway. They weren't in uniform, but something about the way they wore their dark suits and trilbies suggested they weren't ordinary civilians. The tall one had his face half-hidden, black moustache just visible beneath the shadow of his hat, and the shorter one, with fair hair and a ginger beard, held an unlit pipe balanced between his lips.

Jack looked alarmed.

The two men were about to come in, until they noticed the children.

'Excuse me for a moment,' Jack said to Eleanor.

Her gaze flicked between him and the children. They were so very tired that they paid little attention to the visitors, while outside the doorway there seemed to be some kind of disagreement going on.

After a few minutes, Jack returned and began packing away his equipment, then paused to slowly roll down his sleeves. He seemed composed but his movements were hurried and clumsy, and he fumbled over his shirt buttons.

'Here,' Eleanor said, moving towards him, 'let me help you.'

She felt his eyes on her as she finished them.

'Thank you,' he said when she fastened the last one.

The smell of turpentine and tobacco had been replaced with something more—the scent of Jack.

'It's a pleasure,' she said, gazing up at him. An hour earlier, she had never set eyes on Jack Valante, and now she felt as if she couldn't let him out of her sight.

'I'm afraid this can't wait,' he said.

'Can't they see you're busy?'

'These chaps don't take no for an answer.' He glanced back through the doorway to where the men waited, their eyes fixed on him.

The atmosphere in the room had changed; the gentle chorus of nursery rhymes had given way to an uneasy tension. Jack looked over at the children, then picked up his jacket, draping it casually over his shoulder, and walked towards the door.

When he reached the doorway, he stopped and turned. 'It was a pleasure meeting you, Miss Roy. I hope you find your artist.'

Surely there must be something she could do or say? It was unclear whether Jack knew the men or not—he was reluctant but not refusing to go. Yet with barely any time to react, she just looked helplessly at the teacher, and listened as the trudge of footsteps on wooden stairs faded, and, with it, her chance of signing the artist.

Two

Back at the office, Maura insisted that Eleanor tell her all about the trip, but she had decided to keep it to herself: at least until she figured out who the two men were and why Jack had been compelled to go with them. The whole affair had been rather strange, and on the journey back she had wondered if Maura might be right about the building—that spies and traitors were tortured there.

'Aye, you're a dark horse, Eleanor Roy,' Maura said, brown bobbed hair bouncing as she tilted her head to one side. 'What is it that you're not telling me? What have ye been gettin' up to?'

'Oh, you know, just the usual—tea at the Criterion and then an exhibition at the National Gallery,' Eleanor replied with mock formality, adding her jacket to those already piled on the wooden coat stand.

Clive had actually made good time, only getting delayed in a diversion near the Chelsea gasworks where the army had been detonating an unexploded incendiary that was threatening to demolish the area. Clive had driven the long way around because, as he had so delicately put it, *Miss, wouldn't half know about it if it went off!* She had been inclined to agree.

'You seem different,' Maura said, looking her up and down with alert grey eyes. 'Yes, there's definitely something different about you . . .'

Maura had a small frame and so could wear anything she wanted, yet she always found something to say about Eleanor's appearance; it was as if the slogan *Make Do And Mend* had been created with Maura in mind: that and the fact her mother worked in a laundry and often brought home damaged clothes that Maura versioned into something far more original on the family's old Singer. And sometimes with surprising results—a floral blouse under a corduroy waistcoat, or a man's jacket teamed with a silk pencil skirt. It was also one of the reasons that Maura had developed an obsession with magazines; she fawned over actresses' organza ball gowns and polka-dot tea dresses, and envied their pleated skirts and sailor pants. She had told Eleanor, on more than one occasion, that she was going to get a job in a fashion house as soon as the war was over: *Everyone will want to brighten up their wardrobe and their lives!*

But although Eleanor usually trusted Maura's opinion on these matters, she couldn't see what was so different about her appearance this afternoon. All she could think of was that her wavy blonde hair fell around her face rather than being pinned back as it usually was, and shiny black leather shoes replaced a worn-out pair.

'No, still the same old navy suit,' she said with a smile. 'Only the shoes are new-ish.'

'Are you sure you didn't stop off somewhere else?' Maura asked suspiciously.

Perhaps Maura had picked up on her anxiety about Jack not signing the contract . . . or perhaps her eyes were small and puffy because of her interrupted sleep.

'The only place I would go,' Eleanor said, 'is back home to check on Cecily.'

Eleanor wished she could have stopped by to see how her sister was getting on, but the Bayswater flat they shared just wasn't on the route back to the office.

'Don't tell me she's sick again?' Maura asked.

'Yes, I'm afraid so.' Eleanor sighed. 'She was coughing all night. It seems that she's spending more time nursing her own colds than anyone else's.'

Ever since Cecily had started her nursing training, she had been sick with one thing or another; the doctors had told her that her immunity would build after a year or two, but it seemed their mother's concern that she had conceived her fourth child too soon after giving birth was unfortunately being proven right.

'Steadman wants the information about the new lithographs double-quick,' Maura said. 'He says the memorandum needs to be sent out to the boroughs today.' She spoke with an exaggerated seriousness so that Eleanor couldn't tell if she was joking. 'Honestly, Miss Roy!'

Eleanor couldn't see what all the fuss was about; they were already doing what Lord Woolton had asked of them. She glanced at the framed letter kept nearby as a daily reminder of their duty.

> *At the present time, two of the Ministry of Food's British*
> *Restaurants a day are being opened in this country. May I*

*venture to impress upon your Council, if it is proposing to
bring into existence any new British Restaurants, the importance of ensuring that these places shall be so designed
and decorated internally as to give an air of brightness and
cheerfulness? I believe that it would add to the morale of the
country that these war-time creations for communal feeding
should be pleasant to eat in and that the design should be
suitable for the purpose for which they are created.*

'Well,' said Eleanor, 'I'm sure Steadman can wait a few more hours.'

'Aye, if you say so,' Maura said breezily, all solemnity forgotten.

Mr Steadman was in conversation behind the glazed door of his
office, and Eleanor strained to see if she recognised the visitor from
his voice or silhouette. When she couldn't, she gave up and went back
to her desk.

Back when the Ministry had first approached her about the decoration policy for British Restaurants, she had been surprised. It took
her barely a moment to agree, and she soon realised that it was Aubrey Powell, her professor at the Slade, who had put her forward for
the scheme. She wrote home immediately to tell her parents about
the new role, and of the fifty-five boroughs she would have to visit
and the hundreds of pictures and lithographs they would need to
supply. There were murals by students from all over London, and it
had sounded simple enough: she would visit the restaurants, assess
their requests and make sure their conditions were satisfactory—not
too much condensation or dust—and then report back directly to Mr
Steadman, the chief divisional officer for London.

The job had been a challenge to begin with, and each week she
wrote home with details of her new responsibilities. She'd hoped it

would prove her father wrong for writing off her desire to be an artist as a waste of time, but he still insisted that her place was at home and helping with the family business. It seemed as though he would never be satisfied with her choices or accept that all their lives had changed—especially women's—but now she also had concerns over whether Mr Steadman would keep her on after she had failed to sign another artist.

Across the room, coats dangled unevenly on the wooden stand, and she went over to rearrange them as neatly as if they were flowers in a shop display. She couldn't bear the way the other office workers had no interest in their surroundings. At least these rooms were bright and recently painted, the high ceilings with pillars and cornices a slightly darker shade of cream for contrast, and with brass fixtures and fittings that reflected the fleeting sunlight. Even the solid wood bureaus and desks were arranged neatly, some looking old enough to have been there as long as the building had, as if they had taken root. Even in sparsely furnished government buildings, a little beauty could be found if you knew where to look: a small painting here or there, a window that offered a view of the treetops or a panorama of the city's skyline—you just had to use a bit of imagination.

'I say, you don't fancy having a go at the memorandum yourself, do you?' Eleanor asked Maura as she slid into her seat and placed the folders on the desk's scratched leather surface. 'There's a packet of ciggies in it for you if you do.'

'You must be desperate. What are you working on that's so important?'

'I've got more visits to make and, well . . . there's just a lot to think about.'

But it wasn't only the workload. Eleanor knew she was being melodramatic, but she couldn't stop thinking about Jack and what had become of him. Who were those men? He'd appeared to go with them willingly, but it was so abrupt. Where had they taken him? Perhaps she should tell Mr Steadman after all—ask what he thought, at the very least.

The memory of Jack's pictures was distracting her too, and how he had made it all look so easy. Her own brushstrokes were clumsy and childlike in comparison, and she'd meant it when she told him that she no longer had time to paint; now that they were working every hour God sent, she wouldn't have time to complete any of her unfinished paintings, let alone start new ones.

Eleanor reached into the side drawer of her desk and pulled out a linen-bound sketchbook. She placed it on her lap, half-hidden from view, and looked through the pages; they were sketches, pencil figures, roughly drawn in pen and ink, all images from streetscapes and parks around the capital. Mild depictions of war and the struggles on the home front, not the grand records of combat that war artists like Pitchforth, Bawden and Cundall had produced, of men and their machines.

Maura tutted. 'Eleanor . . .'

'Just a minute,' she replied, searching the drawer again. She pulled out a book of earlier sketches and flipped through until she found the picture of a female worker at the wool mill her family owned. Her fingers traced across it; she had embellished only the fabric with colour, a pastel watermark staining the page, and had left the worker in black and white. The worked-up painting from this draft, *The Factory Worker*, had secured her place at the Slade, from where she had been recruited for the Ministry. It was a privilege to be working here, but to be offered a contract for her art, to be contributing paintings to the schemes that would help improve wartime morale—that was all she hoped for, and she just couldn't understand how Jack could turn it down.

'Come on, what is really so important?' Maura asked.

Eleanor took the contract from her satchel and passed it to her. 'Can you file this with the others, please?'

Maura looked at the empty signature line and back at Eleanor. 'But he didn't even sign it . . .'

Eleanor shrugged, not sharing the fact that she wanted to be able to find it again soon.

'And what's wrong with your filing, anyway?' Maura continued. 'Or have you forgotten the alphabet? It goes under "V".'

'"V" for very funny,' Eleanor said, smiling. 'So, what's in the diary for later?'

Maura picked up her teacup, narrowing her grey eyes at Eleanor over the rim as she drank. Despite being employed as a clerical assistant, Maura still didn't like taking instructions from Eleanor and she considered herself to be on an equal footing—even though she was far less qualified and a little younger.

Maura's parents, Patrick and Caitriona Sullivan, came from Kilkenny—just south of the River Nore, she always specified—and had moved to Greenwich just after they were married. Before then, her father had worked for the local brewery and her mother the wool mill, so Eleanor believed that she and Maura had something in common—although she had only three siblings in contrast to Maura's five, and her family owned the wool mill where they worked. Because Maura had grown up living hand-to-mouth, she made no secret of the fact that she couldn't wait to move, and that her upward mobility would require as much instruction and help as Eleanor was willing to give.

Maura drained the cup, making Eleanor wait for her to reply. 'You've got the restaurant in Finchley this afternoon. It's your third visit, isn't it?'

'Yes, hopefully they'll have sorted themselves out this time. Far too steamy for any of the paintings, though maybe not for a lithograph or two.'

'But before that, you are going to tell me what happened today,' Maura said. She stretched herself over the top of her Blue Bird typewriter, part of her upper body nearly disappearing into the machine's cavity.

Eleanor tried to compose the memorandum and field Maura's questions at the same time.

> *In connection with the decoration of British Restaurants, I am directed to bring to your notice a series of colour lithographs specially designed by modern artists and published by the Council for the Encouragement of Music and the Arts (CEMA).*
>
> *These reproductions are now becoming available. In general, the pictures have as a subject the 'occupation of the months' e.g. October Tree Felling and May, a Picnic. They have, therefore, a popular appeal. The size of the prints is 40" x 30" . . .*

'Well?' Maura asked impatiently.

'"V" is actually for "very confusing", if you really must know,' Eleanor replied as she carried on typing.

'Aye . . . and?' Maura asked more urgently.

'And . . . I'm sure you will agree with me, if you ever get to meet him.'

'Really? Why?' Maura said, abandoning the typewriter altogether and coming to sit on the edge of Eleanor's desk.

A group of pigeons shuffled noisily on the windowsill outside, and Eleanor tapped the glass in an effort to shush them away.

'Just ignore them,' said Maura. 'Come on, tell me!'

'I don't really know what to say.'

Eleanor was tempted to tell her friend about the meeting and Jack being spirited away, but Maura wasn't known for her discretion.

'Well,' Maura said craftily, 'you could start by telling me what he looks like . . . and what he was wearing.'

'I suppose you would say he is rather good-looking. Maybe Italian heritage.' Eleanor pictured his dark hair, sun-tanned skin and steady gaze.

'Can't you be more specific?' Maura asked, growing irritable.

'Maybe I should draw you a picture!' Eleanor replied with a trace of sarcasm.

'Now there's no need to be like that. I just want to know the basics. You know, the important ones like hair colour, eyes, that sort of thing.'

'Sorry,' Eleanor replied guiltily.

'Go on . . .'

'Well, he has dark hair and two eyes,' Eleanor said good-humouredly.

'Aw, you know exactly what I mean. What colour are they?'

'I didn't notice.'

Maura scowled. 'Why ever not! What were you looking at instead?'

'Alright, green. They were green. And I was watching him paint. He was just so . . . so patient with them.'

'With whom?'

'The children, of course!' Eleanor said, as if Maura should know exactly what she was talking about.

'Aye, but what did he say to you?'

'Well, not that much, really. He was painting, and I didn't want to spoil the moment.'

'Honestly, Eleanor, what's got into you?'

'You don't understand. I was just standing there watching him, but it seemed so . . . intimate. I didn't want to intrude.'

Maura sighed. 'And that's why you didn't manage to get the contract signed?'

'No, I didn't get the contract signed because he didn't want to sign it—there's really not much that one can do in those circumstances,' she said, knowing it to be half-true.

Clearly disappointed with the lack of any remotely interesting details, Maura returned to her typing. 'Aye, come on then, better get this sorted before Steadman finishes his meeting. And well done, Eleanor. It's another artist you haven't saved from extinction.'

'Oh dear, Steadman's not going to be very happy with me, is he?' she said, worried all over again. 'Who is he in there with, anyway?'

'Don't you know?'

'No.'

'It's Sir Robert Hughes.'

'Really?'

'No, I just made it up!'

Eleanor looked alarmed. 'What do you think he wants?'

'I have no idea, but they've been talking for ages. He arrived just before you got back.'

Sir Robert Hughes was the chairman of the War Artists' Advisory Committee, and he had never visited their office before. His wife, Lady Hughes, had been advising Lord Woolton on the decoration policy in British Restaurants, so perhaps Sir Robert was getting involved now too.

Eleanor was growing excited at the thought of meeting the man she had read and heard so much about, when the door opened and Sir Robert walked out. He was taller than he looked in any of the newspaper articles. His hair was thinning across the crown, but he had the confident walk of a man with authority. Before he reached the door, he turned and smiled.

Eleanor smiled back. As soon as he had gone, she gave Maura a meaningful look, snatched the memorandum out of her Blue Bird typewriter and hurried into Steadman's office.

'What do you *mean* Mr Valante wouldn't sign the contract?' Mr Steadman said, astonished when Eleanor broke the news. 'What did he say?'

'He simply said that he didn't want to. He said he would rather . . . How did he put it?' She fiddled with the string of the manila folder. 'He said he would rather be free to work with whichever department he chose.'

Steadman pursed his lips and frowned, wrinkling his unusually youthful features, before selecting a pen and scrawling a quick signature at the bottom of the memorandum. He wore his usual dark-grey pinstriped suit with a white shirt, red tie and matching pocket handkerchief. Middle age suited him, his fair hair and boyish features giving him an attractive youthfulness.

Eleanor was toying with how to explain what had happened next; it sounded so implausible that Jack had been virtually escorted from the room by two men who weren't even in uniform. She was beginning to think she had imagined the whole thing.

'Really!' Steadman continued. 'What sort of chap is he? The nerve of it . . . Hold on a minute—' he peered at Eleanor over the top of his glasses '—what did you say to him, exactly? You *did* have the right contract with you, didn't you?'

'Of course I did. I know all the different contracts, including the Ministry's one for artists working on the decoration policy.'

Its terms weren't as generous as the six-month commissions that the WAAC gave—six hundred and fifty pounds a year with transport, accommodation and meals included—but it offered some security at a time when there was little else for artists.

'That's right,' Eleanor said, 'I remember now—he said he'd rather take his chances and submit work to the various departments than be tied to what and when to paint.'

Steadman stood up and walked to the window, gazing out thoughtfully over the square below. The grassed area had been replaced with a Victory Garden, and a few lunchtime workers were tending the beds. Eleanor stared out too, her eyes fixed on a woman who was turning the soil with a small hoe, nestling seedlings into place.

'Is that really what he said?' Steadman asked, looking over his shoulder at Eleanor.

She knew that she had to tell the truth now or her chance would slip away. 'Yes, that's exactly what he said,' she replied, losing her nerve. Her attention came back to Steadman, noticing that his thumbs reached for his waistcoat pocket and missed.

'And there's nothing you can think of that would make him change his mind?'

'I don't think so, Mr Steadman. He seemed quite decided. But maybe if I try him again?' She had already made up her mind to take the contract and find Jack; that way she could learn what had happened to him and convince him to sign.

'Very well, what else is there to do?' Steadman asked. 'Nothing, it seems.' He answered his own question, as was his habit.

'So, I'll try again in a few days then, Mr Steadman?'

'I don't think so, Miss Roy.' His pale eyes lingered on her.

'I am sorry—'

'It is a shame, especially in light of my discussion with Sir Robert, but it can't be helped.'

She waited for him to explain, then asked, 'What can't be helped?'

'Never mind, we won't waste any more of our time on Mr Valante. I am sure that there will be someone else suitable who can take his place.'

Of course, there were artists ready to fill Jack's shoes—ones who were now free from their advertising jobs, former art-college teachers, commercial artists with no one to buy their work—the country was full of them. And there were no longer books for them to illustrate: the paper ration had seen to that. Artist friends of Eleanor's who had earned upwards of twenty guineas for their work on magazines such as *The Tatler* or who had been regular contributors to *Picture Post*, *The Sphere* or *The Illustrated London News* were now all unemployed—but none of them were Jack.

'Excuse me.' Mr Steadman retrieved his coat and hat from a hook on the door. 'If you don't mind, I'm late for a meeting. Please close the door on your way out, Miss Roy,' he said abruptly, as he left the office.

Eleanor returned to her desk, frustrated and confused; what had he meant by 'in light of my discussion with Sir Robert'?

'Aye, I think he's really cross,' Maura said. 'Your Mr Valante has set the cat among the pigeons. I don't think anyone has refused an offer before.'

'No, I don't think so either.' But Eleanor didn't believe that Mr Steadman was so worked up because of Jack; it was more likely something to do with Sir Robert.

'Come on, Eleanor, what aren't you telling me?' Maura said. 'There's something more to Mr Valante . . .'

Eleanor agreed, but right now she was more concerned about letting the department and her family down—and about how she could find Jack and make him change his mind.

Three

It was barely a ten-minute motorcycle ride from the Patriotic Building to Queenstown Road, but the bulky materials strapped to Jack's back slowed him down and made steering awkward. There had been hopes for a warmer spring, but despite an excess of sunshine, the roadside trees were still host to only small buds, and the birds that usually sang the evening song were sheltering from the rain. The roads were already congested with late afternoon traffic, and as Jack weaved through slow-moving cars, racing the dark clouds that chaperoned him home, his thoughts kept circling back to Miss Roy.

By the time he reached Battersea it had started to thunder, and he pushed his Triumph motorcycle through the gate and up the brick driveway just as the rain began to fall.

The narrow Victorian terrace was at the Battersea Park end of the road and was no different from millions of others in the capital; except it was his family home and the only one Jack had had for close to thirty years. Most of the houses in the street appeared empty, windows shattered and roofs reduced to skeletons, newly created amphitheatres of war. Battersea was on the 'pointy end of it', he'd explained to visitors from out of town, and he wasn't exaggerating: their part of London had been especially badly hit during the Blitz, and even now the water service was irregular and the electricity came and went as it pleased. He had tried to persuade his mother to move on many occasions, but she refused; he had come to understand that the noise of the trains, a nuisance to anyone else, gave her a reassuring connection to the outside world. She measured her days by the time the trains rumbled in and out of Waterloo Station, and she didn't need to use the brass carriage clock that sat on the mantelpiece.

He propped the Triumph on its stand, took off his helmet and goggles, and let himself in. He smelt cooking as soon as he opened the door, then something else—camphor—and found his sister in the kitchen, stooped over the stove.

'Thank you for dropping by,' she said pointedly. Her dark hair, usually smooth and neatly pinned, was frizzy around her face, her olive complexion moistened with steam from the pot she was stirring.

'I'm sorry, Beth. I got held up—'

'Really, where was it this time? The Rose & Crown or the Star & Garter?'

'It was a rare finch, if you must know. Spotted him in the trees just off the common.' Jack pulled a small sketchbook out of his top pocket and flipped open the page at a pen-and-ink sketch of the small bird, with detailed markings on its breast and wings. 'Thought they had all left—pretty little thing, he was. Not shy at all.'

'Yes, he is pretty,' Beth remarked, forgetting she was cross with him. 'Definitely male then?'

'Of course,' Jack replied with a smile.

He was relieved that he'd been able to get away as soon as he had; he had only been working with the Special Operations Executive since February but the demands on his time had already increased so much that he was having to make more and more excuses to his family for his long absences.

'It *is* only the animal kingdom, you know, so there's no need to despair,' Beth said.

Jack looked quizzical.

'We'll find a mate for you yet,' she added.

'It's okay, Beth. One wedding in the family is enough for now, thanks,' he said and meant it. He appreciated her efforts to fix him up, but he knew he had no time for relationships, especially since he'd be heading overseas at some point soon.

'You don't know until you try it,' she said.

'So, what did you manage to get hold of?' he asked, looking at the lumpy brown mass inside the pot and trying to change the subject.

'It's scrag end, if you must know—and I had to queue for half an hour, so mind your cheek. Anyway, go and see Mum. She's not good today.'

He made his way noiselessly down the dark hallway and into the living room, where Anne Valante sat in an upholstered armchair, her head tipped back, mouth slightly agape. Her breathing was shallow and he thought she must be dozing; he moved the wheelchair aside so that he could sit on the stool next to her.

The room was modestly furnished with a long-neglected piano against one wall, a sofa and two armchairs around a coffee table in front of the fire, and a side table where the wireless took centre stage. The floral curtains had faded but the pale cream walls lent the room a real warmth, as well as a neutral backdrop for the many pictures that his mother proudly displayed: Jack's framed book covers, individual lithographs and nature illustrations. On the mantelpiece, beside the carriage clock, stood a number of framed photographs of Jack in black tie at formal events alongside others of Beth's wedding and the children's christenings.

A copy of the *Daily Mail* lay open in his mother's lap, and a thick film had formed on the cup of tea that had grown cold on the table beside her. It touched Jack that despite being house-bound, she insisted on getting dressed every day. She looked quite demure in a maroon cardigan and grey dress, with lambskin slippers on her feet, although one had fallen off. She could almost be a duchess taking tea—or, at least, his mother when she'd still been mobile.

He'd bent down to fit the slipper back on when he realised that she was looking down at him. 'You would make a good spy, creeping up on people like that,' she murmured.

'I thought you were asleep,' he replied, the irony of her words not lost on him—if only his mother knew.

'I wish I could sleep, I really do.'

'Not a good night?'

She shook her head.

'Is it the pain, Ma?'

She nodded, lips pressed together as if she was bracing herself. 'It keeps me awake at night and then the drugs do during the day.'

His mother had been diagnosed with a degenerative disease when he was still at art school, her movements growing more and more restricted until she finally became wheelchair-bound. For a while the doctors had seemingly given up on finding out what was wrong or any remedy, but they were eventually able to give her disease a name: multiple sclerosis. But it seemed to Jack that medicine had not caught up with the number of people suffering from it, because his mother was told that her only treatment option was the introduction of drugs to dilate her blood vessels, and the love and care of her family.

'Is there anything I can get you?' he asked, fighting the urge to take her hand and pull her out of the chair, ready for the afternoon walk they always used to take.

She shook her head.

'Do you want me to massage the camphor into your legs?'

'No, pet. You can show me what you did today . . .' The tiredness had taken its toll and she looked pale against the cheerful floral fabric of the sofa; even her usually blue eyes were a dull grey.

He wasn't sure if he should show her the pictures of the orphans when she already seemed so low, so he came to stand beside her and pulled out the quick sketches he had done of the Patriotic Building. He had yet to shade the towers with the yellow wash of Yorkstone and paint the roof a wintry grey, but he had captured the building's grandeur.

'Do you remember,' he said, 'you used to take us there for picnics?'

'So we did. You've got a good memory,' she said, hands barely gripping the book. 'Just as well, I suppose . . .'

'I remember how everyone said it was haunted, and Beth didn't believe it and went inside anyway.'

'And got lost,' his mother said, smiling.

'We always used to take extra bread to feed the ducks.'

'Wouldn't be able to do that now.' She tried to summon another smile.

He thought of how full of life she had been; how he would do anything to see her like that again. 'Maybe I'll borrow a car and take you there at the weekend. What do you think, Ma?' He put the pad away and stifled a yawn.

'I think you're both working too hard. I've told Elizabeth that she mustn't come every night, but she won't listen to me. Will you have a word with her?'

'I've tried but you're right, she won't listen. Anyway, it's my fault—if I could be here more often, she wouldn't have to come.'

'You do more than enough,' his mother said, taking his hand. 'I don't know what I'd do without you.'

'It would help if I was a better cook, at least,' he said, bending to kiss her forehead.

Beth looked after their mother as best she could, but she had her own family to look after too and her job. Jack worried that it was all too much for her, and it still wasn't enough care for their mother.

The hands on the brass carriage clock slipped over to the six, and it began to chime.

'I can drive you to dinner, madam,' Jack said, setting up the wheelchair and pulling the footholds round so that he could help her into it.

'Would you mind if I ate in here tonight, luv? You two can sit together.'

'Really? We could come in here . . .'

'No need—Gracie Fields is on soon and I want to listen. Do you mind?'

'Of course not, Ma. Whatever you want. Gracie is probably much better company than us, anyway,' he said, forcing a smile.

He knew not to insist: some days she needed to be on her own so she didn't have to mask the pain. He just wished there was something more he could do to help.

Dining with his sister turned out to be a good idea, as they were able to catch up on family news. The scrag end tasted surprisingly better than it looked, and the dimly lit kitchen, which he usually found so dreary at night, seemed brighter. Beth was so animated when she talked about her husband, Henry, and her children, that for some reason Jack couldn't even explain to himself, he found himself telling her about Miss Roy. He related the whole encounter: their conversation and how the attractive young woman had wanted him to sign a contract for his lithographs—and how she had lingered so long watching him work.

'That's marvellous, Jack,' Beth said, scraping the leftovers out of the pot and onto her plate. 'So how much does the Ministry pay?'

Jack glanced away.

'What? What is it?'

'I didn't sign it, Beth. I couldn't,' he said, looking back at her. 'I'm away too much . . .'

The Special Operations Executive had first approached him in January when he had been working at the Chatham docks on a commission for the Admiralty. The angular lines of the ships and cranes had given him his first clue to the artist's potential for recording details that might count for so much more.

He wasn't allowed to talk to anyone about his work for the SOE, or about the upcoming training—the two agents had been quite adamant. All Jack knew was that he had passed the first phase of training, an induction into armed and unarmed combat skills, and that he would now attend a course in security and tradecraft before his final specialist training—if he made it through. It was a process that had required him to summon all his inner and physical strength, mastering new skills and techniques. He'd also had to develop the wherewithal to lie, or stretch the truth, to explain his frequent absences. And now he would need an explanation for his longer absence the following week too.

'What do you mean you couldn't sign it?' Beth asked, sounding exasperated. 'Have you thought about what we're going to do?'

'What we're going to about what? Ma?'

Beth narrowed her eyes. 'Yes, about Ma.'

'There are some really good facilities out of London,' he said. 'She would be safer . . .' He thought about the rural house in Buckinghamshire that he had attended for SOE training, and how it wasn't so different from the special-care facility he'd visited for his mother.

'They cost money,' Beth said. Now she sounded cross. 'Money we don't have, especially if you keep turning down work.' New lines appeared on her young face as she scowled at him.

'I know, Beth . . . I just couldn't do it.' He knew she would understand that no monetary value could be put on what he was doing—if he could only tell her the truth.

She threw up her hands. 'Anyway, I'm not going to put Ma into care. We've talked about this before. You've heard about these places . . . how they treat them.'

'That's why we start looking now; find a good one . . .'

'I'm not going to do it, Jack,' she said, eyes full of tears. 'That's final.'

He reached across the table and covered her hand with his. 'It's okay, Beth. We'll find a way, I promise.'

She used her other hand to wipe the tears away, just like one of his nephews might do. They were silent for a while, Gracie Fields' muted voice drifting through from the radio in the front room.

'It's not just Ma.' Beth sniffed. 'You can't let this stop you, Jack. Pretty soon you'll have no choice. You can't keep turning things down.'

'It's okay. I know what I'm doing.'

'Do you?' She sighed, reaching in her pocket for a handkerchief and blowing her nose. 'You know you'll get called up eventually.'

'Exactly,' he replied. 'Isn't that why it's better to get Ma settled somewhere now where she can be looked after properly?'

'We can manage—we have up until now,' Beth said. 'Anyway, where do you think we're going to get that sort of money? I thought you said that no one is buying art.'

'That's true. I've had a few commissions, but there's not much money in it. Not after all the medicine and specialists . . .'

She was right: they didn't yet have enough for full-time care, and he didn't have the heart to tell her that he had only sold four paintings in the past year. But there would be a regular income soon from the SOE and he was on the verge of telling her so.

'Well,' she said, 'that's all the more reason you should take an artist contract if you are offered one—you'll be on a salary.'

'It wasn't the WAAC, it was some other scheme I hadn't heard of.'

'Does it matter who it is, as long as you're earning money? Isn't it better that you work as an artist rather than get called up as a soldier? How long do you think it will be now?'

He couldn't tell her that the SOE was training him to run reconnaissance in the field. Journalists and photographers weren't always accurate, and Jack could offer another means of surveillance—one that would provide a much more detailed account of foreign territory and the enemy. He had the ability to record the status of a campaign, and produce thumbnail sketches bearing cryptic notes that offered vital clues once they had been couriered back home and deciphered by the SOE.

'I will go, Beth,' he said, knowing that the moment he might have told her had passed. 'And I will get the money we need. We just need to get Ma used to the idea of moving first.' Jack glanced at the open door through to the hallway. Grace Fields was still singing, and he hoped that their mother hadn't overheard their conversation. He rose and softly closed the door.

'You know if there was any way I could have her at my house, I would,' Beth said, sniffing again, 'but not with Henry's mum and the kids . . .'

'It's okay. I know there's no room. It's impossible, and you do enough, Beth, you really do. No one could ask for more.' Jack stroked her hand.

She looked up at him, her tear-streaked face making her seem childlike. 'I know you think you should be here to help, Jack, but you've got a life as well and a responsibility to all of us . . . and your country, not just to Ma.'

He knew this all too well, but he couldn't tell her why.

Four

As Eleanor struggled to keep the picture upright—and her fingers from getting bound by tape while Maura secured the brown packing paper—she couldn't help but think of the men and women at other government institutions whose sole function was to take care of important artefacts, packing and transporting them, whereas here it fell to her and Maura to service all those needs.

'Watch out! You nearly snipped my finger,' she shouted, pulling her hand from the path of the blades. 'I thought you were supposed to be good with scissors!'

'Aye, I'm sorry,' said Maura, 'but it's not really my fault, is it? I mean, you said yourself that it doesn't seem fair that we have to do *everything* ourselves. There's just not enough time.'

'Well, we don't really have a choice, do we? And I don't think it's too much of a sacrifice,' Eleanor replied shortly.

Maura glared at her and they carried on in silence.

The storeroom was quiet, tucked down in the basement away from the offices and close to the underground shelter where they were sent during air raids and for practice fire drills. The basement hadn't been decorated as recently as the floors above, and its walls were yellowing, the wooden floor knotted and rough. With only a few prints—reproductions of famous pictures—and no windows or natural light, it was a gloomy space, and Eleanor always hurried their work so they could leave quickly. Even the usually comforting smell of old wood was tinged with a mustiness that made her want to cover her mouth.

For now, the basement was the only room available for storing the artworks that were constantly trafficked between the artists' studios and the British Restaurants. There were dozens of them: watercolours, posters, and a large stack of lithographs propped against the wall, the top one depicting a harvest with a bounteous crop from the English countryside. It was to be packaged and sent to a restaurant in Clapham where conditions were unsuitable for a mural; Eleanor had visited and decided that a full-colour lithograph would enliven the space instead.

'You know that Clive is coming for this now, don't you?' Eleanor reminded Maura.

'Aye, well, this isn't going to give them much to think about over their eggless puddings, is it?' Maura sighed as she took hold of the other side of the frame.

'What's wrong with it?' Eleanor said, considering the scene.

'Well, nothing . . . and everything. They're a little traditional, aren't they?'

'I think it's wonderful to have a pastoral scene over lunch,' Eleanor said with an air of authority. 'If only more of our war artists would get on and paint some of our domestic scenes rather than just aeroplanes and battleships.'

What she really thought was that it was wonderful to have art coming out of the galleries and museums and into their everyday lives—not only the elite could enjoy art now. Of course, she didn't want to say this in front of Maura for fear of sounding just like one of the snobs they encountered in those galleries.

'I think it's interesting to see what's helping win the war for us,' Maura replied. 'It's comforting to see the machines we've got on our side and—'

'Shhh,' Eleanor said, turning up the wireless. 'It's the one o'clock bulletin in a minute.'

'Oh good, can we listen to *Battle of the Bands* after?' Maura asked, looking up at the ceiling as the lights spluttered and nearly went out.

Eleanor nodded, eager for Maura to be quiet so she could hear the news. It was only a few weeks ago that the Japanese had made a surprise raid on the harbour and airfield at Broome in Western Australia, destroying planes and boats. If that wasn't bad enough, they had taken Batavia, the capital of the East Indies. Only yesterday, the BBC World Service had reported how their aggressive campaign was intensifying. There were fears that they were advancing on Port Moresby and that this held a threat for Australia.

Eleanor's two brothers were in the navy, and so was Mr Steadman's only son—and on a ship that had taken part in the Dutch East Indies campaign. Squeezing onto the stool close to the wireless, she clutched her knees as she listened, planning to telephone her parents that night to see if there was any news of Clarence or Francis. A fingernail played between her teeth as she fought the urge to bite it off.

She was anxious about Jack too. It had been almost a fortnight since her visit to the Patriotic Building, and she had failed to find him. She had contacted the War Office, the Admiralty and the Ministry of Information, but there was no record of him having submitted any of his work. She thought that if she could just talk to him again, then she might get him to change his mind—to submit some of his work for the scheme, at least—and show Mr Steadman that she had tried.

'As bad as you thought?' Maura asked when the bulletin was over.

'No, worse than I thought. And I was also thinking about Jack . . . how he seems to have disappeared.'

Eleanor finished securing the package, tying it with a small knot that the carrier could place their finger through, and passed it to Maura.

'Perhaps he has joined up,' said Maura. 'Now they've extended conscription to forty-five, he might have got the message that he is actually needed. Who knows, maybe he's been posted already . . . ?'

Maura was probably right: there was a good chance that he had enlisted. Sir Robert's scheme to protect artists by giving them the role of recording the war, rather than becoming cannon fodder, wasn't for everyone.

'But if you're right,' Eleanor said to Maura, 'don't you think I would have found mention of him at the Records Office?'

'Aye, I would have thought so, but you know how mistakes can get made. Just face it, Eleanor,' Maura said matter-of-factly, 'you've missed your chance with him. Best get on with things and forget you ever met Jack Valante.'

But Eleanor couldn't forget about him—she had thought about little else over the past fortnight. It was irritating, not least because danger was all around her and here she was worrying about an artist, albeit a handsome one, whom she barely knew.

She had only been in her role for six months and really wanted to do well. It wasn't just to prove her father wrong but also to show him that what she was doing was worthwhile, even if she wasn't a proper war artist yet, and that Francis and Clarence weren't the only ones contributing to the war effort. It was expected that her brothers would continue their education and go into the family's textile business but little had been imagined for her and Cecily. Her success at school, the scholarship, and the acceptance to art school, all of it had been a surprise—except to her. She thought with her paintbrush, saw the world more clearly once it had been committed to paper, or slate or linen or whatever was available, even when it had been off-cuts of fabric from their factory floor.

A picture on the wall caught her eye: a David Bomberg print. Its depiction of Canadian workers had caused a major stir because of its futuristic impressionism. She looked at the diverging lines, considering how she would feel if Jack had changed his mind and gone to fight. She wouldn't think any less of him for it—probably the reverse, in fact.

'If Jack has gone overseas, maybe he's working for the WAAC and signed a contract after all,' she said, thinking aloud. There was a chance he had refused her contract in favour of the one offered by the WAAC; after all, their terms were better.

'Well, that's another good reason to forget about him then. You don't want someone who is so easily swayed, one minute thinking one way, then changing his mind the next.'

'That's not what I was thinking at all—have I really taught you nothing?' Eleanor replied, propping another packaged lithograph against the wall and standing up straight. 'If he had registered with any of the services then I really think I would have come across his name by now, so the fact that I haven't must mean that he has stuck to his principles.'

'Which means that you want to find him even more . . .'

Maura was right about this, but it wasn't just because Eleanor wanted to sign him; she also wanted to make sure he was safe.

Suddenly, she needed to get out of the basement. 'I need a distraction,' she said, picking up Maura's handmade jacket and handing it to her. 'Come on, let's go and see Myra.' The celebrated pianist Myra Hess was playing another recital at the National Gallery.

'But what about Clive?'

'He'll be fine—he should know where to go. And if not, he can just drive around in circles for a while,' Eleanor said, giggling.

'I'm really not sure I fancy it, to be honest with you,' said Maura. 'I had a bit of a session last night . . . my feet are still killing me.'

She did look a little the worse for wear: her usually neat brown bob hung limply against her neck, and her suede shoes had lost their sheen and some of the tassels were missing.

'Alright, we can hop on the bus then,' said Eleanor. 'I'll even treat you to a sandwich.'

It was only ten minutes to the National Gallery, where lunchtime concerts were held now that its vast rooms were empty, the precious artworks transported away for safekeeping. Eleanor knew that Maura would enjoy herself once they were there—the raisin and honey sandwiches alone were worth the trip. The recitals had become hugely popular, and so too had the temporary exhibitions by visiting and emerging artists.

'I wonder what the Picture of the Month is?' Maura asked.

'I did hear that there's an exhibition of work by CEMA, although I'm not sure we'll have time to look afterwards.'

'Really? I don't think Steadman will be back until much later . . . and you *are* in charge,' Maura replied authoritatively.

'I'm not sure I like what you're suggesting,' Eleanor said, narrowing her eyes at Maura, 'but let's wait and see.'

It was an unusually blue spring day. The bus didn't come straight away, so they were running late for the one o'clock performance by the time they reached Trafalgar Square and the rudimentary brick walls of the surface air-raid shelters came into view. The statue of Charles I was safely cocooned in stacks of sandbags, while nothing could be done to protect Nelson's Column towering above, so it had been put to good use: its base was covered in posters to advertise for urgently needed nurses and volunteers.

Eleanor tried to tally up the hours and days that it must have taken, and still took, to safeguard the nation's monuments and paintings—whole government departments were involved. It was important to preserve their culture, just in case Hitler succeeded and the worst imaginable outcome became reality—wasn't that what Churchill had said?

Trafalgar Square was hectic. Office workers mingled with off-duty soldiers, and mothers pushed prams past arm-in-arm couples. In the middle was the incongruous sight of a group of women engaged in their lunchtime stretching class. Eleanor and Maura made their way past a small stand of fundraising servicemen and women, then headed to the gallery entrance. A queue stretched all the way from the imposing portico and around into Charing Cross Road where the empty theatres stood. As they drew closer to the entrance, Eleanor grasped Maura's hand and pulled her to hurry up the stone steps.

Just inside the grand neoclassical columns, two women stood collecting the entrance fee, bold black letters on their collection boxes announcing that it was for the Musicians Benevolent Fund. Eleanor showed her government pass and then pressed two one-shilling coins through the slot.

'Thank you, Miss Roy. Enjoy the concert.'

She escorted Maura up two flights of steps towards the Barry Rooms where the lunchtime concerts took place. They strode quickly past hollow galleries now out of bounds, where the walls were still decorated with frames like empty eye sockets, their treasured paintings gone. In another larger gallery to the right, grand gilt frames stood statesman-like against bare walls.

During the First World War, major artworks had been evacuated into the disused tunnels beneath the Strand. This time, the underground was needed for shelter during air raids, so Wales had been chosen as the destination for the nations' treasures; Eleanor knew this because she had applied to be part of the curatorial team dispatched with the artworks to manage their safe transport and storage, but she had been deemed too young. Now she liked to visit the gallery regularly, and she considered herself to be a cultural caretaker here instead.

The piano music grew louder as she and Maura carried on down the marbled corridors, the air growing rich with the scents of tea and tobacco. As they approached, Eleanor saw through the half-open door into the brightly lit Barry Room where the audience was seated on wooden chairs, the concert well underway. Once inside, Eleanor realised that the room was absolutely packed, so they squeezed into the standing area at the back. Despite the Home Office mandate that no more than two hundred people should gather in a public place at any one time, there were at least twice as many here, and all equally transfixed. Everyone was sculpturally still.

Installed neatly behind the Steinway grand piano on a makeshift platform, her black hair middle-parted and pinned into its signature waves, Myra Hess's head was bowed in concentration as she played. Eleanor wasn't surprised to see Miss Hess in her usual black tailored jacket, white silk blouse with a bow and string of pearls, but today the sunlight shone down on her through the octagonal glass dome as if she was blessed.

Maura's dark eyes darted about, taking it all in.

Eleanor looked at her and smiled. 'See,' she whispered, 'I told you this would do us both the world of good.'

The crowd included men and women of all ages, servicemen and civilians, bald heads and horn-rimmed glasses, faces creased in concentration, smooth-skinned young women with necks craned, older ladies in flowered dresses and smart jackets, hands pressed in their laps, heads tilted in quiet contemplation. There were many other girls just like her and Maura, Eleanor guessed, who would rather substitute music for their lunch.

A woman sitting in the row in front of them had her head angled to one side, her hands resting under her chin, statuesque. Eleanor understood how she felt—that there was something quite sacred about this experience; other than church, this was the one place where people could forget, where music could reach through the numbness. Eleanor had brought her mother here when the string quartet had played Mozart and Sir Henry Wood had performed, and her mother had agreed that her spirit had soared. But Myra was still Eleanor's favourite, even if there was never a chair to sit on, and she favoured Brahms over Schumann. Thankfully, Miss Hess was playing Mozart today, his Piano Concerto No. 17 in G—Eleanor's wretched piano teacher had made her play it for years. In a stroke of luck, and with surprise, she realised she was not sick of the sound of it.

She took a deep breath and exhaled; she could listen to the music and focus on the present. If she could just stop thinking about Jack and concentrate on their catalogue of work, then when they returned to the office she would be prepared and able to get on with everything. It would be her own overture of sorts.

As Myra's practised fingers danced across the keys, and the audience's attention was held, Eleanor leaned her head back against the wall and looked up at the frescoes and curved panes of glass. No matter how many times she visited the gallery, she could never comprehend how craftsmen could produce such intricate works; it left her feeling overwhelmed by the accomplishments of her fellow human beings. How did those nine pieces of glass become one smooth dome assembled so precisely that it never fell down, despite the heavy storms and bomb blasts? And the frescoes—how had anyone achieved that detail over a hundred years ago? Sometimes it was too much to think about and she had to turn her mind to something more manageable, such as the mural she was currently overseeing at the restaurant in Barnet. That was simple enough: the artists chose their subjects and stood on ladders to complete them, as with all the other murals she had overseen. There must be dozens of them by now, and she slumped against the wall and tried to picture each and every one.

It seemed like barely five minutes, but it must have been fifty-five, when Maura nudged her. 'Better be getting back.'

Miss Hess was playing the first chords of 'Jesu, Joy of Man's Desiring', a sign that it was the end of the program and that others would be leaving too.

'Let's just hear this,' Eleanor insisted.

The music reached its crescendo and the audience was still enraptured. Then Eleanor thought about Mr Steadman arriving back at the office and finding it empty.

The final notes spilled from the keys as Myra transported the audience beyond the confines of the gallery and away from the battlefields. As clapping replaced the fading music, Maura and Eleanor made their way out through the audience who lined the back wall.

They were nearly at the exit when Eleanor caught hold of Maura's arm. 'Let's just have a quick look.'

'But what about our sandwiches? I'm starving . . .'

Eleanor smiled. 'Just a glimpse . . .'

She couldn't resist the Picture of the Month exhibition, and so they turned back the way they'd come, detouring to the left through an archway and up a flight of steps. The applause was subsiding from the floor below, and the scraping of chairs and the rumble of voices reverberated through the century-old stone.

Now they were in rooms thirty-four, thirty-five and thirty-six. The galleries that had been given over to the exhibitions on war were wide and connected like honeycomb, with carved woodwork, ornate brass and twenty-foot glass ceilings creating an easy space to navigate.

Eleanor and Maura walked around freely, spending several minutes looking at the works on display, until the crowd grew and the swell of people behind them struggled to get a view. There were shared whispers and murmurs of appreciation, some artworks earning more enthusiastic praise than others. Eleanor saw the reactions and felt a reverence—a renewed understanding of the value of the war artist's work.

The crowd had its own momentum, pulling her along and drawing her towards a series of pen-and-ink pictures and watercolours: small but vivid depictions of St Paul's. This exhibition would be going on tour to America, so the pictures weren't just about improving morale here but also promoting Britain overseas.

'Don't you think we should be getting back now?' Maura asked worriedly.

'In a moment,' Eleanor said, without looking round.

She was totally absorbed in the picture in front of her. It was only a small watercolour but it captured the setting sun so vividly that it was like seeing a sunset for the first time. It took her back to her childhood and the memory of her father's anger at her staying out to paint too long. There had been spectacular colours in the dyes at her parents' woollen mill and in the skies that changed so dramatically from rose to storm grey. She and her siblings had wandered the foothills of the Pennines for hours, Francis and Clarence exploring, while she and Cecily recorded the tones and textures in their sketchpads until only a fraction of amber was left in the sky.

Maura was getting restless. She clearly didn't share Eleanor's sentiment about these paintings, and how could Eleanor explain how they made her feel? That she would do anything to sit in place of these artists, to have the chance to capture the images as they had? Instead she could only stand there and close her eyes, imagining it to be her fingers guiding the brushes, filling in the details and blending the tones.

Eleanor believed that she could produce pictures like these, that she could paint and draw as well as any of the war artists whom she had seen; but she also knew that only a few women were working as war artists, and none yet had gone overseas.

Five

ENGLAND, SEPTEMBER 2010

There's solidarity among strangers when you are sharing stale air with them. Kathryn often eyed fellow aeroplane passengers closely and could tell when they were doing the same. Just over twenty-four hours ago, she had surveyed the queue at the check-in counter, examining their clothes and faces for any sign of who they were and what they might be carrying: she could be sharing her last moments with these people!

She had catalogued the amount of hand luggage they carried and judged them on it—selfish if they carried too much and lacking in personal hygiene if there wasn't enough to sustain them through their long-haul flight. Forget the disposable toothbrushes and miniature tubes of moisturiser, real travellers brought their own. She should know, she had been doing the trip for long enough, but she was still just as relieved each time they lurched forward when the wheels touched down and the brakes locked in.

This wasn't one of her usual trips, though, and back in the moment she took a deep breath as she guided her suitcase across the baggage hall, relieved to be through customs before the crowds from other international flights could swallow her up.

Earlier that week, she had stood in her lounge room looking at the silhouette of London's skyline, the sunset a crimson smudge on the horizon that set the buildings in the centre eerily ablaze. Two tiny figures were on a rooftop, bold strokes of paint softening towards the edge of the painting, the blacks and greys of the buildings graduating into amber and yellow from the middle of the frame, the miniature initials 'J.V.' in the bottom right corner. The oil, *The Crimson Sun*, was small—only 10 x 13.5 inches—but the standard size for a Second World War painting of its kind. Kathryn had regarded the artwork silently until she felt her husband, Christopher, come to stand beside her.

'So, tell me again what's so special about this one,' he said, handing her a mug.

'Thank you,' she said, glancing at the milky tea. She was trying not to focus on the negatives, but after more than a decade he should be able to make it the way she liked it. She looked back at the oil painting. 'I don't know,' she told Chris. 'I know it's not one of his official war pictures, though. Anyway, I'm sure I'm going to find out . . .'

'And this is why you're abandoning us?' he said, half-serious.

'That's right. There seems to be some rush to find the artist. Not sure why, but I'm sure Eleanor will tell me when she's ready.'

At the kitchen table behind them, Oliver was chasing Pokédex on his Nintendo DS, the noise echoing through to them even though the volume was set typically low. Kathryn's eyes were still fixed on the painting; while she had no idea how to play the video game—she left that for Chris's bonding time with their ten-year-old son—there was little that she didn't know about the effects of colour and form and composition, and how their combination could have an emotional effect on an individual. It was what she had learned as part of art therapy—and what using it with children like Oliver had shown her.

'You know how selfish old people get,' Chris said, unable to conceal the irritation in his voice.

She let the remark go. Her grandmother had always been very private—and she had always put others first. That's why Kathryn had been so surprised by the phone call asking her to bring the painting home. She had been even more surprised by Eleanor's tone; she had never heard her so insistent about anything before. *I need your help, Kathryn; you have to find out what happened to Jack—and you must bring the painting with you.*

'She knows it's term time,' Kathryn said, 'and I've told her that we're under pressure with the appeal, so it must be important.'

'Have you told her about us?' he asked.

'No,' she said, turning to meet his gaze. 'I wanted to tell her in person.'

Kathryn had made her mother, Abigail, promise to keep their separation quiet for the time being, at least until they had worked out if it was going to be permanent—and she needed the time away to help figure out whether she wanted it to be.

They both stood silently, observing the picture. She had always admired it—felt an affinity with it—but now it made her feel sad, the two small figures seeming as remote now as Chris felt to her.

'How can she even be sure that he's still alive?' Chris said, breaking the uncomfortable silence. 'I mean, how many of these nonagenarians are there?'

'She's managed that much research, at least—the registry confirmed there's no death certificate for Jack Valante.'

'Maybe he died abroad. Or in the past week. It's possible . . .'

'Anything is possible, Chris, but she has never done anything like this before.'

It wasn't what Eleanor had said, it was how she had said it: *I've never asked you for anything before, dear, you know that, but now you must trust me.*

'Maybe I'm mistaken, though,' she said, eyes lingering on the two figures. 'I always thought it was his artwork that was special to her— but maybe it was him.'

This felt like an apology rather than an explanation.

The painting had hung on the wall of their home since they'd arrived in Melbourne. Eleanor gave it to her when they moved, and it had always felt like a connection to her, and the home Kathryn had left behind. It was a link to the country and people she yearned for. It was now displayed in the home Christopher had designed and built for them in South Yarra—and that they might soon need to sell.

Kathryn took a sip of her tea, thinking about the phone call and the two years since her last trip back to the UK.

'Still, it's a bit much to ask,' Chris continued. 'How can she expect you to just drop everything. Drop Oliver . . .'

'I'm not dropping him! Stop being so dramatic. I'll only be gone for a week, and Oli will be fine. Anyway, you'll be busy practising for your piano concert, won't you, darling?' she said, glancing over at their son.

Oliver looked up from his game, grey eyes pronounced against his deep black lashes. 'You go, Mummy, if Granny needs you. Daddy and I will be alright.'

'Thank you, darling,' she said, smiling until she caught Chris's eye.

'If you insist,' he said, 'but you can let her know that I'm not very happy about it—'

'I'll do no such thing! What on earth could I hope to achieve by doing that?'

Kathryn held her breath, trying not to react, feeling the bitterness and insecurity that had begun to bloom like a mould in their relationship. Since he had reluctantly agreed to the separation, she knew he was worried that her trip would cement her concerns over their marital issues and her homesickness, and that the split would become permanent.

'I'm sorry,' Chris said, 'It's just . . .' He looked at Oli and lowered his voice. 'The terror attacks and the plane crash in Libya—I just don't like thinking of you all the way over there.'

'I'm not going to Libya,' she whispered, 'and it's not as if you won't know what's happening. You can check 24/7, and we can Skype and talk.'

'You've never been away from us before . . .'

'I know,' she said, softening.

Oliver had finished his Nintendo game. He measured out the precise half teaspoonful of fish flakes before sprinkling them into the tank, the three fish angling their mouths upwards to take big gulps. This meant that it was nearly time for dinner; her last one until she returned, and the thought of it brought a sense of ceremony to the occasion. Of course she was worried about travelling and the security risks too, but it was good timing for her to go away and think about the future.

And so here she was, safely landed at Heathrow and navigating her way through Terminal 3 with hundreds of conversations buzzing around her in dozens of languages, mobile phones connecting them in an invisible spider-web across the globe. Far from making her nervous or homesick, the energy around her was electrifying.

'Darling, you're here . . .' Abigail trilled when Kathryn answered her mobile.

'Yes, Mum. Remarkable, isn't it? Only twenty-four hours and a winter wardrobe later, and it's as if I've never been away.'

Switching on her Bluetooth so that she was hands-free and able to guide her luggage through the obstacle course of trolleys, Kathryn headed down the concourse towards the car rental kiosks. It wouldn't be long before the rush hour started, and she wanted to get to her grandmother's house before commuters choked the roads.

'How was your journey?' her mum asked.

'Good. Qantas kept their promise, delivered on the Chardonnay and plenty of pretzels and mixed nuts—and I got some work done.'

'Are you rested?'

Kathryn hesitated. Did she mean had-a-sleep-on-the-flight rested, or caught up on the days of sleep she had missed during Oliver's recent bout of chicken pox and Christopher's inability to cope? 'I'll have a nap when I get there, Mum.'

Her mother couldn't always handle the truth, and so Kathryn had learned to filter what she told her. The long distance frustrated both of them—Abigail eager to help but practically unable to, and Kathryn needing the support that her mother was unable to give—so now it was just easier to pretend that everything was okay.

'Well, I wouldn't bank on that, darling,' Abigail said with a proprietorial sniff. 'Seems as if the old girl is going to put you straight to work.'

'How is she?'

'I'm not really sure. This whole business is rather perplexing—she's got your father and me completely flummoxed. I mean, why wait nearly seventy years to tell us about this man, and then all the sudden urgency to find out what happened to him? It just doesn't make any sense.'

'But she's okay?'

'I suppose so . . . She's vacillating between sleeping a lot and being quite anxious. Desperate to see you, though.'

Kathryn pictured Eleanor's shrunken frame cocooned in her fluffy Marks & Spencer dressing-gown. It had been a shock when her mother called to say that her grandmother needed her home; she had been ill for so many years with one thing or another that Kathryn had thought her indestructible: angina, arthritis, chest infections, but nothing that would kill her. Or so she had thought. *A creaking door never breaks*, was what Eleanor always said to her, and she found it comforting to think like that: Eleanor would always be there, just a little creakier. Then Kathryn had discovered the reason for the request and her concern for her grandmother's health had intensified—why the sudden urgency?

'I'm hoping the journey won't take too long. Google Maps doesn't seem to think so, anyway. When are you back?' Kathryn asked into her Bluetooth.

'I'm not entirely sure, darling. We've got some important guests here until Friday afternoon so hopefully we'll fly back at the weekend.'

It was always the same with her parents' businesses: at first unpredictable, their hotel was now always booked out and its demands were relentless. It seemed as though Kathryn hardly ever got to see them.

'That's a shame,' she said, disappointed that she would have to wait another four days, if she saw them at all. 'Never mind, at least you're coming down at Christmas, that's not too long. Oliver is planning your days already—he can't wait to see you.'

'Yes, your father and I can't wait either.' Abigail sighed. 'We really need a holiday, and it will be good to get some sunshine. How is the little pickle?'

'Oh, you know . . . still a pickle.'

'And Christopher—how are things? Is he being more supportive now?'

Kathryn hesitated. 'I'm not sure I would use that expression. More accepting, maybe . . .' She was nearing the front of the car rental queue and would need to hang up soon; and besides, she didn't want to discuss her marital problems so publicly. 'Anyway, there's still nothing you can think of to help me with Gran? Nothing you ever heard about Jack?'

Kathryn placed her phone on top of the trolley and pulled on her worn leather biker jacket, tugging the arms down so they covered her fingers—she had forgotten the penetrating chill of these autumn mornings.

'No, darling,' said her mum, 'I haven't got a clue about any of it, and I'm not altogether sure it's not another of her ruses to get your father and me running around after her.'

'That's not the impression she gave me. And didn't you say she seems quite anxious?'

'Yes, I know. Well, see what you can do, pumpkin. If anyone can sort this mess out, you can.'

The conversations around Kathryn had grown louder, more intrusive, and her vision was undulating a little. As she got to the front of the queue and reached the Avis counter, the last of her energy slipped away. Perhaps it was the jet lag kicking in, or maybe the thought of a world without Eleanor in it.

Kathryn was relieved to see Oliver's pixelated face, even though the sound kept dropping out. She hunched over the wheel of the stationary Volkswagen Golf, straining to get Skype on the terminal's free wi-fi. Kathryn wasn't pleased about the dark circles beneath her son's heavy eyes, despite the time difference and the fact that he was already in his *Simpsons* pyjamas.

'Are you okay?' she asked.

'Yes, Mummy. We had pizza!' His voice sounded younger than his ten years, although maybe it always did and she just didn't notice when she was with him all the time.

'Lovely', she said, 'don't tell me—margherita . . .'

'And I had an ice cream.'

'How was Finn?'

'I wasn't with Finn. Look what I made.' He held up a small, intricately built Lego car and then started driving it frantically around and around the computer screen.

'Who were you with?' Kathryn asked.

'A man and lady from Daddy's work.'

'Oh, why didn't you go with Bill and Amy?'

They spent most Friday nights with Bill and Amy—their son, Finn, was one of the few friends that Oliver still had.

'Don't know. Daddy picked me up and we went to his work. I think he was cross, though.'

'Why do you say that?'

The Lego car was picking up speed, moving faster and faster as his arm rotated, swirling dozens of mini Bart Simpsons rapidly in front of her.

'Oli, can you please stop that? Why did Daddy get cross?'

'I don't know,' Oliver said as he banged the car on the desktop, some of the Lego bricks splitting apart.

'But everything's okay?'

'When are you coming back?'

'I won't be long, sweetheart. I miss you.'

He was no longer looking at her, but pressing the pieces back in place. 'When are you coming back?'

'I told you, sometime next week. I'm doing something for Granny, remember—it's a sort of treasure hunt.'

'So you've hidden something and Granny has to go and look for it?' he asked, dark shaggy hair suddenly filling the screen.

She had his attention again. 'Yes, Oli, something like that. Only I'm the one doing the searching.'

'And what are you going to find, Mummy?'

'I'm not sure, but it's very precious to Granny—that's why I need to stay here. Until I've found it.'

'That's okay. I don't mind.'

'Thank you, Oli. Now, is Daddy there? Can I have a word?'

'Yes, Mummy.'

'Love you.' She reached out to touch him but the blue and yellow cartoon collage was already spinning down the hallway.

The small video box at the side of the screen showed her reflection and the traces of black under her eyes. She used her fingertips to wipe away the smudged mascara but unfamiliar shadows remained;

hopefully it was the car's lighting, because surely she couldn't have aged that much overnight. Brushing her long blonde fringe to one side, she tucked the stray strands behind her ears and sat up taller in the car seat.

She heard voices in the background and then footsteps on the floorboards moving towards their office. It was supposed to have been a bedroom for their second child but when the problems with Oliver started she'd wavered between wanting another child, to normalise their lives, and then feeling guilty because she felt that way. In the end she was too exhausted to try and too scared in case the baby developed autism too; not to mention that Christopher might respond in the same way as he had with Oliver, burying himself in work.

The strain showed on his face as soon as he sat down. She could see the remains of dinner on his shirt, red streaks on white as he placed his glass down.

'How are you?' she asked.

'Great! Bloody marvellous, in fact!'

'Oh, you're joking.'

'The whole bloody night was a joke.'

She tried to ignore the drumbeat of her heart and focus on all that was good about her husband. 'What happened?' she asked, fiddling with the tassels on her scarf.

'It's probably my fault,' he said, pulling his fingers through his hair. 'It was Jenny and Scott—I couldn't reschedule so I thought we could just get an early dinner. It was a nightmare. This really is the worst time for you to be away, with the appeal . . .'

Kathryn understood his frustration. Nautilus was a sustainable housing development that had been his passion project for as long as she could remember, and it had been a mammoth task to get it this far. She had also invested excessive hours of her own time designing the interiors. Losing the appeal would cost them a fortune personally and put the practice back years—it had also been one of the pressures on their marriage.

'Christopher, please,' she said. 'We've been through this.' She knew her increased heart rate was in anticipation of this, the inevitable confrontation about her being away. She took a deep breath. 'Just tell me what happened at dinner.'

'Oli went nuts when the pizza came. They brought him a pepperoni one by mistake. He picked off every single piece and then scraped the topping off because it was too soggy. It went everywhere!'

'But he's okay?'

'Yes, of course he's okay. I made him some toast when we got home. We had to leave the restaurant, though—he caused such a scene.' Chris took a large gulp of red wine. 'I don't think we've got a hope in hell of winning this appeal, I really don't.'

Kathryn struggled to keep her cool. 'He's just out of his usual routine. Did he sleep last night?'

'Yes, of course he did.'

'Don't say "of course". There's never any certainty with Oli, you know that. What about tomorrow, what are you going to do?'

'I don't know, maybe we'll spend the day at Luna Park and eat a shitload of lollies! What do you think?' His sarcasm stopped being funny after the first couple of drinks.

'Maybe call Amy,' she said calmly. 'Finn could come over for a few hours—'

'Maybe.' Christopher leaned back and the office chair creaked as he took another slurp of wine. 'How's everything with you? How was your journey?'

'Fine. I'm heading to Gran's now. In fact, I'd better get going before the M25 gets too clogged.'

He raised an eyebrow. 'Really?'

'Yes, anyway, I'm sure Oli would love you to read with him.' She didn't want to talk to Chris when he was like this. Besides, he did need to make sure Oliver was in bed: it was way past his bedtime, and he was already clearly struggling without his usual routine.

'Okay,' Chris said, 'will you Skype when you get there . . . or to-morrow?'

'I'll try, but I might stay in London tomorrow night.'

'Oh, who with?'

She ignored the implication. 'You *will* read to him, won't you? He's really into the Percy Jackson books.'

Chris stiffened. 'Yeah, sure. Don't worry, he'll be fine.'

'Okay. And I've nearly finished the Nautilus concept documents. I'll email the draft when I get to Gran's. If you look at it then, I can do any changes for you tomorrow morning.'

'Thanks, Kat,' he said, leaning forward, roguishly handsome face filling the screen. 'And, Kat, I do still love you.'

'I know.' He looked so different when his features weren't cor-rupted by stress and anger. 'I've got to go. Let's talk later.'

'Okay—but, Kat . . .'

'Yes?'

'I do know how important this is to you.' There was a loud noise from the other room, the TV bursting on, and he glanced over his shoulder. 'But you will try and hurry back, won't you?'

The motorway south was already heavily congested as she slipped into the merging lane behind a convoy of trucks. Even on the inside lane it was nerve-racking, and so she pulled into the middle only to become sandwiched between two towering vehicles, their trailers wobbling precariously as they ignored the speed limit and urged each other faster. Deciding to take her time and get there safely, Kathryn pulled back into the inside lane and continued on, part of a metallic serpent carving through the lush green countryside.

A light summer shower had just passed and the fields had a glossy sheen, making them even and contoured like a prestige golf course. It was this sight that welcomed her home—the scene she first saw from the plane and the one that she thought of whenever she felt the stirrings of homesickness. She had a collection of curated images: London's historic buildings, stone Cotswold homes, the vast waterways of the Lake District, and the Camden home she had once lived in. They were pictures that could be in any tourist brochure but hers were real, memories still alive with sensations: the well-known footholds of rural walking tracks, the nutty cream bite of the local cheese, the smell of the canal from the London flat that she and Chris had shared, with its soundtrack from the nearby nightclubs.

It was another hour to her grandmother's house in Kent, so she settled into the drive, flicking through the radio stations until she found Capital and acclimatised herself to the unfamiliar accents. The traffic report never seemed to change—the M25 with its gridlock at Junction 10 and congestion at the Dartford Tunnel tolls—and she wondered why the broadcasters didn't save themselves some time and money by replaying it.

Driving this familiar route through Surrey shifted her thoughts back to when she and her brother, Tom, had travelled this way as children, when their excitement signalled the beginning of the school holidays and a week away at their grandparents'—or a lucky two weeks in the long summer break. Days when they could roam free, ride tractors, and help look after the animals, with no school, no rules, just Eleanor's wonderful cottage pie and the best apple crumble in the world.

At last the land buckled and fell away to a plateau where the farms sat, and Kathryn noticed how changed the countryside was. The fringes of the towns bled into the green spaces, and new mock-villages amputated the fields and rivers on which farmers and their livestock had once thrived.

On the radio two political commentators were discussing the Greek debt crisis, and she turned up the volume. One was outlining the impact on the rest of the EU members, while the other was arguing how they wouldn't suffer from the financial contagion, only benefit in the long term. It reminded her of her family's concern for how her grandparents had coped over the years with each EU farming subsidy withdrawn or quota placed. Through their troubles, Edward and Eleanor had always seemed so happy together; they had been a strong team who had made it all appear like an adventure to her younger self—the two of them against the world.

The commentators' voices crackled as the signal kept falling out, so she turned off the radio and drove the last few miles in silence, stopping to buy flowers at the service station. There was only a spindly bunch of pink chrysanthemums, but at least they were her grand-mother's favourite colour and the cellophane wasn't too garish a shade of orange.

At last she was balancing her handbag and the packaged painting in one hand, the flowers and her luggage in the other, as she crossed the driveway to Eleanor's home. Halfway across, the sight of the old stone farmhouse made her stop; as a child she had always loved it, and now she appreciated it even more after the arbitrary modern architecture of Melbourne's CBD and the irregular homes of its suburbs. Because the farmhouse looked just the same, the imagined smell of the old place rushed to greet her—but she realised that the scent of cows and pigpens, the fragrant orchards and fields of cereal, was overpowered by the reek of fuel and exhaust from the motorway. She closed her eyes for a moment, enjoying the stillness, despite the smell and the noise from the traffic, an irritating insect hum.

The front door was already open, and she made a mental note to remind her grandmother to make sure she kept it locked. Then Kathryn stood on the threshold and took a long look around. The dresser was in the same place, crowded with photo frames and wonky pots and glazed bowls proudly given to Eleanor by her pupils, alongside Kathryn's own clay sculpture of the farm horse, which looked more like a mouse. The flagstones were covered with the same kilims collected on rare exotic holidays, and the oak hall table was piled with Eleanor's specialist art magazines.

Paintings cluttered the walls, giving no clue to the colour that lay behind. Her grandmother's handiwork was instantly recognisable, with the entire left wall dedicated to the watercolours that she had painted while living there, a homage to the seasons and lifecycle of the farm. The remaining walls were a montage of the works she had collected over the years from fossicking in shops in the local villages and towns as well as from art fairs, many of which Kathryn had been taken to. It was a shame that her grandmother had never been able to open a gallery as she'd always hoped to do, although Kathryn knew she had her own rewards from being an art teacher and a farmer's wife.

Kathryn listened out for the sound of movement but it was still early and she guessed that Eleanor was asleep. Picking up the flowers and Jack's bound painting, Kathryn gently pushed open the lounge-room door.

Since her last visit the bed and a dressing table had been moved in alongside the sofa and coffee table so that the room felt cluttered, shafts of light creating glitter in the dust-flecked air. Eleanor was dozing on top of the bed with her black-and-white cat, Mickey, curled up on the end. Kathryn propped the flowers on the table and opened the window. The cool air came rushing in, sucking out the stale and rustling the newspaper that lay on the writing bureau. It was surely here that Eleanor sat and scratched out those letters that Kathryn had to decipher as she read them to Oliver.

'You might not feel the cold, but old people do!'

Kathryn glanced round. Eleanor's eyes were wide open, a plume of fine blonde hair forming a golden crescent around her head.

'Gran, you have got the worst bed head I've ever seen! Are you going to let me wash it for you?'

'Certainly not, my nice young man is coming on Friday. I wouldn't want to deprive him of the pleasure.'

Kathryn grinned. 'So, you've still got a thing for him, have you?'

'Yes—I don't think it's reciprocated, though. Even if I were twenty years younger! Anyway, aren't you going to come over here and give your old grandmother a hug?' she asked, arms outstretched.

'I thought you would never ask.' Kathryn bent down and squeezed her gently. Eleanor was the only one in the family who liked a cuddle, and Kathryn missed her even more because of it.

'You look tired,' Eleanor said when she released her. 'Is everything alright?'

Her grandmother smelled of lots of familiar things: roses and malted milk biscuits and laundry, but she also felt uncharacteristically slight between Kathryn's arms. Her frame was smaller than Kathryn remembered, her ribs obvious through her dressing-gown.

'I just got off a twenty-four-hour flight and drove halfway across the country to see you; of course I look tired!'

'You know what I mean—is everything alright at home?'

Kathryn was going to shrug it off but knew her gran would see right through her, so she sat on the edge of the bed. 'You know how things are, Gran. You were married for fifty-five years.'

'I know, Katie, but you've only been married for ten, and you know I don't respond to platitudes, so come on—the truth?'

Eleanor was gazing at her, waiting for an answer, her face radiant even with delicate skin loosening across high cheekbones, strong wide brow above hazel eyes.

'We're not here to talk about me,' said Kathryn. 'Anyway, you know how hopeless men are—Chris just finds it hard to cope without me.'

She had thought about little else on the drive down except what life would be like for Oliver if the separation was permanent, but she didn't want to go into those issues now; she would talk to her gran later, once they'd made some progress with Jack.

'The break will do you both good, you'll see,' Eleanor said matter-of-factly.

'Maybe,' Kathryn replied. She hoped it would; she certainly needed the space and time to think. 'Anyway, you look really well.' She meant it—there was a slight change in her grandmother but she couldn't pinpoint what it was.

'I'm all the better for seeing you, dear. Thank you for coming all this way. I know how busy you are.'

'It's not a problem. I'm looking forward to spending the time with you. It will be a real treat.'

'Have you spoken to your mother?' Eleanor asked.

'Yes, she called when I landed. Doesn't think she'll make it over until the weekend, though.' Kathryn sighed. 'I have a feeling I'm going to miss her this time.'

'That's a shame, but you know how busy she is too. Anyway, how rude of me, I haven't even asked how your flight was.'

'It was good. I slept a lot, which is unusual. Must have been tired.'

'And have you got the painting?' Eleanor asked, suddenly animated.

'Yes, would you like to see it?'

'Please, dear. If you don't mind.'

The packaging came away easily. Kathryn moved to place the picture on the writing bureau and Eleanor stopped her.

'No, dear, can you give it to me?' she said, hands outstretched.

Eleanor rested it on her lap, frame clasped between her hands, eyes roaming across the small canvas. Kathryn watched as she studied the shadowed figures on London's rooftops and the crimson smudge of the sunset on the horizon, her gaze at last falling to the initials at the bottom of the canvas.

'Do you remember how I used to try and copy it when I was young?' Kathryn reminded her grandmother. 'It always was our favourite picture, wasn't it?'

'Yes. Yes, it was . . .'

'Why, Gran? Why is it so special?'

Eleanor didn't answer her at first, thoughts probably still anchored in the London landscape of the past. 'In a minute, dear,' she said, at last meeting Kathryn's gaze. 'I know you have questions for me but I think we had better have some tea before we do anything else, don't you?'

'Alright, Gran, I'll put the kettle on, and then you can fill me in.'

Kathryn had started towards the door when Eleanor spoke again. 'Before you go, just tell me,' she said, still clutching the picture, 'have you found out anything about Jack?'

She sounded so hopeful—Kathryn hated to admit that she didn't have much news. 'Not yet. I've done an internet search but there's surprisingly little about him, especially given he was as important an artist as you say he was.'

The search had only revealed a brief bio and a few images from Jack Valante's post-war work as an artist and photographer. Kathryn had seen some beautiful photos of his oeuvre but little about the man himself.

'I thought that might be the case,' Eleanor mused.

'Why?'

'Because it confirms what I have always thought.'

Kathryn waited a few moments for her to say more and was met with silence. Eleanor usually enjoyed telling a story, but she clearly wasn't in any hurry to share this one.

When Kathryn returned from the kitchen, she placed the tea tray down and retrieved the folder of research from her bag. 'This is pretty much it,' she said, opening the folder to reveal a thin stack of papers. 'Like I said, there's not much here.'

Eleanor turned the pages slowly, looking over the Wikipedia printouts and the few photocopies of paintings, until she came to a photograph of Jack.

'He was an attractive man,' Kathryn commented.

But if Eleanor felt anything at seeing Jack's young face or his work, she certainly didn't show it.

'I thought they might try to conceal him,' she said, closing the file and looking up at Kathryn, 'but I didn't realise they would go to such great lengths—or do such a good job.'

Kathryn's eyes were twitching, tiredness gripping her in waves that threatened to pull her under. She loved her gran and wanted to help, but time was limited and she had issues of her own to resolve. She dropped onto the chair opposite. 'Come on, Gran, what's this all about?'

'There's a man that I need you to meet. Stephen Aldridge—he's Jack's nephew.' She paused.

'Why do you want me to meet him?'

'Because he wants to buy *The Crimson Sun*. He says he needs it to complete his collection.'

'That's great.' There was another pause as Kathryn read the look on her grandmother's face. 'Oh . . . you don't want to sell it?'

'No, I don't, but I *do* want to know what happened to Jack.'

'Why don't you just ask Stephen then?'

'I did. But he claims to be working through Jack's lawyers and says that he doesn't know where Jack is.'

'And you don't believe him?'

'No, Katie, I don't. And you know how my instincts are usually right.'

'I know, Gran . . . but I'm not sure I understand. If you don't want to sell it and he hasn't been helpful, why do you want me to meet him?'

'I need you to show the painting to him in person. Once he's sure of its authenticity, then I'm sure he'll be more willing to talk.'

Chris had been cynical about the whole affair and she had dismissed his concerns, but now she was beginning to question Eleanor too. 'Are you sure about this, Gran? It sounds rather . . . well, rather far-fetched that Jack's nephew would hide him from you.'

'Really, Kathryn. That's why I asked for your help, not Abigail's. I knew your mother would just pooh-pooh the whole thing, but I thought you might understand—'

'I'm sorry, Gran, but I don't understand why Stephen wouldn't tell you if he knew.'

'Nor do I—unless he has something to hide . . .'

Kathryn's head was clearing, her imagination firing again. 'But do you have any reason to be suspicious? Why would he hide anything from you, especially Jack's whereabouts? It's been nearly seventy years since you last saw the man.'

'I don't know, dear. That's what I need you to find out.'

Kathryn regarded her carefully. What had her grandmother got her involved with?

'Well, why don't you just tell me what you know?' Kathryn said. 'Start with when Stephen first contacted you—what was it, a phone call or a letter?'

Eleanor insisted Kathryn sit beside her as she took her through the sequence of events in a hushed tone. She described how she'd received the phone call a few months earlier asking if she was *the* Eleanor Roy, and then her surprise when Stephen Aldridge's letter arrived and made a formal offer for the painting. Next she reached into the deep bedside drawer, bringing out an envelope and handing it to Kathryn.

She scanned the letter. 'Gosh, Gran, that's a *lot* of money.'

'I know, subject to viewing.'

'So all you want me to do is meet Stephen and show him the painting but not sell it to him?'

'Yes, and I want you to find out what happened to Jack.'

'Alright, so how do I then explain to Stephen that he can't have the painting?'

'Just don't agree on the price—later you can blame it on me. Say I don't want to part with it after all'. The main thing is that Jack isn't dead, Katie. I know that much, and since Stephen is family, he must have some idea where he is.'

Kathryn's head was thudding now; jet lag and dehydration were affecting her ability to think. 'Why didn't you tell me any of this before?'

'Would you have come?' Eleanor asked, her expression unreadable.

'Probably not,' Kathryn said lightly.

'You can see now, though, can't you, dear? Why you have to go to London for me.'

Kathryn nodded. Now that she was here, of course she would meet Stephen. 'But is that all you're able to tell me?'

Eleanor seemed thoughtful.

'If Stephen hadn't contacted you,' Kathryn continued, 'then you wouldn't even be looking for Jack.'

'Maybe, but he did—and perhaps it's a sign. If only I had contacted him earlier. How many "if onlys" are there in someone's lifetime, Katie? How many are we allowed?'

Kathryn knew what she meant. Her mind was full of 'if onlys'. But she couldn't allow herself to go down that path: no good could come of it, and it wouldn't help her decide what to do about her marriage. She stood up and walked over to the window, looking out across the garden at where the sun had elongated the orchard's shadows. She was certain of something—she had come halfway around the world to help her grandmother, and she deserved to know more.

'So if you're that bothered about this artist,' she said, 'then why didn't you look for him years ago? Why now, Gran?'

Eleanor glanced away, avoiding eye contact. Then, as if thinking better of it, she looked up. 'You'll know why, Katie—when you meet Jack.'

'And you really have no idea what happened to him?'

'None whatsoever,' Eleanor replied, shaking her head. 'I am sorry if you don't like playing detective, but I didn't know who else to ask. Your mother is always so preoccupied with the hotel, and I *need* to know, Katie. I need to know what happened to him.'

Six

The Etch A Sketch still had Oliver's name imprinted on its screen in thick dark letters and the Rubik's Cube was almost complete, left just as it was when they'd last visited two years earlier. Kathryn picked up the View-Master and placed the Bambi card in the slot, clicking through as she watched the 2D images in the eyeholes. She loved how the bedroom had never changed, not since she and her brother Tom were kids, so that when Oliver and his cousins visited they played with the same games and toys. There was a tin of Tom's khaki plastic soldiers, half-reclining figures designed to fire a gun, the rest balanced precariously on bent legs so that they would always topple over. And there, bravely in among them, were two of her treasured Barbies. Opening the lid of another box, she smiled as she noticed that the game of Operation still had only a few of its bones and organs missing.

Kathryn closed the wardrobe door and went to sit on the bed, nestling with the dozens of fluffy toys. They tickled her nostrils with dust and fluff. Leaning back, she realised that she was responsible for nearly half of them. To her left were all the usual suspects—misshapen fairground wins, Easter bunnies, Christmas reindeers, a variety of cats and dogs—while on her right was a growing colony of antipodean animals: koalas, kangaroos, echidnas, emus and crocodiles, nearly all acquired on trips to Melbourne Zoo. They'd been left here at Oliver's insistence, to keep his great-grandmother company.

It struck Kathryn as simultaneously odd and amusing that these furry creatures had managed to express what she'd been so reluctant to put into words—how frustrated she felt being in neither one place nor the other. She missed her life here, her friends and that intangible sense of Englishness, but she had grown to love the openness of the Australian landscape and the people, even though it still didn't feel quite like home. When friends and colleagues asked her if she would ever be back, she couldn't tell them, and it felt as if she was being disloyal, or ungrateful, or both.

She sank further into the musty pillows and stared up at the stippled ceiling, relishing the sense of freedom that came from returning to her family home, despite the unsightly seventies décor that her clients would abhor. She had already explored the other rooms, which were all just the same—only a little more dusty—but it was in here that time truly stood still. It was the place that she liked best, where she could imagine herself down the decades. She felt good to be back inside her twelve-year-old self: she was carefree, with no worries about money or responsibility, and the unexpected gift of time.

She dozed off, and when she woke the sound of a TV was coming from Eleanor's room downstairs. Kathryn shook her head, trying to dispel the fogginess, and walked unsteadily into the bathroom to splash cold water on her face. The mirror cast back an image that she didn't recognise, with uneven skin tone and dull, bloodshot eyes. Perhaps a shot of caffeine would liven her up. She headed to the kitchen to make more tea, hoping that her grandmother would be more alert and willing to talk now.

When Kathryn pushed open the door with the tea tray, Eleanor was sitting in the armchair fully dressed, a jigsaw puzzle spread out on the card table in front of her.

'How did you sleep?' she asked brightly, turning down the TV with her remote.

'It was a snooze, really . . . I think I got an hour.' Kathryn yawned. 'A little helps, but too much is dangerous.' She hated the way jet lag left her head swimming for days and her body struggling to keep up, but she knew she had to get to work instantly, so there wasn't time to think about how she felt.

Setting the tray on the table, she came to sit on the footstool beside Eleanor, studying the picture that was emerging from the puzzle pieces. 'What have you got there?'

'It's the *Seascape* by Van Gogh. You sent it to me last Christmas, don't you remember?'

'Of course I do.' Kathryn smiled, recalling how Oliver had helped to choose it.

Eleanor had completed a large section of the purple and green ocean, its white-foam waves curling towards the shore. Kathryn noticed a piece from the sailing ship, so she reached out and slotted it into place.

Eleanor picked up a similarly patterned piece and placed it alongside. 'Your mother won't let me have a computer—she says old people and technology don't mix: Eleanor sniffed as if to demonstrate her consternation. 'So I'm afraid it's cards or puzzles for me.'

Her mother had told Kathryn as much, with the footnote that a computer was just another thing she would end up looking after and she simply didn't have the time.

'And the TV,' Kathryn said, glancing at the screen, 'you still have that, and the radio.'

The TV was showing images from a war zone. Lines of displaced civilians walked along a dusty roadside, injured victims lay in unsanitary conditions: similar images to those Kathryn had seen so many times before. Then the visual cut to a reporter standing in front of a camp, flimsy tents shifting precariously in the wind.

She picked up the remote to raise the volume but Eleanor reached out to stop her. 'Please don't, not today, it's all so depressing. And I want to find out about all of you.'

Kathryn glanced down at her iPhone's home screen: a photo of the three of them taken on Oliver's birthday at a teppanyaki restaurant in Hawthorn. Chris and Oliver's faces were screwed up in delight as the food bowls came raining down.

It would be early morning in Melbourne now and they'd be fast asleep, all quiet except for the screech of fruit bats in the park next door, which would splatter their courtyard with fruit in their nocturnal ritual.

'You can see for yourself later,' Kathryn told Eleanor. 'I've got my laptop, so we can Skype with them . . . I mean, you can talk to Oli and see him at the same time.'

'Thank you, dear. I may be old but I'm not senile—I do know how Skype works.'

Kathryn smiled as she poured the tea; her mother was right, there was nothing wrong with Eleanor. 'I'm sorry,' she said, handing her grandmother a cup.

'Thank you. So, where do you want to start, young lady?'

Kathryn planned to get as much background as she could before meeting Stephen Aldridge, then she planned to visit the Imperial War Museum. Trove had been useful for general information, but she hoped the correspondence and journals from the time would be more revealing. She'd have a lot to get through, but maybe she'd be lucky and find a lead that might help her discover what had happened to Jack.

First, she needed to ask Eleanor about something else that had been playing on her mind. 'What did Stephen Aldridge mean by "are you *the* Eleanor Roy"?'

'I'm not sure, dear.' Eleanor picked up her cup and sipped slowly, and Kathryn sensed that no more information was forthcoming. 'Anyway, where shall we start?'

'You could start by telling me more about Jack—you said you first met him in March 1942?'

'Yes, dear, but I didn't see him again until a few weeks later.'

Kathryn laid the iPhone on the table and pressed record. She intended to transcribe the notes while Eleanor slept so that she could double-check everything before she made any inquiries or researched any leads.

'What was he like?' Kathryn asked. 'Tell me about him.'

'You'll have to give me a minute, dear,' Eleanor said, taking another gulp of tea. 'Well, he was a mystery at first. His paintings were so beautiful—but him, he gave nothing away. Not until I knew him. Then . . . then it was a whole different story.'

She placed the cup down and leaned back in the armchair, eyelids closing. Kathryn watched her breathe, the faintest movement of her chest, lilac silk blouse barely moving. Outside the overflow of noise from the motorway was building, the guttural growls of the trucks, the school pick-ups that preceded rush hour.

As Kathryn waited for Eleanor to rouse from her nap, she realised that something else was bothering her, something that she hadn't thought to ask yet. There had to be two sides to the story. So why hadn't Jack looked for Eleanor?

PART II

The Crimson Sun

'Only the artist with his heightened
powers of perception can recognise
which elements in a scene can be
pickled for posterity in the magical
essence of style. And as new subjects
begin to saturate his imagination,
they create a new style, so that
from the destruction of war something of lasting value emerges.'

War Pictures by British Artists,
OXFORD UNIVERSITY PRESS, 1942

Seven

LONDON, MARCH 1942

'Jesus, you're a bit tardy, aren't you?' Maura said with a scowl when Eleanor arrived half an hour late.

The atrocious weather meant that it had taken her much longer than usual to get to work, sandbags causing the smaller roads and pavements to flood, so she'd had to zigzag her way along Praed Street and down the Edgware Road rather than cutting through the back-streets as she usually did.

'Good morning to you too,' she replied, shaking out her wet mackintosh while resisting the urge to tell Maura how unbecoming her expression was. 'Do you have a headache?' she asked instead.

'No, although this is enough to give you one,' Maura replied, dropping the paper on the desk. 'Honestly, why on earth don't they just speak the King's English?'

'You're not reading one of those American magazines, are you?'

Maura had been lucky enough to find a GI willing to trade copies of *Good Housekeeping* and *Vogue* for shared martinis, and so she had accumulated a stack of them in the past few months.

'Beauty is our duty, remember,' she said, pouting as she repeated her favourite slogan. 'And no, I'm talking about this letter from the head of the Wartime Meals Division.'

'Oh, he does use the King's English,' Eleanor said. She stood closer and peered down at the piece of paper. 'Just not the sort of plain English that most English people use.'

'So, which part of this do you understand?' Maura asked, picking up the letter again and reading it aloud. '"No doubt you will be surprised to discover that Toft's letter to you on the subject of paint for stencils, about which you wrote to Taylor this week, falls not within his province but mine, and I can imagine your being tempted to quote 'You wrong me in every way' (if not, 'Ye Gods!' Must I endure all this?) . . ."' She looked up at Eleanor and grimaced before continuing in her best English accent. '"With the copy of my reply to Toft, which I enclose, I am therefore sending you his note to explain that Taylor is only concerned with expenditure incurred directly and that he is not therefore interested in the purchases for which other Divisions of the Ministry are responsible . . ."'

Eleanor had thought it sounded fine when she'd read it through with its creator's voice in mind, but she could see how it did sound rather bizarre now.

'Do you understand what any of that means?' Maura asked.

'It's their repartee . . .'

Maura frowned at her.

'It's just their way of entertaining each other,' Eleanor said, 'keeping their spirits up.'

'Oh.'

Eleanor walked over to the window and looked out at the rain as it fell heavily, bouncing off buildings and turning gutters into streams. 'It has taken me a long time to get used to the different departments too,' she said, looking back at Maura. 'Not to mention the names of all the departments and divisions.'

'What, you mean you don't know the difference between His Majesty's Stationery Office and the Public Relations Division, Miss Roy? Or the difference between the Ministry of Food and the Wartime Meals Division—I am surprised at you!'

'And what about the Ministry of Supplies and the Ministry of Information? Oh dear, Miss Sullivan,' Eleanor said with mock horror. 'And, don't you know, there's a new one—the Ministry for Ministries,' she added, giggling.

While this was amusing, Eleanor was secretly quite worried about the paint situation. There had been a volley of letters recently between Mr Steadman and HMSO regarding the large quantity of paint that had been used in London, some fifty-three pounds more than originally ordered: an amount that was considered 'excessive'. She had sent off letters assuring them that there was no wasted pigment, and they had calculated the cost—including labour and materials, each picture worked out to be ten shillings and sixpence. Even so, Mr Steadman had commented that they might be refused the paint they needed and that decoration could come grinding to a halt. If she was honest, the choice between painting a Spitfire and a few more lithographs wasn't a difficult one, but she was there to support the department, even if she still yearned to be producing her own art—if not overseas, then in the fields and factories, or ports and airfields like Ethel Gabain and Dorothy Coke.

Mr Steadman's head appeared around his office door and he fixed her with his eyes. 'Can I see you in my office please, Miss Roy? I need to speak with you.'

'Certainly, sir. I'll just be a moment.'

'What do you think he wants?' Maura asked when he had gone.

'I don't know.'

Hoping he hadn't overheard them larking around, Eleanor headed straight for the ladies'. She quickly pulled a comb through her hair and powdered her nose with her mother-of-pearl compact, then snapped her tan crocodile handbag shut. While her mother sent her money to buy new clothes, she had no time for that, but the bag— which she'd inherited from her grandmother—smartened up most outfits.

She had woken in the early hours to find her sister sprawled across the end of the bed, fast asleep in her nurse's uniform, a red ambulance blanket barely covering her. Eleanor had bundled Cecily in the eiderdown and placed her arms around her, listening to the air whistling in and out of her nostrils as she slept. Cecily's nightmares had worsened in recent days, in part due to the arrival of more wounded soldiers from the front, their injuries so severe that Cecily refused to talk about them. That morning, Eleanor had tried to pep her sister up with a boiled egg before realising the time and dashing out into the pouring rain. She glanced again in the mirror: her blonde hair was still a little frizzy and the grey woollen suit slightly crumpled, but it would have to do.

Gathering her notebook on her way back through the office, she racked her brains about what Mr Steadman could *need* to speak with her about. The completed murals at the British Restaurant in Acton had been a success and more were planned for later that month; and she'd made certain that all the essential artworks and lithographs were in place. She couldn't think of any reason to be worried; she had signed up several new artists—even though she'd been unable to locate Jack—and she didn't think the paint shortages had slowed things down.

Then she noticed a copy of the *The Illustrated London News* on her desk. It had run a major feature on the Acton restaurant opening and the murals by the local art college, so it might not hurt to have it ready to show Mr Steadman. She tucked it under her arm.

He answered as soon as she knocked. 'Come in, Miss Roy. Take a seat.'

Thankfully the windows were open, treetops just visible, because Steadman was seated behind his desk smoking, the end of his cigarette flaring and fading as each pull made the smoker's lines around his mouth even more pronounced.

His large desk and the sizeable proportions of the other furniture made him appear to be in miniature and always caused her to think of *Alice in Wonderland*, not to mention feeling wonder at how the movers had fit all of it through the door.

'How are you, Mr Steadman?' she asked brightly, taking a seat opposite and hoping her still-damp clothes wouldn't leave any marks on the leather upholstery.

'I am very well, Miss Roy. You got caught in the rain, I see.'

'Yes, I think I shall be getting the bus home tonight,' she said, smiling. 'Anyway, how is George? Any news?'

It was a coincidence that his young son had joined the Royal Navy at the same time as her brothers. George was crew on an escort carrier securing safe passage to the navy's other vessels, while the Roy brothers were on board destroyers. They were defending the supply routes against enemy attack, which gave Eleanor and Mr Steadman plenty to discuss.

'He doesn't seem to be coping too well with the seasickness, to be honest,' said Mr Steadman. 'Funny, isn't it? All the things you worry that will happen to them—it's not the journey itself that would seem the most difficult.'

'No. Still, I understand there's a remedy for it?'

'Nothing that appears to have worked so far.' Mr Steadman sighed. 'And what of Clarence and Francis?'

'They're alright, as far as we know. Mother is awfully worried, as you'd expect. In fact, I was hoping I might be able to get back home for a few days, if you can spare me.'

'Oh dear, I'm afraid that won't be possible. I have some exciting news, and you are going to be very pleased, I'm sure.' He paused, taking another pull on his cigarette.

The rain was coming down harder, a noisy drumbeat on the slate rooftop. It stole through a half-open window, splattering the papers on the sill. She raised a hand to close the window as Mr Steadman continued.

'It has been a remarkable few months, Miss Roy. You really have made an impact on us with your work here. Mr Powell was quite right about you.'

'Thank you, sir.' She was grateful to her old professor too, but she wondered what this chat could have to do with him.

'Do you feel that things are progressing well?' Mr Steadman asked.

This wasn't a trick question, she was sure of it; his approach had always been very direct. 'Well, yes, Mr Steadman, I do believe things are going well. Of course, we could do with more help from Supplies with getting paint—and transport is sometimes still a bit of a problem,' she went on cautiously. 'Is Mr Butterworth happy?'

'Oh yes, Mr Butterworth is delighted.'

Eleanor was relieved. Although the Ministry's art adviser on British Restaurants rarely appeared at the office, he was prolific with his letters, circulars and memorandums. Each day they received one or more of his communications relating to the demands of the restaurants and the pressure on supplies.

'It says here—' Mr Steadman picked up a sheet of paper '—that you have arranged for the distribution of Old Masters carried out by the collotype method for eight shillings each and of lithograph copies of living artists for three shillings. All in all, close to three thousand pictures for display in British Restaurants.'

'Yes, Mr Steadman, that's right. London had the most, but the North, Merseyside and the Midlands received about half, and then Scotland and Northern Ireland fewer . . . on account of them having fewer British Restaurants, of course.'

'Yes, indeed, Miss Roy. And it's not been too much of a challenge for you getting around to the different London boroughs?'

'Oh no, not with Clive's knowledge of the city . . . and his useful short cuts.'

'Jolly good—'

'Although I was hoping to take my test soon, so I can start driving myself.'

'We'll see, Miss Roy. We'll see . . . And how are you proposing to keep up with the demand from restaurants now?'

'Art colleges, sir. They've had good results in Sheffield and Scotland with the murals. And it's wonderful that we can now commission our own.'

A real highlight for Eleanor had been working with the students and watching their murals evolve. She thought that if there could be one good thing to come of the war, it was that art had come out of the galleries and museums and could now be appreciated by everyone—well, anyone who frequented a British Restaurant, anyway. It was heartening that the general public had also found a refuge from war in art.

'I agree with you, Miss Roy, but that's not why you are here,' Mr Steadman said, standing up and leaning over the desk towards her. 'You are here because of these commissions . . .' He placed a copy of *The Illustrated London News* in front of her, the same article that she had brought to show him.

'Is there a problem, sir?' she asked.

'No, not at all. Quite the contrary—it is because of the great success of the murals that you have come to the attention of the War Artists' Advisory Committee.'

'Oh . . .' she said, straightening.

'They are impressed both by the initiative and its success. And I know that part of your work here is already overlapping with that of the Ministry of Information. That you have been required to do extra.'

'Yes, sir, but I don't mind . . . I don't mind in the least.'

'Well, that's what I need to talk to you about. The committee has asked if you can attend their weekly meetings. It's a clerical role, but they need someone to work as an administrator, and they have chosen you. Apparently, they have more submissions from artists than they know what to do with.'

'Really?' she said with relief.

'Yes, your hard work has not gone unnoticed. I realise that you are overqualified for the position, but your experience with artists and your background really set you apart,' he said proudly. 'In fact, there really was no competition—and Sir Robert felt inclined to agree.'

So that was what Sir Robert had been doing in their offices. She didn't know what to say; it was flattering and exciting, but also a little concerning. 'That's marvellous, really marvellous, but what about my work here? How will I manage to get it all done?'

'It's only a part-time role and you will delegate more of your administrative tasks to Miss Sullivan.'

Maura wouldn't be happy; the last thing she wanted was to do more of the paperwork when she had already told Eleanor that she was looking forward to the day when she could get out on the road, visit the restaurants and become more involved with the artists.

The leather cushion creaked as Eleanor leaned back into the chair, working out how she would be able to fit it all in. There certainly wouldn't be any time for her to paint, and she considered telling Mr Steadman about her hopes to submit her own work to the committee one day in case this might change things; it was too soon to know if this would be an advantage, although at least she would be in direct contact with the people who made the decisions, the ones who nominated the war artists and selected their works.

She quickly decided that she would just wait, that when the time came she would be able to offer her work just as she had always intended to. 'I don't know what to say . . . Thank you, Mr Steadman.'

'That's quite alright,' he said. 'You are going to be a very busy young lady. Far too busy to be driving, in any case.'

Her father wouldn't be pleased, of course—this would mean she'd have less time to keep an eye on Cecily, but she would talk to him and make him understand.

Mr Steadman continued. 'You will spend two days a week on the committee's work, the weekly meeting included. Maura will be here to help on those days.'

'And when does the committee meet, sir?'

'Today, Miss Roy. You need to get to the National Gallery by ten o'clock. And you might like to borrow an umbrella—first impressions and all.'

'Quite,' she said as she stood, realising there was barely any time.

'Just a moment,' he said, coming around the desk. 'A word of advice: discretion is the other prerequisite for the role. It's not just because of the sensitivity of the information, Miss Roy, but also the departments and personalities involved.'

'What do you mean, sir?' Eleanor asked worriedly.

'You have some of the most powerful figures in government working together. I'm sure there will be many challenges and discussions in the months ahead.'

'I believe that's the case for everyone, Mr Steadman,' she said, growing more anxious at the thought.

'Yes, but there is fact and there is subjectivity. I didn't want to spell it out for you, but if I must—do you remember the outcry when David Bomberg's work was banned by the WAAC for being considered too abstract for public tastes? And the uproar between the Ministry of Information and the Air Ministry when they reported that Nash's pictures of aeroplanes were not realistic enough?'

Eleanor nodded, remembering the scathing press reports on it and criticism of the WAAC's decisions. *The Tatler* and *The Illustrated London News* had dedicated a whole page to a cartoon caricature of the people involved.

'I see, yes,' she said. 'There will be a great deal of debate, I imagine.'

It was not something she had considered before but he was right; with the War Office, and representatives from the different museums and art colleges as well as other government departments, it struck Eleanor that there would certainly be some different points of view. War art was the public face of the warring nation; its visible response to the conflicts and a reflection of national grief. There would surely be many sensitive matters at hand.

'There will be a secrecy paper that you will need to sign but I am confident that you will use your upmost discretion. And it may be as well to remember the high regard in which Sir Robert and the committee are held.'

'Thank you, sir. I certainly will.'

As Eleanor left she thought about Mr Steadman's words, about the people she was about to meet, and considered whether or not she was ready for the challenge.

Eight

The young woman sat astride a bronze lion, waving her placard high in the air, ignoring the pleas of the young red-faced policeman to get down. Another woman, in the grey-green Harris tweed overcoat and grey beret of the Women's Voluntary Services, climbed into the empty fountain and was joined by other supporters wearing blue and red armbands. It was Warship Week, and members of the Greater London division of the WVS had overtaken Trafalgar Square, a sea of people reaching as far back as the spire of St Martin-in-the-Fields Church in the east to the arches of Pall Mall in the south. Despite the serious purpose of the event, and the continuing rain, they were singing and in high spirits.

Eleanor watched for a few moments, moved by their actions in raising money to build a battleship. If these past few years had taught her anything, it was not to be surprised by the strength of her fellow countrymen and women.

She turned towards the National Gallery. Morning visitors were already crowding the wide steps up to the portico, and so she found her way to the staff entrance at the side to which Mr Steadman had directed her. A security guard greeted her, escorting her up the main staircase and into Staircase Hall, passing dark rectangles where the portraits of former gallery directors had once been. She shadowed him along private corridors and through closed galleries, marvelling at the frescoes overhead, noticing the institutionalised smell of this inner sanctum and the increasingly loud voices from the room ahead.

The guard left her at the threshold, where she saw through to the committee, already assembled around a long wooden table. The eight men were deep in discussion so she waited, examining the pictures on display and trying to identify the names of the war artists.

Then Sir Robert looked up. 'Ah, Miss Roy . . . Come in, won't you? No need to hover. I'm Sir Robert Hughes,' he said as he stood, extending his hand. 'So pleased that you agreed to join us.'

After installing her on the chair next to his, he introduced her to the other seven committee members. She studied their faces as he spoke, attempting to remember each one by a distinguishing feature: the gentleman in the formal dark suit was Edward Rothwell, committee secretary, then there was Ceri Phillips, with fine red hair, whom she knew as the esteemed First World War artist and trustee of the Imperial War Museum. Next to him was the artist James Hazelton, almost bald but with a moustache that looked set to take flight, the principal of the Royal College of Art, and then the artist Louis Sepple, keeper of the Royal Academy Schools. The other men were Alasdair Palmer, war office representative, and Henry Tonkins,

Admiralty representative. And, of course, there was Aubrey Powell, Slade's fair-haired professor of Fine Art and her former mentor—she smiled briefly.

Then Eleanor had a better idea and took out her notebook, scribbling down their names and drawing a quick caricature beside each of them; it was intimidating enough being in the same room with these men let alone worrying about forgetting their names and titles. She had heard of and read about some of them since she'd first become interested in art, long before she started at the Slade; she knew what they had done for their institutions and their country.

They were all still talking, but when she looked up Sir Robert was gazing at her, his face so familiar from the newspapers and magazines that she couldn't help smiling back.

He leaned in and whispered, 'We are pleased that you are here, Miss Roy, but since there's a lot to get through, why don't we get started and then have a chat afterwards. Does that sound like a plan?'

'Yes, sir.'

He handed her the agenda, and her eyes flickered down the page.

MINISTRY OF INFORMATION

ARTISTS' ADVISORY COMMITTEE

Notice of Meeting and Agenda

The meeting will be held at 10am on Tuesday March 24th

in The National Gallery

AGENDA

1. Minutes of last meeting

2. Matters arising out of the minutes

3. Selection of Artists

4. Any other business

5. Date and place of next meeting

'And the only other thing that I have to say is that we have a certain way of doing things,' he said, loudly enough for the others to hear. 'Quickly and with enthusiasm!'

There was a ripple of laughter.

'Alright, let's get started then,' he said. 'Please take the minutes, Miss Roy. You will then need to type them up and distribute them this afternoon. Will you be able to do that?'

'Yes, but—'

He raised his eyebrows and she decided that now might not be the time to tell him that she couldn't do shorthand; luckily her handwriting was so fast, he might never notice.

'Is there an office here, sir? One with a typewriter that I can use?'

'Yes, there is. It's all been arranged.'

The other members were sharing an amusing anecdote about a less-than-popular admiral, and she listened to the tail end of the conversation, thinking how surprisingly unconventional they all seemed.

Close up, Sir Robert appeared far younger than in any of his photos. In profile his wide forehead and slicked-down hair made his face seem rounder and smoother. He was long-limbed and graceful, leaning forward with his arms crossed over each other and elbows resting on the table. She tried not to stare but she hadn't been in such close proximity to anyone famous since she'd met Tommy Trinder at the opening of a British Restaurant.

'Come now, I would like to call the meeting to order,' Sir Robert said and waited for his colleagues to settle. 'I think we should combine items one and two into matters arising out of our last meeting:

the issue of donations that need approval. I have the accounts here that list the major contributors as the RAF Benevolent Fund and the National Gallery concert funds. We have also had the WVS for two mobile canteens, the YMCA and the YWCA, the SOS fellowship and British Red Cross Prisoners of War Fund, and Mrs Churchill's Aid to Russia Fund. The amounts are listed in your information.'

They moved quickly through the agenda items and Eleanor managed to keep up, but after an hour of note-taking her hand began to ache.

'Let us take a ten-minute break,' Sir Robert said, noticing as she rotated her wrist.

When the others moved away from the table, Eleanor took the opportunity to look at the pictures on display, crossing through to an area of the gallery that was closed to the public. The image that captured her eye was Cliff Rowe's original picture of *The Call-out*, a scene of the National Fire Service crew, dark except for a menacing glow in the background.

'I don't suppose you ever needed shorthand at the Slade?' Sir Robert said as he approached.

'Is it that obvious?'

'Yes.'

They both smiled.

'It's quite alright,' he said. 'Half of what these old fools say isn't worth recording, anyway.'

Eleanor relaxed, and they were silent as they studied Rowe's lithograph. It had become a well-known image over recent months. The fact that Rowe had been a politically active communist artist supporting refugees was not wasted on her, and she decided it must be a sign of the progressiveness of the committee and a good omen for her.

'It's a real privilege to be working with you, sir,' she said, her confidence bolstered. 'I think the work of the committee is envied by the rest of the world.'

'Come now, Miss Roy, do we have any other choice?' he said, turning to her. 'When people's lives and possessions are being destroyed, who in their right mind would be choosing to buy art? If we don't look after the artists, then who will?'

His frankness surprised her, so she replied with honesty too. 'But don't you think that people are more interested in culture now, not less? They know that it's part of what they are fighting for.'

He looked at her intensely. 'Yes, I do, Miss Roy, but where is the money for this art or the means to produce it?'

She knew he was right, but people found a way to do what they believed in; they always had. 'I've read the article you wrote in *Apollo*, sir. You encouraged buying art. Don't you think that people still want to read, to be entertained—that they need to be informed and distracted?'

'Yes, I certainly do, but how can we do so with fewer books being published?'

'But art is still being created.'

'So you are not one of these people who believe that war is the enemy of creativity then?' he asked.

'Not at all, sir, on the contrary—it is for all of us that the war is being fought. And the role of the artist is to record it.'

'Very well spoken, Miss Roy. Which conveniently takes us back to where we started,' he said, smiling.

Further encouraged, Eleanor continued, 'Have you ever thought of extending the scheme to lesser-known artists . . . perhaps to the émigré artists?'

'There are enough out-of-work British artists, Miss Roy,' he said, suddenly frowning. 'It would hardly be wise to encourage a whole new generation under the current circumstances, don't you think?'

'I know, sir, but the old masters are in Wales, safely out of the way, so you are making room for new artists anyway, are you not?'

'Yes, indeed,' he said with a near-imperceptible twitch. 'You are quite right, but it is one thing promoting a few well-known artists and quite another promoting a whole new generation of lesser-known ones.'

'Even if you featured a new artist alongside the Picture of the Month?'

'You are full of new ideas, Miss Roy. I can see why Mr Powell recommended you.' But his expression didn't support the compliment and he was circumspect before continuing. 'Take a regular artist—I don't mean Nash or Cole, or Anthony Gross, for that matter; not a prominent artist but a regular artist who could have got thirty guineas for his work in a magazine like *Tatler* or *Picture Post* before the war. What hope is there for that now? We need to look after these men in the best way we know how. Not be irresponsible and encourage unknowns or émigrés, Miss Roy.'

'But—'

'Remember, it is because of your background that you are here, not your opinions.'

The committee members were reassembling, taking their seats and glancing over in Eleanor and Sir Robert's direction.

'I think we had better get back to business,' he said, his face devoid of a smile now.

Eleanor took a seat next to Aubrey this time, away from Sir Robert. She felt as if she had ruined her chance to make a good first impression, and she felt guilty that she had let Mr Steadman down. What was it that he had said to her? *And it may be as well to remember the high regard in which Sir Robert and the committee are held.*

The meeting carried on good-humouredly, although her pen struggled to keep up with the speed with which they spoke and with deciphering the artists' names, only some of which were familiar to her. It had already been explained that item three of the agenda, 'Selection of Artists', was the time to meet artists and see their work, and that the following week the committee would decide on whether to give them a commission—overseas or at home—or to purchase their works outright. The process followed meant that some artists would be offered permits to access restricted areas and rationed materials, while others would just be grateful to get payment for their submitted work.

Suddenly tired, and still disappointed in herself for her lack of discretion, Eleanor sat back and glanced up at the black marble doorframes as the oversized doors swung open and the artists walked in. There was a few dozen—young men in suits, men in uniforms, and men in manual workers' clothes—who filled the chairs at the end of the table, the overflow standing against the walls.

From where she sat next to Powell, Eleanor listened, guessing at which hopeful would be offered a full-time salaried contract and which would secure short-term work. She didn't recognise any of them from the art societies and organisations she belonged to, although a number of new ones had sprung up in recent months.

Then Eleanor froze: leaning up against the back wall, head turned towards them, was a man who resembled Jack. She had to keep glancing up from her note-taking and, while she'd only met Jack briefly, it was hard to believe that the man was anyone but him.

His thick dark hair fell forward in a familiar unruly way, his stance was the same as Jack's, and although his clothes were smarter, the way he moved was identical—time studying forms had taught her what set people apart.

Eventually she had to give up trying to look. It was too distracting, and she reasoned that in all likelihood the man was just someone who looked like Jack, since she had searched so hard for him and hadn't found a trace. If he meant what he'd said about not signing any contracts, then there was no reason for him to be here now. Of course, it was possible that he had changed his mind and was offering his work to be purchased—or perhaps her eyes were playing tricks, or it was wishful thinking. Her father had always told her that Newton's third law stated that every action had an opposite reaction, so if she wanted to see Jack again then surely she wouldn't. She reasoned that maybe she should hope that she would never see him again, in which case she would.

The debate about the artists had become heated. Aubrey was talking, then Alasdair Palmer, their voices raised. She tried hard to follow, but her attention was broken. Unable to deny herself another look, she glanced up, but this time Jack's double had gone.

'Did you get that, Miss Roy?' Aubrey asked.

'Yes,' she said, repeating the line she had scribbled down. But Aubrey's gaze followed hers as she looked to the doorway again, and she knew that he had noticed her distraction.

The sky behind Canada House was stained orange and London was hurrying home by the time Eleanor left the National Gallery. Too long indoors and the intense concentration had left her light-headed, so she put out a hand to balance herself, breathing in the cooling air. It had been a curious day: memorable because of her new role with the committee, but disappointing because of the poor impression she had made. Not that she'd intended to offend Sir Robert, and who could blame her for being unnerved at seeing Jack's lookalike? She could have told Aubrey why she was distracted but then she would have needed to explain that Jack was an artist who had got away.

Now that the rain had finally stopped, all she wanted was to catch the last of the sunset and walk back to Bayswater west, along Piccadilly and through Hyde Park. Her route would take her past the Ritz, where she could see the guests; it was one of the ways in which she had learned to live well vicariously since Cecily had moved in.

Agreeing to look after Cecily while she attended nursing college had curtailed Eleanor's social life. And she wasn't entirely sure if it was worth it: the training didn't seem to be going at all well, and her sister seemed just as fragile as when her boyfriend, Giles, had first been killed in combat. If anything, Cecily was probably worse, so much so that Eleanor couldn't imagine how her sister could offer the capable presence that a wounded soldier required. Coping with her anxieties was one thing, but it really was quite wearing on Eleanor to continually try to buck Cecily up. Eleanor had again invited friends over that night for a meal and a game of cards in the hope that this might help.

She was about to set off when a figure appeared from behind the pillar.

'Jack,' she said, startled and almost dropping her files.

'Glorious evening, isn't it?' he asked with a smile.

'Yes, yes, it is, rather . . .'

'I'm sorry if I gave you a fright.'

'So I should think,' she said, smiling back.

He was wearing a black fedora and worn tweed jacket; the hat suited him but it was also one of the reasons she hadn't been certain it was him earlier.

'So, it was you in there?' she asked.

'Yes, I noticed you. I thought I should explain . . .' He moved onto the step below her, so he was much closer. 'What you said, when we met—you made me think . . .'

'And so you decided to come and see for yourself?'

'Yes, let's say there are a number of reasons why it seemed to be the right time.'

'And what do you think?'

'I can see the value of the work,' he said, meeting her gaze, 'and I can see why it would be an honour to be part of the scheme.'

She was surprised: not just that he had come today, but also that he felt he had to tell her why.

'Well, that's wonderful, but you really don't have to explain yourself,' she said, then instantly regretted it. He had been so certain in his refusal before, but now that he had changed his mind she was interested to know why.

'No, maybe not, but you have some explaining to do too.'

She raised her eyebrows. 'What do you mean?'

'I've explained why I'm here, but why are you here? I thought you worked for the Ministry of Food.'

'Ah, yes. Well, I did—I mean, I do. I work for them both, actually.'

He was still staring at her, waiting for an explanation, but she had barely registered the appointment herself. What terrible timing; she would love nothing more than to talk now. Having just found him again she was reluctant to let him go but she really did have to get going. 'It's a long story,' she said finally.

'It's okay. I've got time.'

'I'm awfully sorry, but I haven't—I need to get home,' she said, knowing that she needed to help Cecily prepare the food and imagining her sister already becoming stressed.

'Then perhaps I could walk you?' Jack said, loosening his tie. 'You can tell me on the way.'

'Yes . . . but what if it's not on your way?' she said.

'Well, since I don't have any plans this evening, it doesn't really matter. I can keep you company.' He smiled.

As well as the known number of friends arriving at her place, others often dropped by unannounced—old classmates from the Slade, other artists who were always looking for somewhere to talk and play cards—and it was all she could do to fight the impulse to invite him too.

'Of course,' she said, setting off with Jack across Trafalgar Square. 'Is Bayswater on your way home?'

'Absolutely,' he said.

They followed the shadows west, Eleanor explaining the day's developments. They soon reached Pall Mall, then went on past St James's Palace and through the entrance into Green Park. From their left, a distant hum of traffic filtered between the trees from Constitution Hill, and to their right came the buzz of Piccadilly warming up for the night.

Vast canopies of foliage cantilevered overhead, enticing them further into the park. Squirrels danced up and down a tree trunk, but raced away as Eleanor and Jack wandered past. They discussed the committee and their work, inquiring about each other, until it seemed the right moment for her to ask him what had happened the day they'd met.

It was a moment too long before Jack answered. 'Those men were business acquaintances. You know how impatient some people can be—they want everything straight away,' he said, glancing at her and smiling. 'I'm sorry that I had to leave you.'

'That's quite alright,' she said. 'So does this mean that I'm going to be able to talk you into doing the lithographs now?'

'What, lithographs for you and a contract with the WAAC? I don't think so.'

'Really, I'm sure you can manage it,' she said with a laugh.

'I can see why they gave you the job!'

For months, Eleanor had been keeping a curious eye on artists who worked for the War Office—Freedman, Ardizzone, Gross and Lamb—and how they were covering actions in Britain and overseas. It seemed to her, from the pictures that were coming through, that their kind of work was an opportunity most artists would be keen to take advantage of. She had also learned that both the Admiralty and the Air Ministry were looking for artists to accompany them, so it was good timing if Jack decided to sign up now.

'How come you never wanted to join the WAAC before?' she asked.

'It's hard for me with my family,' he said matter-of-factly. 'They would find it very difficult if I went away.'

'Oh . . . yes, I'm sure,' she said, glancing at his ring finger with sudden jealousy. She hadn't noticed a wedding ring when he was painting but perhaps he took it off while he worked.

'My work as an artist has served my family well,' he continued. 'I've done short contracts for the navy and the army because of the flexibility, but I'm not sure it can last.'

'Why do you say that?'

'There are pressures on all of us to do as much as we can, sometimes more than is really possible. You know that—you discovered it today!'

He was right; her new responsibilities were still sinking in, and she was yet to see the effect of her extra work on her family.

She and Jack had made their way in to Hyde Park and were approaching Duck Island, the isthmus on the lake. Soon the dark inky water surrounded them, the sunset casting an orange and lilac shroud over the trees. The shrubs and bushes cocooned the two of them from the outside world, just as the sandbags and armaments were supposed to on the streets a short distance away.

'Beautiful, isn't it?' she said as they came to stand by the wooden fence.

Music floated across the lake from the bandstand where couples danced. It was a wedding party and the light sheen of the bridal dress was luminous in the moonlight, snatches of laughter and chatter reaching across the tranquil water.

Another couple stood on the Blue Bridge up ahead, and when Eleanor noticed Jack watching them, she smiled. 'So which part of this would you paint?' she asked.

'You . . .'

His answer was so instant and unexpected that Eleanor's cheeks flushed red and her reply came in a whisper. 'Thank you.'

'What about you?' he asked, perhaps sensing her discomfort.

'The bandstand, for sure. I love them . . . Although they do look better with their balustrades.' She was referring to the wrought ironwork that had been taken away, along with the rest of the city's signs and railings, to make arms and ammunition.

'How can you see from here?' he asked.

'I just can—good eyesight; it's hereditary. And for what it's worth, I think you're doing the right thing.'

'What, wanting to paint you?' he said, smiling.

'No, deciding to go. I wish I could.'

'Really?'

He appeared genuinely surprised.

'Of course, why not?'

'It's just I haven't met any female war artists yet.'

'Well, there are some—Dora Meeson and Ethel Gabain, for a start—but I don't want to paint the Wrens or the Land Army like they do. I want to go overseas.'

'You mean like Laura Knight and Doris Zinkeisen did in the First World War?' he asked, suddenly thoughtful.

'Yes. Working as a real war artist in the field and with regiments, just like Bawden and Ardizzone. Like you'll be doing soon.'

Jack fell silent for a moment.

'And you're confident that you know what's required of a war artist?' he said at last.

'Yes, and I'm learning.'

'And what do you think you need to know?' he asked and moved a little closer.

'As far as I can tell, it boils down to three things,' she said, focusing on the layers of inky sky in the distance. 'They must be able to convey their image, it must be convincing, and lastly . . .' She paused.

'Yes?'

'Lastly, those two things must be connected so that they create a unified experience, so that they don't seem disparate. In short, there must be truth, integrity and splendour.'

He seemed to be listening, but she couldn't tell from his expression if he was taking it as seriously as her.

'But it can't always be all three,' he said.

'Why not?'

'Because some situations demand that the artist must improvise, when its not always possible to paint what's in front of you. Then reality is the artist's interpretation of events.'

Eleanor thought for a moment. 'Well, of course, Jack,' she said. 'That's a given. It needs to be a record as well as a work of art.'

'The hand records what the eye sees,' he said. 'So perhaps you should go in my place.'

Her lips curved in a half smile. 'Maybe I should.'

'You're working with the committee now. Why don't you talk to them?'

'I've only just started. Besides, it's not that simple. There are procedures and rules. I had intended to submit a painting, but then I got offered this role and I'm needed there.'

'It sounds as though you just need to be patient,' Jack said with a meaningful look that she found hard to read.

'You're right, but it's hard when you're surrounded by pictures from other artists, and you feel that yours could be just as good as any of theirs.' She sighed and leaned further over the fence, feet close to the water's edge.

'I would love to see some of your paintings,' Jack told her.

'Really?' she asked, now certain that he was flirting with her.

'Yes. It only seems fair—after all, you've seen mine. And what if yours are better? Then I could ask that you should go instead of me.'

'Didn't anyone ever tell you that it's not kind to tease?' she said, laughing lightly.

'Who said I'm joking?' he replied. He looked at her intently. 'Although I'm sure there would be a lot for you to think about. You would need to consider sleeping arrangements, for a start. I shouldn't imagine you'd be able to bunk in with the other chaps, even if there was room', he said with a sheepish smile.

She shrugged. 'All that could be worked out. Surely the most important thing is whether or not my pictures are good enough.'

'You mean if they have truth, integrity and splendour?'

The light was nearly gone and she still couldn't tell if he was just humouring her.

He took a cigarette packet from his pocket and offered her one.

'No, thank you.'

Jack leaned back against the wooden fence as he lit his cigarette, the smoke circling upwards into the fading light. 'So, what do you say? Are you going to show me?'

She didn't say anything for a few moments, still trying to gauge his mood.

'Anyway', she said eventually, 'even if they liked my painting, they would never let me go abroad. I may have only been working with them for one day, but I already know that Sir Robert is not someone who bends the rules.'

'It doesn't hurt to have another artist supporting you, though, does it?'

'No, I suppose not. Anyway, tell me one of your better ideas', she asked with a grin.

'You could have dinner with me . . . and I really would like to see your work.'

She pretended to take time to consider his proposal, hoping that her excitement wasn't too obvious. 'Well, that would be rather nice, and I do have a couple of pictures at home that I could show you.'

'Tomorrow then,' he said, suddenly animated again as he dropped his cigarette, grinding it out with his shoe. 'How about we meet tomorrow?'

'I could meet you after work,' she said. 'About five o'clock?'

'Okay, so where shall I meet you tomorrow at five, Miss Roy?'

'Let's meet at the Ministry office. Come to Portman Square.'

She smiled to herself—signed contract or not, she didn't much care—she just couldn't wait to see Jack again.

Nine

Every time Eleanor crossed the road into Cleveland Square, she thought how attractive the Georgian terraces were—numbers four, five, six and seven, all connected in a most unusual curve. Their construction looked as if it defied logic, although she supposed that stonemasons could create any shape they chose, just as she could mould her materials in any way she liked. She felt an urgent and irrational desire to ensure that the homes would survive the war unharmed and go on to outlast her family, who had owned one for as long as she could remember. Even the blackout blinds and the tape that crisscrossed the windows like bandages didn't detract from their appeal. Unlike with many of the other houses in the square, the designers hadn't gone overboard: the masons had only carved ornamental wreaths on the balconies, not great swathes of fruit and bouquets. The large double doors at the entrance were decorated in a practical way, with functioning parts of brass rivets and bars, together with a large doorknob that she turned to let herself in.

Expecting Cecily to be back from her shift, Eleanor raced upstairs to the front door of their flat, trying to beat the timed light before it went out. There were only ever a few seconds to spare before they were plunged into total darkness, so she held the key ready before quickly unlocking the door. She dropped her coat and bag on a chair and went in search of her sister.

Halfway down the hall, Cecily popped her head out of the bedroom door.

'Hello,' Eleanor said brightly.

Everyone said that Cecily was a petite version of Eleanor, small-boned and thin, whereas Eleanor looked slim but strong in comparison. And Cecily's dark blonde hair, usually tucked beneath the nurse's hat, was less abundant than her sister's. They had no idea from which side of the family Eleanor had inherited her voluminous golden curls, but she guessed it was from her mother.

'Good day?' Eleanor asked, following Cecily down the hallway into the lounge room.

'Not especially,' Cecily replied. She took off her glasses and wiped them on her cardigan. 'How about you?'

'Fine, everything was fine,' Eleanor said, thinking better of sharing her news straight away. It had been such an eventful day for her but since Cecily always seemed so vulnerable, Eleanor worked hard to avoid upsetting her.

Cecily had laid the dining table with their pale blue cloth and napkins, and placed a small vase containing daffodils in the centre.

'What a good idea!' Eleanor said. 'They're lovely.' She poured herself some water. 'Where did you get them?'

'One of my patients.'

'How nice.' Eleanor smiled at her. 'Your bedside manner must really be improving.'

Cecily didn't return the smile. 'No, not really. He didn't need them anymore. He died.'

So much for not upsetting her sister; some days she could never say the right thing. 'Oh dear, I am sorry.'

'It's okay,' Cecily said with a sigh. 'I suppose I shall get used to it.'

Eleanor gave her arm a comforting squeeze. 'Do you want to sit down and you can tell me about it?'

Cecily explained how it had been one of the worst days so far. The hospital had brought in a whole train full of troops just back from overseas, and she had worked as a theatre nurse, helping with operations that were performed back to back. Teams of surgeons barely finished one before moving on to the next—amputations, grafts and fracture fixation—trying to finish some of the work the mobile teams had begun.

Cecily's expression grew ever more grave as she told Eleanor how, as soon as the wounded soldiers arrived, they were triaged, the scale and severity of their injuries were assessed and an action plan was decided on. In a few cases there had been no hope, and it was the nurse's job to make the men as comfortable as possible for as long as possible. But for most of the soldiers, there was some chance of a future with surgery. Cecily demonstrated, with shaking hands, how she'd used compression to help a poor young chap she had come to know as Bob Compton. He had lost too much blood—the stump of his leg was no more than a gristly lump of bone, cartilage and muscle. She had felt his pulse weaken and held his hand as he'd finally slipped away.

'So,' she continued, her voice rising and wavering, 'thanks to Sergeant Compton, I haven't had much luck with dinner, but we have some rather nice flowers—' And promptly, she burst out crying.

'Oh dear, Cecily,' Eleanor said, moving to console her.

She cradled her for a few moments while Cecily sobbed and she gently stroked her hair. 'You will get used to it. It's an awful thing to say, but you have to.'

'I can't.' Cecily wiped her hand across her nose like a child.

'There's no such word as *can't*, Cecily. Remember what Father always said—'

'I don't care about what Father said. I'm not strong like you.'

'But you are, don't you see that? You are the one at hospital, not me, and you are doing all those things you said you never could—there's no question that you *can.*'

Cecily's eyes were large, watery moons.

It was Eleanor's turn to sigh. 'Let's get you cleaned up before the others get here, and what about this supper then—is it mock duck again?'

'I'm afraid I haven't been very successful with that either.' Cecily sniffed as she led Eleanor over to the kitchen bench. 'This is all I could get . . .' She unwrapped a small piece of meat and laid it on the brown paper.

Eleanor leaned forward and sniffed it.

'Ugh, is that really necessary!' Cecily said, turning her head abruptly and nearly losing her glasses in the process. 'Anyway, who did you say is coming tonight?'

'Lindsay, Pauline, Frank and Harry . . . and Heather said she'd try, but she wasn't sure. She's supposed to be on fire-watching duty.'

Cecily had met Lindsay at nurses training, but Harry and Frank were Eleanor's friends from the Slade. Frank had started courting Pauline when the troupe began following the Seven and Five Society. That was back when their ambitions of transforming traditional sensibilities into abstract ones had driven their artistic endeavours. Now all of them were involved in completely different work—except for Eleanor, who had managed to establish a career in art, and they taunted her mercilessly because of it.

'That's seven, including us,' Cecily said. She folded the paper back around the meat. 'Let's hope no one's very hungry.'

'Oh, don't be like that. Where's that cookery leaflet you brought home the other day? There was a lovely sounding stew. We could do it together.'

Cooking had been a late discovery for Eleanor. At their home in Bradford, their cook had prepared all their meals, and their mother hadn't thought it was an important skill to teach her daughters— along with housekeeping and laundry. She believed her girls were destined for far greater things and would be in charge of their own households one day, with the necessary staff to do those jobs for them.

'Really?' Cecily said, looking at the narrow galley kitchen that had been inserted into the lounge room of the apartment. 'So, what, I can peel on the sofa and you can sauté in the kitchen?'

'You know, your cynicism might just see you through this war,' Eleanor said lightly.

As their parents had come to spend less and less time in London, their father had divided the property into apartments and rented them out, keeping this one for the family. Each of the six floors was now home to an apartment with a different configuration and with kitchens that had been difficult to install; adapting the plumbing and electricity of a bygone era had ushered in so many unforeseen problems that their father had handed the job over to someone else. He had then been quite surprised to arrive for an inspection and find that half of the grand old ballroom at the front of the first floor had been given over to a kitchen that was totally out of keeping with the rest of its architecture. The elegant crystal droplets of the ornate chandelier were constantly coated with condensation from cooking pots.

Eleanor and Cecily had decided that as soon as the war was over, they would hire someone to reconfigure and redecorate. For now, the three-bedroom apartment was home for them and a revolving door of friends and family.

Eleanor reached out to the window ledge and brought in a bottle of gin and some tonic water.

'Glasses?' Cecily asked.

'Of course! First things first, get the cooks taken care of.'

It took them less than half an hour to get the meal prepared and in the oven, and for Eleanor to change clothes and freshen up, just before the doorbell rang.

'I'll go,' Cecily shouted from the hallway.

Their four friends arrived together, Frank bursting through the door first with Harry in tow and Pauline and Lindsay trudging behind. There was good reason Frank usually led the pack; unlike Eleanor, he always found the right thing to say. And he knew the latest places to go but he also looked the part; from his smart blazer and light-coloured trousers down to his brown Oxford shoes. It was no surprise to see Harry in another patterned knit sweater over his shirt and tie, his small dark beard and moustache unsuccessful in making him look any more than his boyish twenty-two years. Lindsay was air-raid-siren-ready in her usual attire of kangaroo cloak and clogs, and an odd contrast to Pauline, who must have used up all her clothing tokens since she was overdressed for the occasion in red turban, teal cocktail dress and cork wedges.

'You've been to the pub already,' Eleanor said, catching the alcohol on Frank's breath as he kissed her on both cheeks.

He grinned. 'We were merely testing the nearby public houses to make sure their evacuation procedures were up to scratch. It's all for your benefit, my dear.'

'You know there hasn't been a raid in seven months, four days and twenty-one hours,' she replied.

'That's very specific, Eleanor,' Frank said with surprise.

'It's a very important fact. Why would you forget it?'

'Quite,' agreed Cecily.

'Besides, when one knows things,' Eleanor continued, 'one needs to use them to inform others.'

'Hear, hear,' Harry said, flushed from the alcohol and the exertion of the stairs.

'Where's your loyalty?' Frank said, shooting him a look.

'Here, we brought you a present,' Harry said. He scowled at Frank before taking a glass bowl full of nuts out of his pocket and placing it on the kitchen bench.

'That must be quite some public house—I take it you brought those as opposed to bought them?' Eleanor asked, crossing her arms and pretending to be annoyed.

'Yes, indeed,' Harry said as he flopped onto the sofa.

The others sat down, and Cecily helped Eleanor fix a round of gin and tonics while the friends caught up on the week's events. One drink became three, and by the time they had eaten and were relaxing on the sofas, they were sated and sleepy.

Harry leaned back in his chair and lit another cigarette, watching the smoke perform like a ballerina, twisting and curling until it escaped through a small gap in the window.

Eleanor waited for a lull in the conversation before she said, 'I've got some news,' and paused to take a sip of her drink.

'Well, come on then,' Frank said lethargically. 'You know we're all in need of a drink or sleep!'

She placed the glass down slowly, enjoying keeping them all in suspense.

'You are looking at the new art administrator of the WAAC,' she announced.

'Well, well, Eleanor,' Harry said, 'you're going to be running the country before we know it!'

'You kept that quiet,' Cecily said, looking wounded. 'When did all that happen? You didn't even tell me you were looking for something else.'

Eleanor rubbed her eyes. Why couldn't she ever predict how Cecily would react? 'I wasn't. They approached me.'

'When did you leave the Ministry?' Lindsay asked. 'I thought you were enjoying it.'

'I am, and I haven't left. The WAAC role is part-time, so I'm able to do both—for the time being, anyway.'

'How exciting,' Frank said, suddenly perking up. 'So, what's he like?'

Eleanor couldn't think clearly. 'Who?'

'Well, Sir Robert Hughes, of course. Is he as charismatic as they say?'

She thought about the run-in they'd had, and of her glimpses of the austere private man. And then she remembered Mr Steadman's warning about the need for discretion.

'Very,' she replied diplomatically. 'He's exactly as he's portrayed to be.'

Frank reached over and topped up their glasses, finishing the gin and raising his drink in the air. 'I would like to propose a toast,' he slurred. 'Here's to Eleanor and her extraordinary success!'

'To Eleanor,' the others echoed, clinking their glasses.

'Now, you know I'm only a simple chap, Eleanor,' Harry said, 'but I have to ask . . . why are you arranging to exhibit other people's work when yours is so damned good?'

'Hear, hear,' Pauline said, stumbling as she made her way across the room to Frank, nearly losing her turban.

'Say, steady on, old girl,' he said. 'There's a word for a lady like you.'

'And don't you just love them,' she said and bent to kiss him on the lips.

Eleanor had looked forward to seeing her friends, but now she was growing impatient. They were smashed and becoming rowdy, and she wanted them to leave so she could look through her paintings and decide which one she would share with Jack.

The next time Eleanor glanced up, Pauline had draped herself across Frank's lap and they were kissing as if they were the only ones in the room.

'*Must* you two?' Eleanor asked.

'Why ever not?' Frank said, surprised.

'Because you can and we can't,' Harry suggested.

'Or because you can and you choose not to,' Frank said, raising an eyebrow at him and looking over at Cecily.

Harry blanched and stared at the floor. It was no secret that he had feelings for Cecily, or that it was reciprocated; the fact that he hadn't acted on it had become a source of amusement for Pauline, Frank, Eleanor and a few others in their group.

'Say, we've run out of gin,' Pauline exclaimed, tipping the empty bottle over her glass, 'and Eleanor's news deserves another toast.'

'Sound the alarm!' Frank shouted.

'Shush,' Eleanor said. Her head was pounding. 'I think it might be time to go home.'

'Or to the pub,' Harry said with a smirk.

'Excellent idea,' Frank said. 'Come on.'

He jumped up and knocked Pauline off his lap. She scowled at him and he steadied her, then he pulled Harry to his feet. Cecily stood up too. Eleanor watched as they stumbled into one another, retrieved their coats and prepared to leave.

'Are you coming?' Cecily asked as Harry placed her coat around her shoulders.

'No, I'm staying in. I've got some work to do.'

Cecily's bottom lip protruded. 'Really?'

'Yes, really. You don't mind?'

'I do. Please come, *pleease* . . .'

'Not tonight, Cecily—but I won't do the clearing up either, I promise.' Eleanor winked at her sister. 'It will still be here for you when you get back.'

As soon as she'd closed the door behind them, Eleanor went to the old oak wardrobe in her bedroom and brought out a large leather portfolio. She laid it on the bed and carefully unzipped it, taking out five pictures, all roughly the same size.

Once they were propped up against the wall, she regarded each of them unhurriedly. The first was a scene of fire crews struggling to keep a flaming building under control. The next was of Belgrave Square as it currently looked, taken over as a tank park, with the strange juxtaposition of mothers pushing prams past the giant machines. The third was a more recent picture of a makeshift baseball pitch that the American GIs had set up in Hereford Square, and the fourth a painting of the barrage balloon in Cleveland Square, one that she had stood on the balcony to paint a few weeks earlier.

The last painting was the one that she planned to show to Jack. It was of a destroyed building and the wreckage from a double-decker bus twisted into the earth, bewildered pedestrians staring at the mangled girders and inverted ground. She had started it in pen and ink, giving detail to the startled onlookers, but the brutality of the scene lay in the carnage at the centre of the frame, which she had conjured from layers of oil. She usually worked in watercolour, the favoured medium on the battlefront where artists had no time to wait for thick oils to dry. In the field, artists also made thumbnail sketches on scraps of paper that they worked up later back at base or when they returned from their trip.

She thought about the scenes that Jack had captured and the ones she'd seen by exhibiting artists at the National Gallery—they were powerful depictions of the atrocities of war. She felt this fifth picture was the most similar to them and gave her the best chance to impress Jack. But was it really good enough? She ignored the sinking feeling that told her the answer was no and instead looked at the picture again, knowing she had to do her best—if Cecily had to hold the hands of dying soldiers and could nurse others back to health, then Eleanor should certainly be able to paint a picture that was good enough to hang alongside those of other war artists. Surely this was it.

Her only alternative would be to paint a better picture, but how? She had barely any time before her dinner with Jack, her studio was full of half-finished canvases and her materials were dwindling; she realised there might not even be an unused canvas left, only paper. But paper would have to do as she felt compelled to paint something new. She would work right here in the apartment, on the dining-room table under the light of the chandelier.

Usually she took as much time to clean brushes and mix paint as she spent on the actual work. Now there wasn't any time for that, so she quickly laid out her materials. Last weekend she'd stretched some De Wint paper, but the glue had pulled loose and she had to do it again. The paper still looked wrinkled, but she considered this might be an advantage: its roughness might hold the pigment of her Conté crayons.

As she arranged the crayons carefully in order of the colours she most often used—black and white first and then the sanguine, bistre and grey—she meditated on her subject. She was drawn again to the blimp tethered nearby in Cleveland Square. She would keep the palette a simple black and white; it would allow her to show the metal cables. Even when she couldn't see it, she could still hear it, the clinking of the metal that strained like a great animal against its captor. This was another sort of picture that the committee often wanted: a mechanical image, a triumph of man and machine, a reminder of the energy and apparatus of war.

Eleanor worked long into the night, and although she was satisfied with the result, her mind kept coming back to the children in the attic the day she'd met Jack. She had wanted to paint them since she'd first seen them—the contrast of their melancholy faces and the hope in their eyes.

She put the blimp picture to one side and laid out another sheet of De Wint, arranging candles around her workspace for extra light. While she usually used the crayons to under-draw on canvases for her sketch paintings, today she would use them to complete her picture; the layering gave her the detail she needed for the stark imagery she was aiming for.

Then she began to sketch—the rough outline of a figure, the edge of a face—and her years of life-drawing classes and studying subjects were all collected in that moment.

She laboured for hours, with a flick of her wrist here, a darker shading there, until she had captured the scene of the children in the attic—the intense mustiness of the room, the fractured light across the floorboards, the expression on their young faces—it had been more than just seeing them: she'd experienced an emotional connection to them.

Eleanor didn't notice the time, or that Cecily came back and saw her working and went quietly to bed. All she remembered was waking up the next morning at the table, paint smudged across her forehead, and the certainty that this was the picture she wanted to show Jack.

Ten

Eleanor emerged from the Ministry of Food's grand marble doorway, a paper package wedged under one arm, handbag in the other. 'Hello again,' she said to Jack, smiling.

It was a few minutes before five o'clock but he had been there for nearly half an hour, pacing back and forth in front of the offices. It was inconceivable to him, really: she was virtually a stranger, yet he'd felt compelled to see her again. The second time they'd met had been a happy coincidence, but this time—for him, at least—it was the fulfilment of a frantic need, one that he hadn't experienced before. And it was despite the fact this might be one of the last few days before he left on his mission—time he should spend addressing what would happen to his mother.

'Are we destined to always meet on steps?' he asked Eleanor as she drew closer.

'I can think of worse places.'

Her grey raincoat was pulled in tightly at her waist, while a red felt beret, perched on the side of her head, gave her a coquettish air; he felt like kissing her there and then. Instead he just replied, 'Yes, so can I.'

'Don't you have an umbrella?' she said, glancing at his grey trousers, long patches stained darker with rain.

'Afraid not,' he replied. 'I wouldn't even know how to put one up.'

'Well, it's a good job one of us is practical.' She opened out a large black umbrella and handed it to him. 'I wouldn't want to damage my picture.'

'Certainly not. I'm looking forward to seeing it,' he said, nodding at the package. 'But before that we need to work out where to go; the place I planned to take you is a bit of a hike in the rain . . .'

'That's alright, there's a cafe on the corner,' she replied.

It was a short walk from Portman Square and she clutched his arm tightly as he guided her along the pavement, trying to avoid hitting other pedestrians with the spokes. He liked how it felt having her beside him, the pressure of her arm on his, her light floral scent: not the sickly fragrance that other girls wore but one that summoned up fields and woods.

'Here we go,' he said, opening the door, relieved they'd made it without incident.

The cafe was frenetic with after-work trade, the air milky with smoke and condensation. Round tables and chairs cluttered the middle of the room, while around the edges rectangular tables and benches were framed with rails and curtains as in a railway compartment's dining car.

Eleanor and Jack followed the manageress over to a large booth by the front window, and Eleanor took off her coat before sliding into the seat opposite him. Moisture had built on the windows, obscuring the street, but as Eleanor ordered the tea, Jack could just make out the heavy rain splashing off the wheels of passing cars, drenching pedestrians on the pavement.

'Well, are you going to let me take a look then?' Jack said with a smile.

'Maybe,' Eleanor teased as she nudged the package very slowly across the table.

'Thank you,' Jack replied, fingers stretching out and pulling it towards him. 'Well, perhaps you should give me some background first; tell me about the artist,' he said, hands resting on the painting. 'Do you remember the first picture you ever painted?'

'You mean as a child?' she asked with a surprised laugh.

He nodded, her laughter enveloping him like a hot summer day.

'It was probably our house or the dogs, I imagine.' Her eyes crinkled as she concentrated. 'I really can't recollect . . .'

'What about the first painting you saw that you liked?'

'I suppose it was the portrait of my great-grandfather—he was a colonel in the Royal Air Force. We all thought the artist must have tied him to the chair and tortured him, there was such a look of anguish on his face.'

'Handsome chap then?'

'No, not really. It was in the entrance hall, so you couldn't miss him!'

Jack leaned back, the leather booth squeaking as his weight shifted. He loosened the tie he had worn for her benefit, which seemed so unnecessary now.

'So you come from a military family?' he asked.

'I suppose I do. My father served with the RAF in the Great War, but my brothers chose the navy. I don't think he's really forgiven them yet.'

'And what does he think about your hopes to see some action?'

She looked suddenly startled, wide-eyed like an animal, before the waitress arrived and set the tea tray down clumsily, spilling the contents on the formica tabletop.

'Milk?' Eleanor asked as soon as the waitress had stopped apologising and left.

'Yes, please. And if there's any sugar, I'll have a dozen scoops.'

'Will you now; you don't want to share it round then?' she said with a small smile, stirring in half a teaspoon of sugar. 'And what about your family?'

'I have my mother, Anne, and a sister, Elizabeth, and two nephews.'

'But no wife?' Eleanor asked, glancing at his left hand as he took the cup she offered.

'No, our mother is an invalid so I'm still living with her at home. We can look after her best that way—Beth does what she can in the day and I'm there at night.'

'It must be hard.' She looked sympathetic.

'Yes, it is. If I'm honest with you, it's why I haven't signed up yet. There's no one else to help and it's a lot for Beth.'

'I can imagine. We don't realise how important our loved ones are until they're not there anymore.'

Those were his exact thoughts. He had spent most of the night wrestling with his decision: should he find a way to stay and look after his mother with Beth, or complete the final part of his SOE training and go abroad?

After he'd said goodbye to Eleanor last time, he had crossed the city to his shared studio in the railway arches under Clapham Junction. The night air was freezing, and Fred and Johnty—the artists he shared the studio with—rarely chose to work late, so he was alone to check through his equipment and pack the supplies he would need in the field.

As he filled his trunk with the bare essentials—brushes and pencils, Conté and charcoal—he believed he had made his choice, even though the second stage of his training the week before hadn't shored him up as much as he'd thought it would. Rather than giving him skills and tools, it had made him realise how lacking in knowledge and strength he really was. If he did need to defend himself, or anyone else, he wasn't sure how well he would fare.

But that was immaterial now that everything was in place. He had nearly completed the training and he'd already signed the WAAC contract, so he had the cover he needed to work as an agent in the field. All he needed to do was figure out how to care for his mother.

'Jack?' Eleanor was staring at him. 'You were miles away. I said, they must miss you when you're not around.'

'Yes, they do.' He swallowed, trying to put thoughts of leaving to the back of his mind. 'And what about you?' he asked before he drained the last of his tea. 'Is it just you and your brothers?'

'No, I have a sister too, Cecily.'

'Nice to be part of a big family. I imagine it was a lot of fun.'

'Well, my mother knew she couldn't stop once she set eyes on me—only she got more than she bargained for!'

'And how did you all got along?' he asked.

'Not terribly well,' she said, shaking her head and frowning. 'My brothers were so bossy they would never let us join in, so Cecily and I made our own fun.'

'I suspect you were leader.'

'How can you tell?' she asked, a smile playing on her lips.

'If you spend enough time looking at people, you get to know things about them. But, then, you understand that, don't you?' he said with a knowing look.

'So what else can you tell about me then?' She tilted her head as she studied him.

'I can tell that you stayed up late last night working . . . and that you don't have any turpentine.'

She frowned and then followed his gaze. Her hands were covered in paint, fingerprints as visible as if they were an X-ray.

'Yes, I did, rather,' she said, picking at the paint.

'I think it might be time to open it now,' Jack said, grasping the package with both hands. 'But am I allowed one last question?'

She nodded solemnly.

'What was the painting you saw that made you want to paint?' he asked.

'I don't remember it being any one particular painting,' she said, gaze darting up at the ceiling then back to him. 'It was the illustrations in my books. My mother collected children's books for us, and they had the most beautiful coloured lithographs and prints—*Peter Pan* and *The Secret Garden* were my favourites. They transported me as much as the words did . . . It made me wish that I could do it.'

'It's a long way from children's illustrations to war pictures,' he said. 'Do you really think you could?'

'Am I strong enough, you mean?' she said, looking squarely at him. 'Don't let these hands and this face fool you. I am very determined when I set my mind to something.'

'I can see that. No, I mean, do you have it in you to see what happens to people in battle—to stay calm and record what you observe?'

'I've seen my fair share with the air raids and rescues, and I worked with the ambulance service . . .' She paused, staring down at her hands before carrying on. 'It was ghastly. We rescued lots of families, and reunited mothers with children—dead and alive. But do I have it in me to stand by and watch men kill each other, as shockingly brutal or unforgivable as it may seem?' She stared at him. 'Yes, I think so.'

He nodded. He didn't doubt that she could.

After sliding his finger under the paper, he opened the flap, careful not to rip the painting as he pulled it out. He recognised the setting instantly and glanced up at her, before his gaze moved slowly across the woman and the children's faces. The composition certainly drew the eye, the tones were warm and the scene gestural, but there was enough detail and variation to focus the viewer.

'Is this the only one you brought?' he asked, finally looking up at her.

'Yes.'

'So, you consider it to be your best?'

'Well, yes . . . I do,' she said hesitantly.

'Does it compare to the exhibitions you've seen, the ones at the gallery?'

'Well, it's my best. And I think it compares to one of yours, but everyone's view is different, it's subjective—you know that.'

He glanced back down, examining her painting once again. What she had chosen to leave out was as revealing as what she had included: the focus was on the children, and she hadn't drawn Jack. The burnt umber, reds and oranges gave it a warm tone, despite the meeting having been in the middle of a cold day.

Eleanor was watching him expectantly. 'The committee meets again next week, so what do you think?' she asked. 'Do you think it stands a chance?'

'Of course. You should let me submit it as one of mine; they wouldn't think twice about it.'

'Come on, I'm being serious,' she said, rolling her eyes.

'So am I,' he replied, realising that he meant it too.

'So what are you suggesting?' she asked.

'That if they accept the painting, then I shall nominate that you go instead.'

'Now you're just being daft.'

'Why? It seems like rather a good idea, if you ask me. And where would the harm be in expanding their selection?' Jack said. 'Surely it would be a good thing?'

'It would be a deceit.'

'Well, I won't say anything if you don't.'

He smiled at her, guessing at how she might respond. She had already told him that she'd heard of artists being excluded from the establishment for forging paintings and even though substitution wasn't that kind of deception, it would involve pretence when he knew that she wanted her art to be included on its own merit.

'You don't believe it would just cause embarrassment; that they would look on me less favourably than before?' she suggested.

He wasn't sure how to answer that. Looking at those children's faces had made his thoughts turn to the war that needed to be fought. There had been wins and losses on both sides, but the Axis position was strengthening in the East, and the Allies' casualties had been particularly heavy over the past few weeks. Among them were many of the boys Jack had grown up with, leaving families and girlfriends behind.

And here he was, allowing this crazily optimistic, darling girl to distract him. What for, he wasn't completely sure—even if they managed to pass her work off as his, they would have to admit the truth in order to give her the chance to become a war artist; and she was right, who was to say they wouldn't get into trouble then?

'I don't know but I know that your work is good enough,' he said.

'Thank you,' she said smiling.

She appeared more relaxed, all traces of her initial nervousness now gone.

'If I do submit this to the committee and they like it,' Jack said, unable to dismiss the idea, 'I shall have to train you. Get you ready.'

As she looked back at him earnestly, he realised this was serious—what had started as a wild idea had taken on a life of its own.

'And it's a risk you're willing to take?' he asked.

'I suppose so,' she said.

He wondered if she was just getting swept along, but then she added, 'Yes. Yes I am,' and he knew she was truly on board. Even though they both knew the consequences, they were ready to set things in motion.

Jack made himself taller, shoulders stretched back, his eyes locking with hers. He didn't know if he would even still be here in a week when the committee met again, so he would need to contact Aubrey straight away, ensure there was a chance to present his paintings before he left. After all, what was the worst that could happen?

Eleven

LONDON, 2010

The coffee aroma was the same, and the trendy boutiques and crowded pavements could be mistaken for those of Chapel Street, Kathryn's neighbourhood shopping precinct in Melbourne, but that's where the similarity ended. The chatter of latte-sipping Aussies and flocks of cockatoos were replaced by the distinct accents of north London hipsters and the sight of scavenging pigeons. But even if Hampstead had changed since her last visit, the parade of shops she passed was reassuringly familiar: Oxfam, Hobbs, Whistles. There were just so many more cafes and restaurants than she remembered— nearly every other shop was a new food outlet.

It was a cold, crisp morning, the sun was shining, and she wasn't due at Stephen Aldridge's house for another fifteen minutes, just enough time for a takeaway and to carry on browsing along the street.

Luckily there was still a Pret a Manger, and Kathryn couldn't pass one without stopping for a coffee and pain au raisin. There hadn't been any seats on the train and she'd been in too much of a rush to eat or drink anything before she left Eleanor's farmhouse, so she desperately needed caffeine.

She and Eleanor had sat up well into the night, her grandmother sharing fragments of her past and of her London life during the war. Still, there had been no dramatic revelations and little to inform Kathryn why it was so important to find out what happened to this particular artist among all those Eleanor had known and worked with. Kathryn had deciphered as much as she could about Jack, and had come to the conclusion that with Stephen as the only family lead, this morning's meeting was important and she needed to be alert.

Her map showed that she was getting close. As her footsteps quickened along the busy pavement, she held her breath, hoping to conjure Oli's warm morning smell, but all that came was the snort of diesel fumes from the bus lane.

She wished she knew what Chris was planning to do with their son. Before she'd left, he had mentioned taking Oliver to an AFL game, but he hadn't returned any of her calls last night or that morning, even though he needed to talk to her about work. Worryingly, Amy had emailed them both that morning asking Chris to pick Oli up by 9 a.m. Chris was already relying on their friends' generous offers of help and sleepovers.

Walking hurriedly, Kathryn reached the intersection she'd been looking for and tucked the fold-out London guide back into her pocket. She'd been reluctant to use Google Maps since her last overseas trip, when she had run up a hefty bill while forgetting to turn off the data roaming—Chris had banged on about it for months.

Stephen Aldridge's two-storey house was in an enviable location, just minutes off Hampstead High Street, but it was a poor relation to its neighbours. It still bore the look of a handsome aristocrat, only a little shabbier, with walls of cracking paint, where crisp white or sophisticated greys covered the woodwork and render of other houses up and down the street. Inside, frayed curtains hung, where blinds or plantation shutters dominated windows nearby. Even the garden looked neglected; it didn't match the gravel drives, topiary, miniature bay trees and lavender hedges that the other houses boasted.

Kathryn knocked at the door and waited.

These were the kinds of homes and gardens she would want to live in when they came back—if she stayed with Chris, and if she could get him to agree. The Victorian terraces were like those in Camden where they'd once lived and still held the same appeal for her.

The door opened, interrupting her reverie.

The figure on the threshold didn't look at all as she had expected from their phone call the afternoon before. He was significantly younger than he'd sounded, around sixty, with small eyes peering from tinted glasses, and while his beard was whiskery and grey, his hair was still a deep chestnut brown.

'Hello, Stephen,' she said, offering her hand. 'I'm Kathryn.'

'Yes, of course. So good of you to come.' He shook her hand, his eyes moving to the large hessian bag on her shoulder. 'Please, do come in.'

'I appreciate you inviting me here,' she said as she stepped inside.

'Not at all.' He closed the door and ushered her down the hallway. 'I thought it was easier for you than coming to my office—just one tube change—especially when you're carrying fragile goods.' He smiled.

His voice was distinctly upper class, which made her suddenly self-conscious. She thought of her family telling her how much her accent had changed, the ends of her sentences eclipsed by an Australian twang.

'Yes, very thoughtful of you,' she replied. 'Thank you.'

'It's no trouble. I often work from home.' He led her quickly past a separate front doorway and into a room at the back of the house.

French windows looked out onto an overgrown garden, and a moss-covered wooden picnic bench sat just outside the opened doors, which let in a cool breeze. The lawn stretched some distance, disappearing under tall oak trees where a small potting shed nearly hid between the boundary fence and an overgrown vegetable patch.

It appeared as though no one had taken the time to decorate the rooms. But they were clean enough, and she knew from her work and visiting many houses that this was often not the case.

'You have a lovely home,' she said to Stephen, knowing that it could be.

'Thank you,' he said, observing possessions that covered the surfaces like a fine mould. 'It is a little large for me now, but I manage to spread out.'

The room doubled as a dining room and a study, with floor-to-ceiling bookshelves on two of the walls, and a large table filled with placemats, lose pens and piles of papers. The other two walls were unusually cluttered with pictures and brass ornaments, antiquated tools and weapons, leaving only a couple of empty hooks. If she ignored the smell of musty paper and residual cooking, she could envisage how attractive the house would look after a makeover.

'I'm sorry, I didn't ask you on the phone,' she said, 'what is it you do for work?'

'I work at UCL—I'm a history lecturer.'

That made sense with all the books and artefacts, although Stephen didn't share the lived-in look of the house: his designer glasses and the trousers and jacket appeared more expensive than the taste of academics she knew. He hadn't acquired the clichéd look of a history professor—perhaps in a few more years he'd become grizzled, but for now he only had the proprietary air of a lecturer.

'Interesting,' she said. 'So you would know more than most people about the Second World War?' She was conscious of the rising intonation in her voice.

'Somewhat,' he replied, 'although my field is Ancient and Renaissance History.'

'Wonderful—are you going to write a novel and become a bestselling author?' she asked with a smile.

'I think not. Perhaps I'll leave that to somebody else.' He cleared a space at the table. 'Please, have a seat.'

Kathryn sat down, placing the hessian bag on the floor against her chair. Stephen sat opposite, linking his fingers together on the table in front of him. By keeping things light she had hoped to gain his trust and quickly find out about his uncle, but first impressions made her doubt that this plan would work.

'So . . .' he said, taking off his glasses and exchanging them for a clear pair, brown eyes gazing back at her. 'May I see the picture?'

'Of course. But first, I need your help with something.'

'Oh?'

'Well, my grandmother is very keen to find out what happened to Jack.'

'Look—' Stephen leaned forward, pressing his weight onto his hands '—as I told her when we spoke, I'm not in contact with my uncle anymore.'

'When was the last time you saw him?'

'At least five years ago. But I'm not sure I understand why she's so curious. Surely it was a lifetime ago.'

'She just wants to know about his life after the war, and where he might be now. Anything you can tell me. I don't want to let her down.'

'Well, I'll try, but I'm not really sure it will help.'

'Still, I would be grateful . . .'

Her words hung in the air as she waited for him to speak.

'Jack wasn't around a lot when we were growing up,' Stephen said. 'He'd kept our mother company after our father died—they were very close. Then after the war, as far as I know, he continued to work as an artist, always overseas, travelling to remote places for one conflict or another. My mother would have been able to tell you more but I'm afraid she passed away in ninety-one.'

'I'm sorry.' Kathryn's sentiment was sincere but she was also frustrated; he wasn't giving her much more than what she'd found online.

'Thank you. So it seems he never really left the war artist role behind, just picked up a camera instead.'

'And what sort of man was he?' she asked, hoping her question might make him open up a little more.

'Look, he was very private. And you know how teenagers are. We weren't really interested in the war—or anyone but ourselves. It was the seventies.'

'And what about the last time you saw him?' she asked. The glint of a metal sabre on the wall caught her eye; he may not have been interested in the war as a teenager, but he certainly was now.

'It would have been two thousand and four . . . no, two thousand and five.' Stephen sounded vague. 'There was an anniversary exhibition: sixty years since the end of the war. The Imperial War Museum put on an excellent show, and some of the war artists were there.'

'So Jack was included then?'

'Oh yes. Jack just didn't get the same recognition as the others,' he said, unable to disguise the bitterness in his voice. 'Why do you ask?'

'I've found it difficult to discover much about him, that's all. That's why I was hoping you might be able to help. Why do you think he didn't get the same recognition?'

He shook his head. 'I really have no idea.'

'Oh, but I thought you knew all about his work—my grandmother said you were looking to complete your collection with *The Crimson Sun*?'

'Yes, but it's a family matter,' he said irritably.

Kathryn considered him for a moment. He had the outward appearance of having an ordered mind, but something just didn't add up. A famous war artist in the family and you lose touch for no apparent reason? Or, it seemed, there was one that Stephen wouldn't or couldn't explain.

She glanced away, casting around the room for a sense of Stephen Aldridge, the man outside his work. A shelf on the bookcase was given over to framed photos, and there were several of him with a middle-aged lady and two younger women, presumably his wife and daughters.

'Look,' he said, leaning forward again, 'even if Jack's still alive, he would be nearly ninety-three now.'

Kathryn nodded. 'Why did you lose touch, if you don't mind me asking?'

'After the exhibition, he just went away and didn't contact us.' Stephen paused and she could hear a baby crying in one of the neighbour's houses. 'We tried to find him but, as I've told you, we weren't very successful. If my mother, Elizabeth, were still alive it would have been different—as it was, I'm afraid we just stopped looking.'

But surely Stephen must have given it some thought over the years and speculated on what might have happened to his uncle—most family members would. And it didn't seem to make sense, anyway. Why would Jack lose touch with his family just when he was getting old and needed them more than ever?

Kathryn hoped she came across as politely curious. 'Could something have happened at the exhibition to trigger his disappearance? I mean, it is a bit strange, isn't it?'

'I suppose it is,' Stephen mused, 'but we never got to the bottom of it. Who knows what these men went through during the war and it just gets buried. These anniversaries bring back memories they'd rather forget. Open old wounds.'

Now he sounded more convincing: a historian who clearly respected the past and knew its claim on people's lives. And understood people's limitations.

Kathryn didn't want to admit defeat when she had only just started, but couldn't see what option she had. And she didn't want to leave without discovering anything useful, so she needed to think of something, and fast.

'I am sorry,' Stephen said softly, 'and I know it's not what you want to hear, but I don't think you stand much chance now. Some people just don't want to be found.'

'Maybe—'

'I don't want to rush you,' he cut in, 'but can I see the painting now?'

Perhaps he'd reveal more when he saw it. Kathryn shrugged. 'Sure.'

She unwrapped the picture and laid it on the table between them, watching Stephen's reaction as he surveyed the London cityscape and the two figures silhouetted against the fiery skies—sunset or war, she had never known for certain. The one thing she had always been sure of was how closely the figures were connected to each other, of the energy that radiated from them. Even the dark frame was shot through with gold, as if their strength and the sun's rays had landed there.

Stephen picked up a magnifying glass and slowly examined the painting, his attention finally drawn to the initials in the bottom corner. Then he carefully turned it over, running his fingers across the smooth yellowing surface of the original backing paper.

'It's more stunning than I could have hoped for,' Stephen said, finally looking up. 'Thank you.' His smile brimmed with genuine warmth.

Her mouth was suddenly dry and she swallowed, glancing around nervously because of what she was about to say. Her eyes came back to rest on the display of weapons.

Stephen gave her a concerned look. 'Would you like a glass of water or a cup of tea before you go, or should I just get the cheque?'

'No, I'm fine, thank you.' She steeled herself. 'But I can't sell you the painting. I promised my grandmother I'd do what she asked and show it to you . . . but I can't let her part with it—not until she knows what happened to Jack.'

'You *are* pulling my leg?' he said in a tone she imagined he reserved for his students.

'No, I'm afraid not,' she said, ignoring her speeding pulse. 'I made a promise, Stephen, and as far as I can see, you're the only one who can help us.'

His frown deepened. 'But I've already told you, I don't know anything.'

'Surely you could do a little more digging? What about your brothers; maybe I should speak to them?'

'If you want to, but they are both overseas,' he said eyeing her coolly.

She had surprised herself—she'd only planned to question him, then turn him down and leave with the painting—but she couldn't help trying this. It seemed as if there was more to Stephen Aldridge than met the eye. Besides, it was a fair exchange: he wanted something from Eleanor and Kathryn, and they wanted something from him.

'I'm sorry, Kathryn,' he said, sounding firm. 'I think you had better leave.'

'Alright, if that's what you want.' She stood up and pulled the cloth back around the canvas, wrapping it carefully and placing it in the bag. She reached for her handbag—

'Wait, okay. There is something.' He hesitated.

'What?'

'Jack kept some diaries during the war.'

'Really?' she said, excited by the promise of a diary: it could give some understanding of who Jack was, show what kind of man he might have been. 'How many are there?'

'Only two remaining. We have one and the Imperial War Museum holds the other.'

'Oh, I didn't come across it in my search.'

'It's possible that you wouldn't have done. It was for a new exhibition on war artists: they wanted some lesser-known works. We've loaned it to them. No one had ever seen the diary before—it was private, you see.'

'So anyone can see it now?'

'Yes, I know it's been on public display, so you might have to make a request to read it.'

'And is there any mention of my grandmother, Eleanor Roy?'

His brow furrowed. 'Not that I can recall.'

It seemed odd that he wouldn't remember, considering that he'd called her grandmother '*the* Eleanor Roy'. At least this was something, though, and she felt her neck and shoulders relax as her body released some of the tension that had built over the past half hour.

'What about the diary you have; would it be possible for me to have a look at that?' Kathryn asked.

'I don't know,' he said reluctantly, staring at his clasped hands. 'It *is* very fragile.'

'I'll be careful.'

'Okay, at least then you can see for yourself . . . but you'll have to wear gloves.'

He stood up and walked off to retrieve Jack's journal while she remained at the table, feeling vulnerable. His temperament had changed, his original warmth fading, and the unfamiliar surroundings of dark wooden furniture and cluttered possessions were crowding her in. Stephen was shuffling around behind her, a door creaking open, a key scraping in its lock. Then he reappeared, cautiously carrying an object bound in red cloth.

'Have you lived here long?' she asked, trying to shake her unease.

'Yes, some would say too long,' he said as he laid the object on the table. 'Our family grew up here. My brothers both moved overseas, and I couldn't bear to sell.'

'It's a big house for one person . . .' she said, still fishing.

'My children have their own families now, so it's good to have room for them all.'

He opened the red fabric to reveal the poor condition of the diary's linen cover, which was badly stained and scratched.

'Such a shame,' she said, 'although I'm sure my grandmother would still love to see it.'

He stiffened. 'That's totally out of the question, I'm afraid,' he said vehemently.

She decided it might be better to wait and ask again before she left, when he would have, hopefully, loosened up. 'Which year is this?' she said instead.

'It's 1944,' he replied, placing it in front of her. 'The museum holds 1942.'

'And you don't know what happened to the others?'

'Both 1943 and 1945 were lost or destroyed, so we don't get to follow the chronology of the war, but you get a bit of an insight into his work. And into the paintings he went on to complete. Of course, those are his most important legacy—the artworks from his time as a war artist.'

It was a blow that those two diaries were gone forever, but this one could be interesting: 1944 was two years after Jack and Eleanor met.

Kathryn pulled on the white cotton gloves and opened the cover.

'He had been making quite a name for himself as an illustrator,' Stephen told her, 'and not that long out of art school. It was how they found most of them.'

'My grandmother said he was at Chelsea?'

Rather than answering her question, Stephen asked one of his own. 'So, how well does she claim to have known him?'

'Quite well, it seems.' Kathryn smiled casually.

She had finally got Eleanor to admit that it had been more than a friendship, but her gran wouldn't be drawn on how long the affair had lasted or how serious it was.

'Well, I'll leave you to it then,' he said. 'Just shout out if you need anything.'

'Thank you.'

He went into the kitchen and set the door ajar, intermittently appearing as he moved about doing chores. Apart from the creak of the house, and the squeals of young children playing in the garden next door, it was disquietingly still. She glanced anxiously around the room and back through to the kitchen, but there wasn't any time for nerves or second thoughts. She made herself comfortable and carefully opened the cover, searching through the first few pages for Eleanor's name or a mention of a woman. But nothing caught her eye, so she turned back to the beginning and the faded black ink.

> *Tuesday, 11th July*
> *Attended briefing session today and the Anti-aircraft Operations Room offered up lots of possibilities. It's my first subject with the Div. and my first picture is a composition of the men with their maps and the plotting table; a powerful scene of the planning in watercolour and tempera to get richness of tone. Such a treat to paint again, I haven't been able to for weeks because of the constant moving, and there's never enough time for the paint to dry, let alone enough space to carry a board or canvas.*

The entry didn't state a location, but she guessed from his tiny pictures of cypress trees and olive groves that the troops were in Italy.

Thursday, 13th July

A dramatic thunderstorm last night and we took cover in a hotel. Any other occasion and it would have been pleasant but seeing the sickness that malaria brings and the living conditions outside the protected areas is hard. My father's family were Neapolitans and I'm sure would welcome me with open arms if there were ever time to look them up or by some strange coincidence we found ourselves close by.

Saturday, 15th July

When I got back to base I was in the mood to paint (and not for mixing with the men) so I took all the strips of paper with jottings out of my pockets—there were bundles of them, some I don't even remember doing. We had been caught in the middle of a hellish raid but found cover in a deserted village, not before some of our chaps got hit. We saw out the enemy counterattack in slit trenches before the all-clear to march back came. Picked up some Italian prisoners on the way, which took the best part of the afternoon. Luckily, the table, chair and drawing board were still set up just where I left them so I was able to start on the watercolours straight away. The colours as they came to life after the dry dirt of the past few days was a welcome relief, but the blue swirling water put me in mind for a swim, which of course there's not a chance in hell of having!

Kathryn could almost see the aqua droplet forming at the point of Jack's brush, its mark as it met the paper, and the wash as he shaded the cerulean sky. How vivid a portrait of war he painted through his pictures and writing, and how she felt for the men.

Jack's depictions of conflict were no different from the horrific images of today—war-torn areas reduced to rubble, refugee camps, sickness and starvation—but, strangely, those modern images felt less real to her than these impressions from sixty-five years ago. Perhaps it was true that her generation had become desensitised by constant news feeds and being bombarded by footage, but where could they go from here? It was something that preoccupied her more and more, and something she tried to discuss with friends, who only ever gave it a few minutes of their time before focusing on events closer to home.

> *Thursday, 28th September*
>
> *We moved twenty miles today, expected in Naples by Sunday ahead of the 50th Division. Slept fitfully last night because of the heat, and sleeping in ruins next to cookhouse and latrines esp. noisy, so felt rotten today and all I managed were a few brief sketches whenever we stopped.*

A series of hieroglyphic notes accompanied the disjointed entry. It appeared—from the missing weeks of entries between July and now—that his spirits were low.

> *Saturday, 30th September*
>
> *On the move today and I concentrated on the landscape and the abandoned munitions; like the men who have become weathered by the elements, they are rusted by exposure into amber and oranges and reds. Tomorrow I'm taking to the air in a craft attached to the infantry division to make sketches*

of the battlefield, ambulances and tents. It's the first fine day with a break in many days of continuous rain. The terrain is hard, with water from the road covering the floor of the jeep and causing the engine to stall as well as waterlogging the tents. These are extremes we are still ill equipped for and the men are tired. Even the promise of some Vermouth and dancing with nurses didn't muster a smile from them tonight. Will settle for a quiet one although might be tempted by a game of poker at the Guards Brig. H.Q. on the way back.

A detailed sketch of the scene with deserted tanks and guns, one that he had filled in with colour, took up most of the opposite page. Alongside were arrows and notations with names of colours, which she guessed indicated the ones he intended to use when he produced a painting back in his studio.

Monday, 2nd October

My supplies are running low—what I wouldn't give for a new set of Conté crayons and some paper. I haven't told the men that I'm intending to use some of the rations to make dyes and paints; there is only one tin of sardines left and I am keeping it in reserve to mix the olive oil with burnt twigs once my charcoal runs out. They would not thank me for it if they knew, and neither would the M.O.I. thank me if I don't get any pictures through.

It was such a shame that Stephen wouldn't loan her the diary. She would have loved to take it to Eleanor and compare the sketches to Jack's finished work that they had found on the internet.

Her phone beeped on the table next to her: a text from her best friend, Helen, asking to meet in Covent Garden. Kathryn had just sent a reply when an idea struck her.

Of course, how could she have been so dense? She glanced quickly at the kitchen doorway—she couldn't see Stephen—and then picked up her phone, selected the camera option and started taking photos of the remaining pages. She didn't need to ask Stephen for permission and give him the opportunity to refuse her, or request the loan of the diary. This was for her grandmother.

Twelve

Kathryn tried to set aside her concerns as she negotiated the crowded pavements of Covent Garden, but she kept seeing images from Jack's diary, and her thoughts circled back to the idea that Stephen was hiding something. If he was so proud of his uncle, then why weren't any of Jack's paintings in the house? And why didn't Stephen display Jack's photo? Perhaps he was keeping everything sealed in storage for protection.

But the same instincts that had told her Eleanor wasn't being totally honest were sounding again. Perhaps once she had talked it through with Helen it would all seem more reasonable, make more sense.

Even the side streets felt claustrophobic, so Kathryn took the next alleyway, a short cut to Neal Street, and was soon part of the throng that swept into James Street, the main artery to the Piazza. The day had transformed into an unusually humid September evening; it could have been a Melbourne summer night, only without the lemon-scented gum trees and cackle of birds. There was almost a carnival mood. Ribbons of lights twinkled above her, strung from the blue metal girders, and everywhere she looked tourists were taking pictures of the Piazza's cascading flower baskets. The dusk filled with the overlapping sounds of street performers and the melody of voices—couples walking hand in hand over the cobblestones, office workers spilling across tables at outdoor cafes, and shoppers swarming like bees through handicraft stalls. Lovers and friends seemed content to lean against the brickwork, marking time on their phones as they waited for their dates to arrive.

She was due to meet Helen at the Punch & Judy pub and expected that she would be late; she always was. But as Kathryn made her way down into the brick basement, she saw her best friend seated at an outside table.

Helen's face lit up. It had been nearly two years—far too long.

'Let me look at you,' Kathryn said when Helen finally let go of her.

It was maddening the way that Helen didn't seem to change at all, still maintaining her boho charm after all these years. She insisted it was her disciplined yoga regime and organic lifestyle, but Kathryn guessed it had more to do with the fact that she didn't have the stress of a family and had more time for herself.

'It's so good to see you,' Helen said, finally sitting down.

Kathryn sat next to her, looping her bag around her knees; the area had always been notorious for pickpockets. The couple at the table behind shuffled their stools to provide extra room, and Kathryn smiled at them before turning back to Helen.

'I see you've made a start without me,' she said, noticing a bottle in the wine cooler.

'I wanted to get here early and choose a nice French white,' Helen replied, filling Kathryn's glass and topping up her own. 'I know how much you miss them.'

'That's so sweet. Thank you. And clever of you to think of coming here.'

Friday nights after work had often been spent here or in another Covent Garden bar, and then on to a club. That usually meant a sleep-in on Saturday that inevitably led to a late morning brunch at a local cafe, or an urgent shopping mission for an outfit to wear that night. Perhaps it was the long, lazy Sundays that Kathryn had the fondest memories of, though: lunch with friends, a walk through one of the city's heaths or parks, and sometimes a visit to a pub for live music and drinks to round off the weekend. It seemed like a lifetime ago.

'So, how's it all going?' Helen asked as if she'd read her mind.

Kathryn decided to save the harder conversation about Chris until later and talk about her grandmother first. 'It's a little odd, really, to be investigating the past like this, but it's also quite intriguing . . . I feel a bit like Miss Marple! I'm not sure where it will all lead, but I'm doing my best. Anyway, how are you?' she said, leaning over and squeezing her friend's hand. 'It really is so lovely to see you.'

'I'm great, but before I forget,' Helen said, rummaging in her bag. 'This is for you . . .'

She handed Kathryn a round wooden board covered with pictures that were hard to see in the low light. Some were neatly cut, while others had ragged edges as though scissors had been used in a hurry. In fact, it bore a close resemblance to one of Oliver's school projects.

'Thank you, but I don't need a new bread board,' Kathryn said, less than enthusiastic. 'I'm trying to travel light too.'

Helen rolled her eyes. 'It's not a bread board! It's a vision board. It's to help you. And it's high time you started looking after yourself. This is a way for you to focus—on you.'

Kathryn leaned closer, examining the images: Chris, Kathryn and Oliver in the centre, a photo of Eleanor on the left across a decoupage of English landscapes, and a picture of Kathryn and Oliver on the right over simple motifs of Australiana—their photo was from a few years ago, and she was smiling . . .

Kathryn looked back up at Helen. 'I do seem relaxed there, don't I? It's very thoughtful of you, but I *am* focusing at the moment, just not on myself.'

'I don't believe you. Look at you.' Helen's hands wafted the air in front of her. 'Your chakras are so out of whack. Anyway, these are just suggestions—you can choose your own affirmations and put them on. Whatever works for you.'

'Cheers,' Kathryn said, raising her glass and waiting for Helen to toast. 'Here's to getting my chakras straightened out.'

'I'll drink to that,' Helen said. She took a sip and placed her glass down, attention back on the vision board. 'I've given you a harmonious family over here so that you can celebrate them, and—'

'And then just me and Oliver.' Kathryn raised her eyebrows at her friend; she'd only recently told Helen about the trial separation, wanting to make a decision about whether it would be long term without the influence of family and friends, especially the ones who might want her to move back.

'Well,' said Helen, 'you can remove images or add ones that give you clarity. It's your vision of the life you want. Say, if you meditate in the morning, it will help give you the clarity during the day that you need to achieve your goals.'

Kathryn loved that her friend cared so much, but she couldn't explain to her that there was no time for yoga or meditation when she was working full-time and with all of Oliver's commitments, especially now she was looking after him alone most of the time. She and Helen had discussed some of this once before, and it had ended as a married versus single debate; she didn't want to go there again.

Kathryn laughed uneasily. 'Look, I get the family of two or family of three thing—very subtle—but it's the decision that I'm having a bit of trouble with.'

'Positive thoughts lead to positive outcomes. I used one of these boards to help me find a new vocation. It's anything you want it to be.'

'It's very—how shall I put this? Innocent.'

'I know it might seem immature to you, Kat, but it's no different to using Pinterest. This is just more . . . tangible.'

Kathryn supposed her friend had a point. She used visuals all the time for work, creating mood boards for clients to focus on when she responded to their briefs. Some people took one look at the pastiche of materials and loved what she'd produced, while others found them of no interest. Now she divided her clients into two groups: 'too much money, too little time' and 'too much time, too little taste.'

After laying the board on the table, Kathryn leaned over it, studying the intricate pattern of the wood's grain behind the pictures and deciding that there was something quite charming and childlike about it. It reminded her of a doll's house she'd decorated as a ten-year-old, with wallpaper and even miniature books and magazines—she had used hand-cut pictures for all of them. This board had taken Helen some time to make.

And the photos had reminded Kathryn that she was supposed to be working out her future on this trip instead of getting completely drawn into Eleanor's past.

'I love it, I really do. Thank you,' she said, coming around to the idea—then realising it was unlikely to make it home with her, since you can't take wood into Australia. She leaned over and kissed her friend.

'It's a pleasure!' Helen said, beaming back.

She didn't look in the least bit offended, so Kathryn clinked her glass again and took another sip. The cold Chablis was refreshing after the dusty heat of the underground and all the rushing around, and it helped to relax and focus her mind faster than any number of vision boards could have. She sipped it again.

'How's everything at home?' Helen asked with a touch of concern.

'Not yet, let's just enjoy this for a while.' A wave of emotion caused Kathryn's voice to tremble. 'I'm sure once I start, I shan't be able to shut up.'

Helen gave her a reassuring smile. 'Of course. And before I forget, there's a wonderful new cafe I'm going to take you to for breakfast to-morrow.'

'Oh . . .'

'What?'

'I'm sorry, Hels. I have to get the train back to Kent tonight. I can't stay.'

'But I thought we were going to have the day together.' Helen sounded quite put out.

'We were, but something's come up—I've got photos of an old diary of Jack's, and I need to show them to Gran. Can we postpone until Thursday? Would that work for you?'

Kathryn had tried reading the diary entries to her grandmother over the phone, but it was too difficult for her to follow, so she had to see them. Kathryn had also assured Chris that she would finish the Nautilus concept revisions so they were ready for the council meeting, and that would already mean burning some midnight oil.

'I'm not sure,' Helen said, still looking disappointed. 'It's not that easy to drop everything, you know. I'll have to rearrange a few things.'

Helen's Chinese mother and Scandinavian father had given her the bone structure and skin tone that other women envied, but it was her sunniness that really got her noticed, and Kathryn watched it fade.

'I'm sorry,' Kathryn said, 'I didn't mean to—'

'Don't worry.' Helen averted her eyes. 'I was just so looking forward to this. I thought it would be like old times.'

'I know. Me too. But Thursday—I'll definitely come back then.' Kathryn placed her hand over her friend's. It was this feast or famine existence that she found so difficult. She wanted to spend more time with her loved ones here, before it was too late.

When Helen turned back, her eyes were watery. Kathryn was close to tears too, but she willed them away.

Helen wiped her eyes and took a gulp of wine. 'So,' she said after a pause, 'how's my gorgeous godson?'

'He's not too bad. His school has a new support teacher he really likes. I don't have to take him to extra classes before school anymore, which is good.'

'You must be missing him.'

'I am, and it's hard on him too. He gets very unsettled when he's out of routine, and by what he hears on the news. He's trying to listen out for me, hear what's going on so he can protect me, but he doesn't filter information in the same way we do, so everything seems very real to him. Imagine how overwhelming that must be. But, oh, take a look at this . . .' She picked up her phone and scrolled through until she found the video of Oliver playing the piano. Helen watched his first two clumsy attempts at 'Für Elise' until a third attempt when he made it through the piece. 'That's amazing. The boy is gifted!'

'Not really. It's Suzuki method, so he listens rather than reads. The specialist says it's good for him. And he enjoys it, which is the main thing.'

'He's really good. He should be very proud of himself.'

'Well, it's taken nearly a year for him to learn that piece. He has a concert the day I get back—hopefully Chris is helping him with his practice. Anyway, I'll send you a video.' She placed the phone down. 'It's strange, isn't it? Here we are sending videos across the world and getting live feeds from war zones, and seventy years ago they were drawing pictures of battlefields and sending them home, and that took weeks. Then it might be months before they could actually be viewed in a gallery or seen in a newspaper.'

'You really *are* getting into this search, aren't you?'

'It's hard not to. The history is so interesting!'

She told Helen about the second journal, and a little about Stephen Aldridge and his strange house. Then she outlined her plans for the next few days.

'Most of the library and museum archives have been digitised now,' she concluded, 'so it's a lot quicker to find things out. You can become an expert on anything these days.'

'Do you really believe that?' Helen asked. 'Isn't it more a case of jack-of-all-trades and master of none?'

Kathryn thought about this as she watched the silhouette of their candle dance off the brick wall, the basement becoming darker as dusk settled into night and more people crowded the downstairs bar.

'I don't think so,' she said after a while. 'Information is power, so there's power in the hands of many now rather than just a few.'

'I suppose so,' Helen said. 'Although I sometimes wonder how much good it has done us.'

'I know what you mean. Perhaps we've seen so many images that we don't get affected by them anymore. I think that's why the war paintings are so moving—they may be from seventy years ago but they still have a real impact on you. I don't think all the coverage now is necessarily a good thing. Back then there were only a few witnesses to war, and it affected them deeply, being privy to those horrors. It took its toll.'

She knew she was rambling, but she was just trying to make sense of it all, and it was a relief to speak to someone who knew her so well. She was working out her place in the world while trying to figure out Eleanor's life over half a century ago, and the two felt incomparable.

From the corner of her eye, Kathryn noticed the waiter hovering. She beckoned him over and they ordered their favourite: fish pie and pea puree. The waiter topped up their glasses before quickly reappearing with a basket of French bread and a white ceramic bowl of butter that they instantly swooped on.

'Well, I think it all sounds rather intriguing,' said Helen, after devouring her slice of bread. 'Although it might be harder to work out than you expect.'

'I know,' Kathryn replied. 'I'm worried about what it was that made Jack disappear in the first place. He was posted alongside regular soldiers—all the war artists were—but he never fought as one. There must be some guilt, or something.'

Kathryn had listened to the recording of her grandmother's voice again on the train from Hampstead: *He was a mystery at first. His paintings were so beautiful—but him, he gave nothing away. Not until I knew him. Then . . . then it was a whole different story . . .*

Kathryn stared off into the distance, her mind spinning. 'And why didn't he come looking for Eleanor—*if* he was so important to her?'

Helen cleared her throat in quite a pointed way.

'Sorry,' Kathryn whispered guiltily. Even old friends wouldn't listen to rambling forever.

Their food arrived and they ate in silence for a few moments until Kathryn looked up to see Helen watching her, eyes narrowed slightly.

'What?' Kathryn asked, though she guessed what her friend was about to ask.

'Have we had enough wine to talk about the elephant in the room?'

Kathryn was enjoying the smoky taste of the haddock that she so missed, but now she set down her cutlery with a sigh. 'Alright.'

'So how's Chris?'

'Angry, confused, trying . . . but not hard enough. I think he's more worried about losing the house than me and Oli.'

'No!'

'Seems like it.' Kathryn looked down and picked at the pastry that was stuck to her dish. 'I can't blame him in one way. We've only been there for a year, and it's the house he designed and built—his baby.'

'He couldn't stay there?'

'No way,' she said, her head jerking up. 'It's in a very expensive suburb, South Yarra. We can barely afford to be there on two incomes.'

'What's next then?'

'I don't know,' she shrugged. 'I just want to do what's best.'

'For who?'

Kathryn's mind ran in circles trying to figure it out. Did she love Chris enough to stay with him if he couldn't change? Could she cope with Oli on her own—and, if not, would Chris agree to let her bring their son back here? Could she live in Melbourne long term?

Lifting her glass close to Helen's, she said, 'I'm not sure, but I do know one thing. I want to bring Oli over for a visit soon, with or without Chris.'

'I'll drink to that,' Helen said, and they toasted it. 'When?'

'Oh, round about Christmas time,' Kathryn replied, her sigh giving way to a smile. 'And I'd like for it to be a long visit.'

'I do wish you would. I can see how unsettled you are, Kat. You need to make a decision, for your sake and Oli's. At least come for a while to try it.' Helen was getting quite heated, the wine giving her extra fervour.

'I know, but the courts won't allow me to take Oli overseas without Chris's permission.'

'And he wouldn't give it?'

'It's not come to that yet, Helen,' she said, suddenly defensive. 'It is a trial separation.'

'I know, but it's not fair. You've been there for what, eleven years? It's his turn to make a sacrifice, if this is where you want to be.'

But Kathryn didn't want to talk about it anymore. She had spent hours arguing and discussing it with him, and days reeling disconnected as a result. She wanted to enjoy the little time she had with her best friend. 'Enough about my troubles,' she said. 'Tell me what's been going on with you.'

The music changed tempo, rock replacing jazz, as they spent the next hour catching up. Then Kathryn remembered that the fast trains to Tunbridge Wells were only once an hour at night. She paid before Helen had a chance to resist, guilty about letting her friend down by not staying the night. Their honest conversations meant more to her than Helen could ever know, but Kathryn had to make Eleanor and Nautilus her priorities.

'If I run, I can get the nine twenty-three,' she said, checking her phone. 'Are you okay?'

'Yes, you go. I'm going to get the tube, anyway. Love you.' Helen hugged her.

'Love you too.'

'Hey, don't forget your bread board.' Helen tucked it into Kathryn's hessian bag beside the painting. 'And, Kat . . .'

'Yes?'

'You sound so Australian!'

Thirteen

The farmhouse was in darkness by the time Kathryn arrived, and she felt like a teenager as she crept along the cold stone hallway and into the kitchen. Mickey, Eleanor's ill-tempered black-and-white cat, shot through her legs as soon as she opened the door. He stood by his bowl, meowing loudly.

'Shush,' she whispered. 'You'll wake the mistress of the house.'

He answered by meowing even louder and so she went in search of food, finding a pyramid of tins in the cupboard next to the fridge. She selected chicken, hoping it would have the least unpleasant smell.

'You're a funny one, aren't you?' she said to Mickey, tipping the food into his bowl. 'I thought cats were supposed to stay out at night. Isn't that when all the action happens?'

He didn't wait for her to finish, the fork scraping inside the tin as his face brushed her hand and he started eating noisily.

The housekeeper, Mrs Halls, was supposed to feed him in the mornings, so Kathryn guessed that she hadn't come today. It had been a relief when Eleanor relented and agreed to get help—the house certainly needed it. The William Morris wallpaper and floral fabrics had gathered a few layers of dust. They had also regained a vintage appeal, and Kathryn wondered if her gran knew what an accidental style icon she'd become.

Kathryn moved over to the AGA, palms outstretched as if she could feel its warmth even though the oven wasn't turned on. She might have been alone in the kitchen but there were ghosts everywhere: the never-ending trail of farmhands, her grandmother reminding them to scrape their boots at the door, the clatter of feet across the stone, and the scraping of wooden chairs as visitors sat and rose again. She could even hear her grandfather's booming voice over the clinking teapot that was never empty.

After remembering that she needed to email Chris, Kathryn plugged in her laptop. The council had given them lots of hoops to jump through, more than the residential code required, so she had worked on her laptop all the way home on the train to respond to their objections; at least Chris could read it and send her any changes before morning. She wanted to hear Oli's voice but the kitchen wall clock showed that it was ten-fifty—seven-fifty at home—so they would have already left for school. There hadn't been any contact all day, not even the usual text message with the day's highlights; it felt like they were orbiting the same planet but never touching, like opposing moons.

She waited for the kettle to boil, casting glances at her inbox. She was also eager to sit and re-read the diary pages.

Leaving her computer charging, she wandered over to the old oak dresser. It had seemed as big as a skyscraper to her once and was now home to several cards propped against Eleanor's prized Blue Willow crockery. There were Mallorca sunsets from the beginning of her parents' love affair with the place, before they had lost all their money; an assortment of cards from her brother, Tom, in Singapore; and handmade birthday and Christmas cards from his daughter and son. She picked one up that had a grinning oversized head atop a matchstick body—Kitty would have only been eight at the time—and surprisingly neat handwriting inside: *Happy Grandmother's Day! You are the best one ever! Lots of love, Kitty.* Crosses and noughts filled the rest of the page, representing the hugs and kisses the family saved for each other.

Kathryn smiled as she thought of the young woman Kitty had grown into. Several months ago, her niece had stayed with her and the boys in Melbourne as part of a gap year before starting university—Gen Y seemed to be making gap years an art form, and were taking gap years after university too. Perhaps that was what Kathryn should do: have a gap year to give her the clarity she needed. As she made the tea, she thought about what a novelty it would be to have space to think and not to be rushing all the time: rushing to work, rushing for pick-up, and shepherding Oliver from one extracurricular activity or specialist's appointment to the next.

There was still nothing in her inbox from Chris, so she cradled the mug between her hands and looked out eastwards to where the lawn disappeared into the orchards below. It was pitch-black with only a tiny necklace of lights flickering over the hillside, cars travelling on the village bypass. It made her think of the overgrown gardens at Stephen Aldridge's house and his equally improbable home, unkempt and so unlike his appearance. What an ambiguous character he was, at first so keen to help and desperate for the painting, and then so elusive. It all seemed quite unfathomable now, but then perhaps she just needed to get some sleep; maybe wait for Eleanor to see the diaries in the morning and shed some light.

Owls hooted in the woods and then came a high-pitched shrieking, the distressed call of foxes fighting. The wind was picking up, the house so exposed that the slightest gust banged shutters and rattled loose fittings. An outside door slammed. Kathryn pulled down the blind, suddenly feeling vulnerable, disconcerted at the thought of being watched. It was surprising that Eleanor was still comfortable living here on her own; it was so remote, too far from neighbours if she ever needed help.

Mickey was finishing his meal, the steady *tick-tock* of the clock synchronising with his contented purr. She remembered how Oliver had pestered her for a long time about having a pet before she finally bought goldfish for his birthday.

She realised she hadn't been thinking about Oliver as much as usual, and this caught her off guard. It also reminded her of how she needed to keep life in perspective and not make Oli's autism any bigger than it needed to be, or their lives any more complicated as a result. He just had a different way of looking at the world, and now so did they.

After another glance at her inbox, Kathryn settled down to read the rest of the diary entries. They were just as absorbing as the earlier ones. They also made her curious about the 1942 diary, and how she could get it from the Imperial War Museum. She logged onto the museum's website, its navy and orange logo illuminating the dark kitchen as she browsed the catalogue.

Bingo—the diary was in the catalogue but listed as a reference material, together with hundreds of other items relating to war artists. She was interested to see that Jack's lost 1943 and 1945 diaries were mentioned too under the category 'private papers,' although they were listed as unavailable. A notice said that she'd need to request all documents and make an appointment at the research room. She registered, and moments later a chime announced that she had new mail: confirmation that she would hear back with notification of her appointment time.

It was nearly midnight, but she supposed that the time zone and the caffeine were making her feel unexpectedly awake. Another shriek came from the foxes in the woods. Although she knew she should go to bed, she opened a new tab and googled Jack, using information on places and dates from the diary entries. There was still so little information to be found. What was it that Stephen had said bitterly? *Jack just didn't get the same recognition as the others.'* What exactly had he meant by that?

The next morning Eleanor wanted Kathryn to recount her meeting with Stephen Aldridge again, including how Kathryn had surprised even herself with her negotiating skills. Then they looked through the diary entries on Kathryn's computer at the kitchen table. Her grandmother already knew that she wasn't directly mentioned, but she grew quieter as they reached the end. Kathryn interpreted this as disappointment, and she felt the same way—she had hoped some recollection or cryptic clue might spark something in Eleanor's memory.

'Why didn't you tell me about Jack's success as a painter when you first gave me *The Crimson Sun*?' Kathryn asked while she tried to start the AGA.

Eleanor, still in her dressing-gown, was sitting on a wooden carver, her elbows resting on its sturdy ash arms. Mickey purred contentedly in her lap. 'It wasn't really like that . . . we didn't celebrate artists like they do now. They were just doing their job. It's ridiculous, really—now anyone can be famous, and for doing absolutely nothing worthwhile, as far as I can see.'

'I know what you mean,' Kathryn replied, thinking of the awful Kardashians. 'But if Jack was so renowned, why isn't there more about him in the archives?'

'I don't know, Katie, but can you see now why I needed your help?'

'Yes, Gran, but I need you to be totally honest with me. It could take days, weeks even, for me to find anything useful in all the archived documents . . . and I think you probably know things that would be just as valuable.'

Even after going to bed so late, Kathryn had lain awake for a while thinking about this, staring up at the pink blossoms and green tendrils of the William Morris wallpaper. Surely it wasn't that her grandmother was deliberately keeping anything from her—Eleanor probably just didn't understand what might be important. Kathryn was almost certain that helpful memories were locked away, but she wasn't sure how she could unlock them, or prompt her gran to remember.

Mickey stretched onto his back, ears twitching and eyes half-closed as Eleanor rubbed his tummy, and Kathryn came to sit at the kitchen bench next to them. 'Do you see how telling me everything you know will help?' she asked insistently.

Her grandmother gazed at her and sighed, and then faced out across the lawn to where the wood lay half-hidden in morning mist, concealing nature's atrocities from the night before. It seemed as if Eleanor was also hiding her real thoughts, but when she turned back she was more alert, her full attention on her granddaughter. 'Yes, dear, you're right. What is it that you want to know?'

'Just start at the beginning. Tell me again, everything that you knew about him.'

'Alright. I knew that he had trained as an artist, but he had worked as an illustrator before the war. You could see it in his technique, the fine detail of each stroke.'

Kathryn pictured the meticulous pen-and-ink depictions in his diary, the tiny monograms of war. 'What kind of books did he illustrate, do you know?'

'Oh, yes. There were the botanical books, and also anatomical ones were popular at the time, and then, of course, there were the textbooks.'

'Did he ever give you any?'

Eleanor had relaxed back into the chair, elbows resting on the arms, the tips of her forefingers and thumbs rubbing together in her comforting habitual way. 'No, most people didn't have much then, not in the way that people do now. Possessions, I mean.'

'Not even books?'

'No, people couldn't afford them. He had a very reputable publisher, though. He was very proud of them—if only I could remember their name,' she said as she glanced up at the ceiling. 'A lot of people lost their jobs when the war started and they stopped printing books.'

Kathryn felt encouraged. This information about the publisher could give her a lead—an old industry contact to revisit.

'So you don't have any of the books now?' she asked.

'No,' Eleanor shook her head. 'Only the drawings he did for me. You can fetch them later—they're in the attic. I would have brought them down before you came, but I can't get up that ladder now.' A short-lived chuckle turned into a dry cough.

Kathryn's interest spiked, along with a great deal of frustration at why her gran hadn't mentioned this before. Was it really the forgetfulness of old age? She had already confided her belief that Jack's importance as a war artist had somehow been concealed, and that her instinct told her that Stephen Aldridge knew where Jack was, but she hadn't offered an explanation why he would lie. Whatever it was, and her reason for wanting to know what happened to Jack, it was enough to turn down a considerable sum for his painting.

'What drawings?' she asked, trying not to let her annoyance show.

'Just small drawings that Jack gave me. Tiny pictures, they were; just thumbnails, as in the diary.' Her fingers measured out something the size of half a playing card. 'I would find them hidden . . . It's funny, I had almost forgotten about them.' The memory rekindled, Eleanor stared dreamily into space.

'It sounds romantic,' Kathryn said after a moment.

'Yes, it was, rather. They would turn up in the most unexpected places—under my pillow or in the bathroom cabinet, sometimes even in the cutlery drawer, or my handbag.'

'So, are you ever going to tell me how long the two of you were involved?' Kathryn asked, frustration finally creeping into her tone.

'Haven't I mentioned that? It was only a few months, but we saw a lot of each other. Walks after work, galleries, the occasional dance . . .'

Kathryn tried to reconcile an image of the young Eleanor in the capital with the image of a man other than her grandfather, and she found it difficult. It was also difficult to imagine dating someone during wartime. 'But where did you go? What did you do?'

'We went everywhere! In London, that is. We didn't have time to go further afield—we were so busy working, and there was volunteering and Civil Defence work, which everyone had to do. And, of course, we were both painting too.'

Kathryn's annoyance faded, replaced by admiration. 'I can't imagine how you would have fitted it all in. It makes me feel guilty for complaining about my life.'

'It's not the same, dear,' Eleanor said, patting her hand. 'You have different pressures now. I'm sure I wouldn't want to cope with all the problems you have nowadays. Anyway, I want to hear more about Oliver. Will you show me those pictures and videos again?'

'Yes, I will, but don't you think it might be an idea if I go to the attic now, and then we can look through the pictures while we finish talking about Jack?'

'I suppose so, dear, but you be careful.'

It was clear that no one had been into the attic for years, since the wooden door had swollen and wouldn't move. After a good shove, it creaked open to reveal a sparse room with dramatically fewer cobwebs and spiders than expected. Instead of boxes scattered everywhere and baskets of costumes and toys—the remnants of their childhood spilling out—it was disappointingly rather well organised. Only a small scooter, shaped like a ladybird, signposted that children had once lived in the house. An antique desk was pushed against one wall, chairs stacked alongside, while rows of cardboard boxes were piled high against the other wall.

Helpfully, her grandmother had noted the contents and dates on some of the boxes, the faded writing still legible, so it wasn't long before she found the one she was looking for. After some rearranging, she shuffled the box into the centre of the space, where the casement gave her extra light. She was curious to see the drawings Eleanor had described; how wonderfully romantic they sounded, and such a contrast to the scribbled yellow Post-it notes that Chris left her or the hurriedly sent texts with their benign emojis.

Inside the box was a small vintage suitcase in a dark grey fabric with a beige leather strip down the centre. It was in good condition and still elegant enough to use, and she wondered if her grandmother had ever used it to go away with Jack. Her fingers hovered over the locks as she hesitated, considering whether she should take it down for Eleanor to open first. But her inquisitiveness got the better of her, and she quickly clicked the locks and lifted the lid before she had the chance to change her mind.

There were old envelopes full of photographs, newspaper cuttings, and letters; some she recognised as being in Eleanor's handwriting while others were unfamiliar. It would easily take them the rest of the day to look through these properly, but she was keen to see if any were from Jack, so she flicked through them. At first glance there didn't appear to be any small drawings.

The doorbell interrupted Kathryn and she stopped, listening to voices from two floors below. It had to be Mrs Halls, and Kathryn returned to the papers knowing that this visit would keep her grandmother occupied for a little longer.

Now she searched more thoroughly, looking deep inside each envelope, the thin paper crackling between her fingers. Towards the back of the pile was an old book, an edition of *Mr Glugg* but in an unusual format, pocket sized: specially printed for soldiers to fit in their uniform pockets, she had discovered from a visit to the Australian

War Museum. On the inside cover was an inscription in pale black ink: *TO KEEP YOU SAFE AND YOUR MIND FOCUSED*. She didn't recognise the handwriting but guessed it could be from her grandmother to Jack.

Then, among the papers, she spotted an old piece of canvas that looked of little importance, but when she opened it out, part of a faded painting came into view. It was a baroque image: vague figures leaned forward, but not winged cherubs with harps—soldiers in uniform aiming their weapons. It looked and felt so fragile that she carefully laid it out on the floor beside her, eager to ask Eleanor about it.

At the back of the trunk was a larger envelope containing a clump of papers tied with a thin blue ribbon. Among them were several small pictures—caricatures of Eleanor and Jack—along with a faded black-and-white photograph.

The couple were standing inside a pagoda in a park. It must have been summer because Jack wore short sleeves and Eleanor was in a light floral dress. Kathryn wasn't as surprised as she'd expected to be at seeing her grandmother with a man other than Edward. In her mind, she had built an image of Jack from Eleanor's descriptions and grainy shots on the internet, and it was uncannily close to the face she was looking at now: angular, with unruly dark hair and a full, thick brow. No, what surprised Kathryn was how excitedly happy the two of them appeared to be.

PART III

The Bermondsey Rescue

'To-day war has come to civilians.
Subjects for the artist, whether
or not he is a member of the
Civil Defence Forces, are on his
doorstep and, to judge by its beginning the pictorial record of
war on the home front will be a
worthy and impressive one.'

War Pictures by British Artists, BLITZ
OXFORD UNIVERSITY PRESS, 1942

Fourteen

LONDON, JUNE 1942

'It's just not my sort of thing,' Cecily complained, as Eleanor adjusted her sister's hair and stood back to see the results.

'You'll enjoy it once we get there, I promise,' Eleanor said, turning her attention to her own appearance. There were distinct shadows under her eyes but nothing that a dab of blusher and a spot of lipstick wouldn't fix. She applied her make-up, happy that the benefits of being an artist extended beyond transforming a bare canvas.

Although there hadn't been a bombing raid on the city for nearly a year, the sight of the anti-aircraft guns in Hyde Park and the constant radio bombardments were enough to keep her awake some nights—that and Cecily's nightmares. Yesterday her sister had shared her day's events over supper: an artist had visited the hospital to paint faces on masks for disfigured soldiers. Last night Cecily had awoken from nightmares of faceless men, and one of them had been her late boyfriend, Giles.

'Come on, let's go,' Eleanor said. 'I don't want to be late.' She stood by the opened front door, waiting for her sister.

'Is Jack picking us up?' Cecily asked.

'No, of course not, we're meeting him there.'

'Why of course not?'

'Because he has a motorcycle, silly—and it's not a tandem either!'

'Well, I didn't know,' Cecily said, sounding exasperated.

'Cecily, you're whining again.'

Eleanor had warned her about her moaning. So many of their friends took up all the space in the room that her timid sister could easily be overlooked, and she considered it part of her duty to Cecily to make sure she didn't get ignored—not whingeing would help. As would the neat pin-curls, the colourful new neck-scarf that their mother had sent, and the smidgen of make-up that Eleanor had applied.

'We, however, are going to get the bus and then walk,' Eleanor said, 'so that's why we need to get a move on.'

In the ten weeks since she'd met Jack, they had visited dozens of locations and painted several pictures around the capital. He had been as generous in sharing his knowledge as any of the teachers at the Slade had been. He'd also surprised her after work a few times, and they had walked through Green Park or St James's, stopping to feed the Canadian geese or watch the Welsh Guards change. There had been lunches at nearby teahouses and evenings of dancing, but there had also been outings to some of the exhibitions that were springing up in the city, ones where émigrés showcased their versions of the war. Tonight she was taking Jack to see a new exhibition by Polish artists at a gallery in Holborn, wanting to support the émigrés the larger institutions had chosen to ignore.

The bus took the sisters past Marble Arch and onto Piccadilly Circus, passing Charing Cross on their way to Aldwych, from where they walked the last half-mile to the gallery. And although the journey took a long time, it was memorable because they rarely travelled this far east. But as they walked up Kingsway, it was evident that little recovery from the Blitz had taken place—most of the abandoned shops and offices had just been boarded up and left deserted.

Eleanor lingered for a moment, disquieted by the memory of the eerie silences before the raids, the stillness before the sirens would sound and the bombs would begin to fall. Over a hundred of them had been dropped on Holborn, and she shuddered at the thought of the treasured heritage lost as well as precious lives. Many grand Gothic buildings were now just hollow shells, which was saddening but also a reminder that it might still be treacherous to walk around at night.

'Did you remember your torch?' Eleanor asked her sister.

'Yes,' Cecily replied, patting the gasmask box that was slung over her shoulder. 'It's in here.'

'Well, don't forget to shine it downwards if you need to.'

'Stop fussing, Ellie. You're worse than Mother. Actually, I don't think that even *she* nags as much as you.'

That was the point: her mother didn't have to because she wasn't there. Eleanor was, and there had been more concerns lately. Not that she wanted to involve their mother just yet, instead she pretended that everything was fine, but she'd observed telltale signs that Cecily wasn't coping—the panic attacks, the shakes—and Eleanor was certain that the other hospital staff must have noticed too. But when

Eleanor had voiced her concerns to Jack he'd told her that she was worrying too much and suggested they go out and have fun. So here they were, in a fit of concern and goodwill, and Cecily was taking two steps to every one of Eleanor's in a half-run to keep up.

'So do you still get butterflies when you see him?' Cecily asked.

Eleanor glanced at her but carried on walking. 'Is it that obvious?'

Could she really tell her sister that it wasn't butterflies she felt when she saw Jack but as if her heart had missed a beat? That, as clichéd as it was, time stopped when they were together and slowed when they were apart, and that everything he did and said seemed a revelation to her. But how strangely familiar he was too, as if she might have known him all her life. As pigment needed water, and soldiers needed courage, she needed Jack. They were destined to be together—at least for as long as the war and the WAAC would allow.

'Yes, well, it's understandable,' Cecily said. 'Jack makes me quite nervous too.'

'Really?'

Cecily nodded, lips clamped shut.

'Oh, you are funny! I expect it's just because you don't know each other very well.'

'Maybe. I do appreciate you asking me along. I know you would probably prefer to be on your own.'

'Of course not, Cecily. It's an exhibition—dozens of people will be there!'

'You know what I mean,' Cecily said, glasses slipping down her nose again as she tried to keep up. 'You are lucky, though.'

'How so?'

'Well, all week you're surrounded by art. You mix with artists and interesting people, and then at night you get to go to exhibitions too. What do I do? I mop up blood and hold the hands of dying soldiers.'

'Cecily! What has got into you?' Eleanor said, stopping and turning to her.

Even by Cecily's standards this was particularly melancholy; perhaps Eleanor had better talk to their mother after all.

'My work might seem like fun to an outsider,' she said, 'but those paintings depict the men that cause those injuries, the machines that inflict those deaths. You must find a way of understanding your contribution to the war. Can you not appreciate the value of what you do?'

Cecily's face crumpled and her make-up looked suddenly out of place. 'I'm sorry, it's just been a particularly gloomy week. Let's face it, Eleanor, you do see the beauty in this world while I spend my days among the gore.'

Eleanor selfishly hoped that her sister wouldn't continue in this vein when they met Jack, that she would at least try to cheer up—and then Eleanor noticed him across the street. He was leaning against the wall, one hand in his pocket, the other holding a cigarette. His head was angled upwards, attention caught by something in the sky.

She glanced up too, spotting the firewatchers who were still present in every neighbourhood, eyes trained to notice the first flashes that could bring devastation. Then she took Cecily's arm and led her across the street.

'Hello,' Eleanor said softly, hoping not to startle Jack.

His face broke into a wide grin and he bent to kiss her cheek.

'Jack, you remember Cecily . . .'

'Ah, yes, how nice to see you again,' he said, taking her hand.

'Likewise,' Cecily replied.

'I've heard—' they said at the same time and laughed.

A look passed between them, and Eleanor knew that she need not worry; that they would get on just fine.

'Here's the program for tonight,' Jack said, handing Eleanor a printed sheet of paper.

'We are in for a treat,' she said as she glanced over it. 'They've been getting very good reviews in *The Tatler* and *The Illustrated London News*. Sir Robert is being very short-sighted by not visiting this one personally.'

'Shall we?' Jack said, holding out his arm to Cecily.

She looped her arm through his and followed Eleanor into the hall.

The exhibition was in a disused school and the windows had been crisscrossed with tape, the desks and chairs stacked onto the small stage. It was a sad reminder of how few children they saw in the streets, or voices and laughter they heard bubbling up from the city's playgrounds and parks. And a solemn thought to consider how long it might be until plays were performed on this stage again, or carol concerts with nativity costumes that parents would corral their children into.

There were only a few visitors in the hall and the exhibition was easy enough to walk around, the pictures spaced out, beige walls providing a blank background for the art. They worked their way round in thoughtful silence, except when Eleanor referred to the program to share interesting facts with Cecily, lingering on some works while quickly passing others that weren't to her taste.

Eleanor had been involved with the exhibition of Sir William Nicholson and Jack B. Yeats at the National Gallery in January and knew about the hard work involved—how painstaking it was to catalogue the artworks and showcase them in their best light, to negotiate with the artists if the WAAC or the gallery didn't own the artworks—so it was interesting to see behind the scenes at another type of exhibition. The organisers had held various fundraisers for local and émigré artists, ones who no longer had any form of livelihood or stood any chance of getting on the government's 'magic carpet', as the WAAC was known. Feliks Topolski was the only foreign artist who had achieved any success, with his work as an official war artist for Britain and Poland, as well as his drawings in *Picture Post* garnering him a wide audience. That Jack knew and had worked with Topolski only impressed her more.

Tonight's event had been instigated in part by the wife of Ceri Phillips, to support the Women and Children in Soviet Russia. Eleanor found the Eastern European accent at times indecipherable, at others charming, but it never stopped her from enjoying their work or their company.

As the three of them continued around the exhibition, Eleanor drew Cecily's attention to how the artists inventively created art from unlikely materials when the traditional ones ran out. There were drawings on lavatory paper, linocuts made from linoleum, crushed graphite from pencils mixed with margarine to create ink—and, in the centre of the space, the installation of a laundry mangle seconded from a household for use as a printing press. They came to stand in front of it, staring with admiration.

'They're ingenious,' Cecily said, looking back and forth to Jack and Eleanor, who stood either side.

'You can see how it's not always so easy for the artist,' Jack remarked. 'But if they are determined, then they usually find a way.'

'Except for this one.' Eleanor was looking at a sculpture on a plinth, the description announcing that it had been made from porridge. 'I don't think that this one is such a great success,' she said, amused.

It reminded her of the work of the Five and Seven Society and how close she had flitted to the edge. As a student at the Slade she had been in awe of the artists, admiring their bravery in finding new ways to work, but now she felt differently; war had changed her perspective, and she looked at everything through a different lens.

'Are you certain that you can't see the merit in it?' Jack asked, with a mischievous smile. 'Ingenious, really—art that you can eat. They might start giving them out as standard issue. Something to entertain the chaps and that they can eat when the rations run out!'

'Maybe I was wrong,' Eleanor said, considering it again.

'Yes, but you don't even like porridge,' Cecily said with a scowl.

'I know, I think I would prefer to eat my own stockings!'

'If you can get any!' Cecily added quietly.

'I thought you would like this exhibition,' Jack said, turning to Eleanor, 'and you can see how much there is to learn from these men.'

'Yes, they are all men, aren't they?' Eleanor said.

'I didn't mean it like that,' Jack replied.

'I know.' She touched his arm lightly. 'Just ignore me. I think it's marvellous that they are so resourceful. It makes you realise what you could do if you got called up and needed to improvise.'

'I've got a feeling that porridge isn't part of the ration pack, but I know what you mean,' he continued amused. 'It makes you feel confident knowing that you can use your breakfast if you run out of paint.'

Eleanor spun round. 'Have you heard something?' she asked, becoming serious again.

'No, not yet.'

A look passed between them of shared understanding, the knowledge that he could be called away at any moment, that their weeks together could be coming to an end. She had been so keen to encourage him early on, but now she didn't know what she would do when he was gone.

Cecily was chattering away, and Eleanor was so busy following her train of thought that before she knew it they had walked down the street and onto Kingsway without thinking where they were heading.

'Where are we going?' she asked, stopping and turning to Jack.

'To get something to eat?'

'We had dinner before we came,' she replied.

Cecily looked from one to the other. 'How about a drink then?'

They found a pub off Kingsway, and Jack ordered a round of gin and tonics while they hovered by a small round table, waiting for a couple to leave. A carved mahogany bar was almost obscured by the brass-studded stools that were pulled alongside. It was busy, rich with the smell of ale and thick with smoke, and men sat at the tables or stood talking in pairs. There were few women, their fur-collared coats and pinned brooches a clue that they weren't locals.

The couple at the table, a soldier and his girlfriend, started proudly telling Eleanor and Cecily that this pub was one of a handful in the area that had remained intact. They pointed out the original bevelled glass mirrors and cut-glass windows and lights, and the rainbows the lights threw across the walls. But Eleanor wasn't concentrating; she was concerned about Jack and the fact that he was trying to make a joke of everything—and she was sure it wasn't because of Cecily.

The gin and tonics eased the conversation along as the three of them talked about the exhibition and Jack asked Cecily about her work. As soon as Cecily went to the ladies', Eleanor took her chance to talk to him.

'Are you alright?' she asked.

'Yes. I'm fine,' he replied, eyes meeting her gaze. 'You?'

'This can't go on for much longer,' she said, relaxed by the alcohol, thoughts flowing unchecked into words.

'What can't?'

'This. Us . . .'

He frowned. 'Why?'

'Because they need more artists overseas. I think it's going to be soon, Jack.'

'Nonsense, I know exactly what they think of my work and they couldn't care less for it,' he said light-heartedly. 'There are plenty of chaps more qualified than me.'

Eleanor wasn't smiling, though. 'I sit in on the meetings—I know what they think.'

'Yes, I suppose you do,' he said wistfully, taking another sip. 'Say, I don't suppose you're owed any favours, are you? Couldn't you have a word with Sir Robert and ask him to hold off on me for a while? Tell him I've met a gorgeous girl . . .'

She smiled, but it was only fleeting.

Jack narrowed his eyes. 'He hasn't had you doing more of his errands, has he?'

Eleanor shot him a look. She had come home fuming from the last meeting, indignant at the list of chores that Sir Robert had given her—and it hadn't been the first time.

'No, he hasn't,' she said. 'Mrs Hughes is in town, and it only seems to be when she's away that life overwhelms him completely. No, I won't be asking for any favours.'

Jack leaned closer, lowering his voice. 'So I suppose you still don't want me to submit your painting?'

'I thought we discussed that,' she said and finished her drink. 'I'll let you know if it's ever the right time.'

After their initial bravado had cooled, they'd decided that substituting one of her pictures for Jack's was probably too risky; that in time she would submit her own. Of course, she didn't admit to him that she no longer wanted to go abroad—not while he was still in London.

'Whenever you're ready,' he said, tapping his nose and grinning. 'Would you like another drink?'

'I'm not sure I do, to be honest.'

'Can I see you home then?'

'No, Cecily and I shall be alright. You get off.'

'If you're sure.'

Cecily had returned but was being interrogated by two men in the doorway; she didn't look unhappy about it, though.

'I'll see you Friday,' Eleanor said to Jack with a smile. 'The usual place?'

'I'll be waiting,' he replied.

When they left, Eleanor was relieved that Cecily was in such good spirits. Of course, she would rather have been alone with Jack; she felt closer to him tonight than she ever had, but she also felt, more than ever, that they were on borrowed time.

Jack bent over, hands on knees as he tried to catch his breath, knowing that he had pushed himself to his limits. He found that if he ran at least five miles each day he could hope to achieve the level of fitness that the SOE trainers said would be required of him. Of course, it was nowhere near as harsh as the circuits they completed during training, or close to the conditions he would experience in the field, but he was determined to carry on, and sprinted off again.

After his short ride from the pub in Holborn he'd still been pre-occupied by thoughts of Eleanor, and with so much else on his mind he had decided on a run—in spite of the dangers of running at night. He was on the home stretch now, racing through Battersea Park, the shadowy waters of the Thames coursing alongside, the four chimneys of the power station beckoning in the near distance. The surrounding streets were quiet, a recent shower covering them in a translucent glaze, and the air was so crisp and still that all he heard was his own rasping breath. His legs ached and his heart thudded, yet still his thoughts weren't clearing.

Beth lived a few streets away, and by the time he arrived the curtains were drawn and the lights were off for the blackout. He looked at his watch: it was only nine-thirty but they might already be asleep. He was searching the porch for some way to leave a note, when the front door opened and she appeared in silhouette, backlit by the dim hall light.

'Jack, what are you . . . Is everything alright?' she said, her surprise turning to panic.

'Yes, it's fine. Mum's fine.'

'Oh, thank God!'

'I just wanted to see you?'

'That's nice,' she said with a reluctant smile, 'but it's a bit late, isn't it?'

'I know, I'm sorry. I didn't mean to disturb you—' he noticed she was in her dressing-gown '—it's just . . .'

'What? Are you okay, Jack?'

'Is Henry in?'

'He's gone to bed. You can come in, if you like—I'll put the kettle on.'

'No, don't worry. Actually, do you mind if we talk out here?'

Beth stepped onto the porch and shut the door behind her. She pulled her dressing-gown tighter and dropped down onto the top step beside him, so they sat side by side looking up at the stars, just as they had as kids.

'Which is the furthest planet?' Jack asked. 'Do you remember?'

'Neptune?' she replied.

The sky was clear, a honeycomb of stars glinting at them, a waning moon for company.

'And the nearest?' he asked.

'I'm not sure . . . Venus?'

Jack didn't answer. He lit a cigarette, drawing on it heavily before exhaling into the cool night air.

'What is it, Jack? Something *is* wrong, isn't it.'

'No, I honestly just wanted to see you.'

'You've never done this before, especially in the middle of the night.'

'I'm sorry, it's just that I thought, well, there are things that you and I haven't discussed . . . arrangements. If I don't come back. I don't want to leave you to cope with everything.'

'What do you mean . . . arrangements for Mum?'

'Not just Mum. For me too. There's no one looking out for me like you and Henry do for each other, so I want you to know that I've put some money aside. And I've had a will drawn up. All the paperwork is with Mum's solicitor, Wilcox.'

'Oh, Jack, must you talk like this?' she said wearily.

'Come on, Beth.' He turned his attention to her. 'It doesn't do any good burying your head in the sand. If I get sent away we may not have the chance to talk.'

She didn't reply but eased closer to him on the step until their silhouettes merged. 'Have you heard something?' she asked after a short time.

'No. Not yet.' His heart was still pounding, and he had to talk quickly in case he left anything important unsaid. 'I also want to tell you how much I appreciate all you've done for Mum. You are the best daughter, and sister, that anyone could wish for.'

He wanted to tell her about his imminent departure and the work he would be doing, not just for the war artists' scheme but also for the SOE. He didn't want to burden her with his secrets, though; he would have to carry this responsibility alone.

Her breathing changed and he heard her sniffle.

'Hey, come on,' he said, placing an arm around her. 'You're not supposed to be sad. It's a compliment—you're meant to cry when people tell you how hopeless you are, how miserable you make them, not when they tell you how marvellous you are.'

'I know.' She rested her head on his shoulder. 'I just don't like hearing you talk this way.'

'I'm sorry, Beth, but I wouldn't want to talk like this with anyone else.'

Fifteen

It should have been a simple enough route down to Merton from Portman Square—straight through Chelsea and over the bridge, and then on down through Battersea—but there were delays, so Clive had taken another route via the King's Road. Before they knew it they were crossing Wandsworth Bridge Road, when their Austin Eighteen hit some debris and got a flat tyre.

Eleanor had been too distracted by thoughts of Jack to notice as the roads became less familiar and Clive's directions more vague, and she felt just as unable to concentrate and reassure him now.

'Please stop apologising, Clive. These things happen.'

'My eyesight isn't what it was, Miss Roy. I am so sorry.'

Clive had tried his hardest to change the tyre, but the weight of the axle was too much for him, and they'd ended up in a garage beneath the railway arches in Wandsworth.

Eleanor held a cotton handkerchief across her mouth as she coughed. The air in the garage was so thick with oil and grease that it had made her quite giddy when she first walked in, and although she'd become accustomed to it, it was still tickling her throat. Despite the discomfort, she thought this would be an ideal place to be stranded in a raid: the beauty of it being a basement within a basement, with the pits the mechanics used to mend cars providing shelter for anyone who sought safety there.

'It is absolutely fine, Clive, and your worrying is not going to help.' She did wish he would stop talking so she could work out how they could make up the lost time.

'I know, Miss Roy, but you've got to get to Merton, and what about Mr Steadman?'

'Don't you worry about Mr Steadman. You just leave him to me.'

It was proving to be a bit of a struggle balancing the demands of the WAAC with Steadman's work, and even though she was happy to work longer and harder than she ever had before, she still couldn't afford to lose an afternoon sitting in a garage.

The mechanic brewed a large pot of tea, and she spent the next few minutes talking with Clive before she noticed they weren't alone. On the other side of the garage, away from the hulks of the broken cars and vans that floated above the concrete floor, and undetected beneath the drill and screech of the tools, was a group of children. She heard their voices and went to investigate. Eleven lost souls were perched on their suitcases, pale and yawning.

'Hello,' she said, stepping over the metal tools and disused parts.

Then she noticed that a woman was with them, who looked up and closed her book. 'Are you with the bus company?' she asked.

'No, I'm not. I'm with . . . Not to worry, it's complicated.' Eleanor had given up explaining to people that she worked for both the Ministry of Food and the Ministry of Information, and it seemed much simpler to mention just one or neither. Besides, the woman already looked quite overwhelmed. 'Is everything alright?'

'Well, yes and no.' The woman sighed. 'We were on a bus to our orphanage in Richmond when it broke down. Now we've got to wait for a replacement.'

'Oh, I do hope it won't be too long,' Eleanor said, instantly worried on their behalf.

'Sorry, who did you say you were?'

'My name's Eleanor, Eleanor Roy. We've also broken down.'

She offered her hand, and the woman shook it. She was about thirty with alert brown eyes, and chestnut hair that skimmed the collar of her navy coat, and she spoke with a south country accent. 'Miss Short. Pleased to meet you.'

'Likewise.'

'It's a real pity,' Miss Short continued. 'The children were tired anyway and we've been here for more than an hour. They really are getting very hungry.'

Eleanor glanced over to the children again. They were so young, barely more than seven or eight, and they looked exhausted.

'Is there a shop nearby?' she asked. 'I could go and look, if you like.'

'We've been told to stay put. The replacement bus could be here any moment.'

The woman certainly seemed very tense. Eleanor could imagine how stressful it must be to be stranded here with the infants and no way of knowing how long the bus would be.

'Well, aren't you a little poppet,' Eleanor said to a small blonde girl sucking her thumb.

'Don't expect her to talk,' Miss Short said lightly. 'Her name's Mary-Ann but she never takes her thumb out.'

Another girl yawned, then two boys at the back, leaning against the mechanics' bench, began to squabble. Eleanor was hardly surprised that they were getting fidgety with nothing to do. 'I've got some paper and pencils in my bag,' she said. 'Do you mind?'

'Of course not,' said Miss Short. 'I'm not sure you'll be able to get them to draw, though.'

Eleanor took out the drawing materials and garden magazines that she was taking to show the artists in Merton, and she held up a magazine in front of the children. 'Have any of you ever seen a garden like this?'

There were a few shakes of the head. One boy wasn't even looking, too busy examining the end of his finger, the contents of which he had just retrieved from his nostril.

'What about planting seeds or helping to water the plants—have any of you ever done that?' She was choosing her words carefully so that she didn't mention the word 'home.'

A couple of nods and yawns, as mostly blank faces looked back at her.

She turned the page to show a picnic scene and there was a little more interest, a couple of heads bobbing up to take a better look.

'If I give you a pencil and some paper, do you think you could draw me a picture?' she said to the nearest child. 'Perhaps somewhere you might like to have a picnic, and the things that you would like to eat.'

She could see that some of them were thinking, eyes darting around rather than just staring vacantly. A few moments passed, the only sound the clank of metal behind them as the mechanics carried on their work, while the reek of oil and grime was overpowering.

'Tell you what, I'll go first.' She laid down her coat and sat on the floor next to them.

As she started to sketch, the children truly took notice. This gave her the idea of drawing something else—she started on an outline of Mary-Ann's face. The child was sitting just close enough for Eleanor to see her long eyelashes flicker against her cheek.

Eleanor's sketch was simple, just a charcoal portrait, but it caught their attention and they drew closer as she started on a second work.

'Can I have a go?' one of them asked.

With all the children now taking an interest, Eleanor fetched a nature magazine from her bag and some more pencils, just enough to go around. They produced images of bees and flowers, and she took it in turns to praise their efforts and give them some hints, pleased when they became absorbed.

A small boy, who told her his name was Isaac, drew a picture of a woman. Her face was oversized, and the lines of her body were thick and heavy, but he captured real warmth in her eyes.

'That's lovely,' Eleanor commented.

'It's my ma,' he said, proudly holding it up.

Eleanor's heart ached. 'She's beautiful.'

'She was beautiful.'

His response was so matter-of-fact that it surprised her, but then she remembered that this was how it was now. The war had affected all of them, and their friends and families—it had become part of their everyday lives.

'And you are a very clever and brave young man,' she told him.

Another boy, who had been quietly watching, approached her. 'Can I have a go?'

'I'm not sure there's enough time now,' Eleanor said, noticing that Clive was waving at her from the other side of the garage. 'Our car is ready now, so we have to go.'

The boy looked disappointed.

'What's your name?' she asked.

'Billy.'

'Well, Billy, I could come and visit you another day,' she said without even thinking. 'What would you like to paint?'

'My dad's motorcycle—he'd only just bought it. It was a real beauty.'

'In that case, I shall bring my best paints so that you can find exactly the right colour.'

She heard Clive honk the Austin's horn, so she gathered the rest of her materials and said goodbye to the children.

Miss Short walked over with her. 'Will you really be able to pay us a visit?'

'I hope so. Would the orphanage allow it?'

'Yes, of course. The children would love to see you again. That impromptu art class did them the world of good.'

The unexpected encounter had been a tonic for her as well. She had stopped worrying about her deadlines, or that she would ever get to paint as a war artist, and she'd realised that she just needed to stop thinking about Jack leaving and enjoy his company. Compared with the uncertain fate of these poor children, there wasn't any real problem at all.

Eleanor handed Miss Short a slip of paper. 'Can you please write your address and phone number? Perhaps if I call first, make sure it's a good time . . .'

Miss Short scribbled on the paper and handed it back. 'No need to call—any time will be a good time.' She smiled. 'We'll see you soon then.'

'Yes . . . hopefully.'

Sixteen

Theirs was an irregular skyline, with distorted shapes of well-known landmarks recognisable by day, now forming a spider-web that glistened in the half-light. Eleanor and Jack were on the edge of a parapet with a bird's-eye view over the city—and it felt to Eleanor as if she was on the edge of the world.

They had commandeered the firewatchers post on the roof at Portman Square and watched as the sun melted on the horizon. Eleanor had taken to sneaking up here at the end of the day when the sun afforded her the best light to paint. The conditions were ideal tonight, the sun creating bold silhouettes of the buildings, its far-reaching rays reflecting light off metalwork and glass. Eleanor didn't just respond to the glowing colours, but also to the textures they highlighted: the smooth ancient sandstone of the church opposite, the tessellated tiles of the surrounding roofs, the chiselled masonry that sat at myriad angles alongside the carved and painted wood of the shopfronts below. The city was organic, emerging from the ground—rock, wood, glass and metal, then layers of cloud and sky—just like the strata of the Earth itself.

She was waiting until they had finished painting, when the dusk had finally settled over them, to bring out the picnic she had packed to share.

'Don't you think that if you paint it, it somehow helps to make sense of it all?' she asked, looking across at Jack.

They were sitting slightly apart, angled away from each other while they worked on the small canvases balanced in their laps. Jack was thoughtful as he leaned over to refill his brush from the palette at his feet. She hadn't seen him since their outing to the exhibition, and he was unusually reserved, barely reacting when she had told him how the arrangements were coming along for the launch of the war artists' booklets in a few days' time, or how Cecily had got on with her first exam.

'Jack, did you hear what I said? Does painting help you come to terms with things in some way?'

'Yes,' he murmured.

'Really? It doesn't sound ridiculous?'

'Not at all,' he said, still distracted.

'So is that how you feel too?' she asked, pushing him for a definitive answer.

'Isn't it how most artists feel—artists, poets, writers—not just trying to make sense of the war but everything?' he said and glanced up at her. 'Love, loss, tragedy—but this war especially.'

Here was a glimpse of that man again; that special soul who could rouse angels from children. Only a glimpse, though. Today he was not his usual self—he was distracted.

'I'm ready,' she said.

'What for?'

'My next lesson, of course. Painting for the field, part three.'

'I'm glad you find my lessons so entertaining now,' he said dryly.

She had come straight from work and was still in her suit, which restricted her movements, her calf muscles straining as she propped herself against the chimneystack. Jack had been in his studio so his shirtsleeves were rolled up, streaks of paint visible on his forearms, tiny track marks across the coarse hairs.

It was true that at first she had sometimes been reluctant to listen to him, not wanting to be his pupil. But what he had shared about working in the military sectors, and the ports and factories he had visited, was fascinating and sounded so different from painting in a studio.

'Okay,' he said, 'but you know that if you really were in the field, you would only be doing a quick thumbnail sketch now, a pen and ink that you would work up in your studio later. None of this lengthy layering with colour.'

Of course she knew—she had been working with the war artists for months now. He really wasn't thinking clearly.

'Oh dear, shall I wash it away then?' she said, joking.

'No, I think that might be a little extreme,' he answered seriously.

'Alright, so once I have my thumbnail, is that when I ask the press officer to post it home and start on another one?'

'Yes, if you were working on a series, you would. What *is* your series, Captain Roy?'

'Captain?' she asked, pleased to see a sparkle in his eyes.

'That would be your mandatory title, remember?'

'Of course, that's right.'

She thought for a moment, remembering the themes of the upcoming *War Pictures by British Artists* books; she would have chosen 'the Blitz'.

'I shall be doing a series on the capital's treasured monuments: St Paul's, Westminster Abbey and Tower Bridge, as I'm trying to summon a sense of national pride.' She spoke in a haughty voice, parroting the messages that had been written in the press release.

'Excellent,' he said, warming up at last. 'So which building are you working on tonight?'

'I think you should be able to tell that, don't you?'

'Let's see.' Jack moved behind her so that he could check her canvas.

She felt him standing close, his breath against her neck, the smell of him. She tried to ignore his proximity and concentrate solely on the picture, examining it as closely as he was. The mixed tones represented melancholy and hope, but devastated buildings had become such a predictable metaphor for loss and death that she saw through his eyes an image that was unsurprising and technically weak. The realisation depressed her; it was so frustrating not being able to create original imagery, but how could anyone hope to catch the patterns and images of the capital as it was continually reshaped? Was it even possible to show where the bombs had etched their marks, or how its citizens had ground away even more of their precious city as they attempted to rebuild it? Hers wasn't a picture of a particular building but a pastiche of the city she loved: the one that she was hoping and wishing would survive.

'I like it, but I think you should spend some more time on it at home,' he said after a few moments.

'Agreed,' she said flatly. 'I suspect that's my failing as an artist. Can I see yours, quickly? Before the light fades completely.'

Jack tilted his canvas towards her and she saw that the elements of his picture were much simpler than in hers. It was the same city at sunset, but just a stark silhouette against orange skies. He'd created it in the brief time they'd been there, yet it was as accomplished a picture as one that another artist would spend days working on.

She sighed. 'It's beautiful.'

'Then it will be yours.'

'Don't be silly, you'll get a couple of pounds for it,' she said. 'And, anyway, it's not yours to give—the committee have the first right of refusal on all your work.'

She knew the WAAC conditions off by heart: six hundred and fifty pounds a year with transport, accommodation and meals included. She still held onto the idea of being a war artist but of the fifty artists the WAAC had taken so far, only one was a woman.

Jack was shaking his head. 'Not on this one, they won't—it's for you.'

'Really?'

'Yes, really.'

She loved it; not just because it was in his quintessential style, but because it would remind her of all the days they'd spent together—and their time up here on top of the world.

She glanced at the last of the sunset, at the yellow and orange light that speared the sky. 'You have captured the colours perfectly. I shall call it *The Crimson Sun*.'

He held it towards her, and she reached out and took it, but he was still unsmiling.

'Eleanor . . .'

'Yes?'

'I . . .'

'What is it?'

Laughter from the streets stole onto the rooftop, reminding her that this wasn't their kingdom alone. They had been chased away by the security guard on more than one occasion recently, and she was listening out for his footsteps on the metal fire exit stairs.

'Jack?' she asked.

He came to sit next to her. 'Well, here's the thing,' he said, eyes locking with hers. 'I'm leaving . . . I got my papers today. I've got my posting.'

They had talked about him leaving, about how important it was that he contribute, use his skills in the best way he could, but now she just felt numb. She simply didn't know what to say.

'Eleanor,' he said, taking her hand, 'are you okay?'

'Yes, yes, I am.' She finally exhaled. 'It just feels so . . . so quick.'

'I know.'

'When are you leaving?'

'In two days.'

'Just two?'

'Yes.'

She needed to be brave, consider Jack's feelings in all of this, remember that she had been the one who had pushed for him to become a war artist in the first place.

He placed his fingers under her chin, gently lifting her face towards his, forcing her to look at him. Her eyes roamed across his face, taking in the thick dark lashes, the soft crease from his nose to his mouth, the generous curve of his lips, the shadow of stubble just beneath his skin.

'Do you know where you're going?' she asked.

'Not yet.'

'How are your mother and Beth?' Her voice quivered as she struggled to hide her emotion.

'I'll tell them in the morning. Let tonight be ours.'

She gazed out across the skyline at the crimson sun and the dark silhouette of an expectant city, a population who deserved better. She knew that she wouldn't be able to bear the goodbye—but that she should take what little time they had together.

Then they embraced, clinging to each other, her head buried in his shoulder.

'Promise me that you'll write whenever you can and that you will stay safe,' she said as tears stole down her face. 'Don't try and be too brave.'

'I promise,' he replied.

'I'll wait for you, Jack.'

'I'm not asking you to.'

'I know.'

And then he kissed her. It seemed to last longer than any breath she had ever taken, any thought she had ever had, and when they finally parted he looked into her eyes and spoke with utter certainty. 'I love you, Eleanor. And I will come back for you.'

Seventeen

The Barry Rooms were uncharacteristically noisy as artists, dignitaries and the media jostled for space. A small orchestra played Bach, waiters circulated with drinks and canapés, and the visitors animatedly discussed the paintings. Eleanor was completely detached from it all. Even the artworks—vast oils of dockyards and warships, smaller pictures of factories and airfields, intimate portraits of officers and crews, most of them in a limited tonal range that matched her sombre mood—were all reminders that Jack had gone away.

'Good evening, sir, madam,' she said, forcing a smile as the high commissioner for Canada entered with his wife.

Maura gawped so long at the woman's blue gown with its tightly cinched waist that Eleanor had to nudge her and tell her to hand them a booklet.

'Gracious me, I'm surprised Churchill or King George himself isn't here,' Maura whispered as the couple walked away. She was referring to the calibre of visitors attending this exhibition to celebrate the publication of the new *War Pictures by British Artists* booklets: the first four pocket books that the committee had produced to help improve morale—not to mention harness their propaganda value overseas.

Maura and Eleanor were standing at the entrance greeting attendees, while Eleanor struggled to maintain her composure. She had awoken that morning to splintered sun through the blackout blinds, the birds singing their usual chorus and the familiar sound of traffic in the street. It was only when she allowed herself to drift back to sleep again that her eyes startled open with the memory that Jack had left. She must have shouted before the tears came because suddenly Cecily was by her side and Eleanor was sobbing into her sister's shoulder. 'I'm sorry,' Cecily whispered, 'I'm so sorry.' Eleanor's body weakened under her sister's embrace, the knowledge that she didn't know if or when she would see him again.

She'd replayed her and Jack's last moments together after he walked her home; and their shared sense of grief and longing when he left her outside her building. He had told her that he loved her on the rooftop, and that he would come back for her. She held onto that as she eventually collected herself and got ready for work—and she was replaying it again now.

'That *is* Lady Hughes over there, isn't it?' Maura asked, finger angled directly at an elegant brunette standing in front of a painting.

'Yes, but don't point,' Eleanor snapped. 'It's rude.'

'Alright, I'm sorry. It's just . . . I've seen that coat before—I think it's Jaeger.' Maura obviously coveted the fashionable ivy-green coat. 'I'd lose the fur stole, though. It's not necessary.'

'Yes, you're probably right,' Eleanor said in a gentler tone, understanding that these things were important to Maura. 'Just don't stare, and remember to mark guests off and give them a copy of the booklet.'

'I will, and I'm getting loads of ideas, so thank you. I reckon I'll be up all night drawing patterns.' She glanced at Eleanor. 'And I think you're doing really well,' she added with a warm smile.

'Thank you.'

'He'll be back in no time, you'll see.'

Eleanor smiled back but she wished Maura hadn't said anything, a new well of tears springing into her eyes. She dabbed them with a handkerchief, grateful to Maura for volunteering at the last minute. She'd been helpful so far, despite the running commentary on the women's clothes, but Eleanor hoped her friend would stop being so sympathetic or she might cry all night.

As they waited for new entrants, Eleanor watched Lady Hughes progress around the room. She thought about the awful timing of Jack's departure this week: the week of Cecily's exams and the most important event that Eleanor had been involved with. She'd spent weeks compiling and managing the guest list. Tonight she had greeted journalists from *The Illustrated London News*, the *Times*, *Vogue*, *Sketch*, *The Tatler* and *Bystander*, and only a few feet away a reporter from the *Mirror* was questioning an artist about his impressions of life around the capital.

She had every reason to feel nervous too. The leaflets were the culmination of the committee's work, and she was responsible for pulling it all together. The committee had spent months selecting the artists, then reviewing the paintings and drawings they submitted, and, finally, making the difficult choice of which to include. It had been a time-consuming affair, and only once they had come to the end of it had the committee congratulated themselves on what they had achieved and the compendium of hope they believed it would deliver to the public.

A group nearby stopped talking to pose for the official photographer. Despite how Eleanor felt, she couldn't ignore the energy in the room, anticipation palpable among the establishment as the war artists congregated.

'Have you got more booklets?' Eleanor asked when she noticed Maura's empty hands.

'Yes, they're under here,' Maura said, lifting the tablecloth. 'The same as they were five minutes ago, when you asked last time.'

'I'm sorry.' Eleanor rearranged the four stacks of books for the umpteenth time.

As much as she tried to put Jack from her mind, there was the intrusive fact that the only love she had ever known had gone—and there was nothing she could do about it. Thousands of others felt the same as her, more every single day, but what was worse was that she felt responsible for sending him away. If only he hadn't listened to her; if only he had stayed working as he always had and not joined the WAAC.

She distracted herself, picking up the first of the paperback booklets, *War at Sea*. She was relieved that the purple and black cover image had turned out okay after a number of issues with the printing; it befitted the affecting artworks inside. The committee had chosen equally appropriate colours for the other three booklets: flame orange for *Blitz*, gunmetal grey for the *RAF* and red for the *Army*, and she admired them too for a moment. It had fallen to her to liaise with the experts engaged to write the introductions for each booklet, and to arrange the transport of artworks to and from the printers. The committee had wanted to start the collection with a drawing of Air Raid Warden D.I. Jones OBE by Eric Kennington, and it had taken several letters to get Admiral Sir Herbert W. Richmond to write the introduction in time for it to go to print. It was at the eleventh hour that his two-page introduction was delivered to the office and then swiftly transported to Oxford University Press by Clive—and only then because of another of his surprising short cuts, although, thankfully, a more successful diversion this time.

When she opened the cover and started reading the introduction again, it gave her pause.

> These pictures were merely a selection of a greater number of Civil Defence subjects. Many more will yet be painted; and the Ministry of Home Security is anxious that all possible opportunities shall be allowed artists serving in the Civil Defence Forces today. The committee have in mind that some of the best pictures of the last war were painted by members of the Armed Forces. To-day war has come to civilians. Subjects for the artist, whether or not he is a member of the Civil Defence Forces, are on his doorstep and, to judge by its beginning, the pictorial record of war on the home front will be a worthy and impressive one.

Admiral Richmond was right: the pictures from the home front would be worthy ones, but why was it that most of them were still painted by men? It was women who had taken on the bulk of the jobs and duties on the home front; women who had felt the impact of missing fathers, brothers and sons; women who were suffering at home—yet they weren't the ones telling their stories or painting their pictures. She had only obtained pictures from one female war artist, Laura Knight, for this booklet, and Ethel Gabain for *Blitz*, and she wished there could be more. Maybe Jack was right and they shouldn't have waited; she should have just let him submit her picture when they first had the idea and the confidence to see it through—now that he'd gone away that might never happen.

'Aye, it's going really well.' Maura nudged her, looking as pleased as if the artworks were her own. 'They must all be feeling very proud.'

'Yes,' said Eleanor, 'I'm sure they are.'

She could see representatives from all the ministries; if she hadn't felt so remote from it all, she would have been intrigued to meet them—the Ministry of Information, the Air Ministry, the War Office, the Ministry of Home Security, not to mention members of the Royal College of Art, the Royal Academy and the Slade—it appeared as though anyone who was anyone in the art world had congregated in these rooms tonight. Eleanor would usually have talked to each and every one of them and been eager to do a good job, but tonight the images of warfare just made her think of Jack.

And she had another feeling that didn't sit well, like a cloak around her sadness. It was something she couldn't mistake for anything other than envy—she wished Jack well but she also wished that it could be her.

It was almost ten o'clock when Eleanor reached the pub on Praed Street and pushed her way through the smoky, crowded bar. Cecily was sitting alone at the back behind a curtain of raucous young men and women. 'Eleanor—what are you doing here?' she said, her cheeks flushed.

'The exhibition finished early. I wondered if you'd still be here.'

Eleanor had arrived at their flat to find it empty before she remembered the end-of-exams drinks with the other student nurses of St Mary's.

'I'm so glad you're here.' Cecily's smile beamed. 'Be a love and buy me a drink—I've run out of money,' she said in a voice that didn't belong to her.

'No, let's just walk home.'

'I want to stay. I want another drink—'

'Really, I think it's time to go.' Eleanor said quietly, not wanting to draw attention.

'Come on, I bet you if you wanted one, then we could stay.'

'But I don't.'

'Can't you just pretend you do?' Cecily said with a silly grin.

'No, I can't—I want to go home,' she replied, feeling tearful again.

Her sister sat up straighter, looking cross. 'If *you* wanted to stay out, we would. Why can't we now, when I want to?' she asked, tipping her head back as she emptied her glass.

Eleanor had wanted to accompany Cecily to drinks before realising it clashed with the exhibition, so she'd encouraged her sister to go alone; she thought it would do her good, the exams having pushed her hard. Judging by the state of her now, she might have been wrong. Around them the revellers were growing boisterous, young doctors and nurses singing 'Happy Birthday' to a man who was standing on a chair.

'Oh, come on, sis . . . one for the road,' Cecily said, holding the glass towards her.

'How about we have a walk first?'

'No, absolutely not.' Cecily shook her head.

Eleanor felt quite desperate; she had never seen her sister like this before. She looked around for their friends. 'Where's Lindsay?'

'She left . . . with Frank and Harry. They went to another party.'

'Why didn't you go with them?'

'They didn't ask me to.'

'Really? I find that hard to imagine. They wouldn't have left you by yourself.'

'I'm not by myself.' She wafted her arms towards the singing group. 'I'm with my friends.'

'Harry could have seen you home,' Eleanor said louder, her temper fraying as her sister slumped on the stool, head lolling to one side. 'I said, Harry could have walked you home.'

'Harry's not interested in me.'

'But . . . I thought he was. How do you know that?'

'Lindsay told me. Apparently, he's in love with someone but he won't tell her who.'

She sounded angry.

'Well, that someone might be you, Cecily.'

'Don't be silly,' she snapped.

'I'm sorry—I didn't mean to upset you.'

'You never do! I'm not like you, Eleanor. I don't want the things you do. You always want me to be better or different, or be with someone, but that's not what I want. Not if they don't want me.'

'I'm sorry, Cecily. I had no idea.'

'That's the trouble.'

All this time Eleanor had thought she had her sister's best interests at heart. She'd been taking instructions from their mother, doing what her family had asked—and it wasn't what Cecily wanted. For all her parents' fussing, and her chaperoning and worrying, it seemed that her sister knew what she wanted for herself.

'Don't worry, I forgive you,' Cecily said soberly. 'You *are* thoughtful, Ellie, but you've got to stop thinking your ideas and thoughts are better than anyone else's.'

Eleanor bit her lip. She felt close to tears, but she really didn't want to cry; she wanted to focus on giving her sister what she needed.

'Oh God,' Cecily said, clasping her hand across her mouth. 'I forgot about Jack. I'm so sorry!'

'It's fine. I'm here for you, Cecily. What is it that you want?'

Cecily smiled. 'I just want to pass my exams. That's all.'

Eighteen

The explosion happened at 10.28 a.m. An unexploded mortar, the Air Raid Precautions warden said, and now half a ton of masonry and four devastated families were all that was left. The full force had been taken by numbers twenty-four, twenty-six and twenty-eight, the rest of the street buckling under the blast. It was felt as far away as Hendon, where pictures shook on the walls of the British Restaurant that Eleanor was visiting. Apart from the local families killed and homes levelled, a bus driver lost his leg, and in a nearby church the force sent the organ pipes spiralling skywards as if on their own course to heaven. In the pews, those congregated held on to their hats or dived beneath the wooden benches as they waited for another blast. When nothing followed, they stood their Bibles back on the racks and went outside to see the dust swirling like a typhoon.

As soon as Eleanor returned home from Portman Square, she put on the wireless to listen to the Home Service's report on the incident. It was all that anyone had talked of all day—that and the Japanese holding of Guadalcanal and the threat this posed in the South-West Pacific. She wished she could hear something about the British Expeditionary Force she believed Jack had joined but, of course, nothing was mentioned; she knew that specifics never were.

She sat in the armchair, legs stretched out in front of her, a packet of Jacob's Cream Crackers on her lap. She was gazing at *The Crimson Sun*, propped against the sideboard, and remembering when she and Jack had sat on the rooftop at Portman Square. It had been nearly three weeks since he'd left.

She was thinking about where he might be and what he might be doing while half-listening to talk of the Bermondsey blast. Her eyes travelled across the orange glow of the painted sunset and the inky outline of the rooftops as the newsreader described the devastation and the fire, and an idea formed in her mind. It was obvious what she should be doing right now. What was it that Admiral Richmond had said? *To-day war has come to civilians. Subjects for the artist, whether or not he is a member of the Civil Defence Forces, are on his doorstep*. This was also what Jack had said was expected of her.

Gathering her smallest sketchpad, an assortment of pencils and brushes, and the palette of Winsor & Newton watercolours that had been a gift from Jack, she filled a leather satchel and quickly left the apartment.

A taxi carried her across the city, and as they crawled past shadows she summoned all of Jack's tips and instructions to mind. There was so much to think about: recognising her emotional response, judging how streetlights affected the scene, and taking care not to lose detail at night. She would also need to decide whether to use tonal colours for the heat and cold or whether to just quickly capture a gestural scene, but her thoughts all collided so that she felt as though she knew nothing.

By the time she arrived in Bermondsey the rescue crews were winding down, the Women's Auxiliary Air Force and wardens sorting through the rubble, looking for materials that could be taken to the depot and used for rebuilding. Smoke and dust clung heavily in the air, stinging her eyes, and a barricade separated the destroyed houses from their neighbours. The corner shop at the end of the terrace had become a makeshift HQ for workers and civilians as they figured out how to feed, clothe and rehome the locals. Women came and went, armfuls of clothing deposited on the counter, the shopkeeper sorting through them. The wounded had gone, but somehow seeing these donations—for neighbours who had lost everything—left Eleanor as deeply saddened as any of the injuries she had seen.

She noticed a young boy who sat on a stool as his mother kneeled, trying to find shoes from a cardboard box. His long, dirty-blond hair stuck up in tufts and his eyes were fixed in a wide stare as though he was still in shock.

Eleanor didn't feel entirely comfortable, but she knew she had to put her own feelings aside in order to do her work properly. She leaned against the wall outside, sketchpad in one hand, pencil in the other, all doubts about what to do and how to start forgotten as she instinctively began to sketch. She copied how the boy's fingers were so tightly clenched, how his mother's grimy hands moved so protectively across him, and the gentleness of the volunteers' hands as they worked. Their hands weren't just a motif for help, she thought, but an important reminder of what they could all do practically to chip in.

The mother kept glancing up at her. Eleanor smiled when she caught her eye, but the woman didn't smile back. When at last she found a pair of shoes that fitted the boy, she stood awkwardly for a moment then walked out of the shop towards Eleanor.

'You should be ashamed of yourself,' the woman said.

'Why?' Eleanor asked, taken by surprise.

She thought the woman was angry but then noticed the strain of emotion on her face and neck, ropes of muscle pulled taut from her chin to her collarbone. 'Making a living from other people's misery,' the woman said. 'What newspaper do you work for?'

'I don't. I'm an artist. My pictures are to show others what Londoners are coping with.'

'Still . . . maybe we don't want to be painted. Did you ever think of that?'

Eleanor hadn't expected hostility but then she looked over the woman's shoulder at the disembowelled homes on the other side of the street.

'You're right,' she said quietly. 'I'm sorry, I should have asked.'

'Yes, you should've.' The woman's clothes were torn, her hands blackened and her body trembling. 'Who are they for, anyway, your pictures?'

'I don't know yet, but they're to show why we need help.'

'It's not right, though, whichever way you look at it.'

More people were arriving, laden with bags of clothes and boxes of household items.

'I'm sorry, I didn't mean to offend you,' Eleanor said.

'Exploit us, more like.'

Eleanor wanted to explain what she was doing, why the pictures helped, but she didn't think the woman would understand—not now, not when she was still in shock—so Eleanor just removed her coat and offered it to her.

The woman hesitated and then took it, wasting no time putting it on. 'Makes you feel better, does it?' she asked.

'Please, I didn't mean any harm.'

Then the woman surprised her with a small grin. 'None taken . . . and thank you.'

The boy had finished tying his bootlaces and come outside. 'Mum, what're you doing?'

'Nothing, go back inside. I'll be there in a minute.'

Eleanor smiled at him and he half-smiled back. 'I'm Eleanor,' she said, stretching out her hand to the boy's mother.

She hesitated again before she shook Eleanor's hand. 'I'm Rebecca, and this is my son, Patrick.'

Eleanor gave the boy another smile and then turned her attention back to his mother. 'Is there anything I can do to help, Rebecca?'

'You can make me look like Betty Grable.'

Eleanor's smile widened. She felt pleased that Rebecca hadn't lost her sense of humour.

'What are you going to do with this picture?' Rebecca asked.

'I want to work as a war artist, so I'm going to show it to someone who can help.'

'You fancy your chances then?'

'I'd like to have a go. I think I've got as much chance as any other woman artist.'

'Well, you make a good job of us, and you never know.'

'That's very decent of you.'

'You just tell me what you need us to do, then I can try and get the lad a bed.'

'Can you go back inside and just do what you were doing? I'll be quick, I promise.'

Once they were back inside, Eleanor's hand moved with swift precision. The lines grew darker and the shading became finer as she caught their expressions. She was unsure of the results of this new hurried practice, but when she finished and stood back to look she was pleased to see a startling likeness of the mother and son. It was a disquieting scene—the ragged observers of the desolation—but she had also captured their tenderness.

'Can I have a look?' Rebecca asked.

Eleanor tried to say yes but the word caught in her throat.

Rebecca peered over her shoulder at the picture, Patrick by her side. There was an odd expression on her face, not fear or pleasure but a kind of satisfaction. 'Here, I reckon you're pretty good,' she told Eleanor. 'They'd be mad not to take you on.'

Nineteen

LONDON, 2010

The aircraft's wingspan measured nine metres, the grey steel of its body innocuous enough to camouflage it against the dark grey of most European skies. The Harrier Jump Jet was suspended above the First World War Spitfire in the vast exhibition space, a V-2 rocket balancing just a few metres below.

This was the first time Kathryn had been to the Imperial War Museum, and the scale of the warplane and machines overhead filled her with a new sense of awe. No wonder there were men and women who dedicated themselves to becoming experts on the military and for whom these powerful machines held a deep fascination. She'd never understood it before, but surrounded by such might it was hard not to feel the fascination now.

She knew Chris would love it here, with the old brick walls of the original building left exposed next to the glass and concrete of the renovations. And Oliver would be interested in all the hardware. There was a pleasing symmetry to the way in which the old and new materials had been combined: a fitting backdrop to the scale of exhibits from different eras. From the edge of the ground-floor balcony, she could see everything from the fighter planes suspended above to the rusted outline of the Baghdad Car on the lower ground floor. That exhibit had recently arrived amid media uproar: a vehicle destroyed by a suicide bombing in Baghdad.

There was so much to see, but Kathryn couldn't be late for the research session. She would have to take Oliver here on their next visit.

The previous day, she had waited until Mrs Halls had left and then shown Eleanor the papers from the attic. After revealing the photo of her grandmother's younger self with Jack, she'd watched Eleanor's eyes widen. 'Ah,' she'd said, sounding surprised, 'I'd forgotten about that. Look at us—we were so young!' She had given Kathryn a strangely expectant look, before complaining of a headache and taking to her bed. With the odd sense that she had missed something important, Kathryn had spent the rest of the day on the Nautilus project before catching up with Chris and Oli, as well as on much-needed sleep. Her concern that it was already her third day in England, and with so little achieved, had lessened when she got an email confirming an appointment the next day.

It was nearly time—eleven-thirty—so, feeling re-energised, she quickly followed the signs up to the second floor, home to the Second World War exhibitions. The central atrium had been flooded with natural light, but up here, where the displays revealed the intimate details of the conflicts, the machinery and the human cost of war, it was much darker, the exhibits casting their own shadows. Kathryn weaved through a group of schoolchildren, clipboards clutched in their hands, and headed towards the *Family in Wartime* exhibit.

The reconstructed rooms of the Allpress family home showed how ordinary Londoners had lived during the war. In the living room, two armchairs were angled towards a fireplace and a wireless sat between them; it played an original BBC recording, the newscaster's clipped enunciation representing the British stoicism of the time. Kathryn made her way through to the kitchen, where tins and packets of food were stacked on the countertop, the portions of rations measured out on plates alongside. She walked into the bedroom, where life-size models displayed utility clothing and the tokens that had been exchanged for meagre fuel and clothes.

Kathryn would have loved to linger. The exhibit was so evocative, making it easier for her to imagine Eleanor's life back then—but she was now officially late.

The research rooms were tucked into a corner of the museum with the mandatory battered metal lockers outside and the request for no food or drink to be taken in. Kathryn pulled out her laptop and the printed email that confirmed her request for books and papers, then pushed through the glass doors.

The desks were horizontal to the window and a pleasant light fell across the thoughtful-looking people who sat at them. Despite the request for silence, there were hushed voices as well as the tapping of fingers on keypads, and the clicking from cameras and phones.

Kathryn walked to the reception to collect her requested items from a librarian. She was soon seated at a desk with her hoard spread out in front of her: a manila folder of documents and Jack's diary inside a protective plastic wallet. It was the same size and colour as the one at Stephen Aldridge's house, certainly part of the same set.

Around her, other visitors were absorbed in their reading, the air conditioner circulating a welcome breeze. She settled into the space, pulled out the diary and opened its cover. Inside, in the familiar black ink script, it was dated 1942—the year Jack and Eleanor had met. Hopefully it would yield more answers than the 1944 diary.

> *Wednesday, 15th July*
>
> *The men don't trust me yet; not surprisingly they're suspicious of anyone who holds a paintbrush instead of a gun. I firmly believe that I will need to prove that I will honour my pledge, and that I am prepared to lay down my life alongside theirs. I've been told that the days will be quite different from now on; we will be across the border tomorrow night, and that is when the games begin. I have been warned that while they will defend our freedom, the regiment can become lawless against each other, that the lieutenants and sergeants and ranks of officers can't protect them from themselves—that it's every man for himself—but I haven't seen any evidence of this yet.*

This seemed more direct than the other diary, the tone more urgent. At the bottom of the page was a small charcoal sketch of a soldier leaning against a tree trunk, smoking; behind him, a few of the soldiers had set up camp. She guessed that this was a depiction of a man Jack had met; perhaps the symbolic loner, or the expression of every man for himself. It was a revealing observation, penned as it was from a place of hiding, branches and leaves in the foreground, concealing the artist from view. How terribly excluded Jack must have felt, as an artist, from these men with their shared code of honour and rules.

She was tempted to flick through the pages until nearer the end, but something in the next paragraph caught her eye.

> *Friday, 17th July*
>
> *The men had a riot last night watching me try to navigate through the trenches. I did as they instructed, creeping out of each hole, moving flat like a snake, all the while they shouted at me to get down lower and put my weight on the inside of my knees, big toes and elbows, and not to press on my kneepads and palms. I made it over the rise, staying low and bending my body over the top of the bank as if my chest were almost scrubbing it all the way. I was glad that I had left my pens and sketchbook behind and that I didn't stab myself with any of the equipment inside these dozen pockets.*

Kathryn wondered if this was a usual training exercise or if they were initiating Jack in some way.

She could see why the museum had been interested in exhibiting this diary: the descriptions were as revealing as the sketches on each page, and it made her want to read them all the more.

> *Monday, 20th July*
>
> *It's the common cause that unites these men and I must work hard to gain their trust. It's the same as putting your trust in nature, only theirs has a cynical toughness that I have to overcome. My work is still elemental, that part hasn't changed, but my environment has. The adrenaline*

takes over when you are here; it's only afterwards when you
reflect on it that you are able to function and work can start
again. Some of the men get addicted to that. I can relate
to them only in how my own body changes under these
conditions: sounds are more distinct, I can see more clearly,
it's as if my perception has heightened, senses on full alert.

'Elemental', 'perception', 'heightened'—the words seemed to float in midair, suspended like the images he was trying to construct. She felt a connection with what he was saying: she had thought she would get to know him mainly through his paintings, but now his ideas were drawing her in. This is what it must have taken to make a great war artist—one who could see clearly under pressure; one who could stay calm rather than be overwhelmed by the flight-or-fight mechanism. Being out in the field would have been such a contrast to art school: how strange it must have felt to Jack to go from life-drawing classes to life-or-death situations.

She turned the page, wanting to know what happened next, but the ink was a different colour and the entry dated a week later.

Monday, 27th July
The men shared their stories on the way over, the colleges
and jobs they have come from, the families and girlfriends
they have left behind, but once here it is so different, and all
that matters is staying alive. Then food comes next—and
trying not to die. I have spent a great deal of time training,
lifting heavy objects and trying to improve my fitness so that
I can keep up with them. We walked seventeen miles yes-
terday and much of it was difficult terrain but it's how it's

going to be from now on. It is how I must work too, moving
around, having little time to prepare, disregarding the rules
I have learned up until now. I have to live in the instant,
make notes and work when we stop. I am worried about
how I am going to preserve the pictures and will have to
send some home soon, the first in the series for Sir Robert's
'Heroes' Journeys'.

Looking more closely at the fine lines, Kathryn could see that the sketches were in Conté crayon, but Eleanor had told her that he'd worked in pen and Indian ink, then used guar gum—a thickening agent—and watercolour in his completed pictures.

Thursday, 30th July
We have been on the move for three days now and are get-
ting closer to our destination. Only another few days to go,
but the conditions are harder than I am physically equipped
for. The city has been under attack for months and we are
the reinforcements. Yesterday we came under attack from
heavy mortar and were forced to change our route, so it is
expected to take longer now. The men are jumpy since our
position is now known, and until we reach the rest of the
battalion, they say, we are sitting ducks.

The tension in his words was evident, the small sketch accompanying them dark and the lines coarse, showing his strain. But it also looked familiar—similar to an image in Eleanor's home—although Kathryn supposed that many of the battle scenes must look the same. She turned the page.

Saturday, 1st August

I was sketching the unit preparing to move when a mortar hit. Peters and DeWitt were killed outright. I couldn't even paint the scene if I tried although I can't get the image out of my head either, the torment of more lives lost. We have buried far too many already.

The racks of books on the wall, with their aged leather and linen spines that she usually found so appealing, were suddenly reminders of all that was withered and wasted, merely catalogues of the loss of human life. How many millions of lives and deaths were recorded here, and how many more would be added after future conflicts?

Kathryn focused back on the diary, leafing through and reading entries that stood out, taking photos and making notes on certain facts or turns of phrase that she would ask Eleanor about.

When she next glanced up it was nearly one o'clock, time for the research room to close for lunch. The one-hour break would be a welcome opportunity for her to take a walk and have a think. She headed downstairs to the cafe. The route took her past the gift shop and she made a quick detour, hoping to find something for Oliver. Plastic shelves showcased nostalgic British ornaments and books about the wars; round wicker baskets offered up army tanks on metal key chains and Spitfire pencil sharpeners. Walls of posters instructed everyone to *KEEP CALM AND CARRY ON* and *EAT LESS BREAD*: once important propaganda messages, now little more than catchphrases.

As she looked at all the paraphernalia, Kathryn understood how reaching back in time had made her appreciate what earlier generations had been through and the significance of these wars. It wasn't that she hadn't thought about the veterans before; she bought poppies and watched the Anzac Day dawn services, but she had never really put herself in their shoes. Perhaps understanding how Jack had felt was the key to uncovering what had happened to him.

Back in her seat at two o'clock, Kathryn opened the diary and hoped that her patience would be rewarded.

Thursday, 6th August

The supply ship arrived and it was all my Christmases at once: a full set of assorted drawing pens, the choice of artists and draughtsmen the world over. I wonder if Miss Roy had anything to do with it? I have begun a baroque painting on the roof of our tent. The men will get a surprise when they come in and find the dramatic figures of fellow soldiers aiming artillery at them! If it works out well I might suggest shipping it back home and we can then put the canvas up for display—I know that my darling girl would love it! I captured the scene of a recent night battle because of the intense atmosphere and dramatic colour and light, one that I know my fellow journalists could never capture with their cameras. So far it is working very well; I had enough red for the blood and by the time I have finished it I think it would make Caravaggio proud! First batch of drawings sent off, so praying the courier gets through.

She grinned. A few pages further on and there was her gran's name, finally. And also, Kathryn realised, this must be the piece of canvas that she had found in the attic. She re-read the entry and took a photo before continuing to leaf through, taking in each scribbled note and detailed drawing as she hunted for another mention of Miss Roy. But there weren't any. The diary abruptly ended in August, only a month after it had started, with a mere two lines on the page.

> *Sunday, 16th August*
> *Didn't sleep as felt wretched and coughed all night. Most*
> *of the unit down with flu and the Red Cross nurse said no*
> *more hospital beds so I told her to keep mine for some other*
> *poor bugger.*

There was a rough pencil sketch of a group of men around a mound with a white cross at its head. In the foreground was a small tree, a bird sitting on the branch.

Jack's work revealed an unusual empathy, a rare capacity for warmth; he understood emotions. Kathryn realised that not only did she want to find out for Eleanor what had happened to Jack, but now she wanted to find out for herself too.

As she put the diary back in its plastic case, her eyes caught the bound manila folder of documents at her elbow. She leafed through the few newspaper articles inside. Some covered the last war artists exhibition, and others the 2005 anniversary celebrations. She jotted down the names of art and military historians to follow up.

She came across an article with a picture of Jack. It was more recent than the others she had seen online. His full head of dark hair was grey around the sides and there was no hiding that he looked old but he was still handsome.

His image made her think of the black-and-white photograph of Jack and Eleanor and she scrolled through her iPhone until she found the picture she had taken of it. She looked at the younger Jack, searching for the secrets locked behind those enigmatic eyes. Through reading his diaries, Kathryn had come to understand that he hadn't just been a war artist but an artist at war, and his paintings had brought her face to face with its realities. So what had kept him and the woman he loved apart?

Then Kathryn saw it. The memory of her initial surprise at how excitedly happy the two of them had looked made her shiver. How could she have missed it before? There in the centre of the photo, where the couple's hands were clasped, was a small dark grey shape. Kathryn enlarged the picture and kept zooming in until she could be certain. Yes, there it was on Eleanor's ring finger—a diamond solitaire.

Twenty

The heat of the day had gone but the sun was still bright, so Kathryn found a shaded spot beside the lavender beds near the entrance and dialled Helen's number.

Her best friend picked up straight away.

'Hi, Hels, it's me.'

'Hello, me. I thought you were at the museum today?'

'I am, but it just got a bit more complicated.'

'How so?'

'It seems that Gran was actually engaged to Jack—can you believe it?'

'Really? Whoa, never figured your gran as such a dark horse.'

'I know. I'm actually a bit nervous about what I'm going to find next—feels like anything could happen,' she said as she absent-mindedly picked the heads of the lavender.

'Maybe it's time to get a private investigator, Kat. It will be a lot quicker. They handle this sort of thing all the time.'

Her friend was right; Kathryn was out of her comfort zone and wished that her mother could arrive sooner than the weekend. It felt like the right time to tell her about the recent discoveries but not by telephone—she would have to wait another two days.

'I know, but Gran doesn't want anyone else involved. She says it's a family matter.'

'Every family has its secrets, Kat. Look at mine.'

If Helen didn't have a genetic medical condition, her parents might never have told her that she was descended from Scandinavian royalty. As it was, she hadn't found out until she was at university.

'Yes,' said Kathryn, 'I know, but it's still a bit of a shock. And it makes me wonder . . .'

'What?'

'Well, maybe they were married, for all we know. Maybe Edward wasn't her only husband.'

'Don't be ridiculous,' Helen said with a laugh. 'Why would that have been a secret.? It would be fascinating to find out what happened, though. I wish I could be there when you ask her about the engagement . . .'

Kathryn didn't mind Helen being flippant, but as she was missing the point, Kathryn didn't respond.

'Look,' Helen said after a short silence. 'I know this is difficult for you but you just need to be practical. And I know it's a funny thing to say, but try to think laterally, not get too emotionally involved.'

'How can I do that?'

'Well, you could always look at the best- and worst-case scenarios here.'

'Which are?' Kathryn asked as she watched schoolkids clambering over the cannons and taking pictures of each other.

'Best case is that you find out what happened to Jack and he's still alive. Your gran gets to see him and you find out what this is all about. Worst case is he's dead or has severe dementia, or you can't find him.'

'And then what?'

'Well, look on the bright side—at least you get to keep the painting.'

'Thanks, Helen,' she said flatly. 'That was really helpful.'

A pause. 'I'm sorry. I'm only trying to help.'

'I know, just ignore me. I'm having a bit of a meltdown today. I thought I'd have time to think—even look at some schools for Oli, just in case—but this has been all-consuming.'

'I know, I wish there was something more that I could do. Do you want me to come and meet you?'

'No . . . yes. I mean, I'd love you to but I need to finish here. Maybe later . . .'

'Is that if you haven't had a nervous breakdown by then?' Helen said, her voice trembling.

Kathryn was worried that she had upset her by putting her off again but then heard her friend's barely concealed laughter.

'Well, I'm glad I'm such a good source of amusement for you, anyway,' she said, finally smiling.

'I'm sorry. It's just payback, you know that.'

'Yes, it's about time, hey!'

'You know you can always rely on me for the truth.'

Kathryn hung up, feeling a little better and knowing that her best friend was right; something about being back in her homeland made her see things more clearly. It was as if when she was in Australia she had a free pass to live as a tourist, not registering anything as seriously as she should, taking things at face value. Maybe it really was time for her to come home.

Kathryn headed to the bookshop next to the train station and wandered in a daze through the new fiction titles. In another ten minutes, it would be a reasonable enough hour for her to call Chris. For the first time in what seemed like months, she really wanted to speak to him.

She bought a couple of books for Oli, who had recently become addicted to reading. Then she found the bookshop cafe and ordered a skinny flat white—politely explaining to the frowning barista exactly how it was different from a cappuccino or a latte—before setting up her laptop at the furthermost table. Hardly anyone was around, but the hard surfaces of the wooden floor made the sounds even harsher and she didn't want to disturb anyone, or for her conversation to be overheard.

The familiar long Skype tones sounded for a few moments before Oliver picked up. He was in *Simpsons* pyjamas again, probably the same ones from earlier in the week, and his face was unusually red.

'Why are you still in bed, darling?' she asked lightly, trying to mask her concern.

'I've got a cold.'

'Oh dear. Have you got a temperature?'

'I don't know.'

'Well, hasn't Dad taken it?'

'No. He's not here.'

'Where is he?'

'He said he was just popping out, that he wouldn't be long.'

She tried not to show how that worried her. 'Is that what he said?'

'Yes.'

Oliver did seem lethargic, and he was without his usual committee of toys and figurines.

'Are you hot?' she asked.

'A bit.'

'Take your top off. And have you had lots of water?'

'My throat's sore.'

'Too sore to swallow?'

'Yes.' Then he suddenly looked more animated. 'I liked the pictures you sent,' he said. 'I was up really early looking at them with Dad.'

'Great, just stay there a second . . .'

She had dialled Chris on her mobile and was waiting for him to pick up, but it went straight to voicemail. How the hell could he go out and leave Oliver on his own when he was sick?

Oliver kept talking about the pictures. 'I thought the one of London was really good too. Who was it by?'

'What do you mean . . . ? They're Jack's,' Kathryn asked, her mind turning.

What had Oliver picked up on that she'd missed? She'd emailed photos of the 1942 diary to him and Chris from the library; she'd also sent a photo of the anniversary exhibition program.

Her son had always been so intuitive—one of her most precious memories of his early childhood was of when they were in the park at a five-year-old's birthday party and he had asked her why the blackbird wouldn't play with him.

'No, it's not. It's definitely by a different artist,' he told her now.

A door slammed and Oliver glanced over his shoulder. 'Dad's coming back.'

She could hear the footsteps across the hallway.

'Oli,' Chris called, 'who are you talking to?'

'It's Mum.'

Christopher's figure grew larger as he drew nearer, his whole face filling the screen when he leaned over Oliver's shoulder. 'Hi, Kat.'

'*Where* have you been?'

'To the pharmacy. To get Nurofen—the one in the cabinet was out of date.'

'Oh . . .'

'Yes, oh.' But he didn't sound angry. He just smiled and shook his head. 'How are you?'

'Good.' She felt a twinge of irritation because she'd been worried. 'It's usually okay to use, though.'

'Well, I wasn't sure. Best to be safe, hey?' He seemed mellow, more relaxed than he had been since she'd left for England.

'So what's up with Oli?' she asked.

'He came down with a cold yesterday, nothing serious, but I thought it best to keep him off school. I've arranged to work from home so I can keep an eye on you, haven't I, mate?' he said as he ruffled Oliver's hair. 'We're going to have another look through the pictures you sent—Oli thinks he's found something.'

'It's all part of the jigsaw puzzle, isn't it, Mummy?'

'Yes, that's right,' she said, thinking about their conversation just before her departure; Oliver had said he didn't mind her going since it was to help Granny. 'So what is it that you've found?'

'Well,' said Chris, 'there's a picture in the diary that doesn't match the one in the anniversary program. See this one, *The Bermondsey*

Rescue, July 1942—Oli says it's not by the same person. It's not Jack Valante's work.'

Maybe her son was right, but why would that matter? Anything could have happened—the wrong name could have been used accidentally, or the wrong painting sent. It didn't seem to help her. But she still opened the folder of photos on her laptop and scanned through them until she found the one that Oliver was referring to.

'Can you see, Mummy? It looks different.'

'I know, darling, but there's no proof it's not Jack's.'

'But doesn't he write his diary in July?'

'Yes, but . . .' she said, realisation dawning.

'Well, it can't be him painting in Bermondsey then, can it?' Oliver said.

'No, I don't suppose it can.' She was unsure whether she was more pleased at Oliver's cleverness or embarrassed by her own idiocy. She would put it down to jet lag and sleep deprivation on this occasion. 'That's great, Oli. Well done.'

'So you can come back sooner then?' Chris asked eagerly.

'No, of course not,' she said with impatience, although she was secretly pleased that he wanted her to return. 'I still have to find out what happened to Jack. I do know one thing, though—Gran hasn't been entirely honest with us. I'm not a hundred per cent sure, but it seems as if she and Jack were engaged.'

'Really?' he asked, raising his eyebrows. 'Why didn't she tell you?'

Kathryn just wasn't sure, and now she suddenly had lots more questions. She wondered about the mystery surrounding the paintings. Did Stephen Aldridge know that his Jack Valante collection might not all be by the artist himself? And if Eleanor knew that Kathryn would find out about the engagement, was this all part of her plan for her granddaughter?

'I don't know, Chris,' said Kathryn. 'But I'm going to have to stay here until I find out.'

PART IV

A Portrait of Jack

'The very unfamiliarity of this new
type of war picture, with its new
type of warrior, will suggest that
the contest is no longer a matter
of soldiers and sailors and airmen.
In the work of these artists there
is none of the rhetoric of war; no
military bands, no flags, no splendid
horsemen. Yet in the grim realities
which they depict there is a majesty, and a new vision of glory.'

J.B. MORTON, *War Pictures by British Artists*, *BLITZ*,
OXFORD UNIVERSITY PRESS, 1942, PAGE 8

Twenty-one

LONDON, AUGUST 1942

'It is a problem, isn't it, just showcasing the mechanics of this war?' Eleanor overheard James Hazelton say to Louis Sepple. As an artist and the principal of the Royal College of Art, James was well placed to pass judgement, and since Louis was also an artist, and the keeper of the Royal Academy Schools, she knew that he too had been a shrewd inclusion on the committee.

'There are simply too many churches and monuments—surely the public have seen enough of these casualties,' Louis replied emphatically. 'In spite of their symbolic value, I am in favour of some artworks that would humanise the exhibition.'

The oil painting in question was part of a triptych, a vast image of the navy's best defensive warfare—frigates and aircraft carriers, including HMS *Eagle* before it was torpedoed—and its colossal twenty feet took up nearly the whole wall of the gallery. The hard lines and blunt edges of the machines tapered down to an intricate mesh of greys and blacks, crisscrossing until the perspective led her gaze into the distance.

The committee had assembled to preview the exhibition at the National Gallery before it opened in a few days' time, but there was vigorous debate as they walked around, some members insisting that replacements should be made. Eleanor was drawn in by their conversation and she found herself trailing after them.

'And what of these?' James asked as he stepped in front of a series of portraits by Eric Kennington, the Air Ministry's favoured artist for painting any person of note. Kennington's portrait of an officer was unflinchingly lifelike: bloodshot eyes protruding from soft pouches, deep umber paint that gave the skin a reddish tone and the upturned nose its noble air.

Like all the exhibitions that the WAAC put on, this one was ostensibly designed to improve morale and inform the public—but Eleanor very much doubted that would occur on this occasion. She was confounded by the fact that there were no paintings of civilians: neither in the gallery nor on the calendars, postcards and bookmarks that she had helped to organise. These images of war were important, of course, but what about representing the people on the streets? More civilians had been killed at home than soldiers on the battlefronts so far. Where was their story being told?

The committee members continued to move around discussing the impact that the paintings might make. There were depictions of everything from mine-laying off the Norwegian coast to convoys at a Devon port, and in all sorts of mediums: watercolours and gum arabic on board, and studies made with carbon pencil on tracing paper.

And the WAAC still couldn't agree on which paintings should go and which ones to replace them with.

She'd grown used to the committee's heated discussions, but until now none of them had been so fierce as the debate over Henry Moore's underground pictures. Half of the members believed they were works of genius, while the other half thought they were tomb effigies and had no place being displayed as war art.

The current disagreement seemed similar in intensity, but this time Eleanor decided there was something she could do to help. She kept a portfolio of other submitted paintings that would work well as replacements: air raids and barrage balloons, the city under fire, a vista of London with a blood-red sky and searchlights intersecting.

She walked over to where Aubrey Powell and Sir Robert Hughes stood. Aubrey was saying, 'Cliff Rowe is certainly another one to consider for—'

'Excuse me,' she said, interrupting her old professor before she lost her nerve. 'I've been listening to your comments and, the thing is, we already have a great many paintings that you could use.'

Sir Robert raised his eyebrows. 'Is that so, Miss Roy?' He made the question sound rhetorical. She remembered how tall he was and how imposing he seemed, as he looked down at her.

Steeling herself, she said, 'I can show you—right now, in fact. If you could just come over here.' She led them towards an area that was screened off, behind which a number of paintings were set on easels or leaned against the walls. Several were of buildings on fire or the bombed-out shells of homes with denuded rooms, but all of them contained people. The largest was of a chief warden in uniform, furnished with an armlet and a silver badge, his white helmet painted in dark letters. He was a civilian, not one of the grand personalities from the Admiralty, but he seemed impressive and powerful nonetheless.

'Most of these are from the Recording Britain artists,' Eleanor explained. 'They capture the life on the streets.'

The two men studied the paintings.

'Impressive, but these are not the calibre of those that we believe will boost morale,' Aubrey said. 'However, I am sure there will be another occasion when we can use these, Miss Roy.'

She had navigated the difficult personalities on the committee thanks to Aubrey's help, and her subsequent frank discussions with him. He understood the different natures and political allegiances of those men around the table, and he was able to tread the fine line between being supportive or assertive. And while it was in Eleanor's nature to want harmony, if she had learned one thing from her father, it was that when forces were pitted against each other on these important matters, there was no place for defeatism.

'I believe these paintings are what you agreed are missing from the exhibition,' she persisted.

Sir Robert leaned over and grasped one of the paintings on the floor: Eleanor's charcoal of the Bermondsey rescue. He studied the image. In the background were the tarpaulin homes that had been erected for dislodged families, their few possessions visible under the flimsy shelter; in the foreground, Rebecca bent down as she tried the donated shoes on her son, sombre lines detailing their anguished faces.

'It's the East End,' said Eleanor. 'There are streets and streets of people living this way.'

'Well, I've certainly not seen anything quite like this come before the committee,' Sir Robert exclaimed, still examining it.

'There are lots of other scenes worthy of recording—there are families sleeping in disused drains, refugees in their own city—'

'I know, Miss Roy, and it is a desperate state of affairs, but what is it that you are suggesting?'

'That I can do more like this.'

Sir Robert looked at the painting again and then back to her. 'Hold on, am I to understand that this is one of yours?'

'Yes.'

'I am surprised, Miss Roy,' Sir Robert said gravely.

She looked at Aubrey and waited for him to say something, but he just averted his gaze.

Sir Robert continued, 'I would have thought your priority was the artists we represent, not promoting your own work.'

For a moment she couldn't speak, she was so angry. She swallowed her pride and tried to explain. 'But I wasn't meaning to, sir. Most of these works are by other artists; it's just a coincidence that you picked mine.' Taking a deep breath, she decided to be completely honest. 'I'll make no excuses, though—I do want to paint.'

'Miss Roy,' he said, 'we need men of experience who understand the medium, those who are free to move around. We need you here, my dear. You are doing such a good job of arranging things.'

She stared again at her old professor, still expecting him to support her.

'He's quite right,' Aubrey said instead. 'Our artists have seen active service and understand what is required of them. Look at this painting—' he gestured to an oil painting of a brutalised landscape '—Albert Richards is a royal engineer.'

'Yes,' said Sir Robert, 'it is an authentic experience for him.'

'But—'

'Miss Roy, we do not have the resources,' Sir Robert said. 'You are needed here. I'm sorry, but for the time being you will have to be satisfied with hanging your paintings at home.'

'I see,' she said, burning with humiliation.

She pressed her hands into her pockets, finding the sketchbook that Jack had given her and the strength to stay quiet and not say what she really thought: that the two men were wrong about everything. They had to be blind if they hadn't noticed what was going on in the streets, and they were blinded by their beliefs about women's capabilities.

'I think it is commendable that you want to help, really I do,' Sir Robert continued, 'but these reproductions will be very important to us. You make a success out of these bookmarks and calendars, and we'll see what we can do.'

'Thank you, sir,' she muttered.

He was patronising her, and he was wrong: it was an authentic experience for her too. Aubrey knew that, but he just gazed at the floor, receding hairline now visible as he leaned forward, looking as if he was about to launch himself—strange how she'd never noticed his unusual posture before.

Eleanor didn't want to hear any more about it, or from them. Jack would have been furious; he understood exactly where authenticity came from, she thought, remembering their conversation in Hyde Park: *In short, there must be truth, integrity and splendour.*

She followed Sir Robert and Aubrey back to the group, and the meeting continued without any mention of what had just transpired. A few replacements were made from the other pictures that were available.

When Eleanor was about to leave, Sir Robert caught up with her at the doorway, and she thought that he might have changed his mind.

'I know it's not in the job description, Miss Roy, but would you mind terribly picking up these few items for me? Hate to ask, but Lady Hughes is out of town for a few days, and, well . . . you ladies are so much more accomplished in these matters.'

A too-long moment passed as she looked at the slips of paper; it was long enough for him to know how she felt, and for her to register that she could do little about it. There was an order of cigarettes to be collected from Alfred Dunhill, a prescription to be collected from Boots, and some dry-cleaning. Sir Robert might just as well have torn up her painting.

'Of course, sir,' she said, managing to keep her voice even. 'It would be a pleasure.'

Aubrey had been watching from the side of the room and followed her out into the hallway. 'I think it's a bloody good piece, Eleanor. You have captured the mother's anguish superbly.'

She believed him; it was just a pity he couldn't support her in front of anyone else.

'You could have said something,' she told him.

'You won't find Jack by gallivanting off to Europe,' he said, placing an arm around her shoulders and leaning so close that she could smell the bitterness of stale tobacco on his breath. 'You do know that, don't you?'

Eleanor shrugged him off, speechless. As soon as she found her voice, she said with controlled anger, 'That's ridiculous. This isn't about Jack. I *want* to be a war artist. Do you really think that's because I want to find him?'

Aubrey studied her face. 'I don't know, Eleanor, but you must be patient. Jack will be back, you'll see.'

Two months had passed and she hadn't heard from Jack, but what was it to Aubrey, anyway? Jack was only an acquaintance of his. She didn't want to discuss him with Aubrey and it was making her very uncomfortable, but she couldn't let that show—Aubrey might be her only way in.

'And what about a commission?' she asked. 'I only need one chance.'

'You know, if it was up to me . . .' He glanced towards the doorway, bravado vanishing. 'But I'm sorry, Eleanor. If you want to get on the magic carpet, you need to get approval from the whole committee.'

She gathered herself; she wasn't about to give up now. It had been enough for her to see art reach the masses through the British Restaurants, and then to bring artists to the committee and help make the exhibitions a success. But it wasn't enough anymore.

She had always noticed things that other people didn't. As a child she'd been able to draw different species of butterflies where her classmates had managed only one. And now she could provide her unique view of the war, one that the WAAC wasn't exhibiting at the moment—and all she needed was that one chance.

Twenty-two

Jack's absence enabled Eleanor to stay focused on her work. Time they'd spent painting, visiting parks, dining out, dancing and cycling was now spent solely on work for her two exacting bosses, Mr Steadman and Sir Robert. And in the wake of the afternoon's events, she was looking forward to the distraction of the Women's Voluntary Services meeting that night, the first in a long time.

Collecting Sir Robert's order of cigarettes and his prescription hadn't been a problem, but carrying the dry-cleaning through the rain back to the gallery had certainly been difficult. Luckily, Sir Robert wasn't there when she returned, so she wouldn't have to see him or Aubrey again until the opening in a few days' time. Hopefully she would have calmed down by then—or they might have seen sense.

Although the raids on London were over for the time being, everyone's days were still bookended with new domestic and military routines, and then after work it was supper and a quick change of clothes, before they were off again to WVS or Ambulance Duty or the mobile canteens. Eleanor was trying to remember what on earth everyone had done with their spare time before the war, when a figure emerged from the shadows of her building.

Harry Roberts, she assumed: their local warden. He lived in Leinster Terrace and had looked after the local streets and their residents since the war broke out—rarely a day went by when he wasn't visible. Everyone knew he would have signed up if he had been young enough, but for now the First World War veteran contented himself with being a scrupulous member of the home guard.

'I do believe this is the worst day's rain we have had in weeks, Harry,' she announced as she drew close. 'Can you really believe that it's August?'

It was very dark without the streetlamps and the moon was on its new axis, pulling light in the opposite direction.

As she drew closer, the man replied, 'You definitely shouldn't be out on a night like this, Miss Roy.'

It was a voice that she hadn't heard for a long time, and it made her stop.

She had seen Jack everywhere in the first few weeks after he'd left: travelling on buses, in the streets, half-turned faces in cafes that, once revealed, belonged to someone else. Could it really be him now or was it the rain playing tricks? She knew how when you wanted something badly enough, you could conjure up the image of it. But here he was, standing barely a few yards from her.

His clothes were worn and he had grown a moustache, and his face was altered with patches of rough or sunburnt skin. Even his hair was a shade fairer than before.

They took another few steps towards each other, until they were standing only inches apart, rain streaking their faces. She didn't want to blink in case the image disappeared, but then his face broke into an enormous smile and she knew it was really Jack.

He took her in his arms, kissing her forehead and down across her cheeks. And, finding her mouth, he kissed her passionately.

When at last they separated, he cradled her face between his hands, eyes looking into hers. Her fingers explored his face, feeling over the ridges of his ears, through his hair; he didn't look quite the same, but he was definitely Jack. She turned over his hands, exploring the plateaus of his palms and the patterns of his fingerprints, finding the calluses and the cuts, and kissing them through her tears.

'I'm alright,' he said, wiping them away.

'Are you . . . are you really?'

'Yes.'

'When did you get back?'

'About thirty minutes ago,' he said with a smile.

'I want to know everything,' she said as she kept hold of his hand and started walking towards her flat. 'I want to know where you have been . . .' He suddenly stopped, and so she turned. 'What is it, are you hurt?'

'No, and you *will* know everything—all in good time.'

'Aren't you going to come up?' she asked as they approached her front door.

'No, I have to go, but I wanted to see you first.'

She was confused. 'But when will you be back?'

'Soon.'

'Do you really have to go straight away?'

'So a chap isn't even allowed to have a bath and something to eat when he gets home?'

Her eyes widened. 'What, you've come straight here?'

'Yes.'

'What about your mother and Beth? Haven't you seen them yet?'

'No.'

'Well, of course you must go then. Immediately!' She gently poked his chest. 'But I want you to report back to me at twenty hundred hours, freshly shaven with a bottle of something to celebrate, and a ravenous appetite.'

He laughed.

'God, I can't believe you're back.' She pulled him towards her again and kissed him for a few moments longer. Then she let him go and, without even thinking, saluted him and blew a kiss.

With a lazy salute, he spun theatrically on his heels and marched the way he had come. Only when he was a few yards away did he fall into his normal stride and glance round to see if she was still watching.

'Hurry back,' she shouted, and then motioned him away with a flick of her hand.

At the corner of the square he turned to look once more before finally disappearing from view.

Eleanor lingered, watching the space where he had just been, the buildings' shadows now filling in where he had stood. There was so much she wanted to ask him: where he had been, if he was home for good, what it had been like.

But as she turned to her door, she realised her questions would have to wait. All thoughts of him vanished as she considered what she had to do.

Missing the WVS meeting was unfortunate but couldn't be helped; creating something palatable from the remnants of their larder was more of a problem. Eleanor neither enjoyed cooking nor was very good at it—but being able to sort out their flat before Jack's return would be nothing short of a miracle. As it happened, Cecily was glad to help tidy the piles of laundry and then give Eleanor a hand preparing a cod casserole from one of the War Cookery leaflets.

'I think he'll like this,' Cecily said with an air of authority.

'I am sure it's better than whatever else he's been living on,' Eleanor agreed, sprinkling the last of the parsley over the top and placing it in the oven. 'Right, what's next?' She was on a mission now and intended to have everything ready by the time Jack arrived—she didn't want to waste a second.

'Table,' Cecily said, as she riffled through the drawer and thrust cutlery into Eleanor's hands. Then she reached up to open the cupboard doors, which hung at such awkward angles that she had to manoeuvre into a corner to reach the wineglasses. 'Here you are,' she said breathlessly, passing them down to Eleanor.

'Thank you.'

The flat was taking shape. Piles of clothing had been put away, their usual daily mess bundled into cupboards, and the table was set with a linen cloth, real silverware, and candles they had been saving for a special occasion.

'So you don't even know where he's been?' Cecily asked.

'No, I haven't a clue,' Eleanor said, eyes wide. 'And I don't even know if he's going to show up, either. His mother might refuse to let him go!'

'You still haven't met her?'

'No, I was supposed to before he went away but she wasn't well enough, and then he left so abruptly there wasn't time.'

'He's quite a mystery, your Jack.'

'Is he?'

Eleanor wasn't certain if she would call him a mystery: she had found him to be rather uncomplicated, as a matter of fact. She wasn't even sure she could call him 'her Jack'—but she liked the sound of it.

'Thank you so much for the help, Cecily. You really are a marvel when you turn your mind to it.'

Her sister dropped onto the sofa, picked up a copy of *The Lady* and began flicking through. Without looking up, she said, 'I *did* notice the table is only set for two.'

'Do you *really* want to stay?' It sounded more like a plea than a question.

'Well, I don't want to get in the way, but—'

'Precisely, so I've got the perfect solution: you can stay and say hello to Jack, and then you can go to the cinema.'

'The cinema . . . Couldn't I just stay in my room? I'm not really in the mood for going out.'

'Cecily, how long has Jack been gone for?'

'I know, I know, but I don't even know what's on—and what about my dinner?'

'It's the new Deborah Kerr film, *The Day Will Dawn*. It's supposed to be wonderful, and very stirring stuff, by all accounts. I'm sure you will enjoy it. My treat.'

Eleanor knew that Cecily didn't like to be alone, but it couldn't be helped. And besides, her sister would thank her for this trip to the cinema—Cecily couldn't resist a man in uniform and there were plenty of them in the film.

In any event, Cecily didn't get the chance to answer because the bell rang.

'Oh no, he's early,' Eleanor said. 'Can you go and let him in?'

'Fine. I'll go to the cinema then,' Cecily said, as she slipped out the front door.

'No need to sound so excited about it!' Eleanor shouted before going into the bathroom.

She looked at her reflection in the cabinet, then glimpsed a back view in the mirrored door, thinking how altogether different she looked from this new angle. It was the same with painting, when she could spend hours trying to settle on an aspect. She supposed that was why they showed mug shots both ways in the newspaper.

It was then that she realised how nervous she was, her mind catapulting from one idea to the next when she really needed to stay calm and get ready. She quickly changed into a cobalt-blue dress and picked up a lipstick, carefully drawing a thin line around her mouth and filling in the Cupid's bow.

She was still fiddling with her curls when she heard the front door close, and Jack's and Cecily's voices as they walked past the bathroom into the living room. Hearing his voice again triggered a memory of him saying how he preferred her without make-up, so she grabbed a tissue and wiped the lipstick off.

'Eleanor, did you get flushed away?' Cecily's voice from the other room sounded high-pitched.

'Coming!'

Her sister had poured drinks and was sitting on the edge of the sofa, talking with Jack as if it happened every day.

His moustache had gone and he now resembled the old Jack, the one with floppy dark hair and smooth skin, who always wore a scarf loosely around his neck like an RAF pilot; the one who told her how marvellous everything was, even when it wasn't, and always held her hand when they were out.

He stood up as she approached and kissed her on both cheeks.

'Is that something you picked up on the continent?' she asked with a smile. 'At least some good might come of this war, Cecily, if our men's manners are to be improved.'

Cecily rolled her eyes at him. 'Jack was just telling me about their journey across the Channel—'

'And I can see you two made a start on the cocktails.'

'Yes, would you like one?' Cecily asked.

'I wouldn't drink *that* for all the tea in China, or all the whisky in Churchill's bunker,' she said, coming to stand beside Jack. 'There's gin in that cupboard—be a dear and fix me a G & T.' She couldn't care less if she drank water all night, she was so happy, but she had better join them for one.

'So, now the adventurer returns,' she said, turning to Jack and watching Cecily from the corner of her eye. 'And you have been telling Cecily all about your exploits.'

'As much of it as I thought would interest her—I left out the boring bits,' he replied, taking a drink.

'Oh, I never thought of war as boring,' Eleanor said.

'It isn't. There are just some boring bits. Lots of waiting. I hadn't imagined it beforehand.'

'But aren't those boring bits when you have time to paint?'

'They're when you think about what to paint . . . I kept a journal— it helps to record ideas while you wait.'

'Well, it's a pity that Cecily will have to wait to hear about them. You don't want to be late for your film, do you, Cecily?'

'Of course not,' her sister said, handing her the glass. 'I would hate to end up in the back row by myself where all the creeps are.'

'Oh,' Jack said, surprised, 'you're not going on your own, are you?'

Cecily nodded.

'We could come with you, if you like . . . ?'

'I do it all the time,' she lied. 'I will be absolutely fine.'

'Cecily won't be going on her own,' Eleanor said affectionately, handing Cecily her coat and kissing her on both cheeks. 'Harry is taking her. In fact, dear, you had better hurry—he's waiting outside the cinema for you.'

She couldn't be sure whether her sister's expression was that of shock or surprise as she closed the door behind her.

Once she had gone, the flat fell quiet and Eleanor didn't know what to say. Jack must have felt the same because he picked up his glass and walked over to the double doors to the balcony. The rain had stopped and a gentle evening breeze ushered in the sounds from the street. They listened for a moment, happy to be in each other's company again. There were so many things she wanted to ask him but she didn't know where to begin, so she contented herself with watching him, his back turned to her as he looked out. After a short while, he swung round to place his glass on the table, and she noticed him wince.

'Are you hurt?' she asked, alarmed.

'No, I'm fine,' he said, straightening—but his movements were slower, his body stiffer than she remembered.

Was he injured and covering it up? Was he really the same Jack who had left nearly three months ago, or was he altered beyond the physical changes? She had expected things to be different when she saw him again, but now she was panicked; she knew it was selfish of her, but she wanted the old Jack back.

'I'm afraid I don't have much in the way of new records,' she said, feeling awkward. 'Cecily has been borrowing them to play to the patients.'

'That's good of her.' He smiled. 'She seems happy.'

'Yes, she's much better. Still has the odd bad day, but there seem to be fewer and fewer of them.' In fact, since the night at the pub when she'd told Eleanor that she wanted to be left alone, things had improved for Cecily. It had also helped that Harry asked her out at last; that was why Eleanor had called him to ask for his help tonight.

Jack's smile widened. 'That's good to hear.'

'Thanks for being so understanding,' Eleanor said, thinking of the times when Cecily had joined them on their outings.

'That's quite alright. I'd do the same if it was Beth. I was so happy to see her today.'

Eleanor had always guessed it was because of his sister that he felt so relaxed around Cecily—and, in turn, Cecily was comfortable around him. 'And how was your mother?' Eleanor asked.

'Not so good. She's definitely deteriorated since I've been away. I'm going to take her to the specialist as soon as we can get an appointment. It's hard to get one, and it's even harder paying for it. That doesn't matter, though,' he said, shaking his head. 'I don't know why I said it. Come on, let's have some music.'

'So what's it to be then, Glenn Miller or Harry James?' She held up the two remaining records in her collection.

'How about Glenn? I haven't heard him in a while.' Then Jack took out his packet of cigarettes and asked, 'Do you mind?'

'As long as you stand out there,' she said and pointed to the balcony.

She steadily lifted the needle onto the record and then joined him outside, glimpsing the yellow rim of sky before it faded to pink, the music drifting out to them.

'Eighty-five sunsets,' she said.

Jack frowned.

'That's how many you've missed.'

He contemplated the changing sky and then looked back at her. 'I saw as many of them as I could—you make them count when they could be your last.'

There hadn't been any intimacy between them, aside from a few kisses, before he went away, but she felt the need for it now. She wanted him to hold her, to tell her that he wouldn't leave again, but more than that she wanted the reassuring touch of his skin.

She moved closer, leaning her head on his shoulder, and he put his arm around her waist, pulling her gently into him. Their reunion wasn't how she had imagined it to be, but it felt right. They would have plenty of time to talk over dinner, time to find out about the intervening months. For now they stood together and watched the sky rapidly darkening.

'Eighty-five sunsets,' he repeated. 'Don't most artists have a short commission the first time?'

'Yes, your next one is likely to be longer.' She was certain that it would be six months at least, but she didn't want to think about it now. 'Hungry?' she inquired.

'Famished.'

They went inside and she led him to the table.

'Well, I don't want you to get your hopes up,' she said, pulling the chair out for him, 'but I do think it could be better than my usual efforts. It's fish.'

'Smells good.'

She brought two plates over to the table, the casserole crusts a crisp golden brown, green vegetables steaming by their side.

Jack opened a bottle of wine and poured it into the crystal glasses. 'I can't promise how good this will be either,' he said. 'I found it in the kitchen cupboard. Anyway, a toast . . .' He handed her a glass and picked up his own.

'What are we drinking to?' she asked.

'To my darling girl—to us.'

'To us,' she said, clinking glasses. 'And your safe return.'

'Yes, I'll drink to that,' he said and fixed her with his eyes.

They each took a sip, eyes staying locked together.

'I'm looking forward to hearing all your news,' he said, scooping up his first mouthful.

'Don't hold your breath. There's really not anything terrific to report.'

'Why, what's happened?'

'Oh, don't take any notice of me,' she said after hurrying her mouthful so that she could answer. 'It's just been a bad few days.'

'With the committee?'

'Yes, that's what I spend most of my time on now. Maura is de-lighted to be taking things over at Portman Square, as you can im-agine.'

'Still, it must be more interesting for you?'

Eleanor nodded. 'It has been. And there's a new exhibition com-ing up that you must come to. But anyway, stop trying to change the subject. I'm sure you've got far more interesting things to talk about.'

'It's hard to know where to begin,' he said thoughtfully.

He suddenly seemed uneasy, and she thought there might be things that he couldn't or wouldn't explain—but she wanted to know everything so she could be there for him.

'I could always read your journal if you don't want to tell me,' she said, half-joking.

He smiled and shook his head, staring down at his plate.

'Tell me about the people . . .'

'The chaps were how you would imagine, I suppose: some too young to know what to expect, others ferocious in their bravery.'

He started at the beginning, telling her about their journey to the coast, and how the bravado and jokes masked the men's anxieties. He told her about the four sickening days at sea when all there was to do was wait and watch and learn from and about the men. He spoke of their suspicions of him because he carried a pen and not a gun, of his initiation and their tough training practices. He talked of the fear of waiting for the enemy, the anxiety of knowing he was there, and the quiet before the first round was fired. And then of the way that everyone would react afterwards, the resoluteness of the men and their reactions; and of the injuries and casualties. He talked of the dry, dusty heat and the rats that destroyed their supplies, but how there was far worse for local villagers, whose homes were decimated and families killed. And then he wept openly as he talked with difficulty about the day that Peters and DeWitt were killed.

As soon as Jack had finished, she took him by the hand and led him up the staircase, navigating the old twisted and damp boards, the gradient becoming steeper with each step and each step smaller than the one before, the creaks making it seem as if they were about to splinter and give way, until Jack and Eleanor were at the entrance to the attic.

She had commandeered the space ever since she and Cecily had moved in, and her sister knew better than to disturb her while she was up here, but now she wanted to share it with Jack.

'Where are you taking me?' he asked as he balanced on the narrow stair.

'Surprise . . .' She unlocked the door and felt along the inside wall for the light switch, and then ushered him in.

The attic had been used for storing old roof tiles and pots of paint, and it had been cluttered with unwanted or broken furniture from the flats below, until Eleanor had transformed it into her painting studio. It was still rather dismal by day, with its low ceilings and blacked-out skylights, but at night the string of light bulbs that crisscrossed the room, the chaise lounge beside the far wall, and the textiles draped across chairs lent the space an old-world glamour. Together with the half-finished canvases stacked against the walls and the well-used easel and wooden stool, the décor created the effect she had aimed for: that of an artist's bohemian studio.

Once inside, they were greeted by the potent scents of musty furniture and fresh paint, which signalled the blending of the old with the new.

'This is wonderful,' Jack said admiringly. 'Your very own pied-à-terre.'

'I'm glad you like it.'

He grinned and glanced around. 'I do, I really do.'

Eleanor leaned against the doorframe and watched him explore, examining the pictures, poking into dusty corners, and pulling forward canvases that were piled two or three deep to see what lay behind.

Then the painting table and easel caught his eye and he approached them, running his fingers gently over the brushes, opening the battered palettes to look inside.

She sensed his longing. 'You look as if you have missed them more than me.'

'It's been quite some time since I had the luxury of an easel, let alone any paints. Mine ran out after the first month, and what didn't, got left behind.'

'You received the pencils and equipment I sent, though?'

'Yes, I did, thank you,' he said, glancing back at her. 'They came at just the right time.'

He stood back to inspect the half-formed portrait on the easel: one of the orphans she'd met at the garage, Isaac. Traces of his young face were just visible in the charcoal outline; to Eleanor he was a dear child and a symbol of hope—to Jack he was just a boy.

'So you still want to paint me then?' Jack asked.

'Yes, but first I want to show you something.'

The skylight hatch was stiff, so it took several goes before the lock came loose and she was able to push it open and climb out onto the flat roof. Jack climbed out behind her and they stood gazing out at the inky skies.

There was barely any breeze and London lay dozing. It was as if a spell had been cast to silence the city, draining it of colour; it wasn't stark black, and the outlines of cars and buildings were muted versions of themselves. Eleanor thought it mysterious and very nearly beautiful—but, above all, perfectly fitting as the night to welcome Jack home.

She looked at him and smiled. 'Lovely, isn't it?'

'Yes.'

They could see all the way down to Hyde Park in the south, with vast patches of dense black where the parkland and lake would be, and the great dome of the Royal Albert Hall in the west. Dim lights twinkled along the main streets and avenues, the steady hum of traffic filtering up to them. Apart from the occasional shout on a street somewhere, it was surprisingly peaceful.

'Have you missed it?' she asked after a while.

'Not as much as I've missed you.'

Her face grew warm. 'Come on, we had better go down. I can see that you won't be satisfied until you've been allowed to stare at me all night.'

Back in the attic she steered him towards the chaise lounge but changed her mind, deciding he would be too low down. Instead she settled him on a high-backed chair that had been quarantined for having a few loose upholstery pins.

'Don't lean back too far in case you get a nail in your back. That's fine . . . Don't fidget now.'

'But what if I want a drink?' he said, glancing at the unfinished bottle of wine she had brought up and placed on the mantel over the small fireplace.

'You're not allowed to do anything unless I say so, at least not until I've decided which position I'd like you in,' she said, and her eyes glinted with newfound mischief.

'I thought you wanted to be the subject.' He took off his jacket and hung it loosely over the chair.

'Of course not, and since I am not expecting payment for the portrait, I can paint you how I like.'

'Oh, so that's what you're up to. You're not going to flatter me at all then . . . But couldn't you broaden my shoulders a little or add some extra thickness to my hair?'

'No, sir,' she continued playfully, 'you mistake me for a medieval painter who relies on the good humour of his subject. Your portrait will not be an illusion—I am a realist, if you don't mind.'

He pulled a funny face and then grew serious again, leaning forward out of the seat. 'If you really were a medieval painter,' he said, pausing for effect, 'then you would have known that a misbelief of painters is to create beauty where there is none. Are you suggesting that there is nothing here that you find pleasing?' He sat back and crossed one leg over the other, eyeing her coolly to see if she had a ready reply.

Eleanor could tell that he was playing with her now, and it threw her. She was used to having the upper hand, she had even been vain enough to think that her intellect was sharper than his, but she'd been wrong. Now things felt different; something between them had shifted. Perhaps being in combat had honed his mind and his skills, or was it the influence of the men he'd been stationed with?

She distracted herself by lighting candles that she had saved: a trio of them along the small mantelpiece and half a dozen more in an assortment of jars in the empty fireplace beneath—the effect was of brilliant flames dancing on glass.

'There is much that I find pleasing,' she said, placing a new canvas on the easel, 'but I'm not in the business of flattering my subjects with insincere representations. You will get an authentic picture.'

He smiled, seemingly appeased. 'There's very little that you don't know about the history of painting, isn't there?' he said.

'Yes, and very little that would surprise me. Now, will you be quiet so that I can sketch you?'

It was a warm night and, with little space for the air to circulate, the studio was quickly heady with the smell of paint and aroma of candles. Eleanor had grown tired of talking and wanted to get on and paint, although she was uncertain why she had such an overwhelming desire to do so: perhaps in case he left again, or perhaps she just wanted to commit his face to canvas. Either way, she was ready now and glanced over at him, narrowing her eyes, making a painter's estimation of her subject.

'Well . . . perhaps a touch of pink to lighten those dark pouches under your eyes,' she said after a few moments.

'These are hard-earned bags, I'll not have a word said against them.'

'Rightly so,' she said and smiled.

They fell into an easy silence as she mixed paints and changed brushes, and all the time he sat watching her ritual. Once she had laid out her brushes and was ready, she surveyed him again, trying to remain detached and work on the composition of the picture. But the sight of him watching her made her self-conscious—and also filled her with desire.

He followed her every move and she held his gaze for as long as she could—his eyes like dazzling stars in a familiar sky—before she had to glance away. She felt her blood rise and quickly turned back to the painting, counting silently as she took deep breaths, waiting for the blush to fade.

And then she began to paint. First long sweeps of charcoal, a framework to build up the picture, and then the detailed brushstrokes of colour to fill it in.

After a while he glanced over at the bottle of wine. 'May I?'

'Of course.'

He poured two glasses and brought one over, standing it on the table beside her. She expected him to sit back down, but instead came behind her, examining the sketch.

'Hmm . . .'

'Give me a chance,' she said.

She twisted round to see his expression but it was unreadable, so she turned her attention back to the picture, trying to view it through his eyes. There was no resemblance to him yet, only a meeting of lines and a chorus of light and dark, but she knew what she wanted to achieve.

She steadied her brush over the canvas, its faint black line finishing the curve of his mouth—until she became aware of the warmth of his breath behind her, and then the softness of his lips as they pressed into her neck. First, just one tender kiss, then another and another, tracing their way down the nape of her neck—and then his fingers were pulling at the edge of her blouse, his lips searching for more skin.

She had craved him for so long that she only flirted for an instant with the thought of stopping before she was lost in the scent of him, the pressure of his body against hers, and the exhilaration of what might happen next.

Twenty-three

The Royal Institute of Painters in Watercolours stood at 190 Piccadilly, a magnificent four-storey building with carved stone busts on its façade: Turner, Cozens, Girtin, Cox, De Wint, Sandby and Barrett, all luminaries who had been honoured by their inclusion at the galleries. Jack had seen the busts before but they appeared even more impressive today, their usually austere gaze passing as recognition of the importance in which they were held. Or maybe it was because everything held more appeal today; even the sight of troops in the streets, which usually signalled the vulnerability of their city, made him feel safer. The boarded-up shopfronts that showed how their commerce had been destroyed also showed how, after three years of war, they were still standing firm.

Or perhaps it was because of Eleanor, the most enchanting creature he had ever met, and who—for some reason that he hadn't yet figured out—had chosen him.

He was early. Ever since he'd received the telegram from Professor Aubrey Powell the day before, he had wondered at the significance of meeting here: the institute had been founded by artists over a century earlier in response to the Royal Academy's refusal to treat watercolours as 'serious art'. Was Powell trying to tell him something, or was it just a coincidence that the professor had chosen this as their meeting place? And, more importantly, Jack had barely been back a week so what was so urgent that he needed to see him now?

The traffic was flowing freely down Piccadilly and the pavement relatively un-crowded, so Jack saw Powell straight away—he was easily recognisable, after all, in his long trench coat and wide-brimmed hat, pipe jutting between clenched teeth. The professor's trousers swung as he walked and were cuffed, and Jack wondered why he had traded his old suits for the new style and wasn't supporting the war effort as he should.

'Good morning, Professor Powell,' Jack said, shaking his hand. 'How are you?'

'I'm very well, Jack,' he replied, removing his pipe. 'Please call me Aubrey. And thank you for coming—early start, I know. Shall we go inside?'

Jack let him lead the way, following him up a wide carpeted staircase to the first-floor galleries, where doors led off to various rooms. The lobby area was all grand frescoes and gilt cornicing, watercolours by master painters lining the stairwell and walls. Signs for functions in the private rooms stood on easels, and a reception area ran the length of the back wall.

'Wait here for a moment,' Aubrey said. 'I'll sign us in.' He was back after a few minutes and ushered Jack towards the members' lounge. 'Let's go in here,' Aubrey said, holding open the door.

The dark wooden bar, attended by two middle-aged men in white jackets and black bow ties, was relatively empty, but the smell of alcohol and tobacco lingered heavily in the air. Groups of people sat in clusters around low tables and chairs, and the walls were crammed full of paintings by members who had been invited to exhibit there. With all the table lamps and large ferns and palms, they could have been in a colonial hotel in India drinking gin and tonics rather than about to sip coffee in the heart of Piccadilly. And despite the stern dark wood of the furniture, there was an informal atmosphere about the place—and there were a few artists Jack recognised. It had been years since he'd been inside and he looked around at the work as he followed Aubrey to a table at the back, wondering again what this could be about.

'Good spot, eh?' Aubrey said. 'They make a terrific kedgeree too, if you are hungry.'

'No, I'm fine, thank you—just coffee will do,' Jack replied. 'It's a bit of a walk for you from Gower Street, isn't it?'

'All part of the golden triangle, my dear boy: the National Gallery, here, and then the Slade. I can usually do it in half an hour, as long as no demolitions are underway.'

Their table was near a window that afforded a view onto the street, and Aubrey ordered coffees while Jack settled into one of the leather wing-backed chairs and took in the view. He hadn't mentioned this meeting to Eleanor; she would have been even more curious than he as to why her old professor had asked to meet him here.

'You've been in Italy, haven't you?' Aubrey asked.

Jack nodded, although he was interested to know how Aubrey knew. Eleanor had promised to keep their conversations private, and he had told her little else—it was one of the conditions of the SOE.

'And how was it?' said Aubrey.

Jack had done a good job of compartmentalising his work, not allowing his thoughts to dwell on the brutality of what they saw, doing as the other chaps had suggested: walk, talk, eat, sleep. Get up the next day and do it all over again. The odour was the worst; he hadn't expected the smell of dead bodies to linger so long—even when he and the men had driven for miles, leaving the villages far behind, the stench had still been in his nostrils. He wondered if his brain was conjuring it from the images of blackened, limbless bodies in the pictures he'd sent home.

He lit a cigarette. 'It was pretty bad,' he said on a deep exhale.

Then he spoke honestly, telling Aubrey about the barren farmhouses they came across, with families slain beside their animals. How they'd passed battalions on foot that looked as if they were going to fall down and trucks full of prisoners whose expressions showed they knew their fate. He talked of the men's courage and the camaraderie of the other war correspondents when they travelled together, of their feelings of awe, amazement and horror as the sky filled with planes and they watched the dogfights overhead.

He was about to tell Aubrey how he'd seen a group of British men strip and kill a badly injured Italian soldier—and how it had made his blood run cold, but that he'd congratulated them just the same as the other men afterwards and drunk whisky with them back at the barracks—when something made him stop. He had talked for ages as Aubrey nodded and listened; he hadn't even drunk his coffee. And he had a responsibility to make sure that he didn't give too much away.

'I'm sorry,' said Jack, 'I don't know where . . .' The leather creaked as he leaned back in the chair and looked across at Aubrey. He knew the professor had served in the Great War and been an artist too, so he took it that he understood.

'It's fine, Jack. Absolutely fine. I don't have to be anywhere until eleven.' Aubrey leaned forward, elbows resting on his knees, hands clasped. 'You see, dear boy, I know that the War Office doesn't fully prepare artists for what they are going into, but there really is no other way. The alternative is one that would not keep you out of the firing line—at least this way, you are a good distance from it.'

'I know, I appreciate that. It's just that sometimes . . . sometimes you feel that you should be in it. Why do they deserve it and we don't?'

Jack was still speaking honestly, but he sensed that Aubrey might know more than he was letting on. He needed to remain guarded about his operational work and play up his role as an artist. Could Aubrey have any knowledge of his work for the SOE? Could he himself have worked as an agent, or still be involved?

'No one deserves it, Jack. It's war. If you want to get off the magic carpet, then you can, but I suspect that you'd like to keep on it.'

Jack nodded. It wasn't just that this had been his first posting, a venture into the unknown—he had reconciled his roles as an artist and as an agent, but he still felt like a fake soldier when he was in the field. But that was even more reason why he wasn't going to quit.

'I've seen some of your paintings,' Aubrey added. 'They're good.'

'Thank you,' Jack replied, 'but that isn't why you've asked me here, is it?'

'No.' Aubrey cleared his throat. 'That picture you submitted, *Children in the Attic* . . . I know that it isn't yours—that it's Eleanor's.'

Jack clasped his hands together and thought for a moment; he could deny it and Aubrey would never be able to prove him wrong, or he could admit that it was Eleanor's painting. It was Aubrey's fault; when Jack first came home Eleanor told him how Sir Robert had humiliated her and that Aubrey did nothing to defend her. She also told him that it had made her even more determined not to give up—that she needed just one chance. Jack had seized that chance when he had submitted his paintings a few days later and, still fierce with protective fury, he hadn't consulted Eleanor.

'It's not good practice, Jack. If the others knew about it . . . if Sir Robert knew, well, I think you might be off the scheme.'

'I don't understand why. Surely it proves the point—if a painting is good enough to be selected, you can choose it regardless of the artist.'

'She was never selected, Jack. She was never supposed to be part of the scheme. Miss Roy works for the committee, for goodness sake.'

'But she's good enough to be a war artist, so why isn't she one?'

'You and I know that's not possible.'

'Why? There are others. What about Stella Bowen or Kathleen Guthrie—or Dora Meeson, for that matter. Why is Eleanor any different?'

'Yes, she is good enough. But that's not the point. She has a role to play in this war and she is doing it right now.'

Jack leaned forward and spoke assertively. 'She doesn't know what I've done—she can't know. Especially now.'

'You should have thought about that before. What damage you could have done her.'

'Are you going to tell the rest of the committee?'

'No. In any case, Eleanor has already tried promoting her own work, and Sir Robert was not impressed . . . She didn't tell you?'

Jack nodded his head. 'Yes, she did.'

A vague smile played on Aubrey's lips as he recollected. 'She wanted to make replacements at a recent exhibition; one of her pictures was conveniently among those she had selected. Good piece, but even so.' Aubrey paused. 'Anyway, you should talk to her.'

'I have—but she knows what she wants.'

'I know what she wants too, Jack—painting on the home front is one thing, but an overseas posting for a woman?' He looked Jack squarely in the eye. 'It just isn't going to happen.'

Jack didn't flinch. 'Why? They are taking just as many risks here at home, so what's the difference?'

'Come on, you and I know what we're talking about. You don't think you're the sort of man who could ignore a woman by your side, or in the quarters, for that matter?'

'At least I'm standing up for her now . . .'

'So, you still believe she should do it. I thought you loved her, Jack?'

'I do,' Jack said, shifting to the edge of his seat. 'I don't want her to get hurt but I don't see why girls like her don't get a chance.'

He also thought it was extraordinary that so many women were working as couriers for the SOE, and yet they weren't allowed to work as war artists overseas. But he couldn't tell Aubrey about that.

The professor narrowed his eyes. 'Let me put it another way. If you do anything like this again, then she will be out of the Ministry and you will be in the front line. You have committed fraud and Eleanor has committed forgery, and I will not deceive the public or have you make fools of the committee.'

Jack knew that the committee had the power to do what Aubrey was threatening. He was reminded of what had happened to Edmund Wright, the war artist whose brother had painted pictures on his behalf so that he didn't have to fight. Their whole family had been disgraced.

'Do the WAAC know it's not mine?' Jack asked.

'No, and I can keep it that way, but you need to stop this now. The committee was set up to help artists like you.'

'And what will happen to Eleanor?'

'Nothing . . . if you do as I say. The best way for Eleanor to serve her country is by doing exactly what she's doing now—you would do well to remember that.'

Jack wondered whether Aubrey's motive was really that honourable or if he might be more concerned about keeping Eleanor close; he certainly had an odd, almost proprietary way of speaking about her.

Either way, Jack couldn't continue to jeopardise her future, her reputation and her livelihood. Whatever he said now would affect both of them. He longed to keep her dream alive, but for now all he could do was help her keep her job, so he reluctantly agreed to go along with what Aubrey wanted and keep all that he'd done for her a secret.

Twenty-four

Eleanor rarely saw the colour of labradorite in the limited range of their daily palette. It wasn't visible among the muted tones of the uniforms and civilian clothes, or the greyness of their streets and homes, and the sight of it made her smile—it was blue dancing with grey, a hint of luminescence that she had only ever seen in a pearl. The semiprecious stone was set in a silver bracelet that she'd found on her pillow on waking, with one of Jack's tiny sketches tucked underneath. She hadn't taken the bracelet off yet, not even when she'd bathed or slept, or when she'd gone to her studio to paint. Maura had said that the stone held magical powers, but Eleanor thought its beauty lay in the crystal; it looked like a frozen tear and she clung on to that thought, believing it to be one that she had shed for Jack, suspended like a fossil.

She admired it again now as she waited for him, although he was officially late. He had left another picture for her last night: a pencil sketch of Eros and the legend *6.30 p.m.*, so here she was, standing by the statue in Piccadilly Circus. She was watching the pigeons cause their usual havoc amid the early evening revellers when two soldiers approached her, swaggering slightly as they held on to each other. They looked ill suited: one slim-faced and tall with strawberry-blond hair, and the other short and dark with blue eyes and an overly enthusiastic smile.

'You are far too pretty to be on your own, miss,' the short one slurred in a strong accent that she couldn't quite place—it wasn't Canadian but it wasn't any kind of American accent either—and their uniform was an unfamiliar khaki tunic.

'What's your name?' the tall soldier asked.

She was apprehensive—but then something about him reminded her of Francis and thoughts of her injured brother forced her to be as kind as she hoped strangers would be to him.

'It's Eleanor,' she said with warmth.

'Lieutenant Williams at your service,' he replied, saluting her.

The second officer put out his hand and waited until she took hold of it before he bent to kiss it. Williams let out a snigger.

'Private O'Connor, miss. It is an honour and a privilege to meet such a beautiful English rose.'

Eleanor couldn't help but smile, wondering what Eros would make of it all.

'Now, you come along with us, Eleanor,' Williams said, offering her his arm. 'We're going to see a show.'

'No, no, no, Williams,' O'Connor said, taking her gently by the elbow. 'You need to dine a lady.' Then, turning to Eleanor, 'Let's go find some real fine fancy food.'

She loosened her arm and took a couple of steps backwards. 'That would have been terrific, gentlemen, but I'm afraid I've got other plans.' Knowing how the moods of drunks could change, she continued politely, 'Anyway, where are you two gentlemen from?'

Suddenly they both seemed to sober up. They stood stock upright, hands anchored by their sides and chins tilted in the air, as they began to sing.

> Australian sons, let us rejoice.
> For we are young and free.
> We've golden soil and wealth for toil,
> Our home is girt by sea.
> Our land abounds in nature's gifts
> Of beauty rich and rare;
> In hist'ry's page, let ev'ry stage
> Advance Australia Fair
> In joyful strains then let us sing
> Advance Australia Fair.

Eros's shadow was lengthening as the sun slipped further down the mackerel sky, and the day's unexpected heat lifted. Williams and O'Connor were attracting a crowd—soldiers and others in uniform surrounded them, joining in as they began the second verse of the well-known patriotic song, their voices even louder than before.

> When gallant Cook from Albion sailed.
> To trace wide oceans o'er.
> True British courage bore him on.
> Til he landed on our shore

Then here he raised Old England's flag.
The standard of the brave.
'With all her faults we love her still.'
'Britannia rules the wave.'
In joyful strains then let us sing
Advance Australia Fair.

The crowd was rallying by the end of the verse, their chorus loud and the mood jubilant as the streetlights spluttered to life. Then Eleanor saw Jack walking towards her. The emotion of the lyrics, the atmosphere of the crowd and thoughts of Francis lying injured in a naval hospital somewhere had stirred something in her, and her eyes were moist with tears.

'What's the matter?' Jack asked as he reached her, taking hold of her arms.

'I'm fine—I just got caught up in it all. Blame it on those soldiers, Williams and O'Connor.' She sniffed, nodding at the men, who were being swept away by the crowd.

'Come on, let's get you inside.' Jack took her hand and led her towards the Criterion Restaurant, and she laughed in surprise as he whisked her through its revolving doors.

It took a moment for her to adjust to the change in atmosphere and the golden glow of the décor. The white-jacketed maître d' showed them to a table on a raised platform overlooking the restaurant. 'It's beautiful,' she said, gazing around.

The friezes and entablatures that she had glimpsed outside seemed inconspicuous compared with the opulence of the interior, the ceiling of gold mosaic casting them in a glorious halo. The restaurant was famous and she knew they were in good company; she had read that Winston Churchill and Lloyd George regularly dined here, and that it was where the women's suffragette movement had many of their afternoon teas.

'My darling girl,' said Jack, 'are you alright now?'

'Yes, those boys were really very sweet. It's just, one of them reminded me of Francis.'

'Still no word?'

'No, Father is trying to find out which hospital he's in. And we still don't know how badly wounded he is, so we just have to carry on and hope for the best.'

Jack reached across the table and squeezed her hand. 'He's alive, Eleanor—that's what you have to hold onto.'

When the waiter brought menus, Jack sent him away with an order for house cocktails. As she watched him, she noticed how tired he looked, sallow skin under his eyes. 'And are *you* alright?' she said brightly, trying to hide her concern.

'Yes, although I am a bit tired.' Jack ran a hand over his face. 'But I finished another painting today. I'll be on track for the exhibition at this rate.'

'That's marvellous. You must have been burning the midnight oil, though?'

'Not at all,' he lied; she knew he'd gone straight to his studio from her flat the night before and the one before that. 'Anyway, I'll be able to move in to my studio once the paintings have gone.'

'Will I be allowed back in too?' she asked.

'You know that you're welcome any time—although it's not nearly as impressive as yours.'

She smiled at him, and then decided to change the subject. 'Have you seen the papers today?' she asked.

'You mean about Dieppe?'

She nodded. 'What's going to happen, Jack? Things aren't going our way, are they?'

August had not been a good month for the Allies: first the carrier HMS *Eagle* had been torpedoed on its way to Malta, and then thousands of British and Canadian soldiers were killed or captured in the Dieppe raid. The truth was, there hadn't been any good news in weeks, only worrying headlines and bulletins of mounting casualties, and the terrifying rumours of extermination camps and gas chambers that had been heaped on the horrors that the Nazis had perpetrated.

Jack reached out and clasped her hand again, fingers wrapping tightly over hers, his paint-stained fingertips making her all the more tender towards him.

'I thought we could go to Kew tomorrow,' she suggested, 'and walk back along the river.' She no longer wanted to dwell on what they had no control over. Sometimes it felt as if they had to fight just to stay on two feet; if they didn't, their new world would overwhelm them like a tidal wave that they would disappear beneath.

'That's a nice idea. We could stop at Battersea on the way back—Mum and Beth are desperate to meet you.'

'Yes, me too.'

They had tried to arrange it in all the months they had been together, but their jobs, or his mother's illness and doctor's appointments, had got in the way.

'Good, that's settled then. So what are you going to have?' He glanced at the menu.

There was a lot to choose from but she was more interested in looking around, still mesmerised by the gilt and mosaic. The Criterion was renowned for its neo-Byzantine architecture, and everywhere she looked was a vignette of exquisite semiprecious stones—jade, turquoise, mother of pearl—all begging for her to paint them. She and Jack might have been in the Roman Empire, rather than a London restaurant in the midst of war. If only she was dressed like a Roman empress instead of in this old suit, she thought, noticing how dressed up everyone else was.

When the waiter reappeared with the cocktails, she suggested that Jack order food for them and sipped her drink, studying him.

'So, what were you working on today?' she asked when the waiter had gone.

Jack hesitated before answering Eleanor. He was thinking of Freddie—and he was thinking of the painting he had just finished.

Freddie, a young corporal, had been part of the unit assigned to look after Jack and the other war reporters. They'd spent every day and night together, jammed into the back of armoured vehicles, hiding out in dusty buildings or tightly packed as sardines in tents. They had all been so relieved to make it out alive from a day's raid, but then their jerry cans had leaked, with most of the water lost.

'A man's fortune can change in a heartbeat when he's out there,' Jack said.

Eleanor's brow furrowed. 'What are you talking about?'

'Ignore me,' he said, trying to smile. 'I was just thinking out loud.'

It had been an eight-mile walk back to base with nothing left to drink let alone moisten their lips with. He didn't want to tell her how they were on the home stretch when the younger soldiers decided to head out in front—how Freddie stopped to tease Jack and tossed

Jack's empty water canister around. He didn't want to relive the moment when Freddie spotted an object on the ground and decided to improvise a game of soccer. But more than anything he didn't want to picture it when they'd all realised it was too late, and the landmine had blown up.

Jack took a large sip of his cocktail, waiting for the next numbing hit of alcohol, but the swirl of orange became red and then transformed into blood.

'Jack, really, are you alright?' Eleanor asked insistently.

'Yes, I'm fine,' he said and pushed the drink away.

'And what about tomorrow?' she asked. 'If I come by then, what will you show me?'

'Probably one of the paintings I did in the mess. Some of the officers still like their portraits painted. In fact, they are worse than the Air Ministry. It's extra money, so I can't complain.'

He didn't have any choice: he needed the money for his mother's medicine and doctor bills, and that was why he had been up most of the night painting, and the reason he'd had to sell his treasured motorcycle. Anne's drugs had become even more expensive, in short supply as more and more medical resources were directed to the war effort. Even the diet the doctors had recommended for her to get rid of toxins was proving difficult to follow on the weekly ration.

'Perhaps you had better not tell me after all,' Eleanor said, an eyebrow quirked. 'You know you're supposed to offer all your work to the WAAC if you're under contract, don't you?' she teased. 'Anyway, cheers,' she said and raised her glass. 'Here's to your exhibition. I wondered what you had brought me here to celebrate.'

'Cheers,' Jack said, reluctantly picking up his glass.

This evening wasn't going as he had planned. He *had* brought her here for a special occasion—but he couldn't ask her now, particularly since he was still wrestling with his conscience. He couldn't decide whether to share the details of his meeting with Aubrey. There were already enough secrets between them, weren't there? Wouldn't it be better to try to help Eleanor and fail rather than hide more information from her?

Jack tried to put the matter out of his mind, concentrate on what she was saying and enjoy the food—especially since it was costing him the price of a day's medicine for his mother—but it was hard to focus. When they talked about the war he had to censor his replies, only giving her the sanitised version of events without the brutal and bloody truth, and without mention of his complicity in it or the missions he had run. Still, by the end of the meal her face looked so shocked and saddened at the glimpses he had offered that he knew there and then she couldn't possibly go to war, and that he should never have tried to help her. His darling girl had a talent, of that he was certain, but it was madness to think that she could go overseas. He couldn't bear the thought of her seeing what he had seen—or believe that it had taken him this long to realise it. Aubrey was right; Eleanor was in the best place for her with the committee, so he would do as the professor asked and protect her reputation and her livelihood.

Twenty-five

Jack cycled along the deserted streets, the few delivery vans materialising through an early morning mist, creating a surreal landscape. He had half a mind to sketch it if he hadn't been in such a hurry to get home. He had talked to his mother about Eleanor many times since they had been together and in all that time they hadn't met, but he was excited at the thought they would today. Making an arm signal right, he moved into the centre of the road, pedalling faster, adrenaline and excitement surging through his body at the thought of how they would get along.

When he turned into Queenstown Road and neared his house, he noticed the ambulance outside and was overtaken by a terrible sense of dread, and of deja vu. An ambulance had been at their door on two occasions over the past few years: the first was when his father had a heart attack, and the second when his mother had begun deteriorating and fallen down the stairs. The sight of it now made Jack sick with panic and he rode as fast as he could, demounting quickly at the gate.

He saw two ambulance-women walk out of the neighbour's front door carrying a stretcher, then lifting their neighbour, Mr Walsh, into the back of the waiting vehicle.

Jack reached up to support himself on the doorframe, eyes cast down as he caught his breath. Then he watched as the ambulance doors closed, the driver took her seat and they drove away. Only when they were out of sight did he feel recovered enough to go inside.

It was too early for his mother to be awake, so he washed and changed before heading to the kitchen to make a start on her breakfast, but she was already there in her wheelchair, measuring oats into a saucepan at the kitchen table.

'Morning, luv,' Anne said.

'Morning, Mum,' he said, bending to kiss her forehead. 'How are you?'

'Better—I treated myself and took a sleeping pill,' she said sheepishly.

'That is allowed, isn't it?' he asked, a little worried.

'Once in a while is okay—it just sets me up if I have a good night's sleep. Talking of which, where did you get to last night?'

He frowned, feeling even more worried. 'Didn't Beth come?' he said.

'Yes, Beth came. She brought round a lovely rabbit stew. Oh, and before I forget, this came for you . . .' She picked an envelope off the kitchen table and handed it to him.

It was on War Office stationery, and so he quickly put it in his pocket.

'Well, aren't you going to open it?' she said, after letting a moment pass.

'It's okay. Let's have breakfast first. There's no rush.' Except that whatever the letter was, his new orders or posting, he hadn't expected to hear so soon.

'Do you want some porridge?' she asked.

'Yes, please,' he said and watched as she measured another cupful of oats into the saucepan, her unsteady hand spilling some cereal across the table.

The letter had come before he'd had the chance to look for a care facility for Anne, or for him and Beth to talk to her about the idea of leaving her home. And before she had met Eleanor.

'I'm really glad you had a good night, Mum, because I'm going to bring Eleanor back to meet you later . . . if that's alright with you?'

His mother smiled. 'Of course it is, dear. It will be lovely. You know how much I've wanted to meet her.'

'I know,' he said, smiling. 'She's looking forward to it too.'

'I haven't got anything in. Can you pop down the shop and get something?'

'Like what?'

'Something we can offer her with a cup of tea. I don't like not having anything for visitors. It's not very welcoming.'

'Mum, Eleanor isn't going to mind. She's coming to meet you. Look, I'll try and pick something up on our walk. I've got to go to the studio first . . . there's something I need to finish off.' His fingers brushed the envelope in his pocket.

'Sure. You go and get yourself sorted. I'll have this ready in a tick.'

Jack went upstairs to his room and sat on the end of his bed, looking around at the place where he had spent most of his life. His football trophies were still on top of the dresser, his graduation certificate from Central Saint Martins School of Art and some art prizes on the walls. His Chelsea football scarves and paraphernalia hung from the back of his door, the locked cabinet holding cameras and binoculars, shelves of art equipment too valuable to be left at his studio. This room had taken him from boyhood to manhood, from civilian to war artist, and hopefully from bachelor to husband—but first he needed to know what the SOE had planned for him next.

He took the envelope out of his pocket and slid his finger under one corner. The instructions were brief, only three lines in thick Courier font. He re-read them and then tore them up as he'd been instructed to, placing the paper in the grate and setting it alight, pausing to light a cigarette as he watched it burn. He inhaled as he glanced around again and then crossed the landing to his parents' old bedroom.

His mother had moved downstairs the day their father died; she hadn't wanted to sleep in the same bed they had shared for thirty years. Her condition had made the decision absolute. The curtains were partly drawn and the room held the spell of life suspended—thick dust, little air circulating. He went straight to the dresser where she kept her jewellery and, opening the drawer, took out the small black leather box. Inside was the engagement ring she had promised him: a thin gold band with a diamond solitaire. It had cost his father three months of wages at the brewery, but it had also earned him a dressing-down when his mother had discovered the cost.

Jack put the ring inside his jacket. The war had shown him how almost nothing was certain anymore, but there was one thing he could be sure of, and that was his love for Eleanor. His mother had always intended him to have the ring but he wanted to surprise her, so he would let her know that he had taken it once she had met his darling girl—and once Eleanor had said yes.

He and Eleanor had arranged to meet beside the Serpentine in Hyde Park at two o'clock and take a bus to Putney. They would walk the rest of the way along the river to Kew Gardens, if the weather held. An artists group—botanical illustrators, mostly—met there regularly and Jack knew quite a number of them from before the war, when most of his time was spent on book illustrations and lithographs.

After the visit with his mother he'd once again worked longer at his studio than he'd intended, struggling to complete the portrait that a colonel had commissioned. The fee would only be enough for eight weeks of medicine, and he needed more, since there was no knowing how long he would be gone.

Then he had double-checked all the equipment he was given at his last SOE briefing: the radio transmitter, the Fairbairn-Sykes fighting knife, the US pistol, the materials to make invisible ink, and the measures of silk, which he had discovered were more effective than paper for printing ciphers and not nearly as noisy as paper when hidden beneath clothing. He had carefully concealed all of this in his artist's chest alongside the traditional art materials.

He was a few minutes late, and Eleanor was already on the bench alongside the lake waiting for him. Her face lit up. She was wearing an outfit he hadn't seen before: a floral dress with red velvet ribbons at the neckline and around the end of its long sleeves, and a red felt hat slouched to one side.

There was a warm breeze. Summer was just loosening its grip, even though some of the trees already looked sparse and the birds had started their migration south. The lake was dotted with dainty white boats, and Eleanor and Jack walked arm in arm along the path, watching boaters churn the surface with their oars, meandering across the grey lumpy surface.

Jack still hadn't worked out how on earth he was going to do this. Should he start by popping the question or by telling her about the War Office letter? Both seemed of equal importance, albeit in different ways. Before coming here he had tried to figure it out while finishing the colonel's oil portrait, but he had become too distracted and made a mistake; in fact, most of his work had involved toning down the yellow with green.

A small troupe of actors was performing *A Midsummer's Night Dream* to an audience in a semicircle of red-and-white striped deckchairs, and Jack and Eleanor watched for a few minutes. The hand-drawn posters declared the performers to be the Bayswater Amateur Dramatic Society, and one of them was a fairy who shook a tambourine vigorously at dramatic intervals, alongside a young man on a French windpipe that gave an ethereal air to the proceedings.

Jack had to prise Eleanor away. She was still recounting Shakespeare's verse and describing her childhood attempts to put on the play with Cecily—without great success—when they reached the bandstand. Jack had made his decision about how to proceed. He stopped and turned to her. 'Will you please just stop talking for one minute and come with me?'

He knew her well enough to know that she was torn between keeping quiet and being cross, but she kept her lips closed as she followed him up the steps.

The bandstand was empty but the pipe music followed them and they could hear brief snatches of the actors' dialogue as the wind rose and fell. A honeyed light from the low autumn sun reached through the iron-work, creating patterns across the timber floor and speckling their clothes.

Eleanor looked more beautiful to him today than ever. He drank in the delicate golden weave of her hair, her Botticelli lips, and the high arch of her brow that made it difficult for him to read her. He would never tire of her face.

'Do you remember the day we first met, when we came here?' he asked, gazing down at her.

'It wasn't the first time we met! You were actually quite rude and walked out on me the day we met.'

'Well, it was after the committee meeting, when we walked through Hyde Park.'

'Yes, I remember.'

'And do you remember standing over there?' he said, pointing to the isthmus on Duck Island.

Eleanor looked eastwards to where the trees had created a grotto of shade and light, and the water created striations of colour where it met the fauna on the bank of the lake.

'Yes,' she said, 'we stood and looked over here at the party, won-dering who they were.'

'And we watched them dance,' he said, reaching towards her.

She glowered at him and then took hold of his left hand, letting him place his right hand around her waist.

Then they began to move, her footsteps following his: first just one step to the right, then forward, then to the left and forward again, until they were waltzing around the bandstand in time with the French windpipe.

At first Eleanor laughed, but when she saw how serious he was, how fixed his gaze on her was, she grew serious too.

After a few minutes the music stopped, and their dancing slowed until they were standing motionless together. He knew that this was his moment—that it was now or never—but the words wouldn't form and his mouth was completely dry.

'What is it, Jack?' she asked. 'Whatever is the matter?'

'Do you remember why the couples were here?'

'Yes, it was a wedding party.'

He was still holding her as he felt inside his pocket for the leather box.

'Eleanor, I know we've not known each other for very long,' he said, 'and that I'm probably not the first chap who has asked and you've turned down, but you are the only girl I have asked—' he smiled '—and the only girl I have ever loved . . . could ever love.'

He brought out the box.

She still hadn't spoken, so he carried on, nervously filling the silence. 'This was my mother's ring. I would have bought you one, but it means a great deal for me to give you this . . .' He waited for Eleanor's reaction. Her eyes were focused on the box, so he opened it. 'Will you please answer me?'

'But you haven't asked me anything,' she said with a smile.

'Eleanor, will you—?'

'And you need to be kneeling,' she said.

He went down on one knee, taking her hand with his free one.

The path had grown busy with workers on lunchbreaks, nannies pushing prams and walkers enjoying the scenery, and he noticed how people were looking in their direction. He needed to hurry up before his nerves gave out; he hadn't even stopped to think that the answer might be no and what he would do then.

He took a deep breath, noticing the pink flush that had appeared on her face. 'Eleanor, will you marry me?'

Her cheeks dimpled as her face broke into a huge smile and she squeezed his hands. 'Yes, Jack. Yes, of course I will.'

He was on his feet again and lifting her off the ground, twirling her around as they kissed. He let out a whoop of delight, and she threw back her head and laughed. Once they had stopped spinning and laughing and had caught their breath, he took the ring from the box. She held out her hand and he slipped the ring easily onto her finger.

A couple on the grass clapped and some passers-by stopped to see what all the excitement was about, an amateur photographer among them. He caught Eleanor and Jack in the flash of his bulb.

Then Jack noticed something about the ring. 'Oh, dear, it's too big,' he said.

'Don't worry, a jeweller can fix it.'

He found it amusing to watch her admire the ring on her finger, looking at it from different angles. Then she took it off and gave it back to him.

'I had better not wear it until we get it fixed—I would hate to lose it.'

'Well, yes . . . but no, we can't . . .' he began, feeling very awkward.

He hadn't wanted to tell her yet. He'd wanted to enjoy the moment and talk about their plans, but now he felt that it was wrong to make her wait.

'Why ever not?'

'I've got my posting, Eleanor. I leave in three days.'

'Where to?' she said, her glow fading, a pale hue taking its place.

'I'm not sure yet, but I suspect North Africa,' he lied, wishing he could tell her the truth.

'But, but . . . you can't go now.' She averted her gaze.

'I have to, Eleanor.'

Her mouth was slightly open in what looked like disbelief. She fell quiet and he supposed she was considering the news reports that had been coming in about the heavy casualties in Malta.

'Is it what you want?' she asked, lips quivering as she struggled to stay composed.

'I don't have any choice, my love. None of us do—it's our duty. Isn't that what you've always said?'

Her whole demeanour had changed and he wished he could have taken it back, that they could have shared their moment just a little longer, extending the memory of being together—and of planning a life.

Twenty-six

LONDON, SEPTEMBER 2010

Kathryn hurried out of Euston Underground and headed east towards the British Library, umbrella protecting her from the large barbs of rain and the fumes from the traffic crawling along Euston Road. Her grandmother had been encouraging about the diary and the War Artists booklets when they had talked by phone, so Kathryn had ended up staying the night at Helen's in order to get to the library early.

Kathryn hadn't wanted to ask her about the engagement until they were face to face so she decided to wait. Instead she voiced Oliver's theory about *The Bermondsey Rescue, July 1942* to her grandmother, but Eleanor had dismissed it. And because her grandmother had always prided herself on being a well-respected art teacher, Kathryn knew better than to argue with her.

Kathryn still didn't have any clear knowledge of what had happened to Jack or proof that he was alive. Chris remained convinced she was on a wild-goose chase. But at least the past few days had shown her how much he had meant to her gran—which was a shock, given the happy marriage she knew her grandparents had had. She had also come to believe that part of Jack's life had been covered up: it was as if someone didn't want him to be known or found. The other major war artists had been properly commemorated and celebrated in the anniversaries of the Second World War, whereas Jack's work appeared to be lost or hidden in the archive, and she had to search hard to find anything. She secretly thought that she might uncover some of his valuable missing artworks but, at the very least, she hoped to stumble across something exciting today since she had learned that the library held the best records and kept every publication ever produced in the UK.

Most of all, though, she hoped that she could find out about Jack before she caught the plane home, keeping her promises to everyone.

It was the first time she had visited the new British Library, and the elegant gothic towers of St Pancras station still overshadowed the harsh angles of the building's twenty-first century replacement, with its blunt edges and boxy design. The rainfall grew steadily heavier and she pulled her raincoat tighter, walking quickly past the bronze statue, across the red-and-cream brick courtyard and towards the entrance.

A wide foyer sat at the foot of vast columns of glass, sentinels guarding the King's Library, its thousands of rare books and pamphlets in glorious full view. Chris had been intrigued by the design when the building had been planned and built a few years earlier, and had reminded her of it when they'd spoken the night before—and asked her if she could take photos. She angled her iPhone to get the best shot but the reflection of the low-hanging lights on the glass made it awkward. Still, she had a couple that would do.

She muted the phone, tucked it inside her bag and made her way to the reception desk on the lower ground floor. The online registration had taken ten minutes, but she still needed the library card, so she joined the queue to get her photo taken.

Sitting on the row of plastic chairs, waiting for the photo to be processed, she was alert to the faces around her. An Italian family sat on the chairs ahead, the teenage boy and girl clearly arguing, though it still sounded glorious to Kathryn's ears. Even the voices of the staff at the inquiry desk sounded interesting to her, with their wide-ranging dialects. Why was it that she didn't respond this way to accents when she was in Australia, recognising the different ways of speaking and searching out her own, feeling happy to hear the English brogues? She kept catching herself thinking about how natural it felt to be back. How it didn't do anyone good living in limbo, not being able to commit one way or the other, always the outsider and never quite at home.

Chris had been conciliatory on the phone last night, even showing an interest in what was happening in England generally. And so she was entertaining the thought that maybe they still had a chance.

Finally, her name was called. She collected the card and headed upstairs, through the glass double doors into Research Room One. A long counter ran along the left wall of the huge reading room, the signage helpfully offering guidance, so she got in line and took in her surroundings. The room was filled with avenues of wide beige-wooden desks and pale green carpet, impressive banks of brass sockets and number plaques where visitors sat. Most of the desks were stacked with books and folders and open laptops, the students so absorbed that barely any glanced up when she walked past. Trolleys creaked along, groaning under the weight of their books-in-waiting; others were left unattended beside the large columns that reached all the way to the ceiling. Air-conditioning grilles sat like ship portals along one wall, quietly gurgling as they sent out an excessive chill.

Despite the cold air, Kathryn felt a warming familiarity being in this environment again—it was reminiscent of her university days.

After the librarian handed her three bulky folders wrapped with elastic bands, she settled down at a desk to look through them. At first glance she didn't think the library had fulfilled her request—that not all the items were there—but when she opened the second folder she noticed it contained all the War Artists booklets that her grandmother had told her about. She took out the first one, *Blitz,* and examined the list of contributing artists, looking for Jack's name. The booklets were only small, 19 x 12 cm: small enough to fit in your pocket, according to Eleanor, and at only one shilling and threepence, affordable for the majority.

Blitz was one of four produced in the first set, titled *War Pictures by British Artists*, along with *War at Sea, RAF* and *Army.* Then she moved on to the second series: *Women, Production, Soldiers* and *Air Raids.* There was Clifford Rowe's depiction of a National Fire Service crew responding to a call; Charles Cundall's *Study for St Paul's Cathedral*; and pictures by Denys Wells and Claude Francis Barry, Harold Arthur Riley and Rudolf Sauter, all names that had become familiar to her.

Then she came to pictures that she instantly recognised: *Fire Drill at a School, Auxiliary Fireman,* and a third, *Streetscape After a Raid.* These were certainly Jack's work—they had his name on them and were in his traditional materials of watercolour, India ink, pencil and chalk on paper, and they were signed. But a fourth image, *Children in the Attic*, didn't fit with his works: something in the style was different—something that resembled *The Bermondsey Rescue*.

Kathryn flipped back and forth between the pages, making sure it wasn't a trick of the eye or a printing issue, but it was clear that the lines were blunter, the distinction between the images in the foreground and the background less clear. This was more like her grandmother's work in its detail, the familiar figure shading. Oli had been right, the picture wasn't Jack's but it could be Eleanor's. She rested back into the bow of the chair and wondered if it was possible—had Jack submitted Eleanor's pictures as his own? And would that have caused problems severe enough for him to disappear either by force or by choice?

She was struggling to understand why he would have done this when it occurred to her that hardly any women artists were featured in the booklets. Evelyn Dunbar and Ethel Gabain were two she recognised, but they were only two among the hundreds of well-known male war artists whose work was represented.

Kathryn opened *Women* and read the introduction by Dame Laura Knight:

> *The pictures in this volume provide a small cross-section of the whole gigantic contribution being made by the women in response to the ever-increasing demand for war supplies—and for more women to fill the places in the Services at home of men who have been called to the battlefronts.*

The words were certainly stirring, and Kathryn could see how they would have been good propaganda because even now they were affecting—especially the final paragraph. She re-read it aloud, slowly, under her breath.

> *After what she has done in this titanic struggle, will she not guard what she has gained, and to Man's effort add her own? If she can do what she has done in war, what may she not do in peace?*

Eleanor had been quite adamant about the power held by the WAAC and the force of the personalities involved. What if Jack and Eleanor's deception had been on the verge of becoming public? Could this have threatened the committee's credibility—or even its very existence, which Sir Robert Hughes and the other members had reportedly fought so hard for?

Or perhaps Eleanor had at first been furious with Jack for submitting her work. He might not have asked her permission. Maybe they had fought, and Eleanor had come to regret it—but this just didn't seem to ring true with what Kathryn knew of them.

Gazing at the sky through the roof-lights, Kathryn tried to picture her grandmother sixty-eight years ago. It would have been difficult to be acknowledged as a woman artist alongside the likes of celebrated male war artists—especially if you were working for the committee who selected them. But there might have been advantages too. A cloud passed overhead, throwing the library into momentary gloom, but Kathryn felt as if something had lifted. Having started down this track, her thoughts were racing, picking up threads and clues. Could this really be the reason that Eleanor had lost touch with Jack?

Her attention kept being pulled back to the picture, to the children lying on the attic floor, drawing. The more she looked, the more convinced she was that it was Eleanor's work. She knew how hard her grandmother had always fought to protect her privacy, but why hadn't she told Kathryn about this? It seemed she'd even lied outright.

This thought made Kathryn's heart sink. Suddenly she felt as if the grandmother she had known and loved growing up wasn't the same person anymore. The emotion of the trip was most likely getting to her, and maybe she was confusing Eleanor's feelings with her own, but the sense of betrayal still hurt.

The morning passed quickly as she looked through the rest of the booklets. She turned to the pictures she believed to be Jack's and the one she believed to be Eleanor's and recorded them on her iPhone. She also photocopied them so that she could more easily show them to Eleanor. But then she had a thought: Oliver could probably determine if the paintings were by the same hand. She hastily emailed him: *Are these paintings by the same artist? Love you, Mum xxx.* This way she wouldn't be relying on her eyes alone before confronting her grandmother.

She put the booklets back in their folders and turned her attention to the third folder. To her surprise, it contained an academic thesis about the WAAC by a British professor, Alexander Gower. This was a stroke of luck: here was detailed information about the committee and from an expert, somebody who had sourced material that she hadn't found in any online archives and who had interviewed the committee's surviving members. The problem was that the thesis had been written eighteen years ago. She knew that the committee members had all passed away now, so would the professor still be alive?

It was a large document of some six hundred pages. She searched through but nothing jumped out at her, so it seemed like a good time to take a break; she could google the professor and check on Eleanor. As soon as she was out of the reading room, she dialled her gran, but the number just rang out. She decided to get a coffee and some food, then try Eleanor again.

The pendant lights hung low over the cafe tables, bringing the spectacularly high ceilings only a fraction closer but still affording a clear view of the King's Library. The structure really was magnificent: thousands of books behind gleaming glass, shining like a jewel-encrusted crown. It gave her an idea of how to bring more light into the Nautilus development, how the living areas could be opened up by replacing some of the walls with glass; she would update her plans and send them to Chris tonight.

Kathryn called Eleanor again, listening to the rain hit the glazed roof hard, a rhythmic drumbeat that accompanied visitors hurriedly arriving with wet clothes. There was still no answer, so she pulled out her laptop and googled 'Military Historian Professor Gower', spooning the chocolate froth off her drink as she waited for the page to load. When his Wikipedia page popped up at the top of the results, something twigged—she realised that she recognised it from the anniversary exhibition program.

The biography was brief:

> *Alexander Geoffrey Gower (born 19 July 1956) was born in Surrey and served with the Welsh Guards before becoming a journalist and broadcaster. He studied at Magdalene College, Cambridge, where he gained a double first in English and was awarded a Fulbright Scholarship in 1978*

*to study at Harvard University. Following graduation, he
became an academic, teaching English literature in the US
before moving back to the UK.*

The professor looked all of his fifty-four years, and a full head of
curly grey hair and a small grey beard concealed much of his face.
Along with his bio, this made Kathryn think that perhaps he wasn't
the life and soul of the party—that was until she read his bibliog-
raphy. He specialised in books about military disasters with titles
that Oliver and Chris would appreciate: *The Big Book of Military
Madness, Great Blunders of the Twentieth Century* and *Lost Battles
That Changed History*. Further down was a snippet from a review: 'In
an era that relies on technology it is refreshing to see attention drawn
to the one underlying component that is present in all conflict: the
human factor.'

There were a number of photographs of battle re-enactments,
men dressed in full military regalia. She had heard about these fan-
atics, men and women who spent a huge amount of time planning
and re-enacting different battles with precision. There was an industry built around filming it too. She clicked on the icon for memora-
bilia; war art, journals and specialist books bought and sold; Professor
Gower was getting more fascinating by the minute. There was also a
link to his website—'Alexander Geoffrey Gower: Military Historian'—
so she clicked on it and found his contact details.

Twenty-seven

'That's the trouble these days,' Alexander Gower said over the phone, 'it's a double-edged sword, the internet—there's no burying the past, no place to hide.' There was a hint of amusement in his voice.

Following a brief explanation of why she needed his help, he invited her to come to his home in London that afternoon and said that he would certainly try to help.

He also told her that he had Jack Valante's 1943 war diary.

Looking at Gower's website on the bus journey over, Kathryn felt like she had hit the jackpot. Not only had he been an attendee at the anniversary celebrations, but Professor Gower was also probably the most qualified person she could talk to about the whole business. She was buoyed by her good fortune. As the traffic lights changed and she crossed Praed Street, she hoped that the professor would be true to his word.

Gloucester Mews was nestled between Gloucester Terrace and Westbourne Terrace, accessible through an archway off Chilworth Street that she would never have noticed if she hadn't been looking for it. The tall, glazed offices of the Paddington Basin now overshadowed the miniature homes, making them souvenir trinkets nearly two centuries old. The small mews houses had intrigued her and Chris when they'd lived here, and Chris had explained how they were originally built as stables from the spare bricks of the larger Georgian terraces they served. And how there was no structural integrity—it was a miracle that they hadn't already come tumbling down.

As Kathryn walked past she saw how varied they still were: an assortment of two- or three-storey homes, a mix of discreet traditional houses with small sash windows and pastel walls next to renovations with bold colours and contemporary designs. Seeing these homes and remembering her conversation with Chris made her think of their marriage. It had solid foundations, they had weathered storms and made changes; surely they could adapt and change again.

Finding the number she was looking for, Kathryn raised the brass knocker and stood back to admire the zinc window boxes overflowing with bright fuchsia geraniums and trailing ivy. As soon as Professor Gower opened the door, she could tell that he wasn't the same sort of academic as Stephen Aldridge: from the Prince of Wales check of his tweed suit and contrasting red-spotted tie and pocket-chief, to his enthusiastic welcome and incongruous hiking boots.

'I have bought a great many books at auction, but that diary is probably the most valuable purchase I've made,' he told Kathryn after their introductions. He had settled her on the sofa and was pouring Lady Grey tea from a lime-coloured Limoges pot while Kathryn eyed off the custard creams in the luxury-selection biscuit tin. Alexander handed her a cup and sat back, balancing his own cup and saucer on crossed knees. 'I'm so glad I was still here. I'm leaving for the Cotswolds in a few hours and I'm not likely to be back until next week, so you were very fortunate to catch me.'

'A stroke of luck,' she said, amazed at the serendipity. Her gaze fell on the diary, which was sitting on the coffee table between them. It was encased in a handcrafted wooden box, the glass panel revealing the red velvet of the bed it rested in.

'I had the case made specially,' Alexander said. 'You have to look after these things, you know. They're irreplaceable.'

'Exactly, I couldn't agree more,' she said. 'And I am so very pleased that you have.'

'So tell me,' he said, fixing her with a mildly curious stare, 'you were saying how you're researching the artist for your grandmother. What's her name?'

'Eleanor McLean, but she used to be Roy. Eleanor Roy.'

He raised an eyebrow. 'Ah yes. She produced one or two pictures herself. Do you know if she has them still?'

'I've seen a few sketches. Most of her pictures are from much later on, though—long after the war.'

'Pity.'

Kathryn nodded, thinking about *The Bermondsey Rescue* and *Children in the Attic*. She would ask Eleanor about them tonight. 'And, of course, you've read Jack's diary . . .'

'A number of times,' he said.

She took his smile as a measure of pride at owning such an important artefact and at having had the good sense to acquire it. She smiled back at him.

As she sipped her tea, she noticed that the *War Pictures by British Artists* booklets that she'd seen on his website were displayed in a glass cabinet, with their distinctive logo of a cannon and aircraft, alongside a range of military books with highly decorative spines. Earlier she had noticed the large collection of military prints on the hallway walls, and there were larger oils depicting battle scenes in the living room. But Alexander seemed too cheerful a character to be interested in war, and she wondered why it appealed to him. Was it a fascination with the machinery or the intellect of warfare? Maybe he came from a long line of military men and it was a family tradition. Or perhaps, like so many collectors, he was interested in the chase as much as the catch. 'I'm afraid I haven't had time to read much of your thesis,' she told him, 'but it looks fascinating. It must have taken a very long time to write?'

'Yes, it did. I can't imagine finding that sort of time now, but back then it was my sole purpose—a luxury, really.'

'And you said on the phone that you met Jack. Is there anything you can remember about him, anything that might indicate where he could be now?'

Alexander reached for a biscuit. 'Goodness, not off the top of my head, I'm afraid. A number of artists attended the celebrations, but unfortunately I wasn't able to talk to everyone.'

'Do you know of anyone who might still be in touch with him?'

'I'm sorry.' Alexander shook his head. 'You could call anyone whose name was on the guest list.'

She let out a sigh. 'I've already tried.' After finishing her tea, she asked, 'What about the WAAC? My grandmother worked for them, and so did Jack—do you think something could have happened there? It's just very strange that Jack doesn't seem to have been given the same status as the other important Second World War artists.'

For the first time, Alexander looked grave. 'I suspect the committee could have done anything that they chose to, Kathryn. They were a very powerful entity. There had never been anything like the WAAC before, and it's very likely there never will be again.'

'I see.' She thought again of *Children in the Attic* and the trouble it might have caused.

Alexander straightened, gave a hesitant smile and poured more tea. 'But in this case, I think you're barking up the wrong tree. You have to remember they were there to support the artists. Their raison d'être was to keep a whole generation of artists safe, as well as the stated aim to record the war, of course.'

She nodded. 'It was so different then, wasn't it? No brutal images online in those days.'

'Everything has changed, from the way war is conducted to the way it's reported. No one could have imagined back then that soldiers would be able to fire a rocket from a drone on the other side of the world at the flick of a switch.' He sipped his tea and cleared his throat. 'Tell me, do you have a theory about what happened to Jack?'

She decided that telling him would do more good than harm; surely he'd have some interesting insights. 'What if an artist submitted the work of another,' she began, 'and they were found out. What do you think the WAAC would have done?'

He gave a small shrug. 'I don't really see that it would have been considered that serious, unless the chap was draft-dodging.'

'What if the artist was a woman?' Kathryn asked. She knew that he would probably guess she was talking about Eleanor, but she didn't see that it would matter.

Alexander looked thoughtful. 'Well, there were women artists—not contracted by the committee, though. They submitted their work and the committee purchased it if they wished to.'

'But what if a woman artist wanted to work as a real war artist?'

He looked surprised. 'What . . . overseas, in the field of battle?'

'Yes, I suppose so,' she said, knowing her grandmother as she did.

'As far as I know that wasn't allowed until the end of the war. Mary Kessell and Laura Knight were given overseas commissions after the war—Kessell went to the Bergen-Belsen concentration camp and Knight went to Nuremberg.'

At the Imperial War Museum, Kathryn had seen Laura Knight's remarkable *Ruby Loftus Screwing a Breech Ring* and learned how iconic it was. Knight's painting of the Nuremberg trials was also extraordinary—the realism of the Nazi war criminals contrasted with the missing courtroom walls and the backdrop of a ruined city in flames; it conjured the image of hell itself.

'So,' Kathryn said, 'how difficult do you think the committee would have made it for anyone who tried to send a woman artist overseas?'

'I'm not sure there would have been any real backlash in that situation,' Alexander said, with a thoughtful frown. 'You are assuming there would have been animosity rather than commendation for the effort. Don't forget, my dear, thousands of artists were unemployed at the start of the war—people weren't buying books, the country wasn't even producing any. Books were subject to paper rationing from April 1940, and if you had read my thesis, then you would know there was no advertising industry to speak of, no commercial work for the artists. Don't forget, Kathryn, the committee was there to help.'

He seemed quite worked up, so she chose her next words carefully, aware that she still needed to look at Jack's diary. 'That's why I think there must be more to it than that.'

Alexander nodded and seemed to relax. 'It does all sound rather intriguing, and I do hope the diary helps. If not, then perhaps you should read my thesis—I can email it to you, if you'd like?'

'Yes, I'd appreciate that,' she said, trying to sound politely enthusiastic; she would never have the time to read the whole thing. She drained her second cup of tea and motioned towards the wooden box. 'May I?'

'Please go ahead. Take it over to the table—it will be easier for you. I'm sorry, but I can't allow you to take photographs. And I hope you don't mind wearing these?' He handed her a pair of white cloth gloves.

'Not at all.' She pulled them on, waited for the professor to leave the room with the tea tray, and then lifted the lid.

A familiar linen notebook was nestled inside the scarlet folds, and the inside cover read: *Sicily, Italy—1943*. Her grandmother hadn't seen Jack again after this trip.

Kathryn tried to imagine never seeing Chris again, never knowing what had happened to him after an abrupt goodbye, but she couldn't. Her chest heaved and tears pricked her eyes; she blinked them away. She'd grown convinced that Jack must have really loved Eleanor and wouldn't have left without word unless he had a very good reason. Everything her grandmother had said and done was testament to that. Something must have kept them apart.

Although there were ink smudges and yellow-and-brown blooms from foxing, it was clear from the first page that the script was the same as in the other diaries and that the neat black-ink depictions were Jack's.

Sunday, 14th November

Down to my last set of Winsor & Newton watercolours, a single block of paper and only a few pens. There's little hope of getting any more supplies until the ship arrives in a week so I'm going to make thumbnail sketches for the time being and work them up when the supplies get through.

Monday, 15th November

Despite what I wrote yesterday, I've just finished another 8½ x 11¼ watercolour on paper and it's packaged up ready to come home by return. All in all there are fifteen pictures in the batch. Many are only rough sketches but there are eight that tell the story of the confrontations. It is the most detailed one yet and I stuck to black and white on some but the paintings don't spare the bloodshed.

Tuesday, 16th November

Some of the other men still aren't sure of me—I know they resent us and don't see what we've done to earn the stars. I've heard them say it, 'Three pips on each shoulder and as free as the air.' I had a drinking session in the officers' mess a couple of nights ago and even Colonel Watkins told me that painting is a sissy's job. He asked why I hadn't just signed up, that I should be getting my hands dirty like the other men. If only he knew.

Thursday, 18th November

Hoskins stole my journal last night; he thought I was writing a personal diary until he saw for himself it's my aide

memoire. Bugger off you, nosey bastard—that's for you,
Hoskins, in case you steal it again!

Friday, 19th November
Quiet day at camp waiting for supplies to arrive. It's rare
to get the chance to set up the drawing board; I've mostly
had to find a surface to set my material down and a safe
place to sit and sketch. I've wanted to put everything down
on paper that I've seen but that's not possible with such
limited space and time. Saw incredible ruins today, sky
was blush pink and the earth ghostly pale in contrast.
Watkins invited me to the mess for dinner tomorrow, if
supplies arrive.

Saturday, 20th November
Still no supplies and unit was at a real low today. I had to
walk to the new camp because of their bloody-mindedness.
I walked for seven miles before Hoskins turned up in the
jeep and they gave me a lift the rest of the way. So much
for the pips!

Kathryn looked up; the professor was back, reading quietly in his chair.

'What does it mean, "Three pips on the shoulder and as free as the air?"' she asked.

'The military made the artists honorary captains during the war—it gave them access to the officers' mess, privileges that the other soldiers didn't have. As you can imagine, it didn't go down too well with some of them.'

Enough for someone to cause problems for Jack? she wondered. Enough to cause him harm?

Thursday, 25th November

First night on deck was peaceful, even the water was tranquil, but last night we watched the beaches as they got a terrific plastering. Flares and fire all through the night so nobody slept. I sketched the view from our vessel; the silhouettes of the other boats looked very dramatic with the flashes of gunfire and the Verey lights that shone from the shore. The noise died down just before dawn and we watched as the sun rose; it was like a fire burning across the horizon, reminding me of our London from the rooftop.

Friday, 26th November

Some of the unit helped load the injured onto the craft and I went with the other troops up into the village. Traipsed through the walled olive and orange groves, passed abandoned encampments, and dead and wounded on the side of the road. One of them was groaning even though he didn't have a face. We rested in an orchard and the men ate lunch but I couldn't bring myself to eat.

Sunday, 28th November

We returned to the village today and it was a job to protect our belongings. We were hassled constantly by the women and some of the men went off with them, just for a packet of cigarettes or food. I sat in the jeep and sketched them and will threaten to send it to Hoskins' wife if he steals from me again!

Tuesday, 30th November

The men are talking about Christmas, and Colonel Watkins has asked me to paint him a picture that he can send home; that it would mean so much to his family to see where he is. I tried to explain that it isn't why I am here and how much time it would take but he didn't listen. I did one such painting before for another colonel because Mum needed the money and I suspect he has heard about it.

Wednesday, 1st December

An appalling day transporting civilian bodies to mortuaries and seeing the families weep. Everything here is covered in flies—those grieving and the limbless bodies. The smell is worse than anything and thankfully I am unable to capture it.

Thursday, 2nd December

After yesterday I am trying to get my mind focused on the job I am here to do—there is no time for careful selection of materials. I need to be clear-minded and impersonal, approaching my subjects without sentimentality. I paint what I see, whether it's a shattered world, an act of courage and comradeship, or the incredible endurance of these men. That they keep going day after day, week after week, after seeing what they've seen, what I see—the waste and loss—I can only admire their courage.

Friday, 3rd December

*Watkins cornered me again today to ask about the painting;
he said that life could get pretty hard in a unit without
people looking out for you. I know it was a threat but I
don't have the materials to do what he wants me to. The
supply ship was sunk and Belgian linen is a luxury we no
longer have. Painting on anything else would just be a waste
of time.*

Each page of Jack's diary was a private arsenal of drawings: roughly
sketched civilians, picturesque towns, solitary figures, a pictorial
army, an abandoned battlefield or intricate renders of war machines.
A scribbled tank with the note 'Tank transporter' scrawled in pencil
beside it—and, overleaf, the detailed picture of a 'Nijmegen-A Sqn. 7
Recce Regt. Daimler 9 x 11'.

Kathryn looked at the next entry, brow creasing at the images that
accompanied it.

Sunday, 5th December

*Weather on Sicily is cooling down. At night it drops to ten
degrees but luckily I still have the jacket I was issued with
and a jumper that I was advised to take. The men are all
wearing cravats to protect them from the dust. I am teaching one of the corporals how to draw. Benedict, he's only a
boy, two years out of school, and I think it does him good
to take his mind off things especially at night when he says
he can't sleep. He's very quiet around the other men but he
talks to me in the evenings so I give him a lesson whenever
possible. The vistas during the day give ample opportunities*

to paint with all the undergrowth but at night we wonder whether it hides the enemy.

Monday, 6th December
I am hoping that they will not move our camp for a few days since we have not been in the same place for more than one or two nights the entire time. Our position here at the foothills just outside the village is ideal; we are protected, there is a natural spring that we can bathe in and the first fresh water in days. Benedict has set up the equipment inside the tent that I have been lumbering around for the past few weeks, and there's a small table and a chair to paint at and an empty water drum to hold my equipment. His lessons will really come along if we are able to stay here for a few days. Today I'm going to teach him how to do a face and while he does that I will get on with a letter for my darling girl.

There it was, a mention of his darling girl. So it seemed he'd still loved Eleanor, more than a year after saying goodbye. It spurred her on.

Tuesday, 7th December
Tonight Benedict painted a sleeping soldier but then finished off by putting a knife through him so I am going to suggest a still life tomorrow. He says it's not that he can't sleep, it's that he doesn't want to because he doesn't know if he will wake up again. I got him working on structure and composition, and I told him that his first consideration in painting the finished picture is design; that everything counts on this planning of the basic rhythms.

At the bottom of the page, a tiny figure stooped over a wall drawing; Kathryn guessed it was Benedict by the thickness of his hair and the slender oval face.

Wednesday, 8th December
Letters arrived today but nothing for me, and I wonder if my letters have been getting through. Perhaps that's what Watkins meant by making my life difficult although I relented and painted his picture for him. It should leave today and I am sending letters home for Christmas including a card I sketched that should amuse Mum and Beth. It has rained for five days; I am sure that must be more than at home.

Friday, 10th December
I know that it's not possible to feel any worse, now that I've seen so many dead and mortally injured; I know it's not possible to feel two or three hundred times worse if I were to see two or three hundred more dead people but I should like to know for sure. The chaplain spoke of our men tonight, the ones we lost this week, and I can't bear to think about it anymore. I've been invited to the officers' mess and I'm going to take them up on it.

Saturday, 11th December
There were a few sore heads this morning, mine included. We had to buy the gin and lime but I won at cards and was able to bargain for the round. Benedict was not allowed

in but I managed to sneak him out a drink, which he was grateful for.

Sunday, 12th December
I told Benedict that I had no predisposition or special skills. I used to make models like any child, sometimes I would use scale drawings out of magazines but at school we learned to draw anything and everything. I drew my family and other people, and their pets too. I went to work with my father sometimes and drew the men working on their vehicles. I was never very interested in the machinery of war growing up like the other boys, but out here where it wields power, it feels very different. These inanimate objects of metal and man-made materials are used to reduce flesh—there were hours that I spent thinking about the awful irony of it all and how we could not see what we were doing. I studied these machines from a distance but reproduced the images with detail and precision.

Tuesday, 14th December
Benedict has stopped painting; he said that he was glad he had done it because he understood what I did, how I was writing letters home for these people, showing their lives to their loved ones. He said he understood and didn't need my help anymore. I would have liked to share that moment more than any other with my darling girl who has showed me the joy in helping others to paint.

My darling girl: it was as good as seeing Eleanor's name. Kathryn flicked through the rest of the pages but couldn't see another mention.

> *Wednesday, 15th December*
> *Maybe it was good that Benedict stopped coming when he did. I would have soon had to show him my work. The pictures that he hasn't yet seen are pits full of corpses, naked and starved skeletal remains. I would have told him to do as I do, not look on them as bodies but as a series of forms within a picture, nothing more than charred lumpy joints, emaciated limbs. I could show him and tell him that I was giving them a legacy, or I could just keep them hidden for now.*

This was the first time that she had seen Jack write in this way. Most of his other entries were optimistic, certain of his task, and none had been so grim. It seemed the bloodshed had started getting to him—surely it would to anyone, after a time.

She glanced up at Alexander, who had gone back to his book, the falling dusk painting him in half-light. She needed to hurry; she didn't want to outstay her welcome, and there was still a third of the diary yet to read.

'I'm just going to listen to the news quietly,' the professor told her, looking over. 'I'll try not to disturb you.'

'Don't mind me,' she said with a smile. 'I appreciate you letting me be here.'

He turned the television on and the six o'clock news was playing, the suited newsreader standing up from behind the desk and walking towards the camera. The headlines were about clashes in Somalia, and the number of civilians killed. The footage showed distraught relatives grieving over small covered bodies. Kathryn pulled her attention back to the diary, one ear on the unfolding events.

Thursday, 16th December

The air is thick with lemon and frangipani, and I'm finding it hard to reconcile the beauty of this place with what lies beyond the walls—knowing that tomorrow morning any one of these young lives could be taken. Is it enough to merely record this war, is it enough to honour their bravery with a flick of the wrist and a few lines here and there? I have dozens of them, small thumbnails on buff paper; interrupted lives, men re-visioned in shades of light and dark. It's hard not to be melancholy, especially when there is a constant haze of dust and smoke on the horizon.

Friday, 17th December

I am striving for the right combination of design and colour to communicate the sombreness of this place. I have just finished a picture of the horses that we passed yesterday, villages that had been abandoned with animals that had been killed and horses slaughtered rather than have them fall into enemy hands.

Sunday, 19th December

We've been on standby for three days and it's hard to get drawing done on the boat with all the movement. The men are getting a bit jittery, it's hot and cramped and the training exercises have taken up the last two nights whilst the

Canadian nurses have kept the officers busy in the ward-room. I'm too tired to write anymore.

Tuesday, 21st December
We are to move camp so the men are having a quick break-fast of grapefruit juice, fried egg and bacon. I know I should eat too but I can't keep anything down when we are on the move. It's more time to pack my gear and make sure I've got everything I need. Watkins has told me that I'm going in the last vehicle along with the other war correspondents.

Thursday, 23rd December
Thankfully the water is calm now and the storm has settled as I haven't been able to draw for two days with rough seas and the flying spray. We watched the sunset and I sketched our first sunset here; the sun was a golden orb over the indigo sea and some of the biggest cumulus clouds I have ever seen; all number of shades of orange, lilac, grey and mauve.

Friday, 24th December
We pulled anchor at midday and left Sicily. Locals in small boats sang as we left and we were given a special send-off that lifted the men's spirits briefly. It's a shame to be leaving, the landscape is beautiful and I've several thumbnails that I want to work up when we reach our next port of call.

Saturday, 25th December
Christmas Day and I was invited into the wardroom, I thought it would be a chance to cool down but the fans

weren't working and I was forced to buy a round of drinks. Some of them went ashore today so are trading fruit and peanuts instead of money. Bowls of grapes, oranges and melons have been put around but the men are more interested in the rum. The gramophone plays Glenn Miller and Peggy Lee non-stop and outside the searchlights don't look eerie but beautiful instead; it is one of those times when war becomes surreal. I'm not sure I can ever capture that but I must do my best for the men. Their lives are not just shades of light and dark, but lives lived in the full spectrum of colour.

How vivid and beautiful his descriptions were, and how interesting that he was representing them in pictorial form when she would just as happily have read the words and used her imagination—they drew her into the events of war, unlike the coverage now. On TV, the newsreader was talking about ethnic clashes in Kyrgyzstan, and she wondered when she had become so desensitised.

Sunday, 26th December

Boxing Day and Watkins gave me a book to read. I was able to talk to him afterwards, philosophical discussion on the benefits of having a war photographer rather than a war artist after he confessed that he wasn't aware of any real difference. He said he believes that having a photographer who records events is more advantageous than a war artist who is charged with interpreting events, so I think we will need a few more nights of discussion, and perhaps some more rum or gin.

That was the last page. She closed the diary and stared down at its linen cover tasting bitter disappointment—or was it defeat?

What next? There was little to keep her in England now, but also nothing that she could offer her grandmother in the way of answers. Although, with her discovery of the *Children in the Attic* painting and the engagement, hopefully Eleanor would supply some answers of her own.

Kathryn realised that Alexander had turned off the TV and was looking at her expectantly.

'It just ends,' she told him, trying not to sound too disappointed as she placed the diary back in its velvet-lined case. 'I still don't know what happened to Jack. But thank you very much for showing it to me.'

'My pleasure, it was lovely to meet you. Would you like a drink— perhaps a glass of wine before you head home?'

'Thank you, but I should really get going.' She smiled and picked up her handbag.

'Wait a moment,' Alexander said suddenly. 'There's something I forgot to mention.'

'Yes?'

'I didn't buy the diary at auction—it was a private sale. Strange story, really. The seller wanted to remain anonymous. I'm not sure why. It's hard in our small circle. And anyway, as I said, you can't be anonymous with the internet.'

Well, this was intriguing. Kathryn felt a surge of hope. 'So you know who it is?'

'Oh yes, his name is Aldridge. Part of the family, by all accounts— needed the money.'

Her heart started pounding. 'Was it Stephen . . . Stephen Aldridge?'

'No, Timothy. His brother. He lives overseas. The strange thing is, I'm not supposed to disclose the fact that I have it to anyone. You just sounded so desperate that I had to show it to you, but you really mustn't tell anyone that it's here—except your grandmother, of course. It's our little secret.'

'Yes, of course,' Kathryn said as she gave him a reassuring smile. But her mind was racing, wondering why Stephen's brother would want a secret sale: so as not to upset the rest of the family, perhaps, who wanted to keep the diaries safe and private. Or was there something specific about Jack that the Aldridges were trying to hide?

She followed Alexander to his front door and shook his hand.

'I'm glad we were able to help each other,' he said warmly. 'Please get in touch when you've spoken to your grandmother—I would love to come over and see her paintings.'

'Yes, of course. And thank you again.'

Kathryn felt the sudden need to walk, get some air and think. After so much time indoors she was missing the space and light that she took for granted in Melbourne.

The rain had stopped and the pavements glistened in the warm, dusky night. The city felt cleansed, the promise of a clear night ahead, and Kathryn relished the sharpness of her breath as she began to walk. Houses along the mews were lit from inside, throwing crosses from their sash windows onto the road, while classical music from an open doorway created a strangely mystical atmosphere.

It would be an hour's walk to Charing Cross and the train home, but her route would take her down to the Bayswater Road, through Hyde Park and Green Park and along the Mall, where Eleanor and Jack had spent much of their time. Following in their footsteps, Kathryn could imagine herself back there with them while she sifted through the different elements and made sure she hadn't missed anything.

But instead of turning south onto Craven Road, she found she was walking north, turning left into Chilworth Street towards Cleveland Square. The Regency streetlamps flickered, illuminating the road and pavements. She wasn't thinking about dawn on the other side of the world, and Chris and Oliver starting their day; her thoughts were on Jack aboard the ship, watching the Verey lights brightening the skies, and of Eleanor back home, standing at her window as the searchlights crisscrossed the night, and of the thousands of miles between them.

Kathryn reached number eight and stood gazing up at the first-floor balcony, her thoughts fixed on Jack and Eleanor and the time they'd spent here all those decades ago.

She had got to know Jack, listened to his thoughts and seen his work, and in the process drawn her own portrait of a man who cared deeply, who showed a profound humanity—and who wouldn't abandon the woman he loved without cause.

PART V

Barrage Balloons

'Innumerable books will be written about every aspect of the conflict. But it is certain that there will be no more astonishing story than the story which is illustrated in such publications as this; the story of how the humble and the obscure, whose names the world will never hear, and who had never asked anything of life but the opportunity to follow their own occupations and manage their own homes in security, suddenly found themselves in the midst of a besieged fortress.'

J.B. MORTON, *War Pictures by British Artists, BLITZ,*
OXFORD UNIVERSITY PRESS, 1942, PAGE 8

Twenty-eight

LONDON, DECEMBER 1942

Quills of orange light and yellow swords speared the sky as the sun lowered towards the horizon, the paint thinning to a soft peach hue at the edge of the frame, the dark silhouettes of London's buildings catching the fading light. Jack's painting was propped against the mirror on her dressing table, his other canvases leaning on perfume bottles either side, more dotted around the room. Eleanor recalled the night they'd painted together on the rooftop, and what she'd said before he had given her the picture: *You have captured the colours perfectly. I shall call it* The Crimson Sun.

In the weeks since he had left, she'd surrounded herself with his pictures, but they hadn't lessened her sense of loss, the deep, gnawing ache. Even the bundle of his miniature sketches didn't bring the same comfort it initially had. All the same, she carried some around in her coat pocket because it meant something to close her fingers around them, to think that she was touching where he had touched.

'Come on, Ellie. Are you nearly ready?' Cecily's voice sounded from the other side of the closed door. 'We'll be late.'

'Coming . . .'

The truth was that Eleanor really didn't want to go anywhere, she would much rather just crawl back into bed, hide under the eiderdown and not get up until the war was over and Jack was home. But she knew she couldn't do that, that Cecily was relying on her, so she pulled on her jacket, insouciantly applied some colour to her lips and grabbed her leather satchel—stopping only to check that all the supplies she needed were inside. It was larger than the one she usually carried because she had recently started taking a sketchpad, a small palette, wrapped brushes, and a selection of pencils and pastels wherever she went. They were for the detours she made on the way home from work, arriving well after Cecily had gone to bed.

The tide had turned for the sisters. Cecily was now the one in control, telling Eleanor that what she was doing would do her no good; that she needed to get more sleep and look after herself. But Cecily didn't understand how she felt—how could she now that she had Harry?

At least when Eleanor went to the front lines here, it was as if she was closer to Jack; it was easier to picture what he saw, imagine how he felt. Earlier that week she'd been to the Air Raid Precautions depot to sketch the wardens and nurses doing their drills, and at the weekend she had ventured down to Clapham to watch the barrage balloons being hoisted on the common. She'd found herself surrounded by an ocean of them rising from the ground like eerie sea monsters, cumbersome beasts from a children's story. The balloons were filled with helium and then tested, the wire cables checked, and then came the surreal sight of their launch, dozens of them hovering seven thousand feet off the ground, while men and women were in a tug of war, hand over hand hitching them higher.

Intimidated by the physicality of the work, Eleanor had found a quiet spot in the corner of the park where she sat and sketched. She didn't intend to show the pictures to anyone—except to Jack when he came back—but she found solace and purpose in creating them. It had become increasingly hard to find the time, with each day filled with work for the Ministry or the committee, and following the news with a renewed interest, knowing that the papers and wireless would only reveal part of the story. At the weekly committee meetings she listened ever more intently to the members, trying to discern between speculation and fact. There had only been one very brief letter from Jack, and she was desperate for anything that would give her a sense of where and how he was.

There was a light tap at the bedroom door. 'Eleanor, are you okay?' her sister asked.

Cecily was waiting for her, dressed in full nurse's uniform and thick dark cape.

'Sorry,' Eleanor said, mustering a smile.

'Ready?'

'As I will ever be,' she said, pulling on her gloves decisively and walking past her sister and out the front door.

Once on the street they overtook the other pedestrians, walking quickly despite a thick frost that decorated the pavements and windows.

'Slow down,' Cecily said, grabbing hold of Eleanor's arm. 'We've seen more patients injured through accidents than war this week—this snow and ice is lethal.'

'Alright, but if we are late we are late,' Eleanor said, resigning herself and slowing down.

'Well, I can't be late to work,' Cecily said, pulling a face.

'I know, that's why we're hurrying.' Eleanor sighed. 'What is it today, anyway?'

'Theatre nursing.'

'So what are you going to do—a song or a dance?'

'Very funny. No, it's surgical nursing.'

'Oh dear, that sounds much more tricky. Do you want me to test you?'

'It's a little late for that now. A bit of help last night would not have gone amiss.'

'Sorry,' Eleanor said, pouting at her as they carried on walking arm in arm.

'Don't worry, if I don't know it by now, I never will.'

'You were in the St John's Ambulance Brigade—you'll be fine.'

'It is a little different, Ellie.'

'Yes, I'm sure.' She smiled at her sister. 'How about I help you tonight?'

'I've got a day off tomorrow,' said Cecily. 'Actually, I've invited Lindsay and Harry over tonight. I think Frank and Pauline might drop by too if they're not on duty.'

'Oh, really; can't we have a quiet one? Just the two of us?'

'I invited them over for *you*. You can't just hide yourself away—you have a duty to your friends too, you know.'

Cecily was right. Eleanor hadn't seen their friends in weeks, preferring her own company. She had stopped contacting them and so they had eventually stopped calling, and the worst thing about it was that she was pleased; she was getting the punishment she deserved for sending Jack away. It wasn't just that she didn't want to be surrounded by happy couples; if he couldn't see anyone or do anything, then it was only fair that she couldn't either.

'I see', Eleanor replied. 'Well, I thought I was here to look after you. I hope you aren't passing on any of your intelligence to high command—I would hate for Father to recall me if he knew I wasn't doing my job properly anymore.'

'Don't worry, your mission was accomplished,' Cecily said, smiling.

Maybe Eleanor's sister didn't need her quite so much after all. And it would be good to lighten their parents' load—especially with the ongoing concern over Francis's rehabilitation.

'Anyway, this is me,' Cecily said as they reached the corner of Craven Road and Gloucester Terrace. 'I'll see you tonight. And don't forget about supper.'

'I'll try to be there, I promise,' Eleanor called as Cecily walked away, casting a withering glance over her shoulder.

Eleanor fully intended to make the evening gathering, despite the busy day ahead—there was the committee meeting to prepare for and paperwork to complete for the newly redecorated restaurants in south-east London. She was due to visit the last one that morning and file the report in the afternoon—but as soon as she arrived at Portman Square and found Clive idling in the parked car outside, she made her decision.

'It's a supply problem,' she told him as they drove towards Richmond. 'If we can get the younger generation trained and ready, then we shall not run out of pictures, and we know that will be to everyone's advantage—don't we, Clive?'

'Yes, it certainly will, miss, and the younger the better,' he said, nodding.

It had been preying on her mind for some time that they hadn't made it to the orphanage as she had promised. She had twice planned a visit and then had to rearrange it for one reason or another.

There was so little that one had any control over with this damned war that to make a small promise and keep it really seemed nothing at all. Nevertheless, Miss Short looked quite flustered when Eleanor arrived, and quickly showed her through to a small room at the back of the orphanage, where the children were having morning tea. Bare floorboards and cracked windows were doing a poor job of keeping the cold out, and the children were trussed up in their coats and scarves like the Christmas turkeys that very few of them would be having in a couple of weeks. They were eating egg sandwiches and yawning, and the smell made Eleanor suddenly feel quite nauseated; she really would need to have a word with Clive about his driving.

'Good morning, children,' she said, but they just carried on eating.

Miss Short looked apologetic and smiled. 'Come now, children. Remember your manners. Say good morning to Miss Roy.'

'Good morning, Miss Roy,' they chanted, voices barely audible.

Eleanor stood smiling at the front of the class, recognising one or two faces—Isaac and Sally were still here—but mostly they were a different batch of children from the ones at the garage and altogether more timid. And now that she was here she wasn't sure how to begin; she had looked forward to seeing them again, imagining their faces lighting up as they had before, so that she hadn't paid much attention to what she was actually going to do.

Then she remembered Isaac's special colours: when they had met in the garage, he'd told her that he wanted to paint his father's new motorcycle, how its body was a British racing-car green and how the chrome gleamed like the icing on a cake. And how his father would never have the chance to ride it now.

She unpacked her satchel, placing the palette and brushes on the desk in front of her. She was dismally low on paint and had considered putting in a special order with Supplies but decided it wouldn't be looked on very favourably when paint was desperately needed elsewhere.

Getting down on her knees so that she was level with them, she spoke in a soft, low voice. 'Now, last time we met, Isaac had an idea of what he would like to paint, so maybe the rest of you could spend a few minutes thinking about a picture that you would like to paint.'

One boy lay sprawled across the floor just in front, eyes fixed under one of the chairs, while the younger ones cast their eyes about thinking, as if the corners of the room might hold the key.

A moment passed and then one of the girls shot her arm up. 'Please, miss . . .'

'Yes—' Eleanor glanced at Miss Short.

'Daisy,' Miss Short whispered.

'Yes, Daisy?' Eleanor asked.

'How do you know what to paint?'

A simple enough question, but Eleanor struggled to find an answer; it was an instinct to her, but how could she explain that to a child? 'Well, Daisy, you look around and see what takes your interest. And then you think how you might like the shape and the colour of it to appear, how you might paint it the same or make it look different on the page.'

'Is that *all*?' a young fair-haired boy said.

'It can be that simple to decide, but it's a whole different story actually completing your picture,' Eleanor replied.

'Why?'

'Well, there are a lot of important decisions to be made. As the artist, you have to choose how to start your picture,' she said with a smile. 'Do you copy the shapes or the colours? Do you use the same colours or chose your own and use your imagination?'

'How, Miss Roy?' Daisy asked.

'Give them an example,' Miss Short advised quietly.

Eleanor thought for a moment and then told them about seeing the barrage balloons being hoisted—how they were filled with helium and how she imagined them to be sea monsters.

Daisy smiled when she finished. 'How many brushes do you have?'

'Have you got the green paint?' Isaac said, coming forward.

Three other girls also got up from their chairs and came to look at the materials Eleanor had placed on the desk.

Now she could see Daisy properly, she noticed her cardigan buttons were mismatched; the top two were without their buttons and the bottom two without their holes. There was something equally unkempt about the girl: her hair was fine and fair but matted into clumps, her fingernails were black and her complexion was pale, her skin dirty in places. And there was something about her fragility that reminded Eleanor of her own sister, how Cecily had also seemed more vulnerable than the other children.

'Enough for all of you,' Eleanor answered, fuelled by a rush of emotion. She suddenly felt teary, the children exposing a susceptibility that she had been keeping inside. 'This cold weather always makes my eyes water,' she murmured, wiping tears from the corners of her eyes. Then she remembered the few prints that she had ready for inclusion in the War Artists' picture books that were being printed the next day.

'I have a treat for you,' she said, bending down too quickly and becoming unusually dizzy. When she recovered, she showed them a picture of a Women's Auxiliary Air Force opening the air vent from a barrage balloon as it sank to the ground, then a picture of two Wrens transmitting a message in Morse. But the children didn't respond. Next she chose a picture of servicemen working at RAF Fighter Command Station as it came under attack from enemy bombs, and they just gazed at it as if mesmerised by the flames.

'How do these pictures make you feel?' she asked, not yet ready to give up.

'Sad,' said one boy.

'Frightened,' said a girl.

Eleanor glanced at Miss Short, who grimaced.

'Lonely?' Daisy said.

Oh dear, it wasn't going at all how Eleanor had expected—so much for her mother and father's belief that she would make a good teacher, that she was a natural. It was harder than she'd thought. What would Jack have said if he was here now; how would he have tempted them out of their shells? She wondered how he had earned the trust of those children in the attic.

Then she felt for the bundle in her pocket. Jack wasn't there to help her, but his pictures were. She took out the miniature sketches, the representations of London and their life. They weren't faceless depictions of war but the parks and gardens they had walked in, the shops and cafes they'd visited, and the people in their neighbourhood. There weren't any uniforms or soldiers, or battle scenes or devastated buildings; there was no evidence of war, only communities.

She leaned closer to Daisy. 'You're right,' she said, 'these other pictures might frighten you because of what's going on around us now, but *these*—' she passed around the small pieces of paper '—these show that the important parts of our neighbourhoods haven't changed.'

The children handed the pictures to each other, heads bent in concentration.

Daisy clung on to the images for longer than the others did. 'I can paint our garden before they dug it up for the shelter,' she said.

'I'll paint my old dog, Gladstone,' a boy suggested.

Eleanor glanced at Miss Short, who appeared more relaxed.

'Good,' Eleanor said, 'you have the idea now. So who is going to help me fill these jars with water?'

Several hands shot up.

'And who is going to give out the paper?'

Sally stretched her hand so high that her bottom lifted off her chair. 'Can I, miss?'

'Yes, Sally. Of course.'

Eleanor split the paint onto saucers and set them out for the children. 'Now, Isaac,' she said, coming up behind him, 'I've got something special for you.' She opened another palette to reveal a dark green paint and, in the hole next to it, a gleaming silver white.

His face broke into a wide smile. 'How did you get it like that?'

'It's a trade secret,' she said playfully.

She really couldn't tell him that she'd mixed pearl dust through the paint, giving it an iridescent quality; the dust was expensive at the best of times, let alone its premium now for industrial use—as well as for beautifying the necks of Britain's upper classes.

Eleanor didn't know how the morning would go after her shaky start, or if the children would enjoy it, but there were some amazing results. Isaac's depiction of his father's motorcycle was remarkable despite the wonky wheels. Gladstone, the family dog, was coloured with all the brown and white irregularity Eleanor would expect from its eight-year-old owner, and the suburban garden that Daisy painted was complete with vegetable patch and flowerbeds boasting large yellow heads of sunflowers.

When the lunch bell rang and it was time for Eleanor to leave, Miss Short seemed reluctant to say goodbye. 'You know, I've not seen the children so calm and happy in quite some time.'

'That's wonderful—I shall leave you the paints and what paper there is left. Perhaps you can try giving them another lesson?'

Miss Short shook her head. 'It's really not the same,' she said. 'I don't know the first thing about drawing.'

'That doesn't matter, it seems they just need some encouragement.'

'But they respond so well to you!'

'You know that I can't commit to coming again,' Eleanor said in the slow, deliberate voice she had reserved for the children. 'What with the restaurants I have to visit and the work for the committee, there just isn't enough time. I would love to, really I would.'

'I understand,' Miss Short said, 'but will you think about it?'

The children were lining up, eager to show Eleanor their work, and she took turns responding to each one. Sally gave her the picture of her bus and begged her to keep it, and Daisy clung to her arm as she tried to leave. So despite the draughty room, and her concern about the children's futures, she felt warmed—it was the first time since Jack had left that she felt at peace, and that something really mattered.

Twenty-nine

Mr Steadman didn't come into work for the rest of the week, and when he did arrive the following Tuesday morning, he went straight into his office and closed the door. At lunchtime Eleanor knocked gently and waited until she heard the invitation to come in.

'Good morning, Mr Steadman.'

'Hello, Eleanor,' he said, not the formal address he usually used.

The office was unusually warm, the air stale since it had been locked up for days, and Steadman stood behind his desk, staring out of the unopened window, shoulders slouched.

'Is everything alright?' Eleanor asked.

When he turned it was the first time she had seen him without glasses, and his features were softer, eyes more vulnerable.

'George is gone,' he said.

It took a moment for the news to register. 'I am so sorry . . .'

He attempted a smile but it was a grimace, lips tightening over his teeth.

She moved closer. 'What happened?'

'He was shot. It was quick—which everyone keeps telling me we have to be thankful for!'

'They mean well . . . It can't make it any easier, though.'

'I would like to tell you that it does, but it doesn't.'

Eleanor nodded. 'And how is Mrs Steadman?'

George was their only child, and Mr Steadman had often regaled the office with stories of how she spoiled the boy. And George was no more than a boy, just seventeen.

'I don't really know—she won't talk. She hasn't eaten. The doctor said she's still in shock. You know it's hard when you can't see them to know they're gone . . . when you can't bury them.'

Eleanor didn't know but she thought of Jack, and of Clarence. Yesterday her parents had said that Francis was recovering well but that there was still no news of Clarence, and his fleet was part of the same Far East campaign as George's. No one really knew what was happening over there, so her family could only offer each other optimistic clichés of support: *I'm sure he'll be fine*, and, *He's a Roy: he's made of strong fettle*.

'Anyway, let's keep busy,' Steadman said with forced energy. 'Why don't you pull up a chair and we'll review the report together?'

'Of course, Mr Steadman. If that's what you want.'

She took a seat opposite him, pleased at the chance to sit down but regretting she couldn't just leave the report on his desk as she'd intended. There was only so much discussion one could have about cream and brown paint and checked tablecloths. But it wasn't as if she could complain: he needed her. So she told him instead how pleased she was with the way decoration in their region was progressing.

She had to take several breaks to yawn and then apologise. For reasons that she failed to understand—she was eating the same and getting as much sleep as ever—she felt so tired, lacking in energy, so that it seemed more of an effort to do her jobs.

As Steadman flicked through the report, she wrapped her arms around herself and thought about how the contrast between the work for the WAAC and the work for the Ministry could not have been greater. While she was liaising with war artists to submit works for a second set of *War Pictures by British Artists*, she was also talking to Supplies about arranging distemper for painting the restaurants' public conveniences. One day she was liaising with Captain William Coldstream on his introduction for the new booklet, *Soldiers*, and the next she was diplomatically pointing out how one coat of paint wasn't nearly as good as two to an apprentice painter.

'I see from your summary that you are satisfied with the work,' said Steadman. 'That the results are what we hoped for.'

'Yes, sir. In most places they have done a good job of the painting, given the limited choice of colours. You will see that there is only Apricot, Golden Brown and Celadon Green paint, and Ivory, Old Gold and Adams Green distemper to choose from . . .'

'Oh, I see.'

'And I do say that the exteriors are generally a little depressing, owing to the shortage of time and materials, but that it's the right thing to place importance on redecorating the interiors.'

'Quite so, Eleanor. Quite so.'

'The restaurants all displayed the standard signage too: dark red or brown entranceways, and the simple style of lettering on all the signs.'

'So they are all quite uniform?'

'Mostly—a few have displayed some originality,' she said, still cold and decidedly queasy. 'A restaurant in Morden has been adapted from an old laundry, and they have made good use of an unpromising situation.'

She and Steadman discussed the report in detail: the church hall in Blackheath where artists had used the old gold casement cloth to transform the blackout blinds, and painted the walls and ceiling ivory with Celadon Green dado; the Woolwich restaurant that featured an attractive menu board of waxed wood with slots for daily menus, but that she noted could do with some murals; and the Manor Lane restaurant that had five good replica colour panels of Gauguin and Van Gogh.

And then there was the Stockwell Restaurant, part of Stockwell orphanage, which she decided to raise with Steadman.

'The very large hall in Stockwell has been divided in two by a large mural. The artists used stretched hessian and have created a canvas of local interest. It suits the space really well . . .' She paused to take a breath and fight the rising bile. 'They have also covered the blackouts at the windows with pleated blue paper and artworks by the children—'

Eleanor was about to explain what a good contrast it made to the brown walls and ceiling, when dizziness took hold, and her head became so leaden that she had to put it between her knees.

Mr Steadman got to his feet and came around the desk. 'Are you quite alright, Miss Roy? Can we get you something, some water?'

'No, I'm afraid not. I think I'm going to be sick . . .'

'Miss Sullivan, Miss Sullivan! Bring a bowl,' Mr Steadman shouted, flustered and hurrying into the outer office. 'Can you please come and see to Miss Roy?'

Eleanor was wondering what made her feel worse, her embarrassment at being ill in front of Steadman or her regret at eating breakfast at the Stockwell restaurant, when she realised Maura wouldn't be there in time—and she reached for the rubbish bin.

Cecily emptied the contents of her nurse's bag onto the table next to the sofa where Eleanor lay, head tilted backwards to rest on the arm cushion. Cecily had taken her sister's blood pressure and temperature; she had looked in her ears and throat, and even examined her skin for a rash or spots. The thirty-ninth edition of *First Aid to the Injured: The Authorised Textbook of the St John Ambulance Association* lay open alongside as she worked her way through the contents.

'If I didn't know better I would say you are lovesick,' she said, closing the book, 'but I'm afraid there's another much simpler explanation.'

'Can't you just give me a pill or something?' Eleanor groaned. 'I can't bear this sickness any longer.'

'I'm afraid not,' Cecily said, looking earnest as she sat on the sofa and took her hand.

'What is it?' Eleanor asked. She tried to sit upright.

'I haven't been able to help noticing . . .'

'What is it, Cecily? Come on, you're worrying me!'

Cecily had been monitoring her symptoms for a week or so. When at first Eleanor's appetite shrank, her sister had grown worried, and guilty that she might have contaminated her with a disease from the hospital—diphtheria, measles, chicken pox—but Eleanor hadn't lost weight, and there were no spots, pustules or coughs.

'When was the last time you used rags?' Cecily asked.

Eleanor stared at her sister, trying to remember. There hadn't been any need for them last month, or the month before that—but then she had put it down to being exhausted.

Eleanor moved her hands down to her belly and cradled it, noticing that it felt more solid, not as soft as it used to be.

'Really . . .'. She swallowed. 'Do you really think that I am . . . ?'

'I don't know the answer to that, Ellie—only you do. Could you be?'

Eleanor looked at her sister's soft oval face, the pale trusting eyes that returned her questioning gaze, before they disappeared behind a wall of tears.

'Yes, Cecily . . . I could be,' she replied. 'But we were so careful.' The tears were springing from her eyes.

'Oh, Eleanor, why didn't you talk to me? I could have shown you how to be safer.'

But it was too late, and Eleanor was sobbing.

'It's alright, Ellie, you're going to be alright,' Cecily said, stroking her hair.

'What am I going to do?' Eleanor asked between sniffs.

'There is only one thing to do.'

'What?' Eleanor said, nervous of the reply.

'We need to find Jack and get him back here to marry you as soon as possible.'

Eleanor shook her head, her face in her hands. 'But I don't know where he is.'

'Someone must,' Cecily replied.

There hadn't been a letter in weeks, and that had only come through the WAAC via the batch of paintings that Jack had sent. It had included a section of hand-painted canvas, the fragment of a tent that he had painted a baroque ceiling on. Far from amusing her as she guessed he had hoped it would, she could only imagine what had happened to the rest of it.

She would need to ask for Aubrey's help and hope that the professor could use his influence through the committee to find her fiancé.

Over the balcony, the sun was burnishing the treetops, and she stared at its weakening light. In another time and another place, she would be overjoyed by the news that she was to become a mother, by the miracle of a new life.

Eleanor reached out for her sister's hand, clutching it tightly. 'What if I can't find him? What will happen to me then? Father won't want to know me.'

'We will find him, Ellie. Don't worry. We will find Jack.'

Thirty

The sparse office held the lingering bitterness of tobacco and the citrus of Aubrey Powell's pomade. It was his first pipe of the day and he coughed uncontrollably for a few seconds before taking a sip of water and being able to carry on. The courier had delivered the package the night before and it was waiting for him on the desk when he arrived. He recognised Jack's handwriting straight away and slid the silver letter opener along the flap carefully so as not to damage the contents.

These were the thumbnails that he expected but there were also several larger sketches, depictions of manoeuvres in the field, foreign territory, cryptic notes drawn down the sides. Jack was working out better than any of them had anticipated, given the speed with which he worked, the precision of his drawings and the information that could be gleaned from them. But he had also proven effective with counterespionage, drawing the false maps and intelligence that they had handed to the Italian resistance; misinformation that had been passed up the ranks and been acted upon.

Aubrey put the thumbnails back in the envelope and placed them to one side. After studying the larger drawings a moment longer, he put them in a pouch and called through to his secretary. She appeared in his doorway. 'Miss Ross, please can you give these to the courier for Baker Street?' he said.

Aubrey waited for her to leave before turning his attention to the letter addressed to Eleanor—hesitating, on the verge of opening it, but deciding that it would be immoral. Instead he tore it into small pieces and threw it into the fire-grate. He justified this as he watched the paper curl and burn; he really had no choice. The SOE had been quite clear that there was to be no outside contact—not with family or with his fiancée. It was due to a momentary weakness, and an attempt to make Eleanor happy, that he had let one letter through, but there couldn't be any more—no risk of double agents or anyone unknowingly passing on information that could jeopardise their work. Besides, he was saving Eleanor heartache in the long run. And he would stand a better chance with her with Jack out of the way.

The professor put down his pipe and picked up his favourite Sheaffer fountain pen, mentally composing the letter before writing:

> *My dear Eleanor,*
>
> *Thank you for your recent letter and I agree that it is unfortunate that we didn't get to say goodbye in person before your departure. It is with mutual regret that you had to*

leave us and we will miss you greatly, but I am sure that
the valuable assistance you are giving your parents at their
factory will be of equal importance to the war effort as your
work was to the committee. Upon your request, I have made
some inquiries and have it on good authority that Jack is in
good health and is carrying out his duty to his country with
a singular vigour and determination. I am sure that he will
be in contact with you in good time and when his duty al-
lows. Be patient and be proud.
With all good wishes,
Aubrey Powell

At seven o'clock in the morning, a ferocious knocking woke Anne Valante. It continued for the five minutes before she got herself into the wheelchair and manoeuvred it to the front door.

'Alright, I'm coming, I'm coming,' she said as loudly as she could, struggling with the lock.

Two men in civilian clothes, dark suits and trilbies stood just inside the porch. One was unusually tall, his suit sleeves struggling to meet the ends of his arms, wide white cuffs sticking out, and she had to extend her neck uncomfortably to look up at him. His fair hair jutted out at angles from beneath his hat, and long sideburns gathered at the sides of a plump face. The shorter man had a thick, dark moustache above protruding lips and below a prominent nose, and he looked ill at ease.

The taller one appeared to be in charge. 'Mrs Valante? Mrs Anne Valante?'

'Yes. What is it . . . ? Is it Jack?'

'Can we come in, please?'

She was terrified. 'Who are you?' They didn't look like military men, so who in God's name were they and what did they want?

'I have official papers—we need to look around.'

They had squeezed past her and were inside the hallway before she had the chance to object. 'What for? Where are you from?' she asked, swivelling the chair.

The tall man motioned towards the stairs and the shorter man began to climb them.

'He can't go up there . . .' But her protest was ignored.

'Perhaps you and I could go in here,' the tall man said, gesturing to the kitchen.

Anne had little choice but to wheel herself into the room as he followed close behind. She watched nervously when he started opening the cupboard doors.

'Have you heard from Jack?' he asked, pulling out a drawer and shuffling through its contents.

'No, why?'

'Just answer my questions, Mrs Valante.'

There was a loud thud from above, then the sound of furniture being moved and doors banging.

'What's he doing upstairs?' she asked. 'What are you looking for?'

'That's confidential, madam.'

'He needs to be careful, please go and tell him. Those are Jack's things, my things . . .'

Even if she'd been able-bodied, what could she have done? Her fingers gripped the wheels even tighter as she spun the chair and followed the man into the living room.

'Why don't you just tell me what you're looking for?' she asked insistently.

He ignored her and carried on, opening the drawers of the writing bureau.

'Please?' she asked.

'I'm afraid I can't discuss that. Just let us do our job. We won't be here for long.'

The telephone was within easy reach, and it was early enough that Elizabeth would probably still be at home—but then the smaller man appeared at the top of the stairs, canvases tucked under each arm.

'You can't take those,' Anne said, shaken. 'They don't belong to you.'

He glanced at his colleague before answering. 'I'm sorry, Mrs Valante. We have our orders.'

'But those pictures are all that I have of him.' Her eyes filled with tears.

'Again, we're sorry to disturb you. Good morning, Mrs Valante.'

And they walked out, leaving her sobbing in the hallway.

Thirty-one

KENT, 2010

The sickly sweetness of the tiny white flowers overwhelmed Kathryn as she snipped away at the star jasmine and fought the desire to sneeze. She was clearing a view out of the pagoda so that they could see across the length of the garden and up to the house. The old wooden structure was totally overgrown and had fallen into disrepair, and with no one around to fix it, Eleanor had stopped coming down here.

'See, isn't that better?' Kathryn said as she stood back, admiring the view through the newly created window and down the hillside to the orchards.

Eleanor was sitting on a bench at the ornamental table, camel coat buttoned up to her chin and tartan blanket spread across her lap, sipping tea as she took in the vista. To the left, fields undulated away to ancient woodlands; orchards and hills dominated the central land-scape; while on the right, hop farms gave way to the spires and chim-neys of the market town of Tonbridge in the distance.

'I can see you haven't lost your green fingers,' Eleanor said, casting Kathryn a look.

'Green thumbs—that's what you say in Australia.'

'How strange,' Eleanor said, looking thoughtful. 'Can't see how your thumb is more important than your fingers.'

'I know. It's just one of those terms that you have to get used to, like "chips" instead of "crisps".'

Kathryn had got used to lots of things, and Australian native plants were one of them, she thought as she carried on pruning. It had taken her a while to get used to the spiky shrubs and grasses, but now she really liked their structural forms and had evolved her design work to include native gardens if her clients asked for this.

'You know, you could come and visit us, Gran,' she said. 'You could cruise over on one of the big P & O liners, like you and Grand-pops used to.'

'I don't think I've got it in me, Katie.'

'Really? I don't know about that.'

She was convinced that her grandmother wasn't as vulnerable as she'd first appeared. For now she was testing her theory by getting her outdoors; the next step would be a trip to the local village of Pembury.

'See, we'll have this place back to new in no time,' she said, rearranging the chairs around the cast-iron table.

She had washed down the furniture but now more rust than white paint was visible, and the pagoda itself was in need of proper repair. Chris would have to get the hammer and nails out on their next trip—

It was revealing how her thoughts of the future had changed over the past few days, from doing things on her own to doing them with her husband. Maybe Helen's vision board was working after all, or perhaps it was just the time away that had helped.

The sun was slanting through the trees, the crisp air filled with the song of sandpipers and common snipes. Kathryn sat down and drained the remnants of her coffee, watching the delicate movements of a snipe as it hopped from table to branch and back again, eyeing their breakfast keenly.

But while the clear sunrise and cloudless sky promised a beautiful day, Kathryn's mood was confused. She would be back home in forty-eight hours, and although she had learned so much about her gran and herself on this trip, she hadn't been able to keep the promise she'd made six days ago: *I'll find out what happened to him.*

Eleanor was gazing into the distance, and Kathryn followed her line of sight to where the fence emerged from the orchard, running up the crest of the hill and disappearing over the other side. The trees were lush, the kind she never got tired of looking at, always a new shape or leaf colour to notice, a new texture to inspire her. It was no wonder that so many artists took their cues from nature.

The snipe hopped onto the table, grasped a large crumb in its beak and bobbed its head from side to side as if listening. It reminded Kathryn of Eleanor the night before when they had Skyped with Oliver and Chris.

'So, I'll just sit here and not press a thing,' Eleanor had said plaintively.

'Yes, that's right. Just look into the camera and that's what they can see,' Kathryn reminded her.

'I'm sure I must look a lot younger from here, don't you think, dear?'

'I'm sure you will, Gran. Oli might not be able to tell us apart.' Kathryn clicked on the video icon.

'You're too kind.'

'Hold on, it's ringing now.'

The black screen flickered and Oliver's image appeared, bleary-eyed with hair in tufts.

'Hello, sleepy head,' Kathryn said over Eleanor's shoulder. 'Look who's here to talk to you.'

'Granny!'

'Hello, Oliver. What a treat, I get to see you again!'

'I know—see, you are going to need a computer now. Mummy can get one for you before she leaves.'

'I don't think so,' Eleanor said, then changed the subject. 'Have you done your piano practice?'

His grin turned cheeky. 'Yes . . .'

'Who's that?' Chris's voice sounded in the background. 'Who are you talking to?'

'It's Mummy.'

'It can't be, Mummy's on her way . . . Eleanor, it is you,' he said surprised. 'Where's Kathryn?'

'I'm here.'

'Aren't you supposed to be on your way home?' His tone was accusatory.

'Tomorrow, I just extended it by one day. I'll come straight to the concert when I land,' she said and waited for his reaction.

A pause. 'You look well, Eleanor. Looking after you, is she?' Chris asked with a restrained smile.

Eleanor had dressed for the occasion as though she was going out: silk floral blouse, pearl strand and a stab of pink lipstick.

'Oh yes, very well, thank you,' she said. 'Don't worry, you can have her back soon.'

Kathryn hadn't wanted to ask Eleanor about the paintings until she found the right time, but Oliver brought it up.

'The pictures aren't by the same person, Mummy!' he blurted out.

The colour drained from Eleanor's face.

'How do you know, Oli?' Kathryn asked.

'The same as last time—I just played spot the difference.'

There was some scrabbling around and then he held up printouts of two pictures. 'This one's *Fire Drill at a School* and this is *Children in the Attic*.'

'What can you tell me about them, Oli?' Kathryn asked. 'How do you know really that they're not by the same artist?'

He held them closer, squinting. 'They just look different to me. Why does it matter?'

'It doesn't matter right now, but I think you're right.'

They spent the rest of the call doing a run-through on the piano of *Für Elise*, Oliver's concert piece, and then chatted about how the Nautilus project was going, but Eleanor said very little.

'Are you okay, Gran?' Kathryn asked when the call ended.

'I'm fine,' she said tearfully. 'It's just seeing Oliver. He's growing up so fast.'

Kathryn was sure that this wasn't the real reason, but she hadn't pressed the issue last night. Eleanor had gone to bed and Kathryn had called Chris back and persuaded him to support her decision to stay when she explained all that had happened. Then she had looked at the images again. There was little doubt in her mind.

'Gran,' she said now, her voice soft and forgiving, as they sat together in the brilliant morning light, 'it's your picture, isn't it?'

Eleanor wiped her eyes. She seemed to steel herself before she nodded. 'You're right. I'm sorry. Jack substituted the picture for one of his. I didn't know about it at the time but when I found out I suspected that it might have caused problems for us. That perhaps it was why the committee was so reluctant to help me find him.'

Kathryn felt a surge of anger. Why hadn't Eleanor simply told her this in the beginning? Why had she then lied about it? But she didn't know how to ask her these questions.

'Surely your history with the WAAC must have counted for something?' Kathryn said. 'And weren't they set up partly to support artists like Jack and their families?'

'Yes, I'm sure the committee would have helped under normal circumstances, dear, but apparently they were furious with Jack for substituting the picture.' Eleanor spoke forcefully, as if the memory had brought back the frustrations of her own search all those years ago. 'It called their reputation and credibility into question. Imagine it— if one war artist was discovered representing work that wasn't theirs, who was to say how many others were doing it?' Eleanor shook her head slowly from side to side. 'There was concern about how it would damage the WAAC at home and their standing around the world. Sir Robert would never let that happen.'

Her figure suddenly looked tiny in the seat, and Kathryn detected what seemed to be a look of relief flickering across her face.

'I know what you're thinking,' Eleanor said. 'Was that really enough to have them disassociate themselves from Jack?' She sighed. 'I have asked myself that a hundred times and I can't find any other explanation.'

Kathryn followed the path of the snipe as it took off and soared overhead. Were the insecurities of a past generation really to blame for Jack vanishing from Eleanor's life?

'Is there anything else, Gran, no matter how small?'

Eleanor watched the bird too as it wheeled into the adjoining field and made a sudden descent. The sun was warming, and Eleanor threw the blanket off her lap and reached out for Kathryn to help her up. They walked a few steps towards the wood, looking out at the tangle of heather at the bottom of the lawn and the symphony of bees hovering around it.

'Just before Jack left,' Eleanor said, 'in September 1942, I went to his studio. He had been quite prolific in those few weeks he was back: there were lots of paintings he had worked up from his sketches, a few oils too. But there were also some larger paintings, not his usual style. Dramatic battle scenes, the type of thing he didn't usually go in for,' she said, looking at Kathryn.

'Go on . . .'

'Well, when I asked him about them, he said they were private commissions for the officers he served with. I knew he needed the money for his mother's treatment so I didn't think any less of him for it. But after they never reached the gallery, there was some talk. You see, when you were under contract with the WAAC, everything you painted technically belonged to them. He wouldn't have been allowed to sell them privately.'

'I remember—there were salaried artists, short commissions and purchased artworks.' Kathryn had learned as much from her conversations with Alexander, and that the temperament of the artist dictated what contract they were offered.

'Yes. You see, it was considered rather poor form to be moonlighting. Jack's reputation wasn't the same after that. I always believed that was another reason why there was so little assistance when I tried to find him. I felt as though the committee had turned their back on me, excluded me because they blamed me for that too.'

Kathryn recollected one of Jack's entries in the 1943 diary about a colonel pressuring him to paint a private commission. It sounded like a reasonable enough explanation for why Kathryn had found less in the archives about Jack than the other war artists, and why Stephen had been so reluctant to talk about him. Did he know about this and believe that Jack had been disgraced?

'Why didn't you tell me any of this before?' she asked her grandmother.

'I suppose I didn't really think it was important, until now.'

Kathryn tried to piece together the fragments Eleanor had just shared with what she already knew. 'I suppose it explains why there's not so much about him in the official records. But it still doesn't really explain why you couldn't find him at the end of the war.'

'I told you, he lost his studio, and I never got to meet his mother or his sister before he went away. His orders came and a few days later he left. I tried to find his family eventually, of course, but they had moved.' Eleanor shook her head. 'I didn't know what had become of him. I always assumed he was captured. They were confusing times, Kathryn. I'd hoped that even POWs got to write home, but sadly not. And artists in London were getting arrested for being spies. There was no trust.'

The word 'trust' felt loaded, but it had opened the door, and so she felt entitled to ask. 'Why didn't you tell me about any of this before, Gran? Don't you see how important it could have been?'

Eleanor looked unrepentant. 'Because, my dear, I didn't want to have to. I wanted Jack to tell you.'

But it was too late for that. Kathryn's stomach tightened again at the thought of leaving Eleanor without keeping her promise.

She watched her grandmother gaze out at the garden, wondering what secrets still lay locked behind those hazel eyes. What it was that had really happened between her and Jack Valante all those years ago. It looked as if Kathryn would never know now, but she only had one more afternoon to spend with Eleanor and she wanted to make it count.

Thirty-two

The vole lay curled on its side as if sleeping, but as Kathryn stepped over it she saw that half its insides were missing, no doubt due to foxes—the job half done—leaving the poor creature to slowly and painfully die. She walked on quickly, focusing on the beauty around her, knowing that nature was cruel.

There had been a late morning shower, and the woodland glistened like the landscape inside a Christmas globe. She had left Eleanor napping and slipped out for a walk. She hadn't made the most of the countryside—too many trips to London—but now she had walked for miles, through the woods to Tudeley and back, testing her memory of the plants and trees, and getting cross whenever she couldn't remember a name. Larger shrubs on the narrowing track gave way to forbs and grasses that signalled the edge of the wood. How annoying—why couldn't she remember the name of the green-fronded plant with tiny white flowers?

The time with Eleanor had gone too quickly and it seemed impossible that it was their last day. She had planned a trip into Royal Tunbridge Wells for a cream tea—or Tonbridge if her grandmother was not up to going quite that far—and Kathryn wouldn't take no for an answer.

The cool shadow of the canopy ended as she was thrown into the strengthening sun, the woodland floor giving way to long grass that brushed wet against her ankles. After the shade, the heat felt like a caress, and halfway up the hill she caught the scent of lavender. Thrusting her hands deeper into her jacket pockets, enthralled at the kaleidoscope of meadow flowers underfoot, she decided that they would definitely make it to Royal Tunbridge Wells on such a glorious day.

The tiny white flowers were cow parsley, she remembered and smiled to herself—until she glanced up again and noticed an unfamiliar black Mercedes parked outside the farmhouse.

What if her grandmother had left the door open again, and this uninvited guest had let themselves in?

Her feet couldn't carry her fast enough, and she was out of breath by the time she reached the house and was racing around the front. Through the living-room window, the large outline of a man was just visible, his back towards her, bulky frame towering over Eleanor. The front door was still open, so Kathryn rushed down the hallway and burst breathless into the room.

Stephen Aldridge was standing over her grandmother, and they both looked up, alarmed.

'Kathryn! Are you alright, dear?'

'What are you doing here? I told you, my grandmother doesn't want to sell.'

'It's okay,' Eleanor said. 'Stephen and I have been talking.'

'Did you invite him here?'

'No.'

He looked the same as he had the day she'd met him in Hampstead: tailored clothing, an outward respectability. Only today, something about his demeanour had changed.

'I came of my own accord,' he said. 'It's time you both knew the truth.'

'The truth about what?' Kathryn asked.

'About Jack.' Eleanor's face was flushed, her eyes gleaming. Whatever Stephen had already told her, it seemed as if she was willing to accept it as the truth. 'Stephen knows where Jack is.'

'Where?' Kathryn asked Stephen, the knot in her stomach tightening. It was clear that he had been hiding something from them all along; but did he know about their history together—about their engagement?

'Alright then,' Stephen said, 'but you have to know it has only ever been about protecting Jack and his reputation—that was always the most important thing . . . *is* the most important thing. It was never just about the art, though that was one of the reasons I didn't want you to find him.'

'What, because I would work out that some of the pictures weren't his?' Kathryn said. 'And you expect us to believe that you've done this because it would hurt Jack's reputation, not because it would devalue your collection?'

There had to be more pictures: they would be hidden somewhere, squirrelled away like the important artworks had been during the war—and she had a feeling she knew who else might be involved in that.

Stephen Aldridge's face clouded, the crow's-feet around his eyes deepening before he spoke. 'You worked it out?'

'Yes, my grandmother told me. She's already admitted that two of the paintings are by her.'

'Well, you are partly right.'

'You told me that most of his works were lost.'

'Some of them were,' he said and paused to take a deep breath, 'but there are still a number held privately.'

Kathryn's surprise at seeing Stephen was replaced by anger; and a deeply felt frustration at the time he'd wasted by not telling her any of this sooner.

'By you and your family?' she said impatiently.

'And other private collectors . . .'

'Alexander Gower?'

'Yes, he's one of them. We met at the sixtieth anniversary celebrations—he was interested in Jack's work and seemed to know there were missing paintings. Anomalies, I think he called them. Anyway, he offered to help me build the collection by helping to trace the missing artworks.'

'And did he?' Kathryn said, folding her arms as she continued to stand in front of her new opponent.

'To an extent. He knew enough to recognise Eleanor's unsigned paintings—'

'*Children in the Attic* and *The Bermondsey Rescue*?' Kathryn interrupted as she glanced at Eleanor.

Her grandmother was watching Stephen intently, hanging on his every word.

'Yes, but the important thing, which I didn't realise at the time, was that the fiftieth anniversary had marked the end of the Crown

Copyright that covers the work of all war artists. The paintings were even more valuable then.'

'In what way?' Kathryn asked.

'Artists or their estates were free to exploit their paintings—reproductions, postcards, licensing, not to mention selling them to museums and private collectors.'

Kathryn nodded. 'And so Gower would earn more money too.'

'Yes, but it isn't just Jack he's interested in. The discovery of your grandmother's paintings adds to a small body of work by women war artists, and that money and prestige was far too tempting for Gower. Jack's work alone would be valuable, but with the lost art of Eleanor Roy—well, it would be even more so.'

Kathryn sat down, taking in all that he had said. 'Are you still working with him?'

'Look, he's done nothing wrong. In fact, he's in a good position to get the works appraised and exhibited, so you may want to contact him.'

Kathryn looked at her grandmother, but Eleanor's expression gave nothing away.

'Of course, there is someone else I can recommend, if you would rather,' Stephen suggested. 'He runs a fine art gallery in London.'

'Thank you, Stephen, but I think you've done enough,' Kathryn said, her tone suddenly cold. 'This is something that my grandmother and mother can work out together.'

'Certainly, but here is one slight problem,' he continued, 'the copyright period for non-WAAC paintings is actually seventy years, so Gower has a dilemma on his hands. Identifying your grandmother's paintings would mean waiting another five years before the copyright ends.'

'So what do you think he'll do?'

'I'm not sure. I know he wants the prestige of making the discovery, but the rest is entirely up to you, Eleanor—what do you want?'

'I want to know why Jack didn't come to me before . . . or you?'

Stephen sighed and sat down in the chair opposite her.

'I asked Jack about you after Gower suggested I find *The Crimson Sun*, but he said that you had worked for the committee. I could tell it upset him—his mood changed. He told me that he didn't want to rake over the past. I didn't tell him that I contacted you because I thought I was protecting him.'

'But you've spoken to him about it now?'

'Yes, and he wants to see you.'

Eleanor shot Kathryn a look. She had seen her grandmother's emotions fluctuate over these past few days but now there was a steely determination in her eyes, and the promise of a smile on her lips.

It all seemed to fit into place. Kathryn knew how proud Stephen was of his uncle and his achievements, but did he know about the engagement? 'But that's not the only reason you didn't tell Jack, is it?' Kathryn said, fishing.

'No, it's not,' Stephen said, returning Kathryn's glare. 'I'm sorry, Kathryn.' He sounded sincere.

'What for?'

'Because it was my cowardice and greed . . .' He stopped and looked away.

'I don't follow,' she said with a frown.

'I wanted to protect Jack, but I didn't want to share his legacy with anyone either.'

She shook her head. 'But why would you have had to?'

'If people had found out that the paintings weren't all his work, then it would follow that they don't all belong to us.'

'And you would have to give them back,' she concluded.

'Yes.'

'And the reason you kept the diaries hidden?'

'Because I suspected,' he replied.

Eleanor's mouth tightened and she looked down at her folded hands.

Stephen looked at her. 'So it's true?'

'Suspected what?' Kathryn asked.

Stephen kept his eyes on Eleanor, waiting for her reply.

She twisted in her chair so that she was facing her granddaughter. 'Because, Kathryn, Jack is Abigail's father . . . Jack is *your* grandfather.'

She leaned back in the chair and released a long breath: the weight of the great secret she had carried for so long.

First Kathryn felt disbelief, then it took her a moment to register what Eleanor had said, and it began falling into place: the mystery, Eleanor's secrecy, fragments of information shared with her, memories that almost revealed what happened but weren't quite enough.

But why hadn't her grandmother told her? Why hadn't she told any of them?

Then a thought flashed into her head. 'But what about Grandpa?'

'Edward will always be your and Tom's grandfather, Kathryn. The same as he will always be Abigail's father.'

'Did he know?'

'He never knew about Jack. He always thought I was a widow. We loved each other, Kathryn, the same as he loved you.'

'So, this search wasn't about what happened to Jack or selling the painting?'

'No,' Eleanor said forcefully. 'It was about you finding him . . . and telling him who you are.'

Kathryn gaped at Eleanor and then sank back slowly into the chair, her gaze falling on the purple bloom of a flower in the wallpaper, staring trancelike.

The fact that Chris had thought this was some kind of wild-goose chase suddenly struck her as hysterically funny and she fought off the desire to laugh. What would he say when she told him the truth?

Her grandmother's figure blurred as Kathryn fought the instinct to cry, overwhelmed by the sudden sadness of losing her grandfather, not yet able to accept this discovery. 'So that's why you could never let me see the diary?' Kathryn murmured, realising that she and Stephen must be related; that he was a second cousin.

The wooden frame creaked as Stephen shifted to the edge of his seat. 'We guessed that if your grandmother hadn't told you about Jack all these years, she wasn't going to now, but we were wrong. If you don't mind me asking, Eleanor,' Stephen said. 'What made you change your mind?'

'It was my granddaughter,' she said, hands stretching out towards Kathryn. 'I realised that sometimes the future needs protecting more than the past does.'

Kathryn's gaze flicked up to Eleanor and then back down, her lips quivering as she struggled to hold back her tears.

The atmosphere in the room had changed. The tension dissipated, the confrontational mood replaced by one of warmth, and the three of them were silent as they registered all that had changed. Kathryn should still have been angry but there was too much else to think about now and too many questions she had for her grandmother.

She looked at Stephen. 'Can you give us some time alone, to process this?'

'Of course.' He stood and bent forward and took Eleanor's hand between his. 'We'll see you soon, though?'

'Yes, I'm looking forward to it,' she replied, patting his hand.

'I'll leave you to it then,' he said, straightening. But when he reached the door, he stopped and turned to Kathryn. 'I'm sorry, I didn't mean for anyone to get hurt.'

She waited for the front door to close and for her breathing to even out.

'Come and sit down, Katie.'

Kathryn moved slowly. Sitting on a corner of the sofa close to Eleanor, she looked at her thoughtfully. 'There are so many things I want to ask you.'

'I know, Katie. I'm sorry.'

'Why didn't you tell us before . . . Oh my God, does Mum know?'

'No. I couldn't tell you, any of you, not before Edward died. He might not have been blood family, but he was a father to Abigail and a grandfather to you and Tom—I couldn't take that away from him.'

Kathryn glanced over at the window and the footsteps retreating across the gravel drive, the car door slamming and an engine starting. Stephen drove away.

When she looked back, Eleanor was still gazing at her. 'I wasn't going to tell you. I didn't know if you would ever find him. What if you didn't, what was the point?' Her voice cracked. 'You would have all just had a lot of heartache and more questions.' She stopped for a moment, swallowing hard. 'I couldn't risk it until I knew he was still alive and mentally sound . . . I couldn't risk you all hating me.'

'We couldn't hate you, don't be silly,' Kathryn said, with a look of tenderness as she reached for her grandmother's hands.

'You're not angry with me?'

'No, not angry, just a little confused. Pops died five years ago, so why now?'

'I was going to leave it. I thought let sleeping dogs lie, but when Stephen contacted me . . . and seeing you, Kathryn . . . all this soul-searching and uncertainty. I thought it might help to settle you—knowing who you really are, where you came from. I want you to get on and enjoy your life,' she said, gripping Kathryn's hands more tightly.

Kathryn shook her head. 'And what if we hadn't found him?'

'Then you would have just gone home, and no harm done. This really was the only way. I couldn't have found him on my own.'

Kathryn thought about Eleanor's words, *that it might settle you*, but surely it would be far more unsettling for her grandmother— unless she really did want to know what happened to him. She supposed that her instinct to know would have been as strong as Eleanor's.

'So Jack did nothing more than try to help you and paint some pictures for a few greedy officers, and you were both punished by never being able to be together?' Kathryn said, thinking aloud.

'I don't think it was ever anything sinister, Katie. The WAAC just didn't want those things made public. I always assumed they simply didn't want any issues with their war artists distracting from their work.'

She examined Eleanor's face. They might have a different his-tory now but she was still the same grandmother Kathryn knew and loved, and with the same smile; the same one that Eleanor had worn in the engagement photograph seventy years ago. And it was that photograph she would be showing to her mother and Tom in a few days' time.

'You really loved him, didn't you?'

'Yes, Kathryn,' Eleanor replied without hesitation. 'I most certainly did.'

'And when did you give up on him?'

Eleanor's expression changed, and all traces of sadness disappeared.

'I never gave up on him, Katie. I always hoped he would come back. But, when he didn't, my father found a husband for me just as he said he would. Luckily, it was Edward.' And she smiled.

Kathryn felt she understood but there must have been so many times when Eleanor wanted to confide in them—and what about Cecily and her brothers—had any of them known? She would let her mother have that conversation; there had been enough revelations for one day. There was still one question she did want to ask, though.

'And what about your dreams of being a war artist? You had to let those go too.'

Her grandmother was thoughtful for a moment before she spoke. 'Yes, Katie, but I loved being a teacher, and look at what I got in return.' Her hand was gently stroking the side of her granddaughter's face.

PART VI

The Factory Worker

'After what she has done in this
titanic struggle, will she not guard
what she has gained, and to Man's
effort add her own? If she can
do what she has done in war,
what may she not do in peace?'

DAME LAURA KNIGHT, *War Pictures by
British Artists, Second Series, WOMEN*, OX-
FORD UNIVERSITY PRESS, 1942, PAGE 8

Thirty-three

LANCASHIRE, OCTOBER 1943

The spoon tapped noisily against the table as Abigail banged it down, orange goo dribbling from the sides of her mouth onto the white cotton bib.

'Who's a clever girl?' Eleanor said, smiling.

Seeing her mother's face light up, she banged the spoon even harder, squealing in delight.

'Shush, Abigail. Your grandfather will think the Germans are at our door!' Patricia Roy said, half-serious.

'Come on, Mother,' said Eleanor, 'you know he hasn't the slightest interest in what she's doing. I think he's only been up here twice.'

They'd installed the nursery on the second floor next to Eleanor's bedroom, away from any visitor's ears or prying eyes. Today they were in the sitting room, Abigail's wooden highchair pushed up against the round table near the bay window, long pink gingham curtains draped half-open on either side. The pale blue of the carpet was just visible beneath the large oriental rugs and antique furniture.

'You know that's not true. It's just taking him a while to get used to the idea.'

'Pretend she's not here, you mean.'

Patricia narrowed her eyes at Eleanor as if she disagreed but had become tired of saying so.

Eleanor looked at Abigail's plump smiling face and tiny upturned nose and wondered if she had ever seen anything more perfect. When the midwife had first placed the baby in her arms, Eleanor vowed she would never leave her, but it had been ten months in her parents' house with her father's furious gaze and ten months with still no word from Jack. The War Office had been no help in contacting him and, while Cecily had done a good job redirecting her mail from Cleveland Square, nothing had arrived.

'Wouldn't your father love you,' she said, stroking Abigail's silky-soft crown, 'and wouldn't you adore him . . . ?'

Patricia stopped sewing and looked up from her embroidery. 'You know Abigail is safe here and that you're better placed to find him in London. I don't know why you don't just go. Go and find him, Eleanor.'

Gilbert Roy had told his elder daughter that if she didn't find her fiancé by the year's end, he would find a husband for her: one who would take care of her and the child.

'You really think Father is going to do as he says?' Eleanor asked.

'Yes, I do, dear. And I know he already has someone in mind.'

'Who?'

'I can't say, but if you do as I'm suggesting it might not come to that.'

'Please, you must tell me who!'

When Eleanor had arrived on the train back from London, four months' pregnant and as lost as a ship at sea, her mother had taken charge. Gilbert was a devout man and his faith stitched him together as tightly as the fabric from the mill held his clothing, so it wasn't a surprise that he avoided her as much as he did, or when his ultimatum came. So she hid in the house, pretending that her husband was on active service, and kept to her sitting room. She was protected and cossetted by Mrs Percival, the housekeeper, and the maids, who were beside themselves with excitement that a baby would soon be in the house; it was a gift, something joyous to focus on in these dark times.

A Victorian doll's house sat on top of the shelves, front door open to reveal the tiny furniture and figurines inside. She was surrounded by the toys and books she had played with as a child, and felt how strange it was to inhabit the rooms where she and Cecily had put on plays, written stories and dreamt about a far-off day when they would be adults inhabiting an adult world. She would be an explorer living overseas, eventually with a husband and possibly two children; never, ever had she thought it would be like this. Some days she took comfort from having these girlish tokens around her, while other days they seemed to taunt her, as if she couldn't escape from them and her life was to be anchored here, all that she had found and achieved in the meantime reduced to nothing. She had tried to make the space her own, but it was very difficult.

Mrs Percival had retrieved all the old baby clothes from the attic, washed and darned them and folded them neatly into piles. The fact that they were stacked in batches of colour from left to right—white first, followed by yellow, then pink, green and finally blue—pleased her more than she imagined was appropriate, but it was also very useful once Abigail had arrived and she became worn down by the night feeds and the continual crying.

Abigail curled her hand around her mother's little finger and gurgled at her smiling face. Eleanor knew what was at stake: she needed to find Jack rather than be forced to marry another man, but she wasn't ready to leave her daughter yet.

'I just can't—'

'I think you could,' Eleanor's mother said, 'just for a few months. Really look for him, and then come back.'

'But she's in such a good routine now.'

'Even more reason that you should go.'

'Isn't it too much for you, though?'

Patricia Roy was a busy woman: the head of the household, active with the local WVS, the wife of an important businessman. She had more than enough to occupy her.

'Darling, I had four,' she said. 'I think I might be able to cope with just one. Besides, some babies are more troublesome than others and you were my easiest, and I'm pleased to say that Abigail seems to be taking after you.'

Eleanor liked the way the name sounded when her mother said it—*Abigail*—as if it should be sung. She had surprised them all with the name. It meant 'father's joy', and from her mother's mouth it sounded soothing, three syllables broken into a chant, but she couldn't remember her father ever saying it.

She gazed at her daughter's rosy cheeks and long dark lashes, unable to look away. Even Francis, when he was fully recuperated, had come to visit and remarked how Abigail was as delicate as a flower and twice as pretty, and Clarence, when home on leave, had showered her with gifts.

'I'm sure they will have replaced me by now,' Eleanor said, leaning forward to press her lips tenderly against her daughter's forehead.

'You should write to Mr Powell—he always had a soft spot for you. I'm sure he could see his way to finding you something.'

'Maybe . . .'

The committee and the Ministry had no idea about the pregnancy or Abigail. Eleanor had made the excuse of being summoned home to help with the family business. That the textile factory was producing uniforms and that the committee already knew this had worked in her favour, and no suspicion had been aroused.

Eleanor had only taken Maura into her confidence when she'd guessed, and then she'd helped by altering Eleanor's clothes to guard their secret.

'Good,' Patricia said, lifting Abigail out of the highchair and taking her through to the nursery, 'we shall leave you to it then.'

Eleanor found a pen and paper and sat at the desk, listening to her mother sing lullabies in the next room. In front of her was a stack of letters from the War Office, all in response to hers, and all saying the same thing: Jack's unit was in Italy or North Africa and communication was difficult. That Italy had declared war on Germany hadn't helped to ease Eleanor's worries.

She wondered if she would in fact be serving Abigail's needs better if she went looking for Jack and left her daughter behind. The only way that she really stood any chance of finding him was to go back to London, and her mother knew that too.

A week later Patricia ambushed Eleanor after breakfast before she left on one of her lengthy walks. Light rainfall in the night had left the Pennines sparkling and the air pungent with a mix of pollen, moss and wood. There would be plenty of animal life and new fauna to occupy her, and since Abigail's sleeps were the only time she had to paint, she was keen to get outdoors.

'You seem as if you're ready for the Alps,' Patricia said, looking her up and down.

Boots and trousers were a basic requirement for the boggy terrain, but her raincoat and hat were just a precaution, and her satchel of painting equipment a necessity.

'The forecast wasn't very specific,' Eleanor replied. 'Mrs Percival is keeping an eye on Abigail. I'll be back before lunch.'

'Mrs Percival does have other duties, Eleanor.'

'Yes, Mother, I know. It's only once in a blue moon, so I think she can manage.'

'Well, your father thinks that if you are going to stay, you could help teach at the school. There are dozens of evacuees still here and your art classes count for something.'

Eleanor took a deep breath; if she kept her eyes closed and counted to ten, she might stay on speaking terms with her mother. First, Patricia had wanted her to go, and now she was asking her to stay and help, even though she would still be expected to hide Abigail.

She had nearly got used to the idea of going back to London, until she realised what Jack might say if he came back and found that she had abandoned their child—how unkind a mother he might think her to be—and so hadn't sent the letter.

But the idea of helping the village schoolmaster, whose idea of fun was cataloguing the local weeds in his herbarium, might just be enough to make her change her mind.

'And there's a new teacher your father thinks you will enjoy meeting,' Patricia added. 'He is unattached . . . and he likes children.'

'It's all settled,' Eleanor lied. 'I'm going back next week. I've written to Cecily and told her to expect me.'

'Well, that's that then,' Patricia said, beaming. 'It's the right decision.' She patted her daughter's shoulder. 'And it will be good for you to keep an eye on your sister again.'

'Yes, Mother.'

Patricia smiled again. 'And we shall look after Abigail for you.'

Eleanor had written to her sister to raise the idea of returning, and Cecily's reply had been unequivocal: *Why must you come back and put yourself in danger? You are a mother.*

Yes, I am a mother now but that is not all that I am, Eleanor had replied.

Thirty-four

LONDON, NOVEMBER 1943

Her silhouette flickered across the wall, footsteps echoing as she made her way further underground. The temperature had noticeably dropped as autumn surrendered to winter and branches had withered to broomsticks, but down here the chill was absolute, the kind of icy cold that Eleanor knew reached into your bones and held on tight. And with the freezing cold came an increased gloom, as if she was diving headlong into a dark pool, the staircase behind her disappearing in shadows. She held the paraffin lamp higher, the movement shifting the gasmask further onto her shoulder. It seemed ironic that she was carrying apparatus designed to protect them when she was already struggling to breathe, the air thick with ancient dust and a penetrating dampness that leached through the floor. The winter had brought a physical discomfort that was pervasive in a way she hadn't noticed before and, as she reached the bottom step, she wondered, and not for the first time, if she had done the right thing in coming back.

She hadn't managed to trace Anne Valante or Jack's sister Beth either. In fact all she had managed to find out was that Jack might have been with the Eighth Army. As news had arrived of their capturing of Isernia and the Germans' withdrawal, there had been reason for optimism and she'd thought he might come back. But that was weeks ago now. The committee had expected a batch of drawings from him too, but nothing had come, and so she continued to send letters that remained unanswered.

Aubrey had proved elusive and hadn't replied to her letters or returned her phone calls until just last week, when an invitation arrived for an exhibition opening this afternoon—*Anthony Gross: War Artists in India*—so she was hoping to talk with him then.

Her initial excitement at being back at the Ministry was also short-lived. In the eleven months that she had been away, tension had escalated in the city. There were more troops in the capital, more barricades in the streets, and increased air raid wardens on patrol—it was a level of activity that she hadn't seen since the Blitz. She noticed that her colleagues were in a heightened state too as they struggled to keep up with demands from the growing number of British Restaurants amid the ever-shrinking resources. It now also fell to the Ministry office staff to carry out safety checks of the Ministry's basement air-raid shelter.

So instead of being at a meeting in Harrow with the British Institute of Adult Education, Eleanor was studying the framed notice that catalogued the safety procedures under the dim fizz of light. Because she hadn't carried out the checks before, she diligently worked through the checklist: first ensuring that the firefighting equipment was intact, then that the sandbags were in place; next that the emergency lighting was ready, and that the water buckets were filled. And then she bent to check one of the buckets, only to come face to face with a bloated rat floating on the surface.

She jumped backwards, nearly knocking the bucket over. Her chest was moving rapidly, the sharpness of her breath the only sound in the constricted space, and she pulled herself up onto the bench to catch her breath.

It was reassuring to know they had somewhere to shelter when the warning siren came, but she was sure that if they had any more than a few hours down here, they would all suffocate; a junction of grilles and pipes connected them to the outside world but it wasn't obvious how far it went, or how much air it circulated for those inside.

It was then that she heard a scratching sound and realised that she wasn't alone—and that it wasn't clawing on wood or stone but the tearing of paper. Then she noticed the hole in the side of a cardboard box and prodded it with her foot.

There was a scuffling and small dark shapes emerged, quickly disappearing into the corner of the wall.

She pulled her legs up beneath her, clutching her knees to her chest; she could cope with one or two—she had to at home, since Cecily never could—but more than that and she would be running up the stairs.

She waited until there was quiet and then nudged the box with her foot. One of its sides collapsed. The boxes held emergency rations, but clearly the rats had whittled them away until only unopened tins were left. She shunted the box from the wall, noticing a trail of chewed cardboard, like porridge, on the floor, before she heard footsteps above.

'Eleanor? Are you down here?' Maura's voice echoed, then she appeared in the shadow of the lamp she carried.

'Maura, what are you doing here?'

'I thought you might want to know that Clive is looking for you,' she said. 'I've been all over this blooming fortress—I thought you were on the rooftop.' She tiptoed across the damp soil in a maroon suit and high heels.

Eleanor hadn't been on the rooftop since Jack had gone; she couldn't bring herself to, despite wanting to sit in the same spot overlooking London.

'I don't suppose you know where the traps are?' Eleanor asked with a sigh.

'I'm afraid not. Why?'

'Because it looks like the rats have helped themselves to the emergency rations,' she said, pointing at the boxes slumped like concertinas.

'Bit of poison usually does the trick.'

'Really . . . there are nearly a hundred people expected to squeeze in down here?'

'Aye, I hadn't thought of that. Let's hope we don't have to use it, eh?' Maura said, worried. 'Sweet Jesus, Eleanor, it's how those poor souls must feel.'

'Who?' Eleanor asked with a frown.

'The Jews. When they're herded into . . . I can't even say it.' Maura was shaking her head as if trying to rid herself of the image.

Eleanor didn't want to think about it either, yet it had sat there at the front of her mind ever since she'd heard about it; and it was one of the reasons that she wanted to stay and help. Enough of the contents of *Der Stürmer* and German propaganda was reaching London for them to know that the anti-Semitism knew no bounds and that the Nazis had no limits. She couldn't comprehend the latest reports, no one could, but a number of refugee artists had confirmed that they were true.

'Anyway,' Maura said, noticing how pale Eleanor suddenly looked, 'I came to see if you want to come to the parade. They're setting up outside.'

The King had announced awards in recognition of the gallantry displayed in flying operations against the enemy, and this had given them all cause to celebrate. But even though she knew one of the wing commanders who had received a Distinguished Service Order, Eleanor was reluctant to join in.

'Oh no, I don't think I shall,' she said.

'I can wait until you've finished here. Or give you a hand . . .'

'No, you go ahead. I'm supposed to be in Harrow, anyway—I should go up to meet Clive soon. And I really don't think I could face it.'

'What are you going to do about the boxes?' Maura said, looking at the chewed cardboard.

'I'll move the food onto the shelves; then I can get rid of the rubbish before they eat that too.'

'Or make nests from them.' Maura pulled a face. 'Come on, I'll give you a hand.'

'Really? Have you got time?'

'Of course. It's only you who'll notice—the others are all out at the parade!'

They stacked the tins as they talked, the powdered milk and fruit placed on the shelves, unopened boxes lifted onto benches if they were undamaged, the damaged ones emptied.

'I told Clive that I wouldn't be long,' said Eleanor regretfully.

'I could have done the safety checks. You should have asked.'

'But, you know, I wanted to come down here. I know it sounds strange but there's something about being underground that helps me imagine how the soldiers must feel—the dirt, the confined spaces . . .' Eleanor stopped work and looked at Maura. 'It makes me think about my brothers . . . and Jack. Does that sound daft?'

'A bit. Why put yourself through that?'

'I don't know. It makes me feel closer to them, I suppose.'

Maura was giving her a strange look, so she smiled.

'Anyway,' she said, 'we're nearly done.'

'Good,' Maura said, stacking the last of the tins on the shelf. She sat down on the bench and offered Eleanor a cigarette.

'Why not?' Eleanor said, even though she rarely smoked.

The match spat before settling and lighting the cigarettes, and they watched as the smoke coiled upwards, the tobacco camouflaging the damp.

It tasted bitter but Eleanor formed an oval with her mouth, kissing the air and watching as the rings of smoke emerged in front of her and then slowly dispersed.

'So how are you coping?' Maura asked.

Eleanor glanced sideways at her through the haze. 'Honestly? I am eight weeks from becoming a farmer's wife. My father hasn't even allowed me the agreed six months—and he's already told the man that I'm a widow. Imagine it.' She fought back tears.

Maura had matured since Eleanor had been away; she could see it in her eyes and in the way she interacted with the others in the office. There was no hesitation, no room for uncertainty, and Eleanor was pleased to have her company and that she could trust her.

'Well,' Maura said, blowing smoke from the side of her mouth, 'I have my own big moral dilemma to face.'

'Oh dear, what is it?' Eleanor said, worried about what work or guilt her parents had heaped on her now.

Maura's expression was grave. 'I have to decide whether to go out with the officer from Chicago—who can get me *Cosmopolitan*—or Doug from Kentucky, who said he is days away from getting his hands on the October *Vogue*.'

'Maura!' Eleanor said, elbowing her friend.

'What? It's a very serious business.'

'Why?'

'Because it's the first cover by Irving Penn—and it's all about accessories. Think about it, Eleanor, all those handbags and shoes . . .'

Nothing could be further from her mind; the only clothes she thought about were the baby clothes she sent home for Abigail from her lunchtime shopping trips.

Maura certainly had a flair, she thought, glancing at the Irishwoman's maroon tweed suit, and at the skilful pleats of the skirt and the luminous buttons she had cleverly sewn on to make her visible in the blackout. The luminous accessories had been a revelation to Eleanor: she had commissioned Maura to make luminous handbags for all the women in her family and given them as presents.

'What would you be doing now if you had a choice?' Eleanor asked her. The thought that Maura would have a bright future after the war cheered her.

For a few seconds Maura's eyes searched the gloomy space, and then they sparkled. 'Well, I'd like to stick one to Hitler for a start, drop a big one on him, and then I'll open my own fashion house, design and make my own clothes. Hey, I can get my fabric from your factory!'

'And what about family, children?'

'Oh yes, two . . . no, three. And a house with its own bathroom, and an indoor lavatory. And a big bathtub with taps.'

'And what of this husband of yours?'

'He would be a soldier, I suppose, so he would be off fighting somewhere. Doing his bit for King and country.'

'Anything else?'

'No, Eleanor, I'm not like you.' She turned to face her. 'I don't want to save the world.'

Eleanor felt wounded.

'It's not that I'm criticising you,' Maura said apologetically. 'It's great that you want to show people these things, and you're a brilliant artist. I'm just not as clever as you.'

Eleanor didn't feel very clever. She wasn't even sure that she should be here anymore, that she wouldn't be better off back in a house in the countryside too, looking after Abigail.

'I think your idea sounds perfect,' she said, standing up and stubbing out the ghastly cigarette in the sand bucket. 'But I also know that there are three hours before an exhibition opening I have to attend, and a restaurant in Harrow to visit in the meantime.'

'We're all done down here?'

'Yes, and I think Clive has probably waited long enough.'

They were on the A40 on their way back from Harrow, approaching Shepherd's Bush, when Eleanor leaned forward so that Clive could hear her. 'How would you feel about a little detour today?'

She hadn't had the chance to visit the orphanage in Richmond since her return, and she was looking forward to seeing the children again. The prospect of seeing their small freckled faces and hearing their squeaky childish voices, even though they were significantly older than Abigail, filled her with a new sense of purpose.

'I would, miss, but I'm afraid they're not there anymore.'

'What do you mean?'

'The orphanage has gone, shut down. Some months back now.' He sounded solemn.

'But do you know why?'

'No, I'm sorry, miss. I went to drop off the paints you asked me to a few months back, and it was boarded up, no sign of anyone.'

Of course, she couldn't tell him that while she missed the children it was her own child she yearned for.

Clive dropped her off in front of the National Gallery in time for the Anthony Gross exhibition opening. The queue stretched all the way from the bottom of the portico steps up to the gallery doors, and Eleanor joined the back of it, half-expecting to smell the sweet aroma of the raisin and honey sandwiches she and Maura had eaten during the lunchtime concerts.

After only a few minutes of shuffling, accompanied by brief snatches of conversation, the queue funnelled inside and she was making her way up to the first floor.

The exhibition, *Convoy*, was in one of the larger rooms. She looked around for Aubrey but there was no sign of him, only the usual journalists and photographers jostling for a picture of Anthony Gross. He was one of the only war artists to have a one-man show, and his paintings for *Convoy* had been produced the previous year aboard the troopship *Highland Monarch* as it travelled from the North Atlantic across to the Middle East. Working her way round, Eleanor couldn't help but compare Gross's trip and his pictures with those that Jack would have made on his journey and with this came a renewed disappointment that it wasn't his work she was looking at.

A smaller exhibition in an adjoining space caught her eye: a selection of paintings from the second series of *War Pictures by British Artists* booklets: *Women*, *Production*, *Soldiers* and *Air Raids*, published while she had been away. A string quartet was rehearsing Mozart in the same room and she was standing listening, waiting for the crowds to settle, when she spotted Aubrey talking with a journalist.

Keeping him in her line of sight, she made her way through the exhibition and nearer to the musicians. Representations from the first three booklets hung on the closest walls, but when she turned to face the wall that sat perpendicular, she froze.

It was a selection from *Air Raids*, and among it were four pictures she recognised: *Fire Drill at a School*, *Auxiliary Fireman*, *Streetscape After a Raid*, and a fourth, *Children in the Attic*—all listed as works by the war artist Jack Valante.

She stared at that fourth picture for a long time while people moved around her, as the quartet played and hushed conversations whispered around the gallery.

Jack must have decided to submit the painting, but why, and at what cost?

Then she heard her name and turned to see Aubrey. His thumbs were tucked into the corners of his jacket pockets. He held a pipe between his lips, so it was hard to read his expression.

'You see, Eleanor,' he said, 'you are a war artist now.'

Thirty-five

Patricia Roy was doing what she thought any good grandmother should do—giving her daughter written updates on her baby girl—but, the excitement of each discovery, every new word and amusing anecdote increased Eleanor's doubt over remaining in London.

'Listen to this,' she said, reading the letter aloud to Cecily. '"Abigail said 'cat' and now follows Cocoa everywhere. Yesterday she crawled along to the end of the hallway and terrified us all until we found her hiding behind the curtains."' Eleanor smiled at the thought of Abigail chasing the family cat, until she grew worried that she might have fallen down the stairs or plunged off the balcony.

'What else does she say?' Cecily asked, reclining on the sofa while glancing at the day's edition of *The London Gazette*.

'Mother says that Abigail now likes playing peekaboo as much as exploring the garden, and there's a list here of foods she's tried, and the bedtime stories Mother has read her, including *Peter Pan* . . .' And then Eleanor burst into tears.

'Oh, come on, Ellie,' Cecily said as she put an arm around her. 'You've got to cheer up. You've been back three months. You can't carry on being so miserable. I've got half-dead patients who are happier than you!'

'I'm sorry, it's just . . .'

'What?'

'I miss her so much.'

'Of course you do, just the same as other mothers, wives, sisters, all miss their loved ones.'

Cecily was right, but Eleanor didn't feel any better. There was still no word from the War Office about Jack, and it was the not knowing where he was and how he was that made things so unbearable for her—the grief of missing him and now Abigail too.

She brushed tears from her eyes and sniffed. 'Cecily,' she said, 'will you be honest with me?'

'About what?'

'You promise to tell me what you really think?'

'Of course I will. Haven't I always . . . ?'

'Do you think I should stop looking for Jack and go home?'

Cecily sat down on the sofa opposite. 'Look . . . I think you should do what is best for Abigail. And if that's having you here to look for her father, then no.'

That wasn't what Eleanor had expected to hear: was Cecily suggesting that their mother was doing as good a job as she, Eleanor, could?

'But that isn't what you told me before . . .'

'I know but Mother is doing a good job of taking care of Abigail.'

'So you don't think that a child needs their mother?'

'Ordinarily speaking . . . but, as you know, these aren't ordinary times. You're needed by lots of people, Ellie—by the Ministry, by the committee, and, I expect, by the kids who painted these pictures.' She glanced at the orphans' paintings that Eleanor still displayed on their living-room wall.

There was Isaac's picture of his dad's green motorcycle with its large wonky wheels, right beside a painting of a large black-and-white dog. Then, underneath, Daisy's family garden bloomed as it had before they dug the shelter, blue skies studded with plump white clouds.

'And what about you,' Eleanor said, 'do you still need me?'

'No,' Cecily replied. 'I'm okay now. But I did.'

'So you're not going to tell me what to do?'

'No, I'm not. Why don't you sleep on it?'

'Because the situation won't be any different tomorrow,' Eleanor snapped. 'I'll still be here, Abigail will still be without her mother, and Jack will still be missing.'

Cecily stood up and arched her back. 'You know what this calls for,' she said matter-of-factly, 'a cup of tea and some custard creams!'

Eleanor looked at her, speechless. Cecily obviously decided she needed to try harder: she started to sing 'Don't Sit Under The Apple Tree' as she ran the tap and put the kettle on.

As she delivered the last line, Cecily sat on the back of the sofa, spun her legs over and onto the seat, and offered the open tin of biscuits to her sister. Eleanor couldn't help but laugh; Cecily had a truly terrible voice but she supposed the patients didn't mind it, and she appreciated the fact that her sister was trying to cheer her up.

'You've been watching too many musicals!' she said, taking a biscuit. 'And where have you been getting custard creams from, anyway? When you're not entertaining the troops,' she added with a smile.

'Mother's contraband: she wouldn't ever let Father know but she's had rather a good scheme going. She's been sending these down for months.'

'Really?'

'Of course not!' Cecily said, relenting. 'Can you really imagine Mother doing that?'

'No, not really.'

'They're from Mrs Rowley at the WVS—now, there's a group of women who can get anything done if they set their minds to it . . . maybe we should get them to find Jack?'

'Yes, that's an idea,' Eleanor said, warming a little. 'Or we could ask Mother. Black market no, but I do believe that she would make rather a good spy: she's discreet, and she knows an awful lot about not very much, and she knows a lot of people.'

'And what about you then, Ellie,' said Cecily, 'with all your travelling and painting—how do we know it's not a cover for something much more sinister?'

'It's not—I just want to help.'

Her mood had turned serious again, and she got up from the table and walked over to the window, looking out at the encroaching night. She felt less certain of herself than at any time in her life: she had abandoned her precious baby, had let her parents down, and had deceived the institution that she had been so proud to represent.

She thought of a passage by Dame Laura Knight that she had read in the introduction to *Women*:

> *After what she has done in this titanic struggle, will she not guard what she has gained, and to Man's effort add her own? If she can do what she has done in war, what may she not do in peace?*

She had understood more than most how important the war artist's role was. Becoming one had been all that she had hoped for over the past three years, but that had changed.

Her figure was a silhouette against the fading sun, her voice cracking.

'I can't help Jack, but I can help Abigail.'

Thirty-six

KENT, 2010

As his eyes danced across the horizon, Jack wondered, as he had a thousand times, what would have happened if, when he came for her sixty years ago, he had never left. How different it could have been; would she have forgiven him when he told her why there had been such secrecy?

Stephen had wanted to drive, but Jack insisted on driving himself, so his nephew sat silently beside him as he steered the black Mercedes through the country roads. He was used to confined lanes, driving regularly from his Cotswold home to London for visits with the family or an appointment with his specialist, but he hadn't been to Kent in years.

Not since he had tracked her down once before, many, many years ago, and had then got cold feet. Still, he easily relied on his memory to follow directions. He noticed everything; SOE training had given him that, indoctrinating him into registering details, and deepening his powers of observation. He noticed the thrushes on the upper branches of the oak trees they had just passed, the wind-damaged hedgerows outside the priory on their right, and the empty pond that had been contaminated by weeds. He remembered the names of streets he had barely glanced at, and public houses and schools they had travelled by on their journey. He could see how most of the villages showed signs of shrinkage and regrowth, closed primary schools replaced by large private schools, the gentrification of the villages out-pricing the original inhabitants. It was the same all around the greenbelt—London's overspill, and the villages in his home county of Oxfordshire were no different. In some places they had retained the village post office and the occasional tearoom and pub, but the smaller shops and bakeries had closed as the supermarkets laid claim to selling every product under the sun.

It had been a straightforward journey: the A306 from Richmond, a short hold-up on the A3 but a quick trip across on the M25 and through onto the A21.

Jack glanced over at his nephew, at his bearded chin concertinaed against his shirt collar, neck bent as he peered down at his phone, fiddling around with some new map app he couldn't get to work.

'It's only another two and a half miles,' Stephen said without looking up.

It's taken me nearly seventy years to make this journey, Jack thought with a wry smile, fixing his eyes on the road ahead.

Over the Pembury Road roundabout onto the A26; past the vast blue waterway on our right and Tudeley Lane on our left, he thought, recollecting the directions from the map he had double-checked and trying to focus his mind.

But his earlier calm was dissolving, ripples appearing on the steady surface as his disappointment over the lost years reared up. His usual steadiness was faltering, the words he had carefully composed were drifting, tugged by a vindictive wind. And while he drove determinedly, it felt that the nearer he got, the faster he was losing control; with each mile they covered, more of his practised explanations deserted him. It was as if all sense of reason and logic was evaporating, his sound judgement abandoning him.

'Just past Postern Lane now and it's straight ahead.' Stephen's voice sounded distant.

Jack tried to reply but only a hoarse whisper came. He had lived through a world war, had fought for what he believed in, and yet had spent years regretting that he hadn't done more for Eleanor; this was his last chance to find her, tell her the truth and put things right. He had brought her paintings too, *The Crimson Sun* and her precious early artwork, *The Factory Worker*.

There wasn't time for him to rehearse his carefully chosen words again, the white lines counting down the final yards until the church roof and spire came into view.

He had known this day might come, after Stephen had found her; that she might come looking for him. And she had, sending her granddaughter, Kathryn, who Stephen had told him about.

And now his nephew had set things in motion, he needed to carry it through and admit what he had done, as he should have more than sixty years ago. He remembered their last days together as clearly as anything: Eleanor inside the Hyde Park pagoda, twisting the ring loosely around her finger, trying to hide her disappointment that it didn't fit. It was there that she had agreed to become his wife, before the war had kept them apart—as had his own vain morality. He ought to have done just as Aubrey Powell had asked and stayed out of it, let Eleanor carry on as she was, but instead he took her at her word from their last goodbye. *It occurs to me that when you are so short of time, you had better not waste it,* she had said with utter certainty. It was then that he had taken it upon himself to present *The Children in the Attic* as his own work before he left, and Powell had discovered it. It was the only reason he could see why she had gone when he came back, and why the committee refused to help him find her; she had been punished when it should have been him.

Was it too little, too late? He hoped not, and now he wanted to put it right—formally acknowledge the paintings that were hers and make her the war artist that she had always wanted to be.

The fields were broadening out around them, the light brightening as they left the built-up areas behind and the road veered sharply to the right.

Stephen suddenly sprang up in the seat. 'It's the next left . . . just here.'

Jack eased the car round the corner and into the narrow lane, slowing to ten miles an hour when he saw the church up ahead. To their left were converted barns set back from the road, well-tended gardens and low wooden fences, and on their right a conspicuous vicarage with a stooped figure clipping abundant roses. On the surface an idyllic sunny afternoon, he thought, as his eyes combed the road ahead, searching beyond the hedges and brick walls for signs of other cars or people.

He was often told that he had aged well, and he had looked after himself, cultivating good habits in later years, but he wasn't sure he believed strangers, or his doctors, when they said that he could pass for a seventy-year-old. It wasn't as if his thick grey hair and tailored suit didn't count for anything—he wanted to look his best—but he knew that it was what he felt and what was still locked inside that mattered most. He had it all worked out: he would take it step by step, month by month, year by year, explaining what had happened. He would tell her about his role with the press corps accompanying the Eighth Army on their Italian assault, and see if she could understand what it had been like for them, why it had been so difficult. Only afterwards would he tell her about his work with the SOE and the deal that he'd needed to make with Aubrey.

Thirty-seven

Kathryn should have been in the airport lounge waiting to board her flight, arriving home in time to take Oliver to his piano concert, but instead here she was driving along a stony track towards All Saints' Church with her grandmother, to meet the grandfather she never knew she had.

Chris had been as shocked as she was when she called, waking him in the early hours, apology stumbling along with explanation. But as soon as he'd realised that his feelings were insignificant compared with hers, he had stopped the interrogation and asked with thoughtful concern if she was alright—if there was anything she needed.

Time was the only thing that was of any use to her now: time to take it all in, time to be here to support Eleanor when she saw Jack for the first time in countless years, and time to be here when they delivered the bombshell to Abigail the next day. The flight was booked, and Kathryn would be the one picking her parents up from the airport and preparing them before they saw Eleanor.

Today would just be about Eleanor and Jack. They had a lifetime to catch up on, and unanswered questions of their own to be addressed, before they were ready to share their love story with anyone else—even the family they had created.

Kathryn's hands felt clammy, the wheel sliding beneath her grip as she turned it to the right, spotting the sharp angles of the church and spire as they reared over the bank of trees. Her stomach clenched as though she was excited, but that quickly turned to fear and, with it, the vague childhood memory of doing something wrong and the anticipation of being caught.

Eleanor was beside her in the passenger seat, her eyes centred on the road ahead, and Kathryn wondered what on earth could be going through her mind. She had exchanged her usual attire of trousers, smock and house slippers for a cream silk blouse decorated with vertical lines of tiny pink and purple flowers, and a long, straight navy skirt. Large, creamy pearls hung from her earlobes, while a gold locket—a gift from Edward, containing pictures of him and their children, which she never took off—hung loosely around her neck.

Eleanor and Kathryn had looked through the 1945 diary that Stephen had given them after he left and seen more references to Jack's 'darling girl'. And they had learned how Jack had spent the last year of the war: hospitalised in Italy with malaria. But it was his life in between, the one barely touched on by Wikipedia or the history books, that they wanted to discover.

After they had finished, Eleanor revealed something else: she had searched for Jack in London for months and finally given up, returning home to Lancashire for a hastily arranged marriage.

As Kathryn eased the old Rover into the All Saints' car park, they saw the black Mercedes tucked into the corner. She parked close to the church gate and opened the door to help Eleanor from the car, wondering how she was going to explain any of this to her parents when she saw them the next day. New questions constantly sprang to mind: had her great-grandparents known, and what about Great-Aunt Cecily and her great-uncles?

Eleanor had suggested All Saints' because she didn't want Jack to come to the house she had shared with Edward and her family, and it was a comfort that she knew the church well. Even Kathryn had attended services there with her family, when they too had admired the magnificent stained glass. It was lucky for them that it was the only church in the world to have all of its twelve windows decorated by the great Russian artist Marc Chagall; it had been sad, though, for the parents of the young woman who had commissioned the artist to commemorate her life.

Eleanor stepped from the car and pulled her camel coat tighter, as composed and as confident as she had ever been. Kathryn had helped with her make-up: a quick brush of powder and a dab of rouge had given her fragile skin a renewed glow, and the thin line of mascara drew attention to her emerald eyes.

'Are you ready?' Kathryn asked.

Eleanor smiled. 'Yes, dear.'

'How could you have kept the secret for so long?' Kathryn said without thinking.

'You tolerate the sacrifices because of the rewards,' Eleanor replied instantly. 'And because your child is blossoming, growing and becoming more than you ever imagined they could be.'

A flock of widgeons wheeled overhead, passing once before heading east towards the coast. They reminded Kathryn that she wouldn't be travelling home tonight but that it was okay. Speaking to Chris had made her long for him and their lovemaking, and this had surprised her; it was the first time she had felt that way in months.

She had seen the sacrifices that Eleanor had made and knew with certainty that she wanted to make her marriage work. Hopefully, this new discovery wouldn't make the pull to stay in England and find out about her new family any stronger than the one to leave, because she knew that after what her grandmother had been through, she had to do what was right for Chris and Oliver.

The widgeons were mere specks in the distance, their song fading until they finally disappeared from view.

Inside the gate, the graveyard was surprisingly large, with a wide-open lawn: not undulating layers of turf compressed against the church walls, like so many of the ancient parish graveyards, but lush with grass and scattered clumps of buttercups, clover and daisies. A handful of crooked headstones bordered three sides of the stone building, more like primordial signposts, so great were the distances between them, and plump bushes of pink hydrangeas swayed in the spaces between. An ivy-covered porch was visible from behind the low hawthorn hedge, and a noticeboard beside the entrance gave details of the regular services, issuing welcomes in English, French and German.

Kathryn stopped, letting go of Eleanor's arm. 'You go ahead . . . I'll be here when you need me,' she said as she leaned over and kissed Eleanor's cheek.

What was it that she detected in Eleanor's look? Not nervousness but quietude when she smiled and turned towards the church.

As Kathryn watched her walk away, a shiver crept up her spine, setting her hair on end. Eleanor was more courageous than she had ever realised; now she had to find the same strength, and after these past few days, she knew that she could.

⟡

It was after two o'clock and the sun was angling home, throwing its light behind the western windows and casting the church in a rich manganese glow. Blue waterfalls rippled down stone walls, bathing the altar in a pale watery light. The effect was so dazzling that at first Eleanor didn't notice the figure sitting in the middle pews, mesmerised as she was by the stained glass. It told the story of the scriptures, and their words came to mind: *You made him ruler over the works of your hands; you put everything under his feet: all flocks and herds, and the beasts of the field, the birds of the air, and the fish of the sea, all that swim the paths of the seas.*

That was how they all began and how they would end, and that was why she could bear this now; how she had borne it for all these years. She had understood it when she had painted seventy years ago, she had understood it when she had given up looking for him and taken a new father for Abigail, and she understood it now.

And then she saw him, a silhouette in the pews.

He looked up, with a tentative smile. There were flashes of the younger Jack, and memories of the man she had loved so very much.

It took her back to the time she'd first seen him in the attic, surrounded by black-and-white sketches of the children—his art not as beautiful as Murillo's seventeenth-century street children, she remembered thinking, but still mesmerising, a fretwork of greys and blacks, and how she was drawn to the images, the startlingly intricate lines—and then she had noticed the artist as he turned and looked up, his dark hair falling across his face.

His hair was thick, although grey and thinning around the sides. He was still a handsome man. And as Eleanor sat beside him, her composure weakened. Wondering where on earth to begin, she simply said, 'How are you, Jack?'

'As well as you'd expect,' he said with a smile. 'What about you, Eleanor?'

'Really good,' she said, examining his face, noticing how he was doing the same to her.

'Thank you for seeing me,' he said.

'Of course, how could I not?' she replied. 'I'm glad Stephen contacted me.'

'Yes, so am I.'

Eleanor smiled.

'He said you have something to tell me—that it's something important,' Jack said.

'Yes, it is. But before I do, I need to know what happened to you. I tried to find you . . .'

There had been a lifetime between them to arrive at this point, and now it was here he had one more chance to get it right. So he started at the very beginning, from the day he went away. Eleanor listened, interrupting to tell him the parts she had learned about from the diary, or to ask questions, or tell him what Kathryn had discovered. But when he finished, and she knew for certain about Aubrey and the committee, she still couldn't understand why she hadn't been able to find him and why none of their letters had been delivered.

'It was because I wasn't over there just as a war artist, Eleanor. I was part of Churchill's Secret Army.'

She considered him for a moment, thinking that perhaps he wasn't quite so well after all. Perhaps he was suffering from dementia and Stephen had neglected to mention it.

'It was known as that among some circles,' he continued, 'but you might have heard about it as the Special Operations Executive. I was an agent, Eleanor. I was working for the government.'

Then she remembered the diaries and the notations and the intricate drawings he had made. He told her about the Sicily landing in 1943, and how the campaign to secure the Balkans saw him stay until the Axis surrender in May 1945. How he reported to the SOE station in Brindisi, and later to the HQ in Southern Italy, as they fought to control the Balkans. She listened as he described his work in sabotaging the Italians, aiding secret armies that could help liberate the country with the Allied forces, but that he never considered himself to be an agitator, just an agent with special skills.

She was speechless as he described the methods he used and how he helped to pass on intelligence with maps and sketches, cryptic notes, invisible ink and, occasionally, forged identity papers. How he rarely knew what the intelligence was used for or where it went but that they had to stay flexible, responding to the demands from HQ. Only later had he learned how many of his colleagues were women and how so many of them had given their lives.

His eyes never left hers, not faltering for a second, and she could see that he was telling the truth. She felt relief and pride and had a hundred questions, but she still couldn't make the mental leap as to why this had had to come between them.

She finally found words. 'If only I had known.'

'You couldn't know, Eleanor. No one could—not Mother, not Beth, no one. The organisation evolved but there was one thing that never changed: the secrecy. Even after the SOE was disbanded, it was rarely spoken about until much, much later.'

She understood what it had taken Jack to reach the heights that he had, to become a war artist and an SOE agent, to bring credit to his country and his profession, promoting their success and their cause—but she still didn't understand. 'We were engaged, we were going to be married . . . and then I never heard from you again.'

'I found you, Eleanor, but it was too late. I saw you with another man, and a child. And I knew I was too late.'

'When was that?'

'Late 1946. I didn't get back until November 1945—I was sick in hospital.'

'You should have come to me. I always wanted to know what happened to you.'

'I'm sorry, I can see that now, but back then . . . well, I didn't think there was any point.'

'There was a very good reason you should have. One that I know will come as a shock to you, Jack.' She paused, her mouth suddenly dry, knowing she had to speak now before she lost her nerve. 'The child you saw me with then . . . she was your daughter, Jack.'

'We had a child?'

'Yes, Kathryn is your granddaughter. She's outside—she's waiting to meet you.'

'I don't believe it,' he said, casting his eyes downwards. 'I came here to give you your paintings back. I wanted you to have an exhibition so you could finally have what you wanted . . . and you tell me that I'm a father—a grandfather.'

'I have what I always wanted, Jack. I have my family.'

He shook his head as he looked at her. 'I never did. I married but there weren't any children.'

'I'm sorry, Jack. I did everything I could. I looked for your mother and Beth too.'

He leaned back against the pew, his face collapsing, eyes clouding.

'Stephen told me they moved out of London.'

'Yes. Battersea wasn't safe anymore, so they were rehoused in Essex. Ma was in a nursing home there,' he answered, before returning to Eleanor's bombshell. 'And what about our daughter, is she still alive?'

'Oh, yes,' Eleanor said, 'her name is Abigail and she's very much alive. She lives in Spain with her husband, Martin. And you have a grandson too, and three great-grandchildren.'

They sat quietly for a moment and took in all that they had shared.

'Do you want to see a family photo?' she asked.

'Do you have one?'

Eleanor opened her bag and pulled one out from two Christmases ago, the last time they had all been together. She was on the sofa, Abigail and Martin one side of her, Tom and his wife on the other, the grandchildren behind and the great-grandchildren cross-legged on the floor; for once their smiles were synchronised and everyone looked happy.

Jack studied it for a long time before looking back at her. 'Say, I don't think this is a very good deal, actually.'

'What do you mean?' she said worriedly.

'Well, I came here with a couple of old paintings for you,' he said, gesturing towards the package on the pew next to him. 'And you give me a whole family . . .'

She thought her tears could be disguised with laughter, but Jack somehow still knew her well enough to know how she felt and took her hand in his.

What magnificent poetry it was for their lives to intersect again, and who knew what would happen. But, for the most part, she had lived the life she had chosen and she hoped that was how Jack had lived his too—with truthfulness, integrity and splendour.

They had talked for so long that the sun had moved around the building. It suddenly flooded through a different window, brighter than before and capturing their attention with the cadmium yellow, the crimson, and the Prussian blue, yellow ochre and Renaissance gold they had once used to tell their part of a story.

Eleanor looked back at Jack as she laid her hand over his, the church now ablaze, saturating them in colour.

Afterword

At the outbreak of the Second World War, the War Artists' Advisory Committee was established. Its stated aim was to produce a comprehensive artistic and documentary history of Britain during wartime. The objective was to create propaganda and organise art exhibitions in Britain and America, to raise morale and promote Britain's image abroad. An unspoken aim was to create a visual record that may otherwise have been lost and, in so doing, protect the lives of artists who would in all probability be killed and lost to the art world forever.

Thirty-six men and one woman, Evelyn Dunbar, were given full-time contracts by the WAAC. Women artists working without a commission included Doris Zinkeisen, who worked with the Red Cross, and Stella Schmolle, who worked with the Auxiliary Territorial

Service. By December 1945, the WAAC collection consisted of nearly six thousand works produced by over four hundred artists. At the end of the Second World War, two women artists—Mary Kessell and Laura Knight—were finally given overseas commissions.

Eleanor's Secret was inspired by the work of the WAAC and a generation of courageous artists.

Abbreviations

ENSA	Entertainments National Service Association
BIAE	British Institute of Adult Education
CEAW	Committee on the Employment of Artists in War Time
CEMA	Council for the Encouragement of Music and the Arts
NG	National Gallery
RAF	Royal Air Force
SOE	Special Operations Executive
TG	Tate Gallery
UCL	University College London
WAAC	War Artists' Advisory Committee
WAAF	Women's Auxiliary Air Force
WVS	Women's Voluntary Services
YMCA	Young Men's Christian Association
YWCA	Young Women's Christian Association

Acknowledgements

It was a real privilege to research and write this novel, gaining an understanding of the lives and work of war artists, and there are many people to thank. I've already mentioned that the story was inspired by the WAAC and specifically by war artists such as Eric Ravilious, Edward Ardizzone, Anthony Gross, Feliks Topolski, and female war artists Evelyn Dunbar, Laura Knight, Ethel Gabain, Mary Kessell and Doris Zinkeisen, among others. I discovered some of their work at the Imperial War Museum's archives, as well as in other collections that I was able to access or visit for research. My sincere thanks go to the librarians and researchers at these institutions: the British Library, the Imperial War Museum, the National Gallery and the National Archives in the UK, and the New South Wales Library and the Art Gallery of New South Wales, for doing such a wonderful job of looking after our treasured histories and making it possible to share these stories.

These and other sources allowed me to create *Eleanor's Secret* by drawing on paintings, illustrations, maps, diaries, journals and online information to imagine life for artists and civilians all those years ago. Also key in creating the characters was being able to talk to recent war artists Wendy Sharpe and Joshua Yeldham. My gratitude goes to those artists and to Deborah Beck, Dean Cross and Bronwyn Woodley for generously sharing their time, anecdotes, technical information and experiences; and to the British military artist David Rowlands, whose own career as a war artist also helped to colour Jack's.

I am very grateful to Paul Liss of Liss Llewellyn Fine Art for his expedient advice, and help on the detail and history of the WAAC and the art market. I would also like to acknowledge Oxford University Press for kindly allowing me to use the extracts from the *War Pictures by British Artists* booklets.

Thank you to Niamh Brosnan and Catherine and Kate McNulty for background help with 'Irishness', and to Scott Petherick for his insight into life as an architect and the wonderful city of Melbourne.

The team at Curtis Brown Creative—Anna Davis, Rufus Purdy, Jack Hadley and Nikita Lalwani—have provided an amazing story incubator and I want to thank them for their ongoing support, and also Tara Wynne at Curtis Brown Australia for her advice.

I am fortunate to have Ebury Press as the UK publisher for *Maggie's Kitchen* and now for this novel, and am grateful to Gillian Green, Katie Seaman, Sarah Garnham, and all those involved with my books, for all their hard work.

A huge thank you to the wonderful team at Allen & Unwin, including Maggie Thompson and the editorial, sales and marketing teams, for all their efforts to help produce, market and sell our books. In particular, thanks to Kate Goldsworthy for her patience and insights working on this novel, and to Christa Munns and Annette Barlow—a very special thank you for making the magic happen twice. Thanks also to Christabella Designs for creating such an evocative cover for *Eleanor's Secret*.

A sincere thanks to booksellers and librarians for all you do to keep our stories alive. I also want to thank the readers and those who supported me with *Maggie's Kitchen* and now this novel—especially my number one book groupie, Mrs Potter! Lastly, thank you to my friends—local friends and loved ones overseas—and to my sister, Nicky, and parents, Jackie and Moon, John and Brenda, for all your love and encouragement. To Sam and James, I am so very proud of you both, and apologies for writing whenever we are on holiday. And to John, for everything you do.

Sources

Of the books, journals, booklets and papers read for research the most important include:

Edward Ardizzone, *Diary of a War Artist* [London]: Bodley Head, 1974.

Monica Bohm-Duchen, *Art and the Second World War* [UK]: Lund Humphries, 2013.

Suzanne Bosman, *The National Gallery in Wartime* [UK]: National Gallery Company Limited, 2008.

M.R.D. Foot, *Art and War: Twentieth century warfare as depicted by war artists* [London]: Headline in association with the Imperial War Museum, c1990.

Meirion & Susie Harries, *The War Artists* [London]: The Imperial War Museum and the Tate Gallery, 1983.

Sacha Llewellyn and Paul Liss (eds), *WWII War Pictures by British Artists* [London]: Liss Llewellyn Fine Art, 2016.

Eric Newton, *War Through Artists' Eyes: Paintings and drawings by British war artists* [London]: John Murray, 1945.

Alan Powers, *Eric Ravilious, Imagined Realities* [London]: Imperial War Museums and Phillips Wilson Publishers, 2004.

Private Len Smith, *Drawing Fire: The diary of a great soldier and artist* [London]: Collins, 2009.

Catherine Speck, *Beyond the Battlefield: Women artists of the two world wars* [London]: Reaktion Books, 2014.

Angela Summerfield, *The Artist at War: Second World War paintings & drawings from the Walker Art Gallery's collection* [Liverpool]: National Museums and Galleries on Merseyside, 1989.

War Pictures by British Artists: War at Sea, R.A.F., Army and *Blitz* [London]: Oxford University Press, 1942.

War Pictures by British Artists, Second Series: Soldiers, Production, Air raids and *Women* [London]: Oxford University Press, 1943.

Appearing on pages 278–279: 'Advance Australia Fair' written by Peter Dodds McCormick, first performed 1878.